I0607610

TALES FROM THE EDGE
Volume Two

Living on the Edge

A Double-Edged Sword

L.M. SOMERTON

Tales from The Edge Volume Two
ISBN # 978-1-78430-130-9
©Copyright L.M. Somerton 2014
Cover Art by Posh Gosh ©Copyright 2014
Interior text design by Claire Siemaszkiewicz
Totally Bound Publishing

Published in 2014 by Totally Bound Publishing, Newland House, The Point, Weaver Road, Lincoln, LN6 3QN, United Kingdom.

DANCING ON
THE EDGE

Dedication

To those who trust enough to love.

Chapter One

Alistair let the pounding beat of the music soak into his body. The deep thrum of the bass reverberated through his feet, up his spine and into his brain. He moved instinctively, twisting his hips and swaying, lost to the euphoria of the dance. The Underground's dance floor wasn't big, as if it had been deliberately designed to bring overheated bodies closer together. Alistair liked to be in the centre of the press of writhing flesh because there he could be anonymous. Nobody would notice that he was dancing alone. Occasionally someone would slide a sweaty arm around his waist or press a hard cock against his arse — he could just slip free and disappear into the crowd. No offence given and none taken.

It wasn't often that he had the freedom to really let go, but it was his night off and he was determined to enjoy himself. It was so stifling that for a moment he wished he were still wearing the short leather kilt that formed The Underground's skimpy staff uniform. The black PVC trousers he had on were ludicrously hot. Perspiration ran down his bare back and chest and his hair was soaked. It was time for a long, cool drink and he really needed to towel off.

Alistair made his way gradually to the edge of the dance floor. It took a while—the music was intoxicating and hard to withdraw from. He hovered on the periphery for a while, still dancing but aware now of what was going on in the wider room. The stage was empty apart from two men who were manhandling a large wooden cross into its centre, cursing and swearing at the weight of the thing. Alistair knew that some eager sub would be chained to it later, enjoying the kiss of the whip.

Many of the tables that circled the dance floor were occupied. Alistair knew all of the regulars by name and recognised quite a few of the less frequent visitors. A team of waiters, unashamedly employed for their looks and desire to please, attended the tables. On six nights out of seven he was one of them and enjoyed being part of the team. They were well paid and, though subservience was required, they had no other obligation to the clientele. The members were well aware of the rules and kept their hands to themselves, but it was perfectly proper to ask a server if he would be available to play when he got off his shift. Most of the boys Alistair knew were more than willing. For an unattached sub, The Underground was safe. It also attracted dominant men who were committed enough to the lifestyle to pay the exorbitant fees. For those that wanted them, there were plenty of opportunities to test compatibility or just to find someone happy to deliver a sound spanking with no strings.

Alistair had taken advantage of his position many times. He was slim, blond and pretty—all attributes that appealed to a large proportion of the members.

He never had a problem finding a Dom for an evening of fun and games that they would both enjoy. It helped that he adored having his arse paddled until it glowed and if he was tied up while it happened, so much the better. He scanned the room catching several interested glances, but Alistair was only looking for one man. The man who was always present, whomever Alistair played with. The only man he had ever allowed to fuck him. It was dark and crowded — spotlights blinded him as he peered up at the gallery, his stomach knotted with anxiety. Where was he?

Bodies between Alistair and the bar moved apart and there he was — Carey Hoffman — and he was looking directly at Alistair, a slight smile curving his lips. Alistair relaxed as soon as he locked gazes with the darkly handsome man. Carey was his anchor in a bewildering world and there was no way Alistair would have walked across the club alone unless he knew Carey was watching. He began to move, careful not to brush against anyone or make eye contact. He didn't like rejecting people, but he wasn't wearing a collar and that made him fair game. He made it three paces before a huge, leather-clad guy loomed over him with a leer.

"Well, pretty boy, what are you doing here all alone?"

Alistair looked up and took in the extensive tattoos that covered his new friend's heavily muscled arms, then the thick neck and shaved head.

"I...I'm not..."

Alistair flinched as the stranger took his arm, gripping his biceps tightly. "Don't be scared, little one, we can have a good time together." He tugged Alistair towards the tables.

"I'm sorry, Sir, I'm not available tonight," Alistair finally managed to get out.

"Or any night," Carey said as he appeared next to him and stroked his hair. "This one's taken, Frank." The big guy looked disappointed, but he smiled, revealing a dimple that was completely incongruous.

"S'all right, Carey. Haven't been in for a while—didn't realise." Frank released Alistair's arm and stepped back.

"Not a problem. In fact I think Toby over there might suit you." Carey gestured towards a server with dark hair and a cheeky grin.

Frank grinned right back. "Pretty. Is he interested, Carey?"

Carey crooked a finger at Toby and the slight waiter came scuttling over with undignified speed.

"Oh, I think you might say that."

Toby bounced on the spot, his dark brown eyes glinting. He looked like a puppy that had just been given the best treat ever. He disappeared with a squeak as Frank wrapped a beefy, decorated arm around his shoulders.

"My work here is done." Carey sounded satisfied. "Alistair, come." That was snapped out more firmly. Alistair felt his cock jerk. Carey's voice always did that to him, it was all deep and growly—a voice to be listened to and obeyed. He bowed his head and followed the older man towards the bar where Carey gestured to the barman for water then handed Alistair a bottle. Condensation slicked the glass and dripped onto his hand. He unscrewed the cap and took a long, slow swallow, letting the cool liquid bathe his parched throat. He sighed happily, placed the bottle on the bar and looked at Carey who was looking right back with a stern expression on his handsome features. Alistair's stomach knotted, he wanted nothing more than to sink to his knees right there, but it was his night off — he didn't have to do that. Alistair knew that Carey wanted him to have time to himself when he could be free from orders and obligations. What he did on his night off was up to him. The trouble was that Alistair really wanted to tell Carey that he didn't want or need a night to himself. He felt lost without clear orders to follow, but it was a night off for Carey too and Alistair worried that Carey might want the time apart more than he did.

"I can't leave you alone for five minutes, can I, boy?" Carey looked more amused than upset, which settled Alistair's stomach somewhat.

"Sorry, Sir...umm...Carey. He just appeared and I couldn't avoid him."

Carey chuckled. "Frank is quite difficult to avoid — he's built like a barn door. Fortunately young Toby likes his men big and ugly. Still, you shouldn't be in here alone, you know that."

"I knew you were here and most people realise I'm off limits." Alistair tried not to sound petulant. If Carey wanted a night off, he had to put up with the consequences. Carey cupped his cheek with a cool hand and Alistair resisted the urge to nuzzle.

"I just want you to be safe. What if I hadn't seen you?"

Alistair tilted his chin. "I can deal with the likes of Frank." It was all bravado and they both knew it. Carey shook his head and sighed. "Fine. What are you going to do with the rest of your evening?"

Alistair swallowed some more water — he really didn't feel like dancing anymore. "I'm going to take a shower and watch a movie upstairs." He didn't ask if that was okay, though he wanted to. He needed

Carey's permission before he could relax. Carey gave him what he needed with a slight nod. "I'll be up later to give you a ride home."

Alistair could feel the hot burn of tears in his eyes. He turned and ran before Carey could say anything else. The night off also meant a night in his own room in the flat they shared and he hated it. He wouldn't sleep—even knowing that Carey was in the next room wasn't enough. It felt like punishment, only he couldn't work out what he was guilty of.

Alistair didn't have to run far. Carey had a small flat on the top floor of the building that housed The Underground, the club he had owned for more than fifteen years. In the three years they had been together, they occasionally stayed over at the club, but more usually went back to their larger place across town. Alistair let himself in and headed straight for the bathroom. The flat was nowhere near as big or grand as the apartment Carey called home, but it had everything Alistair needed while he waited for Carey to drive him. Carey didn't like him taking taxis late at night so he was stuck until Carey was ready to leave. He stripped off his boots and peeled his trousers down, grimacing as the fabric clung to his skin. He wasn't wearing underwear—there was no room beneath the skin-tight PVC. He showered efficiently, taking no pleasure in the feel of the hot water on his skin. He shampooed, soaped and rinsed in less than five minutes. He turned off the spray and stood there, dripping. On any other night, Carey would have joined him and turned showering into a full-on erotic experience. Tonight everything was falling flat, including Alistair's dick, which had lost all perkiness and hung softly against his thigh.

He shook himself out of his stupor, grabbed a towel then dried off. Carey's robe was hanging on the back of the door so he pulled it on and wrapped the thick, warm folds around his body, breathing in Carey's lingering scent. It was far too big, so he rolled up the sleeves and tied the belt tightly around his middle. He brushed his teeth then rubbed the drips from his hair. It was starting to get a bit shaggy and the ends always curled when it got too long. He'd have to get a haircut soon or he'd start resembling a blond labradoodle. Suddenly tired, he leaned against the sink and watched the last drops of water disappear into the plughole. He thought about making some crass analogy with the state of his life, but it just wasn't true. He had everything he'd ever wanted. Almost.

Alistair wandered into the small lounge and browsed the shelf of DVDs, brushing his fingers along the smooth spines of the neatly alphabetised boxes. That made him smile. Carey was more than a bit anal when it came to tidiness and organisation. Once, when he'd been too bored to bother with self-preservation, he'd put one film back on the shelf out of order just to see if Carey would notice. He'd spent two hours kneeling naked in a corner as a result.

He picked out a copy of *Strike Back*, series one, not because he particularly liked it, but because it starred Richard Armitage who bore a remarkable resemblance to Carey. He slipped the disc into the player under the TV, hunted down the remote, which had done its usual disappearing act under a cushion, then curled into the corner of the sofa. On a whim, he picked up the phone and dialled his friend Olly's number. Olly was a good listener and Alistair needed someone to talk to who wasn't going to laugh at him. He looked at his watch—it was late, gone eleven. Olly was probably tucked up in bed, wrapped securely in the arms of his partner, Joe. Alistair hoped he wasn't interrupting anything. He was just about to put the phone down when Olly said a curious, "Hello?"

"Hi, Olly, sorry—I didn't realise the time. Are you in bed?"

"Alistair? Hey! It's good to hear from you. You can call me any time, you know that. I'm not in bed anyway." He giggled. "I had two cups of coffee this evening."

Alistair chuckled. "How did you get away with that? I didn't think Joe let you anywhere near caffeine?"

"He doesn't, and when he finds out I'm going to be in big trouble!"

Olly sounded absolutely delighted at that thought.

"Isn't he there?"

"No—I think he's over at the main house giving Heath some ideas about how to control Aiden. They could be a while!"

Alistair laughed then replied, "Aiden isn't the subbiest sub in the world, is he?"

"That's this year's biggest understatement. How are you anyway, how's Carey?"

"He's amazing. I love him to bits, Olly." Alistair sighed.

There was a pause. "But? I hear a 'but' lurking there, Alistair. What's going on? Spill."

Alistair sighed. "We aren't full-time, Olly. He insists on me having a night off every week and I hate it. He even makes me sleep in my own room."

"You know he's only doing it for you, sweetie. Have you spoken to him about it?"

"I've tried, but I don't want to hurt him. He knows best, right?"

Olly snorted. "Doms like to think they know best, but half the time they are too blind to see what's right in front of their alpha-male noses!"

Alistair laughed. "I bet you wouldn't say that to Joe's face!"

"The trick is to tell them whilst making them think the idea was theirs in the first place."

"You are a bad influence, Olly."

"Ooh goody! One of my ambitions fulfilled! But seriously, is one night a week off that bad?"

"I feel lost on my own, Olly. I'm not strong like Aiden or confident like you. Oh, I can flirt and shake my arse if I have to, but honestly — I just want to be kneeling at Carey's feet. He gives me peace."

"Then tell him, love. He'll understand. One look at those puppy dog eyes of yours and he'll do whatever you want him to, I promise."

Alistair smiled. "Thanks, Olly, I knew talking to you would make me feel better. I hope Joe doesn't punish you too badly."

"Oh, I do! Ring me soon, 'kay? I'll tell you all about it!"

The line disconnected before Alistair could respond. Olly was always so full of life — he was an instant boost. Feeling a little less edgy, Alistair settled down to watch his DVD. The next thing he knew he was being shaken awake. Carey leant down and planted a gentle kiss on his lips.

"Hey, sleepyhead. Ready to go home?" The little lines around Carey's eyes crinkled as he smiled.

"Oh! Sorry… Must have dozed off."

"Even in front of the gorgeous Mr Armitage?" Carey waved the DVD box at him and grinned.

Alistair couldn't do anything to stop his face heating. Carey knew all his secrets.

"Didn't even get to watch the opening credits. I did speak to Olly, though."

Carey ruffled his hair. "How is the brat? Behaving himself?"

"Nope. He'd had coffee."

"Ah. Did you get any sense out of him?"

Alistair smiled. "Some. Can we go visit soon?"

"It has been a while, hasn't it? I'll give Joe a call and see what can be arranged. I'd quite like to do one of their courses—knot work maybe. You'd look very pretty all tied up like that."

Alistair chewed his lower lip and tried to ignore how quickly his cock was hardening. Thank God for Carey's voluminous robe!

"I'll just go and get some clothes on." He almost ran towards the bedroom, but Carey's low growl stopped him.

"Don't imagine that I don't know exactly what's going on under that dressing gown, Alistair. No touching."

Alistair turned back towards Carey with a pout. "But it's my night off."

"A night off you don't want or need, I hear."

"Oh. I..." Alistair scuffed his bare toes into the carpet. He didn't dare meet Carey's gaze in case he was upset. "Olly has a big mouth."

"Olly spoke to Joe and Joe rang me. That's what friends do, sweetheart. Olly and Joe care about you very much and they don't want you to be unhappy. Neither do I. Why on earth didn't you come to me?"

Alistair felt his eyes fill with tears, but he was determined not to cry like a little girl. "You make the decisions, Sir. I like that...love that, but you wanted the night off and I assumed that was because you needed time away from me."

He blinked away the tears then Carey wrapped him up in the warmth and safety of his arms.

"Sweetheart, I'm much older than you. I wanted you to have a night where you could spend time with people your own age, let go a little. I'm an old-fashioned, traditional Dom — I like quiet obedience. I thought you needed a chance to let off steam. I would keep you near to me every second of every day if I could."

Alistair pressed hard against Carey's body, revelling in the closeness. "I like the quiet too, Sir, and you don't exactly keep me prisoner — I have plenty of freedom. You're not old either — you're not even forty!"

"I'm thirty-eight, that's fifteen years older than you, love." Carey stroked Alistair's neck in a way that made him shiver with desire.

"Doesn't matter. I hate being apart from you — it makes me feel like I've done something wrong."

Carey was pushing the robe from his shoulders. Alistair let it slip down his arms and gravity did the rest, carrying the heavy fabric to the floor, leaving him bare to Carey's touch. Light pressure traced down his spine before Carey cupped his arse with a warm hand.

"Well, boy, you will have to be punished for hiding your feelings, but that can wait until the morning. In the meantime, I feel the need for some quiet time."

Alistair shivered. His cock felt hot and heavy, his balls tight. "Are we staying here tonight then, Sir?"

Carey stroked Alistair's hair. "Yes, we are and I intend to fuck this perfect little arse of yours until you scream. Only you won't be able to disturb my peace because I have a nice new ball gag in the bedroom that I can't wait to try out on you." He smiled. "Are you sure you don't want to reconsider the whole night off thing?"

Chapter Two

Carey decided there and then that he was never going to buy another lottery ticket. There was no need. He had already won the jackpot and his prize was kneeling in front of him, looking up at him with an expression of utter adoration. He couldn't believe how lucky he was. Alistair had been a part of his life for almost three years and he still had to pinch himself occasionally to convince himself that he wasn't dreaming. He could still remember the first day they'd met with vivid clarity and he'd known even then that the sweet, gentle young man was going to have a lasting impact.

The Underground never had a problem attracting staff — in fact Carey received more unsolicited applications than he could deal with — but once a year he liked to have an open selection day. It was a lot more trouble than simple interviews but far more effective — the young men that turned up worked hard to win their jobs and subsequently worked even harder to keep them.

There were usually a couple of spots to be filled as staff members moved on, graduated from college or became part of a permanent couple with a partner who didn't want them flaunting themselves in front of other men. Carey never had to advertise — he just spread the word that there would be a selection day going on and waited for the line to form.

Carey and two of his senior managers conducted screening interviews that narrowed the pool of hopefuls down to ten. The lucky few were invited to stay for a practical trial, assisting with the lunch service. Carey took pride in being able to spot the applicants with the most potential. He gave them staff uniforms, left them to change then lined them up in the club to see how they reacted.

The uniform consisted of a short black leather kilt, which sat on the hips and barely covered the backside, and a net thong. That was it and it took a fair amount of confidence to look comfortable. Staff members who wished to could also wear a club collar, which denoted a status of 'look but don't touch'. Sometimes Carey employed men who were already in loving relationships but who were unable to express their submissive tendencies in them. The Underground gave them a safe outlet for their needs and the collar provided additional protection.

Three years earlier the selection day had attracted over thirty applicants. After the initial cut, Alistair had been at the end of the line of scantily clad young men. Carey could still remember the little lightning bolt that had struck his cock the moment he'd seen him. If they hadn't had three vacancies to fill he would have happily sent the rest of the candidates home without another glance. He recalled lightly tanned, slender limbs and a smooth, firm body. No six-pack, but no flab either, just lots of beautiful smooth skin begging to be touched. Alistair wasn't as pretty as some of the others, but his 'boy next door' good looks appealed to Carey more. He had gorgeous blond hair, neatly cropped but long enough on top to get a good grip, and the most sensuous lips—but it was his eyes that clinched the deal. They were soft and appealing, so full of hope and eagerness to please. Carey couldn't recollect ever meeting a more natural and obvious submissive.

It had taken a lot of willpower to remain professional that day. Alistair had looked like he'd been born to wear the uniform and had seemed totally oblivious to the effect he'd had on the patrons as he'd helped to serve lunch. Every time he'd bent to place a dish down or stretched to reach for a tray, the curve of his arse had been revealed. There had been a lot of people watching him speculatively that day, and Carey had known they would be wondering what the boy was into and how far he would go. There had been no doubt that he would have an eager queue of play partners if that was what he wanted.

Carey had taken a seat at a small table and had watched the lunch service. He'd twirled a straw in his glass of iced water and kept an eye on which of his new prospects had been generating the most excitement. He'd had to rely on Harry, his bar manager, to help him with the selection because his attention had refused to stray from Alistair for very long. He'd frowned as one of the members had put his arm around Alistair's bare waist. That wasn't right. No one else should be touching his boy. He'd allowed himself a slight smile as Alistair had neatly extricated himself and moved away. Carey had caught Alistair's eye and gestured him over. He walked beautifully with just a slight sway to his hips, the lack of obvious exhibitionism making him all the more endearing.

Carey had asked, in what he'd hoped was an encouraging tone, "How are you getting on, Alistair? Any problems?" To his surprise and delight Alistair had sunk gracefully to his knees next to him and had given him a beautiful, open smile. "It's fun, Sir. Everyone has been very kind."

Everything about him was soft and gentle, even his voice.

"So why are you here? What is it you want from the job? And don't tell me you're looking to hone your waiting skills..."

Alistair didn't speak right away—he looked thoughtful. "Two reasons, Sir. I've finished my degree and I want to be a photographer, but it takes time to build a reputation and the field is very competitive. I need a flexible job so I can support myself while I build my portfolio." He paused. "And I really, really enjoy playing, Sir. I've heard that this is the place to find men who can give me what I need."

Carey hadn't been able to resist ruffling his hair a little. "What do you enjoy the most then, boy?"

"Bondage, Sir, spanking. I like a little bit of pain... I need to submit and I like strong, dominant men."

His voice had been clear and steady—no doubts there, Alistair knew what he liked. Carey had wondered how far he'd been pushed, whether he'd been whipped or flogged. There had certainly been no marks on his pristine skin.

"And what about sex, Alistair?"

"Oh..." He'd flushed lightly. "I *really* like that too, Sir, but I understand that you can set limits here?"

"That's right. You choose how far to go and any member you play with will respect your choices."

Carey knew the curiosity in his voice had been obvious.

"For the right person I'd have no limits." Alistair had kept his head demurely bowed. "But otherwise…toys are fine and oral with protection."

Carey had felt a strange sense of satisfaction. In his mind Alistair's perfect arse had already been taken. It was to be his and his alone. He wanted to be 'the right person'. He'd decided to take a chance.

"Would you like to play now, with me?"

"Is this part of the interview, Sir?" There had been a cheeky twinkle in Alistair's hazel eyes.

"No, brat, it isn't. Consider yourself hired. And don't feel obliged to humour the boss either."

Carey had held his breath.

"Then yes, Sir, I'd love to."

With those few words the world had become a better place.

Carey yanked his mind back to the present.

Alistair had changed very little. His face had thinned slightly, he kept his hair a bit longer and his shoulders had broadened, but other than that he was just the same. Carey knew he had been the one to change the most, with a bit more silver in his hair and a few more laughter lines around his eyes, but he kept himself in excellent shape. Lurking in the back of his mind was always the worry that Alistair would trade him in for a younger model. He repressed a sigh and acknowledged for the hundredth time that Alistair was really in charge of their relationship, however dominant Carey might be.

He moved so that he was standing directly in front of Alistair, who was on his knees, waiting patiently and completely still except for his cock, which was hard and twitching, betraying his need. Apart from that, Alistair projected perfect serenity—as if there was nowhere in the world he would rather be than naked, on his knees, in front of his master. Carey had no reason to believe that wasn't true and it was something he loved about Alistair. Oh, the boy could be a brat when he wanted to be, but for a young man, he had a mastery of his body that Carey had never seen matched.

Carey touched Alistair's chin with his knuckles, prompting him to look up. Carey brushed a finger across Alistair's lips and smiled as they parted. Alistair suckled gently, his sighs of pleasure loud in the quiet room.

"Let's move your attention elsewhere, love." Carey sat on the edge of the bed and unzipped his fly, allowing his swollen cock to spring free. Unbidden, Alistair crawled across the room and positioned himself between Carey's knees. He looked up hopefully, making Carey grin and nod his permission.

Carey spread his legs wide and waited for Alistair to work his magic. At first Alistair gave light, tentative flicks of the tongue, then languorously slow licks that travelled Carey's straining cock from base to tip. Alistair kissed the leaking head then took it into the warmth of his mouth. Just the head, nothing more. He sucked gently, putting his hands on Carey's thighs for balance. Carey wound his fingers into Alistair's soft hair, not to force his movement but to let him know that his master was there and paying attention to his needs too. The sucking increased, Alistair's cheeks hollowing as he dipped forward, taking Carey's entire length before drawing slowly back, scraping lightly with his teeth as he did.

Carey's pulse raced—he gripped Alistair's hair tighter, he was getting close. Alistair took him deep into his throat and held him there for a few delicious seconds before pulling back again. He looked up, as if he knew how close Carey was, checking whether his master wanted to come or wait. Carey tugged a few strands of hair, giving Alistair the signal to withdraw. He didn't want to come just yet. He stood carefully, legs trembling a little, and walked across to the chest of drawers where he kept a small collection of toys. The new ball gag sat there, nestled between a pile of Alistair's skimpy underwear and Carey's winter pyjamas.

The black rubber ball wasn't huge. Carey wanted to keep Alistair quiet, not stretch his face into some weird parody of 'The Scream'. Alistair pouted prettily when he saw it, but the dark flush to his rigid cock told Carey that he wasn't really objecting. Carey slipped the ball into place and tightened the straps around Alistair's head, being careful not to catch his hair.

"That's lovely, sweetheart. Now on to the bed, hands and knees. You know what to do if you want to safe word?"

Alistair nodded as he got into position. Carey reminded him anyway, "Good. You bang the bed with your fist and I stop." He was always scrupulous about safety—Alistair had a tendency to be stubborn. Carey stripped down, enjoying the feel of the air on his warm skin. Alistair had managed to get him nicely close to boiling point and he couldn't wait to bubble over, but first he had to pay another visit to the toy drawer. He retrieved Alistair's favourite paddle—it was made of flexible steel sheathed in a thick rubber sleeve and could deliver a painful whack. Although Carey was a strict master most of the time, it was indulgent to give the boy what he enjoyed the most and an occasional lapse into soppiness was allowed.

Alistair was trying to peer back at him—difficult from his current position and he knew he wasn't supposed to look unless he was told to.

"Eyes to the front, boy, or I'll blindfold you as well." Carey kept his tone light and conversational. He never said anything he didn't mean and felt that a raised voice signified loss of control. Alistair snapped his head back into position, but he wiggled his arse cheekily.

"Patience, brat, all in good time. First I need to warm you up a little. Spread your legs wider."

Alistair moaned around the gag but did as he'd been told, resting his forearms on the bed for better stability.

Carey took a nice relaxed stance and slapped the paddle against his thigh. The sound would let Alistair know what was coming. Carey drew back his arm and delivered the first blow with measured force then watched with pleasure as Alistair's pale skin flushed with colour. He gave Alistair a second or two to catch his breath then took up a steady rhythm with the paddle. Alistair's sweet little whimpers turned to moans, but his cock was hard and slick with pre-cum. Carey knew that the moans were more about Alistair's efforts not to come than they were about the pain. He laid the paddle on the bed and pressed his hand to the reddened skin. Warmth soaked into his palm as he gently stroked the curve of Alistair's arse.

"You took that beautifully, love. You really want to come now, don't you?"

Alistair nodded frantically.

"Well then, this will be an excellent lesson in control, won't it? You are not to come until I say so." Carey chuckled at his own cruelty. He could have given Alistair a cock ring, but that would have made restraint too easy for him. Carey loved to watch him squirm and cry with need. The single command to end his frustration was the biggest gift he could give. He grabbed a plastic bottle of lube, popped the cap then slicked a finger.

"Mmm. This smells good—spicy, I think, a hint of ginger maybe? Here, what do you think?" He held the tube beneath Alistair's nose and watched his eyes widen as he sniffed. Carey knew full well that the lube contained ginger oil. It was already making his finger tingle and he couldn't wait to see Alistair's reaction as it coated his passage. Alistair clearly understood what was coming because he gripped the bedclothes like his life depended on it.

Carey fingered Alistair's twitching hole, spreading the lube liberally. He squeezed more of the slippery gel onto his finger then dipped into tight heat, pushing firmly past Alistair's initial resistance.

"How does that feel, love? Is it good?"

Alistair was panting hard, his face pressed into a pillow. Carey withdrew, coated two fingers then plunged back inside him, harder this time. He didn't seek out Alistair's prostate because he really didn't want him to come until he had felt the full benefit of the lube. Carey had tried it on himself and knew that the initial slow warmth rapidly escalated to a tingling, heated crescendo. He scissored his fingers, stretching Alistair out, making sure he was well prepared.

Guessing that the time was right from the way Alistair's muffled cries were issuing from behind his gag, Carey lined his cock up and thrust forwards in one, smooth motion. He felt the mild warmth of the ginger against his flesh almost immediately and it encouraged him to speed up his movements. It took every ounce of his iron will not to come. He held Alistair's hips and concentrated on drawing out the pleasure of being encased in his lover's constricting heat. As he came, with an orgasm that seemed to reverberate along the entire length of his spine, Carey reached beneath Alistair's body and grasped his cock.

"Come!"

It was like magic—the instant the word had left Carey's lips Alistair screamed into his gag and shot hard into Carey's hand. After several shuddering spasms, they both collapsed onto the bed. Regretfully, Carey slipped from Alistair's body and removed the gag.

"Massage your jaw a little, it's going to be a bit sore." He slipped away to the bathroom to clean himself off. He was leaning over the sink, splashing cool water over his face, when Alistair joined him. His eyes were exceptionally bright and his hair wildly ruffled. He tilted his head up expectantly and Carey obliged him with a kiss.

"You can speak now, love."

Alistair kissed him back. "I don't really know what to say, Sir. That was just perfect... I thought I was going to explode!"

Carey smirked. "I was under the impression you just did."

Alistair giggled and let Carey wipe him clean. "What was in that stuff anyway?"

"Ginger oil extract. It's supposed to get you all hot and tingly." He gave Alistair a hug.

"You get me that way just by looking at me, Sir...but it did feel good!"

Carey indulged in some groping and more kissing. He loved the feeling of having Alistair in his arms — he was so willing and pliant.

"Come on now, you're keeping this old man from his bed." He patted Alistair's arse.

"Ow!" Alistair sidled away from him, and Carey had to pull him back and give him another hug.

"You're not old! But you are a mean and cruel Master."

"I am, aren't I? And you wouldn't have it any other way!" Carey took Alistair back to bed and spooned up close behind him.

"I love you, Sir."

"I love you too, boy. Now sleep."

Alistair drifted off quickly, obedient as ever. Carey smiled to himself and wondered just how long it would be before something came along to upset their peaceful, happy world. In his experience, nothing was ever this easy or this perfect for long.

Chapter Three

Alistair woke slowly, persuading himself into consciousness with the lure of Carey's warmth against his back and the potential offered by the iron rod that was sticking into his arse. He slipped quietly from beneath the covers and padded the short distance to the kitchen. Waking Carey with good coffee might go some way towards mitigating the punishment that Alistair knew he had coming. You needed a membership of MENSA to understand the intricacies of the coffee machine, but Alistair had memorised the settings that generated the perfect result. It had taken a great deal of trial and error and several packets of expensive ground coffee to achieve such expertise and he could use his skill to bribe Carey when he was at his most vulnerable—first thing in the morning and desperate for caffeine. He always altered the settings when he was done so that Carey never managed to duplicate his efforts. Carey had never read an instruction manual in his life and wasn't about to start, so Alistair felt safe in the value of his secret knowledge.

He rummaged in a cupboard and found a packet of *pain au chocolat* unopened and in date. Alistair hummed happily to himself as he put two in the oven to warm and finished off the coffee. This combination would definitely put Carey in a good mood. He stacked a tray with mugs, plates and napkins then singed his fingertips pulling the pastries from the oven. The flat was warm, but Alistair was wandering around naked and felt a little chilled so he hurriedly checked the tray and headed back to the bedroom.

Carey was sitting up in bed with a pile of pillows behind his back. His dark hair was tousled from sleep, but he looked wide awake.

"Well, there's a pretty sight first thing in the morning."

Alistair felt his face heat and his cock jerk. Holding the laden tray as he was, he couldn't do anything to cover himself. Not that he would have been allowed to anyway. Carey often kept him naked when they were at home, but though he was used to it, it always made him feel a bit vulnerable.

"Good morning, Sir. I made coffee." He placed the tray carefully on the bed next to Carey and waited for instructions.

Carey patted the bed. "Come and kneel here. You can pour."

Alistair knelt next to the tray, painfully aware of how exposed he was and just how much it turned him on. His slim cock jutted stiffly away from his body, swaying every time he moved. He served Carey his coffee and slid a warm pastry onto a plate for him.

"You're spoiling me, Alistair, or is this a bribe? You want me to go easy on you this morning?"

"No, Sir! I mean yes, Sir. I mean… Yes, I'm spoiling you, but you deserve it, and I did think that if you liked it enough, you might be lenient."

"Do you think you deserve to be punished?" Carey fed Alistair a small piece of *pain au chocolat*.

"Yes, Sir. I kept something from you."

"You did, and that made you unhappy. We've talked about this before, love. I need you to be completely open with me otherwise how can I know what's best for you?"

"I'm sorry, Sir."

"I know you are, and that's more important than coffee. Delicious though this is, it doesn't let you off punishment."

Alistair sat as still as he could and clasped his hands behind his back. Carey continued to feed him and even allowed him a few sips of coffee. He wasn't scared. Carey had never hurt him more than Alistair could bare and never would. His punishments, however, could often be…uncomfortable. Alistair shifted a fraction—his heels were digging into his arse and he was still sore from the previous evening. Carey wouldn't spank him for punishment because he knew Alistair enjoyed it too much. No, discipline would certainly be something he didn't get pleasure from.

"Take the tray and put it on the dresser." Carey wiped his fingers with a napkin, balled it up then tossed it into the bin on the other side of the room.

Alistair put the tray down. "How do you do that without even looking?"

"Natural talent."

Alistair bit his bottom lip to stop himself from laughing.

"Bring me the rawhide thongs from the drawer, please."

Oh. Not funny. Alistair did as he'd been asked with shaking hands. The long strips of leather were coiled neatly and he made sure they stayed that way as he handed them over.

"Thank you. Now stand there, hands behind your back and legs apart."

Carey sat on the edge of the bed and unrolled one of the narrow ties, then proceeded to wind it tightly around the base of Alistair's balls and his cock in a figure of eight. The last few inches of each strand were criss-crossed the length of Alistair's shaft and tied off at the base of the head. More effective than any cock ring, Alistair knew that he had absolutely no chance of coming any time soon. The constricting ties were just shy of painful and held his erection stiffly in place.

"Beautiful." Carey was admiring his handiwork with an evil grin. "I suppose you'd like to know what your punishment is to be?"

Alistair looked down at his bound cock pointedly. "This isn't punishment enough, Sir?"

"The coffee was good, Alistair — it wasn't that good." Carey swung his legs back onto the bed and began to stroke his cock with long, leisurely caresses. He leant back into the pillows and closed his eyes, sighing with pleasure. "First you get to observe while I enjoy myself."

Alistair stared, wide-eyed. Carey jacked himself faster and Alistair moaned as his own cock strained within its prison. It was torment to be able to watch but not touch. He longed to offer Carey his mouth or his hand, but they were not required. Carey didn't need him and that hurt more than any lash. Carey didn't even look at him as his body tensed and he came with a shout of pleasure.

After a few moments of laboured breathing, Carey opened his eyes. "Fetch a cloth, Alistair."

"Yes, Sir." Alistair scurried to the bathroom and returned with a warm flannel and towel. He cleaned Carey up tenderly, spending a little too long on his rapidly softening dick. Carey chuckled. "I'm not your age, Alistair, there is absolutely no chance I'm going to get it up again that quickly. Now put the towel in the hamper and get yourself onto the bed."

A little flicker of hope made Alistair's toes curl. He liked the bed—it held a lot of very happy memories for him. Maybe Carey was feeling mellow enough to go easy on him.

"On top of the covers."

Alistair followed Carey's command and lay down on his back.

"Good. Now relax while I get you into position."

Alistair let his limbs go limp as Carey pulled his legs wide apart and stretched his arms above his head.

"Perfect. Now let's make sure you stay like that."

The familiar hug of leather around his wrists and ankles was comforting, as Carey buckled on cuffs then chained them to the bed frame. There was very little give in the bindings, but he wriggled into a more comfortable position and stilled. There was a dull ache at his groin where his bound cock and balls strained against the leather ties. If he lifted his head a little he could see his cock pointing skyward, the tip glistening with moisture. He dropped his head back with a moan. Being bound and helpless for Carey was as hot as hell, but he had a suspicion that release would be a long time coming.

The bed dipped as Carey sat next to him. Alistair nibbled at his bottom lip anxiously as the lube was snapped open. Carey squeezed the tube and slicked his fingertips with the glistening gel.

"First, a little preparation."

Alistair jerked as Carey spread the cold substance around his nipples, massaging his flesh and pinching lightly. The tip of his cock got the same treatment — slow circles of pressure that drove him wild. He bucked his hips and thrashed, making metallic music with his chains.

"Be still." Carey snapped the words out, refreshed the lube on his fingers then plunged two deep into Alistair's arse. He stroked the inside walls of his channel, stretching it gently, leaving a coating of lubrication behind.

Alistair whimpered. Every slight movement of air set his nipples tingling and his cock jerking.

"Sir! Please!"

"Punishment, Alistair, remember. Do I need to gag you again?"

"No! No... Please don't." Alistair didn't want to be forced into silence. He clamped his mouth shut, determined not to beg. Carey stroked Alistair's hair in a gesture that was so attentive and loving that Alistair almost forgot that he was about to be disciplined.

"Good boy."

Those words always sent a thrill of satisfaction through Alistair's body. He was pleasing Carey, nothing else mattered. He could feel himself drifting into his own private headspace. He never felt safer than when Carey's attention was fixed on him, even if it wasn't for the most pleasant of reasons.

Carey reached down the side of the bed. Alistair was mildly curious as to what his master was getting a hold of, but he was floating and happy — it was too much effort to look. A low buzzing sound started up, which was interesting enough to attract Alistair's attention. He turned his head curiously. Carey was holding the handle of a flexible wand that ended with a vibrating metal lozenge about five inches long and an inch round. Alistair didn't have any time to wonder what Carey was going to do with it. The metal touched his nipple and sent vibrations shooting through his body. It was the most agonising pleasure. His back arched and he jerked his hips, desperate for some friction against his swollen cock, but there was nothing but air. No relief. The wand moved to his other nipple and he cried out desperately.

There was a moment's respite as Carey moved the wand away, but the sound continued. Carey hadn't switched it off, he was moving lower down Alistair's body. Realising what was about to happen, Alistair thrashed as much as the chains would allow. It did him no good. The wand touched the tip of his cock and the lightning bolt of pleasure shorted every nerve in his body. Carey moved the wand away again, but the relief was fleeting. As soon as Alistair's breathing had slowed to a normal rate rather than the kind of hyperventilation that usually required a brown paper bag, Carey touched him again. This time Alistair screamed. His balls drew up tightly, but the leather thongs prevented any release. Every muscle in his body, from the neck down, tensed. He sobbed and panted, incoherent words slipping from his mouth of their own volition. He felt the weight of Carey's hand against his stomach, holding him down, then the wand made contact again. A silent scream chorded his throat and his vision blackened around the edges. It was too much.

Alistair had no idea how long the sweet torture continued. There was no rhyme or reason to it, no rhythm that would allow him to prepare himself. Sometimes Carey would touch him over and over again — sometimes he held the wand against his flesh until his tears ran freely. Then there would be a pause and merciful quiet for several minutes before it all started again. At some point Alistair lost the ability to think at all. He forgot where he was, even who he was. There was just the agonising sensation of being desperate to come but not being able. He was hot, his hair felt damp with sweat, he was exhausted. Then Carey kissed him, long and deep and he thought it was finally over. He was wrong.

Carey trailed the wand the length of his body, tapped his balls then pushed the tip against his hole.

"No! No, please, Sir!"

His slick passage accepted all five inches of the wand's pulsating head with ease. Carey jiggled it slightly then pressed the button that increased its speed. Alistair no longer had the strength to scream. He prayed fervently that he might pass out but wasn't so fortunate. Carey rotated the wand's handle ensuring that Alistair's prostate felt the full benefit.

"I hope you won't keep anything from me again, Alistair."

"No, Sir! No... I promise. Please...!"

"Have you had enough?" Carey withdrew the wand slowly only to push it back in.

"Stop! Please, Sir..." Alistair felt the tears rolling down his face.

The wand withdrew and this time it didn't return. His body was racked with shivers and when Carey began to untie the thongs around his cock and balls he nearly passed out. The orgasm began somewhere at the base of his skull, shot down his spine and exploded from his cock the moment he was released.

His entire body spasmed and it felt like his balls were on fire. The exquisitely painful pleasure was finally too much and Alistair collapsed into darkness.

He hadn't been out of it long, Alistair was pretty sure of that. He forced an eye open, nervously checking to see if Carey was still sitting there with that bloody wand. Even the spectacular orgasm at the end of his punishment did not make up for over an hour of edging. Carey could be deliciously cruel. Alistair's lips quirked and he squirmed deeper beneath the duvet. Carey had unchained him, though the leather wrist and ankle cuffs were still in place, then covered him up. He'd been cleaned off too—he smelt soapy and fresh. He winced as strained muscles reminded him of the abuse they had suffered. He felt like he'd been racked and there were definitely bruises beneath the cuffs where he had fought the restraints. He grimaced—the lunchtime service was going to be a bit of an endurance test.

"If you've quite finished lazing around under there, then get up. We both have to go to work."

Alistair tunnelled up from beneath the covers reluctantly to find Carey standing next to the bed with a glass of water in one hand and a packet of painkillers in the other.

"Thought you might need a couple of these."

"I passed out." Alistair knew he sounded accusing.

"You did." Carey was definitely not remorseful. "You should be grateful I let you get off at all. I had planned to keep you bound up and frustrated."

"Your kindness knows no bounds, Sir." Alistair took the pills and pressed a couple out of the packet. He swallowed them gratefully. "I ache everywhere."

"Good. It'll remind you to behave today. I'd hate to have to repeat that little exercise again this evening."

Alistair shivered. "I'll be good, Sir, I promise." Was it wrong that a little part of him wouldn't have minded a rerun?

Carey smiled and Alistair melted. His master was so handsome and so unbelievably sexy when he was being strict.

"You'll keep the cuffs on during service today and I want you wearing a club collar. From now on, no one else lays so much as a finger on you. I'm not sure I want you to carry on working here either, we'll see how it goes."

Alistair beamed. He longed to wear Carey's collar, but so far the club one had been as far as Carey had gone. He'd worn that the last time they had visited with Joe and Olly and he'd loved the feel of the slim strip of leather around his neck. He slipped out of bed and pulled his club uniform from a drawer. The skimpy net thong was hardly worth wearing, but as he pulled it on he could feel Carey's gaze boring into him. He started to wrap the leather kilt around his hips but Carey slipped an arm around his waist and it fell to the floor in a heap.

"You are so fucking irresistible." Carey bent him towards the dresser, grabbed the tube of lube from the top and snapped it open. Seconds later the thong was ripped aside and a well-lubed cock was probing Alistair's tender entrance. He relaxed and welcomed Carey's swift penetration, bracing himself against the thankfully solid piece of furniture.

Alistair's cock hardened swiftly and Carey didn't stop him when he wrapped his fingers around his shaft and stroked quickly. Carey took him hard and fast, grasping Alistair's hips tightly. A few punchy thrusts later and Carey gasped his release. Alistair felt the heat of Carey's release inside him and shot ribbons of cum down the front of the dresser.

Carey panted. "I'll leave you to clean that up and meet you downstairs." He dangled a torn piece of net from one finger. "Think you may need a new one of these, too."

Alistair rolled his eyes and watched with interest as Carey tucked his cock away and zipped up. He could feel warm moisture trickling down his thigh and needed to pay a trip to the bathroom, but he didn't move until Carey had gone.

* * * *

Alistair bounced down the stairs eagerly. He was still on a high from his morning's activities but was also looking forward to working. When he had first started the job he'd never expected to enjoy it as much as he did. Waiting was only ever meant to be a stopgap, but even when his photography business had grown he'd found he didn't want to give it up. Of course, being around Carey had a lot to do with that. Alistair had never let anyone else at the club fuck him. He had played with a few of the members, but only while Carey watched, and in the last few months they had been completely exclusive. It felt like the latest step to full-time had been the last on a long road of getting to know and understand each other.

Alistair had recognised his submissive nature early. He wasn't like some of his friends who tried to deny it or resist its pull. He was comfortable with who and what he was. That didn't mean that the journey had been easy—it had taken a great deal of trust to put himself in the hands of a Dominant, even a great one like Carey. Alistair felt blessed that he had found someone able to deal with his desire for independence alongside his need to submit. He laughed under his breath and acknowledged the fact that Carey being hot as hell also helped.

The club was buzzing with activity as he joined the waiters' briefing. Harry and the other barman, Goran, and Christian, who handled front of house, were there too. They all needed to know what the specials were that day, anything that was off the menu and what the events of the week were in case of questions. Alistair listened out and scanned the room for Carey at the same time. He spotted him leaning on the end of the bar reading a newspaper with an intense look on his face. Alistair instantly felt more settled just knowing Carey was there.

The briefing finished and everyone started to head off to their various roles. Alistair grinned at Christian. "Ready for the madness?"

Christian's dark red hair glinted as he nodded. "It's going to be busy, it always is on a Friday. What did you do this time?" He gestured at Alistair's cuffs.

Alistair shrugged. "You know Carey."

"I do and he's completely smitten. He checks up on you all the time." Christian sounded a little wistful.

"Hey, you'll find someone too…"

"I'm not down here wiggling my arse like you lot. It's hard to get to know anyone when the extent of your conversation is 'Good evening, Sir'."

Alistair giggled. "You look stunning, Chris, and I know you get hit on all the time." He took in Christian's outfit of tight leather trousers and fitted black T-shirt then looked at his own clothes. "If you wore this get-up at reception you'd die from hypothermia. Still, I hope Carey makes you wear the bloody thong under there. I don't see why you should avoid the chafing just because nobody can see!"

Christian's creamy freckled skin pinked.

"You do, don't you!" Alistair crowed gleefully.

Christian grimaced. "Do you think I could fit anything else under these trousers? Besides, Carey said I have to. I'd better get upstairs—we open in ten minutes."

"'Kay. See you later. We should catch a film soon."

"Sure. Try to stay out of trouble."

Alistair wandered across to the bar, his bare feet sinking into the deep pile of the carpet. Carey looked up as he approached and pulled him into a tight hug. Alistair felt Carey slip a hand under his kilt and fondle his arse.

"Carey! Stop! I can't deal with the lunch rush and a hard-on!"

Carey pouted and Alistair laughed at the expression.

"Do you want me dropping food into their laps?"

The pout turned into a scowl. "Of course not." Carey produced a slim leather collar and fastened it around Alistair's neck. "I just like touching you too much. How's Christian? I saw you two talking."

"Fine, Sir. Lonely, I think. He needs a good Dom to look after him."

"He's a very pretty boy, I'm surprised he hasn't been snapped up already. I'll have a think about who might suit him…"

"You sound a bit distracted, Carey, what's up?"

Carey stroked Alistair's bare shoulder. "It's probably nothing and I don't want you to worry." He opened the newspaper and spread it on the bar. Alistair scanned the articles then spotted the headline that made his blood turn cold.

'Hardliner Easton takes control at EFW'

Underneath was a picture of a man in his fifties, handsome if you ignored the arrogant sneer on his face. Alistair shivered and pressed closer to Carey. "He got what he wanted, Sir, he always does. He'll come after me next."

Carey wrapped him up in a hug. "What makes you say that?"

"I'm unfinished business. My father is now head of the biggest law firm in the city – he'll see me as a loose end that needs to be snipped off. I could damage his credibility. Easton Fisher Weston represents a lot of right-wing organisations with extreme views – you can put money on them not knowing that Edward Easton has a gay son."

Carey sighed. "I'd like to reassure you, but I think you're probably right. I think it might be time we took a break. I'll give Joe a call and book us in to The Edge for a few days. It will give us time to think things through."

Alistair took a deep breath and relaxed. "That would be great."

For the next two hours Alistair didn't have time to think about anything but delivering plates of food to the right people. It was a great distraction and thoughts of his father faded to the back of his mind. It was getting quieter when Harry, the bar manager, called him over.

"Could you take a drink out to Christian? He just rang and asked for a coffee."

"Sure." He took the mug he was offered. "Does this have sugar in it?"

The barman grinned. "Yep. Six grains, just as he likes it."

Alistair laughed. "I don't know why he bothers, but he says it makes all the difference."

He took the stairs up to the lounge area carefully, shivering a little as the warmth of the club was replaced by cooler air in the stairwell. At the top he pressed the door release button and turned to push it open with his backside. He crossed the lounge to the door that led to the reception area and repeated the process.

"Hey, Christian, here's your coffee…"

Alistair turned and froze. A gorilla of a man was holding Christian with a hand over his mouth. Christian's green eyes showed his horror as he struggled in the man's grip. Two other apes lunged for Alistair. He threw the coffee straight into the face of one of them and fought hard, but the other tackled him to the ground and he fell hard. A knee jammed into the small of his back, then there was a sharp pain in his arm. The world started to spin.

"Get the little fucker out to the van!"

That was the last Alistair heard as everything faded away.

Chapter Four

Carey was happily surveying his busy little empire whilst keeping half an eye on the door to the stairs. Alistair out of his sight made him feel uncomfortable at the best of times and after seeing the news about the boy's father he was even more on edge. He knew he was ridiculously overprotective, but that was part of who he was and he had no intention of changing. "Jesus, how long does it take to deliver a cup of coffee anyway?" he muttered under his breath. "Gossiping when they should be working, no doubt."

The door from the stairs swung open, but instead of Alistair, Carey was met with the sight of Christian practically falling through it, his face streaked with blood.

"Fuck!" Carey moved without thinking, catching Christian before he sank to the floor, head lolling. "Harry! Give me a hand here!"

From behind the bar, Harry used his broad shoulders to thrust his way through the gathering crowd of concerned onlookers. He took Christian beneath the arms and hauled him onto a chair, cradling him with a heavily muscled arm. "What the hell happened, boss? He's bleeding all over me!"

Carey took a few deep breaths and did what he did best—issued orders. "Someone put the main lights on. Fetch me a clean cloth and some water. Send someone upstairs to look after the reception desk and *find Alistair!*"

Staff and customers started to run around, doing as he'd asked. The room flooded with light and Carey concentrated on taking a look at Christian, who was barely conscious. Gently he pushed strands of blood-sodden hair apart to find the wound that was bleeding so profusely. Looking after Christian was the only thing that kept him from descending into utter panic. He had to blank thoughts of Alistair from his mind or he was going to be sick.

Carey dabbed at Christian's head with a wet cloth, which came away stained with blotches of crimson.

"His scalp is torn. It's not too deep, but there is a lump. He's been hit pretty hard." He persisted with his efforts and gradually the bleeding slowed. Christian moaned and squirmed in Harry's arms.

"Alistair! We have to help Alistair! They've taken him... Oh God! I couldn't stop them. I couldn't..." Christian sounded absolutely distraught.

Harry proved to be a great calming influence, cuddling Christian close and muttering soothing words in his ear. The younger man slowly stilled and his rapid breathing slowed. His eyelids flickered as he became more aware of his surroundings.

Carey stood up and looked around at the sea of familiar faces, desperately searching for the one person he knew he wouldn't find. Cold anger began to build deep inside him and he realised he was in danger of losing control.

"Harry, can you get things back to normal, please. Give a free drink to anyone that wants one. I'll take Christian into the office and look at the CCTV footage from upstairs. Who's manning reception?"

"Goran went up there. He can look after himself, don't worry."

Carey managed a small smile—the deputy bar manager was six foot seven and more intimidating than a pack of hungry velociraptors. "I'll call him from the office."

Christian was looking a bit more alert, though his skin was the colour of chalk. Carey gave him a reassuring pat on the shoulder. "Come on, Christian, I want you to tell me everything that happened." He helped Christian into his small office and got him settled in the comfy leather swivel chair before retrieving a first aid kit from a shelf. "Now, take your time. What exactly happened?"

"I'm really sorry, Carey, I tried to stop them…"

"It's not your fault, Christian. Don't blame yourself. We'll get Alistair back…but you can help. Every little detail you can remember is useful." Carey soaked a cotton wool pad with antiseptic and swabbed the cut on Christian's head.

"There were three of them. They came out of the lift behind that new member, Jonah Salter. I let Jonah through to the lounge and then asked the others for their membership cards—I knew they weren't members, but I didn't know what else to do. I reached for the alarm button, but one of them grabbed me and held a knife to my throat." He fingered his neck as if remembering. "He was really strong and when I struggled he hit me with the butt of the knife. One of the others said they would kill me if I didn't use the intercom and get Alistair to come upstairs. They had a picture of him…"

Carey could see that Christian was trying hard not to sob. Carey was absolutely furious that one of his staff had been subjected to such an ordeal and automatically blamed himself.

"I should have put bouncers on reception as well as on the street…"

Christian gulped. "We've never needed them at lunchtime, Carey, it wasn't your fault."

Carey applied a couple of butterfly bandages to Christian's head and let him carry on.

"I rang down to Harry and asked for coffee. I told the men that Alistair always brought it up and for me to ask for him by name would be suspicious. I thought the chances of it being him that came up were slim—I hoped it would be Harry or Goran."

"But Harry sent Alistair."

"Yes! As soon as he came through the door they grabbed him and dragged him to the lift. They mentioned taking him to a van, but nothing else useful that I heard. They shoved me into the wall and I banged my head—it was a few minutes before I could get downstairs… I'm so sorry, Carey. Who were they? Why would anyone want to hurt Alistair?"

Carey scowled. "Alistair's father is a powerful man who has recently become a lot more visible. He doesn't approve of Alistair's lifestyle, doesn't even accept that he's gay—I think this is probably down to him. The only small measure of comfort we can take from that is that I don't believe his father would hurt him too badly—not physically anyway."

Christian was shivering from shock. Carey remembered some old promotional club fleeces and pulled one from the back of a cupboard. "Here, put this on. Do you think you can go through the CCTV footage with me?"

Christian nodded. "Of course. I'm fine, really."

Carey made a couple of calls, the first to Goran at reception. Goran had cleared up the mess upstairs and was happily scaring the members as they came in. They expected to see sweet, pretty Christian and instead came face to face with a man mountain of belligerent attitude. It was great entertainment. Then Carey called Harry at the bar and ordered a mug of hot sweet tea, which felt like a cliché but was just what Christian needed.

"Thank God for digital recorders." It didn't take Carey long to find the right section of film. He and Christian watched as the events unfolded. Christian had played down how rough the three men had been and how much he had fought. Carey looked at him with new admiration—the boy had one hell of a backbone under all that prettiness.

"I don't recognise any of them and they clearly didn't care that they were on camera—that worries me," Carey muttered. He watched Alistair appear around the door, took note of the horrified expression on Christian's face then tensed as Alistair was manhandled away. Alistair had managed to throw the hot drink he was carrying into one attacker's face and had fought like a demon as they'd dragged him off. Carey felt a glow of pride for his man's spirit.

"If Alistair hadn't brought that drink up to you, I don't like to think what they would have done to get at him," Carey said.

"What do we do now, Sir?" Christian sounded lost and frightened.

"First I have to talk to the police. This is kidnapping and we've got it on film. Then I have some friends who may be able to help. I intend to pull in some favours."

"I want to help."

Carey looked at Christian's determined face and grinned. "Good. I need an assistant and you are a witness so we need to look after you. You can stay in my flat upstairs for now—is that going to be a problem at home?"

Christian shook his head. "I'll let my roommate know so she doesn't worry."

"Good, that's settled then. Are you up to working?"

Christian nodded. "I'd rather keep busy."

"Go and help Harry behind the bar—with Goran upstairs he's probably rushed off his feet and I trust him to look after you."

Carey reclaimed his chair and replayed the video a couple more times before pausing it on an image of Alistair's face. "I'll get you back, love," he whispered fiercely at the flickering screen. He just hoped that Alistair would believe the same thing.

Late afternoon stretched into evening. The police came and went, taking a copy of the video footage with them. To Carey's surprise they had been attentive and polite. No comments were made about Alistair's state of undress, his job or the nature of the club. As Carey showed them out, the younger of the pair turned and shook his hand. "We'll do everything we can, Mr Hoffman. Say hi to Toby for me and make sure he behaves himself."

Carey's confusion must have been apparent. "I'm sorry, I don't understand..."

"Toby Seddon is my baby brother."

"Ah... I see." Carey smiled at the thought of the bouncy young waiter. "Toby's a good boy, PC Seddon, you don't need to worry about him."

"Thanks to you. Toby was a bit wild before he started working here. He made some poor choices and he was lucky not to get hurt. He tells me you have very strict rules and that's exactly what the brat needs."

Carey frowned. "Safety of the staff is paramount here. We were caught off guard today. It will never happen again."

"Well, I'm sorry it's happened at all. We'll be in touch as soon as we have any news."

Though Carey appreciated their good intentions, he wasn't convinced that the police would be able to help much. He placed more faith in the abilities of his friends. He and Alistair had helped Joe Dexter rescue his partner, Olly, from Olly's psychotic ex a few months earlier. He'd rung Joe straight after the police and now he was on his way, as were Heath Anders and his partner Aiden.

Just knowing that his friends were coming made Carey feel better, but if he stopped to think about Alistair, even for a minute, panic started to build in his gut. Alistair needed him, but he also needed Alistair. Not being able to look at him or touch him was torment. Carey's job was to look after his sub, discipline him, love him, protect him. His absence was a deep-seated ache that no amount of painkillers would get rid of. Joe and Heath were both dominant men living the lifestyle with submissive partners. They were very different to Carey, but they would understand what he was going through in a way that others could not. Carey felt like his world had fractured—a gaping chasm had opened up and he was hanging onto the edge by his fingernails.

Carey checked his watch—it was nearly seven o'clock, four hours since Alistair had been taken. It would be at least nine o'clock before Joe and Heath arrived from Yorkshire as they'd had to make sure everything was under control at The Edge before they'd left, so he wandered back out into the club and took up his usual position at the end of the bar. It was early, but The Underground was already filling up with diners. The main food service stopped at nine and made way for dancing and stage shows so plenty of members came in to relax, eat and chat with their friends before the real action started. He watched his staff as they went efficiently about their business and allowed himself a moment's pride. The Underground was thriving and despite the events of the day was looking scarily normal. He wondered how many other people would consider the scene in front of him normal.

At first glance it could be any private members' club, albeit a very exclusive one. Twenty small tables were arranged around the dance floor. Most of the tables were occupied—one or two with a single customer but most with two or three. A second look and the differences to any other club became apparent. The apparel of the waiters was the most obvious clue. The servers were mainly in their twenties, good-looking and fit. They wove amongst the tables, skilfully depositing plates of steaming food and balancing trays of drinks. They went barefoot and that was one of the reasons that the club was kept immaculately clean. There was no smoking and no alcohol. Carey was ruthless about the rules—safe play and inebriation were not compatible in his book. Ever.

Closer examination of the clientele was also revealing. There was no dress code, but a remarkable preponderance of leather was evident. Not all the members were seated at the tables—some were sitting or kneeling on the floor. Carey discouraged complete nudity unless it was part of a show or in a private playroom, but some of the subs kneeling at their masters' feet wore very little.

He watched men being fed by hand, others were on leashes or blindfolded. Doms stroked and petted their subs. There were men of all ages, sizes and shades mingling in a world that transcended petty prejudices. Carey sighed. For him this *was* normal—but not without Alistair.

A glass of iced water appeared at his elbow, a slither of lime floating on the top. Carey turned to see his bar manager's beaming smile.

"Harry. Are you trying to make me feel better?"

"Nope."

Harry had never been one for too many words.

"I don't attempt the impossible," he said, "and I know damn well that nothing I can do or say will improve your evening."

Carey stared. That was the longest sentence he'd ever heard Harry string together. Carey sipped his drink and watched Christian as he carefully mixed two fruit cocktails with a look of intense concentration.

"He doing okay?"

Harry nodded. "Sure."

"Have you ever considered...?" Carey threw a look in Christian's direction.

Harry shrugged. "I'm not his type."

"You tried?"

Harry nodded. "Who wouldn't?"

Carey looked at Christian a little more closely than usual. His dark red hair was an unusual colour and it suited his creamy skin. There was a light dusting of freckles across his nose and he had beautiful, sensuous lips. His eyes were light green—clear and cool. Carey guessed his height was about five feet ten, and he was very slim. He moved lightly, like a dancer.

"So what is his type?"

Harry shrugged. "Strict."

Carey raised an eyebrow. "That doesn't narrow it down, Harry, most Doms are strict."

Harry chuckled. "I mean *really* strict. In a scene, he likes to be controlled—completely. Joe Dexter would probably get close."

"Joe's off the market—his sub's got him tied up in more knots than your average Boy Scout could produce."

Harry suddenly started polishing glasses that didn't need polishing. Carey shook his head and looked at him curiously. "Love changes everything..."

"Carey! I realise you're emotionally distraught, but *that* is a line from a song and I object to being linked to musical theatre in any way."

Harry snorted into his glass as Carey twirled around.

"Joe! You made good time."

A blond blur shot across the floor and Carey found himself with an arm full of Olly.

"Carey! You must be feeling terrible! I can't believe it—poor Alistair... Poor you... I thought we were all done with drama after Aiden's adventures but now this... But we're here to help and I'm sure it's all going to be okay. It has to be..."

Carey gave the whirlwind a bemused hug.

"Olly!" Joe snapped out the word in a way that suggested he said it in the same tone often. "Drop him." He pointed to the floor next to his feet and seconds later Olly was kneeling next to him, head bowed but resting against a thigh.

Carey shook Joe's hand, grinning knowingly. "It's great to see you both, thank you for coming."

"It's been a while since our lives were last turned upside down, Carey—I was starting to get bored." Another man joined them, his voice deep and soft.

"Heath!"

Something inside Carey settled as he received another firm, assured handshake. Heath's steel grey eyes glittered with resolve. "Anything you need, Carey, we're here to help. You remember Aiden?" The young man standing slightly behind Heath stepped forwards.

"Of course. It's nice to see you again, Aiden." Carey caught a couple of people casting glances at Heath's partner and wasn't surprised. Aiden Keller was a strikingly beautiful man with unusually pale eyes and dark tousled hair. The heavy leather collar around his neck sent a very clear message that he was unobtainable and Heath's calculated glare at certain people reinforced it very well.

"Thank you, Sir. I hope we can help... Alistair's a special person."

Heath put an arm around Aiden's shoulders and pulled him nearer. Carey felt a pang of envy at their closeness. Seeing his friends so happy made his yearning for Alistair all the more painful.

As if sensing his discomfort, Joe gestured at an empty table. "It's been a long drive down, Carey, perhaps we could all sit down with a drink and you can tell us everything you know?"

"Of course. What can I get you?"

"Coffee for me, please. Olly will have water."

Olly looked up with a pout.

"Coffee would be great, thanks, Carey." Heath smirked in Olly's direction.

"Aiden, what would you like?" Carey had no qualms about addressing him directly—if Heath didn't want Aiden to order for himself he would have done it for him.

"Tea, please, Sir, if you have it."

Carey passed the order on to Harry and added another coffee for himself. He watched his four friends settle around a table, observing the dynamic between them with interest. Joe sat first then Olly sank to the floor between his legs and leant back with a happy smile, as if resting between his master's legs was the only place he wanted to be. Heath took the seat next to Joe and grinned at Aiden who was wearing a belligerent expression. He clearly did not want to be put on the floor. Heath relented and pulled the boy into his lap instead, giving his arse a hefty smack on the way. Aiden scowled but settled against him.

Carey laughed to himself. Olly and Aiden were so different. Olly was cute and cheeky—he looked angelic with his golden curls and huge blue eyes but boy, did he need firm handling. Aiden on the other hand was much more reserved and Carey knew that accepting his submissive nature was a challenge he fought every day. Heath relished the fight, though, and the two of them made a stunning couple.

Christian rounded the bar carrying a tray of drinks and followed Carey across to the table. He handed the drinks out carefully, moving with grace and poise. Carey decided that he really would have to put some thought into who might make a good Dom for Christian—the young man deserved some dedicated attention.

"Christian, join us. If you can stand going through your story again."

To Carey's surprise, Christian didn't take the remaining free chair and instead knelt next to Carey. Carey petted him. "You know everyone, don't you?"

"Yes, Sir, I do." Christian met each man's eyes then whispered, "Hi, Olly," under his breath. Olly bounced on his knees until Joe rested a hand on his head, subduing him.

"Hey, Christian, don't look so worried. We're here now."

Carey smiled at how certain Olly sounded and wished he could feel the same.

Heath took a swallow of coffee then put his mug down on the table. He tightened his grip on Aiden who nearly choked on his tea. Aiden turned baleful eyes on his master but didn't try to get free.

"We took the liberty of inviting someone else along to this plotting party, Carey. Aiden's boss should be here any time." Heath kept his voice low.

Carey asked, "You mean Dave Becket? He's a member here."

Olly giggled. "Becket has a proper first name? I thought it was Agent."

Joe tugged a few blond curls sharply.

Carey stifled a laugh.

Heath shook his head and sighed. "We had to let him know that Aiden would need a few days off and when we told him why he got very interested."

Aiden shifted in Heath's lap and spoke, "It could be that my outfit has more than a passing interest in Alistair's father."

He didn't name the organisation he worked for but everyone present, except Christian, knew that Aiden was employed by MI5.

"Well we'd better wait for Becket—no point in Christian telling us everything twice." Joe sat back in his chair. "Looks like we don't have to wait any longer."

Dave Becket was the kind of man that gave off an air of absolute authority. He had the looks to match with his cropped blond hair and piercing eyes. Carey had met him a few times, but he wasn't a regular visitor to the club. Carey stood and extended his hand as Becket joined them.

"Dave, thanks for coming. Can I get you anything?"

Becket shook his head and acknowledged his friends. "I'm good, let's get on." He took the last seat and stretched out his long legs.

Carey nodded. "Okay. I'm going to let Christian tell you what happened today, then I'll fill you in on a bit of background and what the police said when they were here. Christian…?" Carey looked down to where Christian was kneeling between his chair and Becket's, but all the boy's attention was directed at Becket, as if the rest of them no longer existed. Carey threw a 'what do I do?' look at Joe who grinned and shrugged.

Olly snickered. "Aw, that's so sweet."

Becket remained impassive but cupped the back of Christian's neck and squeezed lightly. Christian jerked and looked around at them all, startled. Becket didn't move his hand. "Tell us what happened, Christian, then we can work out how to get Alistair back where he belongs."

Christian inched a little closer to Becket's knee and began to talk.

Chapter Five

Alistair dragged his drug-fogged mind out of a woolly grey haze into the daylight. When his vision finally cleared, he decided that he must have still been dreaming because he seemed to be lying in a narrow single bed in the room he had last seen as a teenager. He tilted his head to one side and winced as a sharp pain stabbed through his skull. "Don't do that again, idiot," he muttered to himself. Every syllable of the whispered reprimand brought with it an agonising beat. Alistair wondered if this was what a migraine felt like. If it was, he never wanted another one, ever again, even if it meant giving up chocolate, coffee, red wine *and* cheese.

If he had still been asleep then his head wouldn't have hurt so much. That meant he had to be awake and either someone had made a remarkable reconstruction of his childhood bedroom or he was at his father's house. Not home. It hadn't been home since he'd been old enough to realise that his father was a cruel, bigoted bully. Not since he'd realised that girls could be great friends but didn't possess the anatomical parts that fuelled his dreams.

It was a nice room. Big and airy with a large sash window that overlooked the park. From what Alistair could see it had changed very little. The dove grey walls had been stripped of his posters and photographs. The shelves above the desk were empty of books. But apart from that it looked the same. Same furniture, same plain navy curtains, even the same blue and grey checked duvet cover. It also had a tiny attached shower room—en suite was far too grand a term for it—with a single shower cubicle, toilet and a tiny sink just big enough to wash your hands in.

Alistair pondered if he could make it as far as the toilet. His bladder convinced him that it would be worth the pain. He pushed himself up to a sitting position slowly and carefully, then spent several minutes fighting back the wave of nausea that swept over him. He felt proud that he didn't throw up all over his bed. It was a small victory but something to hang onto. Three metres across carpet felt more like three miles across mountainous terrain as he dragged himself to the bathroom. He gave himself more points for using the toilet without falling into it then splashed cold water over his face in an effort to clear his muzzy brain.

What the hell was he doing in his old room? He perched on the edge of the bed and tried to assess the situation. He remembered taking coffee to Christian at The Underground, then not much. He rubbed his arm reflexively and found a bruised spot. "They stuck me with a needle. I threw the drink..." He could still see Christian's horrified face. "Oh God, I hope they didn't hurt him." Talking to himself helped. There was no other sound to distract him.

Someone had taken his working clothes and now he wore thin cotton trousers, more like hospital scrubs than pyjamas, and no underwear. He tugged the duvet free of the bed and slung it around his shoulders. His brain was working at the pace of a tranquillised snail—nothing made sense. His father was a bastard, but he'd disowned him years ago. Why had he gone to such lengths to bring Alistair home?

If only Carey were there. He would know what to do—he always did. He was so confident, so certain. Alistair's lower lip trembled. "This is bloody ridiculous. I'm a grown man, not some teenage runaway that can be dragged home on a whim!" He stomped across to the door, pulling the duvet with him, and yanked on the handle. "He locked me in! Jesus!" He retreated to the bed and curled himself up in a tight ball. He couldn't think about it anymore, he had to get his mind somewhere else before panic set in. He shut his eyes and imagined he was with Carey, safe, warm and cherished. Nobody made him feel the way Carey did. Even after three years, their relationship just got better with each passing day. Carey gave him what he needed—boundaries, discipline and control all wrapped up in the deepest, most intense love he had ever experienced. With Carey he had found the peace and calm he craved, far away from the judgemental hatred that had poisoned his relationship with his father.

Alistair shivered. There was something wrong with his father, something broken. He'd tried to convince his only son, Alistair, that he was the damaged one and applied constant pressure to make him conform, make him hide who he really was. Alistair had endured it for two years. He'd come out at sixteen—with hindsight not the brightest idea considering his father's beliefs—but even then he had unconsciously sought approval. His mother was long gone by then, happily remarried to a French banker and living the high life in Paris. Submissive tendencies he didn't even understand manifested themselves in dedication to his studies, a hatred of confrontation and loyal obedience to the elderly bookstore manager who employed him after school. Alistair wasn't weak, though—on his eighteenth birthday he had walked out of his father's house and had never looked back.

Alistair knew he was luckier than a lot of other kids whose parents could not accept that they didn't fit their idea of what was 'normal'. His French stepfather had generously supported him through college and called every week regardless of the fact that they had only met once, at the wedding. He'd be eternally grateful to the man for giving him the means to get away from his 'real' father and study the subject he loved. In seven years Edward Easton had made contact just once. Two weeks after Alistair had moved into his hall of residence at university he had received a letter telling him to expect nothing further from his father and telling him to never set foot in his father's house again. He'd read it and felt absolutely nothing.

There was no clock in the room and it was intensely frustrating to Alistair that he didn't know what time, or even what day it was. The window looked out over the garden, but it was a cloudy day and impossible to gauge where the sun was. He longed for some painkillers, but he could put up with the headache if something would just *happen*. Waiting and wondering was just horrible. He got up, marched across the room and hammered on the door until his hand ached as badly as his head. He crawled back to bed cursing beneath his breath and trying not to cry.

He guessed that another two hours had passed before the door opened. The sound of the key grating in the lock jerked him out of the doze he'd slipped into. He was exhausted and Carey's absence was a gnawing ache in his gut. He didn't recognise the man who opened the door. His face was completely blank, giving nothing away. Alistair caught the thin grey T-shirt that was thrown at him and pulled it on.

"Mr Easton will see you now."

Alistair almost laughed. What a joke. Anyone would think he was waiting for an appointment with his bloody bank manager. He didn't hold out much hope that this meeting would end up with a loan. He followed the nameless servant across the landing, his bare feet sinking into the deep pile carpets. They passed a grandfather clock ticking steadily, telling him that it was seven-thirty, then continued down the wide staircase and along the hall... He didn't need a guide. His father would be in the snug. That was where he'd always spent his evenings and Edward Easton was a man of regular habits.

Sure enough they passed the lounge, dining room and study doors and came to a halt outside his father's favourite room, a place Alistair had never been permitted to enter without a specific invitation. Courage born of indignation crumbled away as the door opened. His sombre escort gestured for him to enter but didn't follow, just closed the door behind him. Alistair felt like he was walking into a trap that he had no way of avoiding and he was scared. He wanted Carey.

"Good evening, Alistair."

Alistair was gratified to see that his father had aged, and not well. His hair had receded and deep lines scored his skin. His eyes had lost their brightness. He was fifty years old and looked sixty-five.

"It might be good for you, father, for me—not so much." Alistair squared his shoulders and stood up straighter. "Why am I here?"

"Because you're sick and need help."

It wasn't the man in front of him that had answered. Alistair had been focused on his father and hadn't realised that there was somebody else in the room.

"I am Dr McBride and I'm here to help you, Alistair."

The doctor took a step forwards and Alistair took one back.

"I don't need any help, there's nothing wrong with me."

The doctor had the kind of voice that made Alistair think of snakes—boas and pythons, constrictors that strangled the life out of their prey. There was an underlying sibilant hiss to every word and it made his flesh crawl.

"On the contrary. You've strayed from the straight path to something twisted. You've lost yourself and I can help bring you back. Your father cannot have a deviant son embarrassing him—"

"My father couldn't give a shit about me. I'm not lost and I definitely won't ever be straight." Alistair startled himself with his own virulence, he wasn't usually so forceful, but the situation seemed to merit it. He turned back to his father. "Just do what you're going to do. You dragged me here against my will, drugged me, you're not going to let me walk away now so just fucking *do it!*"

Easton's response was a cruel smile and a gesture that had the doctor scurrying to open the door. Two of the goons that had taken Alistair from the club filled the doorway with their bulk then manhandled Alistair to his knees, twisting his arms painfully behind his back.

His father jerked his head back by the hair. "You prance around virtually naked. You're on view at that club every day. You let another man touch you and you tell me that's normal?" Easton's voice was getting higher, more strident. "You will not fucking humiliate me now I've got what I worked for all these years."

Alistair struggled, ignoring the pain, as his hair was pulled hard.

"And how exactly do you think I'm going to do that? You've been out of my life for seven years and I'm happy for it to stay that way."

"You don't understand, *son*." Spittle splashed across Alistair's cheek. "I need to be seen to be doing something about you. The firm has clients that expect nothing less."

"Your firm is worse than the criminals you represent!"

Alistair could do nothing to avoid the blow that rocked his head back. His father rarely lost his temper and it was a sign of the pressure he was under. Alistair smiled grimly, twisting the rivulet of blood that trailed from his split lip.

"A few months' therapy will adjust your attitude and help you see things differently. Then we can find you a nice, suitable girl and a respectable job. Dr McBride's facility has a reputation for excellent results."

"You have no right! I'm not a child…" Alistair struggled harder until his father thrust a document into his face. You've signed a voluntary committal to the clinic. I have every right."

"No! I didn't sign anything, you bastard…"

"Enough of these histrionics. Deal with him, McBride. I don't want to see him again until he's suitably compliant and willing to do what's required of him."

Alistair watched in disbelief as his father took a seat in his favourite armchair, shook open a newspaper and began to read. The doctor retrieved a small leather case from the table, opened it and pulled out a syringe and a vial of clear liquid.

"I'm sure our journey will be a little more pleasant if you are calm, Alistair." He filled the syringe and squirted a little liquid through it.

"No!" Alistair tore an arm free at the expense of some bruises and received a kick for his trouble. Pinned once more he could only look on as the needle sank into his arm and the syringe emptied. Warmth flushed his veins and in seconds the world lost its sharp edges and became softer, fading gradually to grey.

* * * *

"No! No fucking way."

Heath looked on impassively as Aiden folded his arms across his chest and put on his most stubborn expression.

"We discussed it yesterday, Aiden. You agreed to help."

Aiden's scowl was impressively dark. "Of course I want to help, but nobody mentioned that I'd have to wear...that!" He stabbed a finger at the short black leather kilt lying on the bed behind him.

"You wear a lot less for me." Heath smirked and waited for the explosion.

Aiden's unusual pale eyes narrowed, but his cheeks pinked. "That's totally different and you know it."

"Why? Because I order it?"

Aiden twitched and lowered his gaze. "Maybe."

"Well I'm ordering you to do this. You offered to cover Alistair's shift and that means wearing the same uniform as all the other servers."

"But..."

"But nothing, boy. I'm not giving you a choice and I think we could use the" — he checked his watch — "forty-five minutes before the lunch session starts for a little reminder of who exactly is in charge in this relationship."

Aiden's exaggerated sigh was all about pushing his luck and Heath knew it. He could see straight through his pretty, scarily intelligent brat. Aiden thought too much, it was Heath's responsibility to take him out of his own head. The last couple of days had been intense for both of them. Carey and Alistair were close, dear friends and seeing Carey attempt to hide his fear and frustration was difficult. Heath knew exactly what it was like to be in a position where he might lose the man he loved. What he had been through with Aiden was different, but he could still empathise with Carey. As a Dominant, Heath felt intensely protective and possessive towards Aiden. When they were separated for any length of time he felt unsettled. Carey must feel like he was missing a part of himself.

It had been nearly forty-eight hours since Alistair's disappearance. The first evening when they had all arrived, there had been a lot of talking around the situation but very little that could be planned without further information. It was comforting for Carey to have his friends around him but annoying for all of them that they couldn't accomplish more. Carey needed someone to cover Alistair's shifts at The Underground and though Olly would have been the obvious choice, he was far too scattered and upset to be trusted with trays of hot food and delicate glassware. Heath had volunteered Aiden. He wasn't particularly enamoured of the thought of his boy parading around semi-naked, but his collar would ensure that he wasn't touched. Aiden could also listen in to conversations around the club. Carey suspected that someone had given information to whoever had taken Alistair. The members would talk to Aiden, he was too pretty to ignore.

When he'd agreed, Aiden had been under the false impression that he'd be allowed to wear the same uniform as the bar staff—black leather trousers and a plain black T-shirt. He'd just discovered that wasn't the case. They were in Carey's small flat above the club. The others were downstairs already, waiting to meet Dave Becket who had called with the promise of new information. Heath had time to give Aiden what he clearly needed.

Heath took a seat in the bucket chair in the corner of the room and stretched out his legs. His trousers moulded to his thighs and the feel of soft leather against his skin put him in exactly the right mood and as he looked at Aiden, shifting restlessly in front of him, his cock began to swell nicely.

"Strip. Slowly." His voice rasped as desire tightened his throat.

Aiden unfolded his arms stiffly, resisting every inch of the way. There was always such fight in his eyes, even as he bent to his master's will. Heath smiled, gentling and calming without speaking, looking for the tiniest hint that Aiden wasn't enjoying every second of their little scene.

The shirt went first and Heath feasted his eyes on smooth, pale skin and nicely defined muscles. Aiden's jeans hung on his lean hips and when he released the stud fastening they slipped a couple of inches. Aiden kicked off his boots and bent to remove his socks, exposing a tantalising V of skin as his zipper parted with the movement. Heath held his breath. He never tired of looking at Aiden's deliciously firm, slender body and basked in the knowledge that it was all his, to do with as he pleased. His lover was playing coy now, chewing his lip and fiddling with his waistband. Heath tapped his fingers on the arm of the chair. "I said slowly, but preferably before I reach my next birthday, Aiden." Oh…that got him a thunderous scowl. Aiden shoved his jeans down and stepped out of them leaving him clad only in his collar and a pair of skimpy briefs that were losing the fight with his rigid cock. Heath licked his lips and raised an expectant eyebrow. "Well?"

Aiden's eyes were a bit too bright. "Make me."

Hmm, Aiden's inner brat had surfaced and was in the mood to play. Heath leant forward just a little. "It's a simple choice, Aiden. Either you're naked and on your knees at my feet in the next ten seconds or I send you down to lunch service without the kilt."

There were only two parts to the service uniform at The Underground, the leather kilt and a skimpy net thong. Heath had a feeling the threat would be effective and it was. Precisely six seconds later his naked sub was on the floor, head bowed demurely.

"Better. Spread your knees wider." Heath used his booted foot to shove Aiden's legs farther apart.

"Look at me."

Aiden peeked up from beneath long dark lashes, but Heath could see the glitter of defiance beneath the subservience.

"Stroke yourself."

"Sir?"

"You heard me, Aiden."

Heath wanted to touch himself but resisted. He watched as Aiden tentatively wrapped his fingers around his cock and began to move. He had beautiful long, slim fingers that Heath had witnessed flying over keyboards, pulling miracles from computers, but now were hesitant and unsure.

"Why are you doing this, Sir?" Aiden whispered.

"I'm not doing anything, sweetheart, you are. Faster."

Heath held back until he judged that Aiden was close to coming. He could see the telltale beads of moisture escaping the tip of Aiden's cock. His muscles were twitching and his face was flushed with colour.

"Stop. Hands behind your back."

Horrified understanding expressed itself in Aiden's whimper, but he did as he'd been told.

"Sir! Please...no!"

Heath chuckled and lowered his fly. He released his cock and gave it a gentle squeeze. Oh, it felt so good. He ached—his balls felt hot and tight. He gave a happy sigh and jacked himself, murmuring his enjoyment. He could feel the orgasm building deep inside, slow but inevitable. Aiden stared at him, biting hard on his lower lip, shifting on his knees, desperate for friction. Heath knew Aiden would get no relief for his straining erection, he'd made sure of that when he'd forced the boy's legs so wide apart. God it was such a turn-on knowing that Aiden was held there, frustrated and hard, just by the power of his word. No ropes or chains, just a simple command. Heath came with a shout. Aiden let out a strangled sob as he came too and drops of cum splattered across his thighs.

"Beautiful. Just beautiful." Heath slipped a simple leather cock ring from his pocket. "Stand up, love."

Aiden rose gracefully, keeping his hands behind his back.

"Sir…please, I need…"

"You need what I choose to give you. If you're good today, I may let you come this evening." Heath wrapped the leather around the base of Aiden's cock and cinched it tight. "Now fetch a cloth for me then you can get ready for work." He leaned in and kissed Aiden hard. "You remember who's in charge now?" He didn't expect an answer, just gave Aiden a firm pat on the arse and an evil grin. "Then we can go and hear what news Becket has for us."

Aiden looked down at his rigid, bound cock and grimaced. "You are a complete bastard, Sir."

"Not something I've ever tried to deny."

Shaking his head in mock disgust, Aiden fetched a wet cloth from the bathroom and handed it to Heath who cleaned himself, then Aiden.

Aiden picked up the tiny thong from the bed. "Just how do you expect me to get this"—he pointed to his dick—"into this?" He twirled the scrap of net from a finger.

Heath grinned at his naked, disgruntled sub and had a moment of uncharacteristic soppiness as he kissed him gently. "You're a clever boy, sweetheart, you'll figure it out."

Chapter Six

The Underground was buzzing and getting busier by the minute. Alistair's disappearance had caused a stir and business was booming. Joe leaned against the bar and made no secret of the fact that he was observing everyone and everything. At first glance, all seemed normal, but Joe was attuned to the nuances of body language and the tone of conversation. Beneath the chatter and background music there was a faint undercurrent of curiosity and speculation.

The atmosphere was exacerbated by the new member of the serving staff. Aiden, in The Underground's skimpy uniform, was the cause of many a cooling meal and forgotten drink as he moved gracefully between the tables. If he bent to retrieve an empty glass or to deliver a plate, the movement seemed to be accompanied by a sharp intake of breath from whoever was closest. Men craned their necks for a peek as his short kilt swung enticingly.

Joe watched Heath watching Aiden and made an effort to keep a straight face. His friend was throwing menacing glances at anyone who so much as looked at

Aiden in a suggestive way. That was a hell of a lot of glaring to get through because virtually every Dom in the place was tracking Aiden with covetous lust. Joe understood the attraction even if he didn't feel it himself. Aiden was gorgeous, but it wasn't just his looks that made him so attractive. He had a unique aura that promised submission with bite, a rare combination. Heath was a lucky man and Joe knew that his friend had nothing to worry about. Not only did Aiden adore his master, but Heath's reputation alone was enough to keep wandering hands away from what was clearly his. That and the heavy leather collar that was strapped around Aiden's neck, of course. On any other sub it would have looked extreme, cruel even, but on Aiden it looked exactly right and he wore it like a badge of honour.

Carey was behind the bar, deep in conversation with his staff. Goran was back in his usual spot as Christian had begged to return to his post at reception. Carey had insisted on putting security staff there to protect him, just in case. Joe frowned. Carey was fraying around the edges, betraying his stress with signs that only someone as observant as Joe would spot. His gestures were a little jerkier than normal — he maintained a professional smile that didn't quite reach his eyes and his fingers strayed repeatedly towards the pocket that housed a creased picture of Alistair. He sighed. He knew exactly how Carey felt. Being forced apart from Olly had been a nightmare and it had happened when their relationship was still new. Carey and Alistair had been together for some time and Joe was amazed that Carey was managing to hold it together as well as he was. He suspected that it wouldn't take much for the man to crumble. Force of will was the only thing keeping him sane and Joe was determined that his friend would not suffer for a moment longer than necessary.

Joe sensed a new presence at his elbow. For a big man, Dave Becket moved remarkably quietly. He always seemed to be poised for something…ready for action. It didn't seem like he ever relaxed. He needed a sub to lavish some of that dedicated attention on. In a rare moment of camaraderie, Dave had admitted to being bi, but his strong preference for men came from being unable to find a woman capable of dealing with his clinically cold and intimidatingly dominant persona. Dave was not the touchy-feely type.

"No Olly?" Becket sounded wary, much to Joe's amusement. Olly had the ability to upset the equilibrium of the toughest Dom with his irrepressible nature and complete lack of political correctness.

"Olly needed a little quiet time." Joe pointed to a dark corner at the back of the room where Olly's golden curls could just be seen in the dim light. He was kneeling, facing the corner, hands loosely clasped behind his back.

Becket stared in amazement. "How the hell do you get him to stay still and quiet at the same time?"

Joe chuckled. "It's a challenge. The trick is to make the alternative a whole lot worse."

"You gave him a choice?"

"Of course," Joe said mildly. "I'm not a tinpot dictator."

Dave looked sceptical. "Tell me."

Joe debated whether or not to keep his friend guessing, then relented. "An hour in the corner or the entire evening gagged. Neither option was particularly palatable to him."

"I can imagine." Becket looked at his watch. "How long has he been there?"

Joe grinned. "Fifty-nine minutes and fifty-five, six, seven..."

Three seconds later a slender blond missile shot across the room and threw himself into Joe's arms.

"That was horrible, Sir. I missed you so much. It was dark and lonely and it felt like forever." Olly pouted prettily.

"I was right here the whole time, Olly, you know that."

"But I couldn't see you so it was like you weren't there at all and I hate that. It was scary and my knees hurt and I'm really, really hard and I need you to... Oh, hi Agent Becket, you're back, where's Christian? Have you fu—" He was cut off abruptly as Joe placed a hand tightly over his mouth.

"Unless you want to spend another hour in that corner, Olly, behave yourself."

Olly nodded, his blue eyes huge above Joe's hand.

"Sorry, Sir." He snuggled against Joe's side and sighed happily when Joe encircled his waist comfortingly.

"Good boy."

Becket shook his head as Olly peeked at him with a mischievous grin. "Let's find a private table. I've got some news."

Joe nodded. "Olly, go and fetch Heath—if he can manage to let Aiden out of his sight for a few minutes." Olly giggled and scampered across the room to where Heath was lounging in a chair trying, and failing, to look nonchalant. Joe beckoned to Carey who stiffened and came over immediately.

"Dave needs to talk to us."

Carey blinked and straightened. "Let's go to the office. It'll be cramped, but there's less chance of anyone overhearing us." He lifted the bar hatch and joined them.

"Go ahead. I'll wait for Heath and Olly." Joe could see Olly talking animatedly to his friend. Heath was clearly feeling resistant. Olly grabbed Aiden's hand as he passed and Joe watched with amusement as Aiden dealt with his overprotective partner. Within a minute Heath was walking towards him with a face like thunder, Olly bouncing and chattering beside him.

Joe patted his friend on the shoulder. "You'll get over it."

Heath growled, "Aiden needs his arse whipped."

"I'm sure he does, and you're just the man to do it, but in the meantime he needs to do his job. Nobody is going to talk to him with you glaring daggers at them."

"They shouldn't be talking, or looking, or even thinking…" Heath craned his neck, looking back to where Aiden was now chatting with a table of attentive Doms. Joe grabbed his arm to stop him from running right back to where he'd come from and steered him towards Carey's office. "You agreed to let him do this, Heath, now leave him be."

Olly took Heath's hand. "You don't need to worry, Heath—with all that leather around his neck, only a complete idiot would think that Aiden is available. Where did you get that collar anyway? It looks…uncomfortable. You won't make me wear anything like that, will you, Sir?" Olly fiddled with the fine chain that hung around his throat and played with the little padlock pendant.

He ran a finger down the curve of Olly's slender neck. "It wouldn't suit you, don't worry, and you know Aiden doesn't wear that one all the time. He isn't complaining, is he?"

Olly shook his head thoughtfully. "No. He likes it. How weird is that?"

"He'll be wearing it permanently if he's not careful," Heath muttered under his breath.

They all crowded into Carey's office where Carey was already sitting in his chair and Dave Becket was perched on the edge of the desk. Heath cleared some paperwork from a low filing cabinet and took a seat on that. Joe took the visitor's chair and Olly sat cross-legged on the remaining square of carpet after he'd pushed the door shut.

Joe rested a hand on Olly's shoulder. "Okay, Dave, we're all yours. What have you got?"

Becket took in the room, quietly appraising them all, his gaze settling for longer on Carey. For a fleeting moment Joe sensed the empathy between the two men. Under Dave's cold, unbending exterior Joe suspected that a soft, warm heart was beating.

Becket began without preamble. "We've been following two lines of enquiry. The first is Alistair's location. The second concerns some of his father's business interests."

Carey put his elbows on the desk and steepled his fingers, listening intently.

Becket continued in a steady tone, "I put surveillance on Edward Easton's house and office as soon as I learned of Alistair's disappearance. I believe that Alistair was taken to the house from here. The CCTV footage of the van that Christian heard mentioned suggested they were heading in that direction."

"You can't be sure?" Heath didn't sound annoyed, just curious.

Becket shook his head. "We didn't get there quickly enough. We think Alistair was already inside the house by the time we got a team in position. What we did witness was the arrival of a man that's since been identified as Dr Duncan McBride, someone we already happen to have a file on."

Joe frowned. "I think I know that name... Why does it seem familiar?"

Becket's lips pressed together in a tight line. "You may well have heard of him because he shares your profession, Joe. He's published various papers on his specialism — reversion therapy."

Joe snorted. "That's it — fucking quack. He gives psychologists a bad name."

Carey spoke, sounding more than a little strained, "Can someone please tell this poor, ignorant bar owner what the fuck you're talking about?"

"Sorry, Carey" — Joe grimaced — "this so-called doctor says that he can cure homosexuality. He sells his services to anyone prepared to pay."

"Being gay isn't a fucking illness. It can't be *cured*," Heath spat the words with venom.

"Of course not," Joe agreed. "And no genuine psychologist or psychiatrist believes that, but there are plenty of families prepared to try anything to make their kids 'normal'. Even some individuals who have been brainwashed or bullied into believing that there is something wrong with them pay for McBride's treatments."

Carey looked very pale. "And what exactly are these treatments?"

Becket shrugged. "We don't really know, but the rumours include everything from shock therapy to chanting and fasting."

"Very few people are prepared to talk about what they've been through. I've heard of hypnotherapy being used, even sensory or sleep deprivation." Joe shook his head. "It's torture, plain and simple."

Carey looked like he might throw up. Olly nudged the wastepaper bin a little closer to the side of the desk with his foot.

Becket continued, "Two cars left Easton's house late last night. They went in separate directions, one towards central London and the other to the north. My tail followed the one going north and sent in the registration of the other car, which was picked up a few miles away. I got local police to stop both of them on the pretext of a drink driving campaign, but there was no sign of Alistair or the doctor. I believe it was a deliberate plan to get us away from the house. They must have known we were watching."

Carey took a slow, deep breath. "You mean you have no idea where Alistair is?"

Joe was amazed that his friend was managing to keep his temper, but he suspected that Becket wasn't nearly as incompetent as his account seemed to suggest.

"We know exactly where he is, but thanks to last night's operation, neither his father nor McBride will have any clue that we do."

Carey took a paperclip from the pot on his desk, straightened it out and began stabbing it into the leather surface. "I like you, Dave, I really do, but if you don't tell me where he is in the next five seconds then assault with a deadly weapon is on the cards."

Joe leant forwards and closed his hand around Carey's fist. "Though I appreciate the drama of death by paperclip, Carey, Alistair needs you here, not in prison, when we get him back."

"When...?"

"Yes, when. Not if. When."

Olly clambered to his feet, edged around the desk and plonked himself in Carey's lap. "I know I'm not Alistair, Sir, but I really need a hug."

Joe squeezed Carey's hand, giving him permission. Carey let Olly snuggle against him and he stroked his curls.

Joe relaxed — giving Olly some attention would be a safe enough distraction for a while even if it did mean another man touching his sub. Olly was a total hug addict, he could snuggle for England and wouldn't consider it a sacrifice to let Carey look after him — or at least let him believe that was what he was doing.

"Sorry," Carey muttered. "Carry on, Dave."

Becket nodded, completely unphased by his close brush with a gruesome, stationery-inspired death. "As soon as McBride was identified, I put surveillance on his clinic in Cornwall. A patient matching Alistair's description arrived there this morning in the company of two men who looked remarkably like the thugs on your security tapes, Carey."

"Go to Joe, Olly." Carey nudged him gently. "I feel a lot better, thank you." Olly gave him a kiss on the cheek and headed straight for his lover's lap where Joe gathered him into his arms.

"Was he okay? Did they hurt him?" Carey whispered as if he didn't want to hear the answer.

"He was walking under his own steam, Carey, I can tell you that, but being held. He wasn't resisting, looked a bit out of it. Probably drugged to keep him compliant."

"So why are we sat here yapping like a bunch of old women, and not on the road?" Carey challenged.

Becket sighed. "It's not that simple. On the surface McBride's business is legitimate. He'll know that Alistair is unwilling, but he'll have paperwork in place to cover his arse. If Alistair isn't completely lucid, we can't just march in there and pull him out without good cause. We need to be a bit more subtle than that."

"Bullshit."

Joe glanced around at Heath, who looked vaguely amused. Becket raised an eyebrow quizzically.

"Don't try to act innocent *Agent* Becket, it doesn't suit you. You're stalling for time. You work for the fucking security services — you could close the place down in minutes or send in half the bloody army if you wanted to. You're a manipulative son of a bitch with your own agenda, so why not just tell us the truth before I decide to use you for a whipping demonstration. Or better yet, let Carey do it."

To his credit, Becket didn't try to bluff his way out of the tight, and potentially painful, corner he had backed himself into.

"Fine. I was coming to part two. I need time to do some digging into a few of Easton's business interests."

"No. No fucking way am I leaving Alistair in that place for a second longer than necessary." Carey was on his feet, face like thunder.

"It *is* necessary or I wouldn't suggest it," Becket responded calmly. "A few days now could make all the difference to Alistair's future. How safe do you think he'll be if you just ride to the rescue? His father has power, money and influence. We have to bring Easton down for Alistair to have any chance of a normal life."

Carey sat down with a thud, compressing the air from his leather seat with a whoosh. "No. I can't. He'd never forgive me."

Joe stroked Olly's arm, enjoying the strength of lean muscle. He glanced back at Heath before he spoke and registered unspoken support. "Carey, who is the stronger in a D/s relationship?"

"The sub," Carey responded automatically.

"Who holds the power?"

"The sub," Carey cursed as he realised what Joe was doing.

"True submissives have enormous inner strength and resilience. Look at what Aiden and Olly have been through—Alistair is no different."

Olly bounced a little. "Alistair's stronger. He has that whole inner calm thing going on. I can't do that without a lot of help...and I mean a lot!"

That got a whole round of laughs that broke the atmosphere down. Olly pouted. "Neither can Aiden," he said defensively. "He submits like a wild stallion— needs breaking first."

Heath choked on a laugh. "Very perceptive, brat, but you're right, Alistair is no delicate flower."

"Of course I'm right." Olly nuzzled beneath Joe's chin.

"Fine, fine." Carey scowled. "I get the point, but I don't have to be happy about it."

"We understand, Carey, really. I hate it when Aiden is out of my sight, let alone hundreds of miles away." Heath's glance strayed towards the door.

Joe decided it was time to move things along. "You presumably have a plan, Dave? Why don't you just tell us and then we can make a more informed decision?"

"Okay. This is open for discussion—consider yourselves deputised."

"Oh! Do I get a badge?" Olly quipped.

Joe growled, "You and I are going to spend some quality time in a private room as soon as we're done here. I may even invite Carey along to watch."

Olly chewed on his lower lip and cast a wicked glance at Carey, "Yes, Sir." He sounded like he'd just got exactly what he wanted.

Becket shifted and got back to talking. "Firstly, I need Aiden back at work. He's assigned to the business investigation and I want him chained to a computer as soon as possible."

He glanced at Heath who nodded agreement. "No problem, we'll head back to Yorkshire this afternoon."

Joe guessed that actual chains were a real possibility.

"Second, we need to get someone into the clinic, ready to get Alistair out of there as soon as we have what we need. My suggestion is that Joe admits a patient on the same programme. As a doctor he then has visitation rights. Joe—you've also got all the credentials we need without us having to concoct too much background."

Joe inclined his head. "Okay, what about my patient?"

"I think Olly can do it." Becket kept talking before anyone could stop him or protest, "He's ideal— medically trained and appropriately bratty. No one will suspect that he's not a genuine case."

Joe gripped Olly's arm a little too tightly. What Becket said made sense, but every protective bone in his body ached at the idea of deliberately putting Olly into the clinic.

"Given what I've just said to Carey, I can hardly refuse—but it's up to Olly, not me."

"Of course I'll do it! I don't need to be wrapped in cotton wool, though it is nice to be pampered occasionally." Olly fluttered his eyelashes at Joe.

"I don't do pampering."

"No, Sir, you don't. Perhaps it's time you learnt?"

Heath chuckled. "You've spoilt him, Joe. Your reputation as the strictest Dom in the club is going to be shot to pieces."

"I hate to interrupt, but while everyone else is helping out, what will I be doing? Sitting here knitting?" Carey looked pissed off.

"Partly, well, not the knitting bit—I don't trust you with a pair of knitting needles—but I do need you to be here, conducting business as usual. You can't go to Cornwall because you may be recognised. However, a little misinformation goes a long way in my line of work, and you will be aiding and abetting." Dave had a glint in his eye that told Joe he was up to something. "I've got another job for you, too, but I'll tell you about that later."

Heath stood up. "I'm going to retrieve Aiden and then head back to your place, Joe, to pack up. Carey— I'll be relieving you of a set of club uniform. Payment for Aiden's services today!"

Olly sniggered and Joe rested a hand lightly, but threateningly across his crotch.

"Olly and I are going to make use of the facilities, then we'll do some character planning. Carey—would you care to join us downstairs?"

"Hmm. I think I would. A lesson from the expert in brat control doesn't come along every day."

Olly whimpered and Joe felt the ridge of the cock beneath his fingers harden.

"Excellent. In that case, Heath—I'll call you tonight. What about you, Dave?"

Becket grinned. "Work to do, people to see, plots to hatch… I'll be back to see Carey again this evening and I'll catch up with you and Olly in the morning."

They manoeuvred themselves out of the cramped office and headed off in various directions. Joe smiled as Heath made a beeline for Aiden who spotted him coming and stood waiting, hands on hips. He looked about as submissive as a spitting cobra, but when Heath reached him, Aiden sank to his knees and bowed his head.

"Half an hour apart and look at them!" It was a good feeling to know his friends were so in love. "Carey — would you like to choose a room for us? It's time Olly had his arse warmed."

Olly bounced indignantly, but his eyes were bright and eager.

"My pleasure... I think the room with the St Andrew's cross might be appropriate, don't you?"

"Perfect. A very pleasant way for us all to unwind before the fun really begins." Joe sounded perfectly serene.

Olly looked from Joe to Carey and back again. "You're teasing me, Sir. Aren't you? Sir...?"

Chapter Seven

Carey adjusted the knot on his dark grey silk tie and folded down the collar of his shirt. A little twist of pain screwed with his guts as, yet again, an everyday act reminded him of what he was missing. Alistair loved to help him dress and managed to turn the whole process into a deliciously erotic experience. Carey reflected that it was a good job he didn't have set office hours because he had a habit of being later than planned every time Alistair got involved in his morning routine. It would start with stroking — gentle touches between buttons, the brush of a thumb across his nipple — then soft kisses to his neck and collarbone before cotton closed over his skin.

Naked and hard, Alistair would drop to his knees and nuzzle, tugging at the fabric of Carey's underwear with his teeth. Then he'd look up with those irresistible, pleading eyes until Carey nodded his permission. Then underwear that he'd just pulled on would be around his ankles and Alistair's sweet mouth would welcome his cock with warmth and enthusiasm. Carey shuddered and tried to think about something less painful. All his focus had to be on doing what was necessary to get Alistair back where he belonged.

Necessary. That was the word he had to concentrate on. He was doing something that needed to be done. He could still see the glimmer of amusement in Dave Becket's pale eyes as he'd briefed him on his part. Carey shook his head and shrugged into his jacket, before doing up the buttons as if they might afford some measure of protection. He gave himself an appraising look in the mirror. Alistair would approve. The charcoal grey and slim cut of his suit accentuated his height and the silvery blue shirt added just the right amount of colour to relieve the relatively staid outfit.

"You scrub up okay for an old man." Carey grinned at himself in the mirror. Alistair would tell him off for the 'old man' comment. Carey didn't look as tired as he felt. He had slept, eventually, but nightmares had prevented real rest, and the constant worry was exhausting. He gave himself a mental slap. "You can sleep when you're dead, Carey, now man up."

As he headed downstairs into the club, Carey straightened his back and cultivated a haughty expression as befitted a Dom. He didn't want anything to betray the depth of his fear. He strolled to the bar and accepted a glass of iced water from Harry before he spoke, "I'm going out for an appointment shortly, Harry, so you're in charge tonight. I'm not sure how late it will be when I get back."

Harry nodded. "No problem, boss."

Carey beckoned him a little closer. "I need you to do something else this evening, Harry. I want you to sow a few seeds of gossip."

Harry grinned. "And what rumour would you like me to spread exactly?"

Carey looked around to make sure that there was no one else within earshot. "If anyone asks where I am, you can tell them that I've gone to a meeting. If they press, hint that I'm seeing a new prospective sub."

Harry's eyes widened. He grabbed a cloth and started to rub at a non-existent spot on the highly polished bar. "You're not...?"

"Of course not! Jesus, Harry!" Carey exclaimed. "I just want it to get around that I'm moving on. You can suggest that Edward Easton is too powerful to be tangled with."

Harry looked confused but nodded. "Okay, whatever you need, boss. Where *are* you going then?"

Carey brushed an imaginary piece of lint from his sleeve. "Can't tell you that, but I've got my mobile with me if you need me. Emergencies only, understand?"

"Sure. You can rely on me, you know that."

"I know." Carey pushed his glass away. "I'd better be off. Have a good evening, Harry."

Carey headed for the exit feeling like a man going to his own execution. He had just ensured that the members of The Underground would brand him a selfish coward. A good Dominant never abandoned his sub. Relationships ended, people moved on, fell in and out of love, but real Doms made sure that their subs were looked after even when they were no longer together. It was aftercare that was just as important as the application of a soothing balm after a flogging. Carey knew that he had just committed the cardinal sin. To all intents and purposes he had just given the impression that he had abandoned Alistair to his fate.

Christian was busy at the reception desk, for which Carey was grateful because it meant he didn't have to lie to the boy. He gave him a brief wave, let the security staff know that he would be gone for a while then stepped into the lift. When he reached the street, the cool night air was refreshing. There was no need for an overcoat. It was a dry evening and, though a little chilly, Carey walked briskly enough to feel comfortably warm. He loved London at night. He could feel the pulse of the place beating through the streets and buildings in a constant, never-ending rhythm. It had a calming effect somehow. In the darkness with less bustle and muted noise it was easier to sense the history all around him. He liked to explore the hidden alleyways and passages that had survived centuries of change to remain concealed, imprinted with the marks of time. But tonight there was no time for wandering. Carey took the most direct route to his destination. He was visiting a place he knew by reputation but had never been to before, and he had to admit, had never expected to see inside.

Carey crossed a wide street edged with anonymous office blocks and turned into a side road. Immediately the atmosphere changed to something that felt much more suburban, even though he was still in the heart of the city. To one side there was a private garden, fenced with wrought iron railings, which all of the street's residents would have access to. On the other, a row of grand Victorian houses that, from the signage outside them, had nearly all been converted into small hotels and guesthouses. Carey stopped outside the first property that didn't carry any information about its vacancy status and walked up to the glossy black front door. The brass knocker and letterbox gleamed in the amber glow of a nearby street light. A small, discreet brass plate to the side of the door was etched with the words, 'Severin's Muse'.

"Hmm. *Venus in Furs*, someone's well read." Carey looked around for a bell. He didn't want to use the knocker and alert half the street. On the other side of the door to the brass plate was an old-fashioned bell-pull. Carey gave it one quick tug and waited. He didn't hear anything inside the house, but then the bell might be sounding in the basement for all he knew. He turned and surveyed the road, which was completely deserted. The cars parked at the kerb looked expensive, the properties uniformly well maintained. A quick glance at his watch told him that it was precisely nine o'clock, exactly the time he was expected. He swivelled back to face the door just as it opened. A young woman, who looked like a stereotypical librarian, stood looking at him curiously. "Mr Hoffman?"

Carey nodded.

"Please come in, Alana is expecting you."

As the solid front door closed behind him, a little shiver ran down his spine. Carey could instantly empathise with any insect that had ever been snared by a spider's web. The hall he now stood in was innocent enough. The carpet was a deep burgundy, the pile thick beneath his feet. The walls and woodwork were painted cream and reproduction paintings by various impressionists dotted the walls. It was all very calm and soothing. Carey didn't feel calm or soothed — he wanted to get this over with.

His escort guided him through the hall to a room that was set up as a cosy lounge. Two comfortable armchairs and a couch surrounded a low coffee table upon which sat a silver tray carrying a coffee pot, cream jug, sugar bowl, two delicate cups and saucers.

Carey could smell the aroma of good strong coffee and relaxed a little. Anyone that served decent coffee couldn't be that scary.

"Please take a seat, Mr Hoffman."

Carey sat. He suspected that the young woman now leaving the room was not quite as demure as she seemed. His suspicions were confirmed when she turned at the door and gave him a wicked wink. He crossed his legs. It seemed the sensible thing to do.

"Jesus, Carey, pull yourself together. They're just women for pity's sake," Carey muttered under his breath. Carey knew that the woman he was meeting was definitely not 'just' anything. Alana French was possibly the most infamous Dominatrix on the London scene.

Carey wasn't kept waiting long. When the door opened, he stood to greet his host. Alana was imposingly tall, helped by the four inch spiked heels she wore. As she turned to close the door, her old-fashioned seamed stockings came into view...and a zip on her pencil skirt ran from the waistband all the way to the hem. A smoky grey silk blouse and a choker of dark grey pearls topped the outfit. The whole ensemble was understated, elegant and, though businesslike, implicitly sexy. Carey had never been attracted to a woman in his life, but he could appreciate what he saw. Alana wasn't beautiful, she was striking. She held out a perfectly manicured hand. Carey took it gently and raised it to his lips.

"Well, Mr Hoffman, you are quite the gentleman." Her voice was a little deeper than Carey had expected, but warm.

"And you, Ms France, know how to make an entrance." Carey allowed his lips to brush her knuckles then waited for her to sit down before he resumed his own seat.

"It's a great pleasure to get to meet the owner of The Underground, though I wish the circumstances were more pleasant. I've always wondered what it would be like to spend an evening there." Alana bent forwards, poured coffee into the two cups then handed one to Carey.

"Then you must be my guest very soon." Carey smiled at her and sipped his drink. It was deliciously bitter and appropriate for his mood.

"I'd like that."

There was a mellow huskiness to Alana's voice that made Carey think of whisky and firelight. His nerves disappeared. "I understand that we have a mutual friend?"

His companion nodded. "Indeed. Members of this country's intelligence organisations move in some very interesting circles, do they not?"

"They do, though I have to admit that I was a little surprised to find that Dave Becket was familiar with your...services."

Alana laughed. "It doesn't surprise me that he didn't make his relationship with me clearer. Dave and I have been friends for years, we met long before I established my current business and much as I would often like to apply my whip to that man's arse, I'm afraid he's rather a lot like you. I don't number that many gay dominant men among my clientele, more's the pity."

Carey chuckled. "I've had cause to think the same about Mr Becket recently. The man brings new depths to the word implacable, but he's a good friend when it counts."

"And he understands the value of exploiting people's compulsions." Alana raised her coffee cup in a toast.

Carey emptied his cup and placed it carefully on the tray. "So why am I here, Alana? Dave said you wanted to meet me and that it was in my interest to be here. He didn't tell me anything else."

Alana crossed her ankles neatly and gave him an appraising look. "I'm sure you understand the value of confidentiality in my line of work. If my customers thought that there was any chance their little secrets might be betrayed, I'd be flipping burgers within the month."

Carey tried to picture that and couldn't force his imagination to make the leap. "I do, but what has that got to do…"

"Tell me about Alistair." Alana leant back in her seat and looked expectant.

Carey absently noted that she had quite large hands… He was avoiding an answer, deciding whether or not to refuse. If Becket said this was a worthwhile visit, then he believed him. He folded his hands in his lap to avoid wringing them as he spoke. "Alistair is a photographer, a very good one. He specialises in urban wildlife and landscape, though he does quite a lot of portraiture—he's built a solid client base since he graduated. His mother lives abroad with her second husband. His father… Well, I'm sure you know who he is. He has no other siblings."

Alana smiled. "Carey, I want to know how you feel for the man, not his life story. He's your submissive, isn't he? That's a very special relationship."

Carey sighed. He was a man, wasn't there a law that said he didn't have to talk about his feelings? He rubbed his chin, easing his clenched jaw, and looked at his hands. "Alistair is creative, gentle, mischievous…and comfortable with himself. I don't think I've ever met a submissive that was more accepting of his own needs. He's independent, but when we're together… He submits beautifully. He's controlled, sensual…but he has an inner calm that I admire greatly." Carey's voice broke a little.

"You love him?" Alana asked gently.

"I do." It was a simple answer for a question that wasn't simple at all. "I feel like a part of myself has been ripped away and I'm slowly bleeding to death. There's no peace in my world without him."

Alana leant forwards and patted his knee. "Thank you, Carey, I'm sure that wasn't easy." She looked around the room briefly. "Well, maybe it was time for a career change anyway."

"I don't understand, Alana…" Carey was genuinely puzzled.

"Edward Easton is a client of mine. I've been keeping an eye on him for a while now at Dave's request. What he has done is unacceptable. Dave Becket asked me if I'd be willing to help, but I needed to know how you felt about your boy before I made such a…life-changing decision."

Carey stood up and wandered across to the window. "That's very interesting. It makes Easton a hypocrite as well as a bigoted coward, but forgive me, Alana— exposing his liking for a Dominatrix is unlikely to put much of a dent in his reputation. Mild embarrassment that can be dismissed as a healthy need to release tension would probably be the extent of the fallout." He turned. "Not that I don't appreciate the offer."

Alana stood and joined him. "But what do you think his clients would do if they knew he was seeing a man?"

Carey stared at her in disbelief. He took a step back, noting her height, large hands and feet and the double row of large pearls that could easily conceal an Adam's apple. "You have got to be kidding me?"

Alana's lips twitched in amusement. She kicked off her heels. "Oh thank God! I have no idea how women manage to totter around in heels all day, they are instruments of torture." She fiddled with her hair and Carey gaped as a wig was removed to reveal short, tousled strands that stuck up everywhere. "I know, I know... I always look like a hedgehog when I take it off."

Carey stared. Alana was as much a man as he was. It was amazing what makeup could do when the face beneath was already androgynously handsome.

"Alan Fairbrother. Pleased to meet you."

There was something surreal about shaking hands with a man still dressed like a woman, but sounding and acting like a man. Carey did it anyway.

"You had me fooled, Alan, you make a very impressive woman." He chuckled. "So are you – ?"

"Transvestite? Transgender? Nope, nothing that interesting. I had ambitions as an actor, spent some time touring with *Rocky Horror* and then met the guy that owned this place. He was the original 'Severin's Muse' and when I came into some money from my grandparents, I bought him out." Alan scrubbed his hands through his hair. "I don't have sex with the clients here, it maintains the illusion nicely. Most don't want that anyway and the ones that do are sent elsewhere."

Carey rolled his shoulders, releasing some of the tension that had built up yet again. "I can see what a useful asset you must be to Agent Becket. I imagine you hear all kinds of things?"

"I do, and it helps the security services to build up portfolios of information that they can use if they need to. You'd be surprised at the number of politicians and powerful businessmen that seek me out."

"Very little surprises me these days, Alan." Carey felt suddenly exhausted. "I miss Alistair. I need him back. I'd like to say that I couldn't possibly ask you to risk everything this way, but I'm too bloody selfish. Anything you can do to help—anything that will protect Alistair in the future—I'll accept with open arms and a great deal of gratitude."

"Well then, that's payment enough. I'll talk to Dave again soon—best you don't know too much about how this will work, not until you need to. Now how about some more coffee?"

They sat and chatted for a while before Alan got up. "I have a client at ten, Carey, and you need to be long gone by then. It's been a pleasure. I hope Alistair is back with you soon and then, well, we'll see, won't we." He gave Carey a cheeky grin. "Now I have makeup to repair and a far less comfortable outfit to change into. Have you ever tried to breathe in a leather and whalebone corset? It's a challenge, I can tell you."

Carey raised an eyebrow, not quite sure how to reply until he saw the mischievous glint in Alan's eye. "When all this is over, you must come to The Underground on an evening when there's a show on. That'll open your eyes to a whole new world."

Alan smiled. "I'll look forward to that, and to meeting Alistair. He must be very special." He pressed a buzzer next to the door and seconds later his assistant returned to show Carey out.

The two men shook hands. "Thank you, Alan, for everything." Carey tried to convey how he felt in completely inadequate words, but Alan seemed to understand. Five minutes later Carey was back on the street, heading to The Underground.

Carey walked slowly, his mind whirling with random thoughts. Despite everything, he was a lucky man. He wasn't so naïve as to think that Dave Becket was acting without some other agenda, but he didn't care. What touched him more was the idea that a complete stranger was prepared to make a huge sacrifice on his behalf. He wondered if there was any way that Alan could be protected—it seemed unlikely. This was the kind of information that the tabloid media would tear into like a pack of rabid dogs. Edward Easton deserved it, Carey had no qualms about that man's reputation being shredded, but Alan would inevitably be collateral damage. He wondered if there was a way that he could cushion the impact... Perhaps there could be a use for Alan's particular skills at The Underground. He'd have to give that some serious thought.

He was jolted out of his musings by the vibration of his phone in his jacket pocket. He stopped in a doorway and pressed it to his ear.

"Hoffman."

"Boss, it's Harry. Now don't panic, but you need to get back here. There's been a fire."

Carey went cold. "What? How? Was anybody hurt, Harry?" He started walking rapidly as he listened.

"No, everyone's fine. It started at the back of the stage. One of the boys spotted it and had the presence of mind to grab an extinguisher. He put it out before there was too much damage—just some smoke and a couple of ruined stage lights."

"All that kit was checked and certified less than a month ago..." Carey rounded the corner. "I'm almost back, Harry." He rang off and turned into The Underground's entrance. He punched his code into the keypad then took the lift down to the reception area. There was no sign of Christian, but that was normal, he would have gone off duty. Security staff manned reception after ten at night.

"Mr Hoffman, welcome back, Sir. You've heard?"

Carey nodded to the burly guy behind the desk. "Just. I'd better get downstairs."

Harry met him at the door and Carey took a quick glance around the club. He could smell the lingering scent of burnt plastic, but everything else seemed normal.

"Glad you're back, boss." Harry ran agitated fingers through his hair. "We evacuated everyone no problem, made sure everything was safe and then let them back in. We had two off-duty firemen in tonight—they took a look and gave us the all-clear. It was all over so fast we didn't even have to call out the brigade."

Carey stomped across to the stage where the blackened lights were sitting in a corner. "I don't get it... This stuff isn't that old and it's not long been checked."

Harry drew him to one side. "The lights were sabotaged, boss, someone replaced the usual gel covers with something flammable. They were in the back corner—if it hadn't been for Charlie, the smoke might have been dismissed as dry ice because the show was just starting. He was waiting in the wings with some props."

Carey swore under his breath—the last thing he needed was another problem to deal with. "Okay, Harry, thanks for handling everything so well. If

Charlie is still around send him into the office — I'd like to thank him personally."

Carey went to his office and shut the door. He hung up his jacket then slumped into his chair and put his head in his hands. His phone vibrated again. This time it was a text message. He took a look and scowled. "Fuck!" He stared at the message in disbelief.

Forget Alistair Eastman ever lived. You've been warmed.

The typo was obviously deliberate and the most chilling part of the text — how could anyone turn a death threat into a joke?

"Sick bastards." Carey loosened his tie and pulled it off. He took a couple of slow, deep breaths. If Edward Eastman thought he could be intimidated then the man was delusional. Carey smiled coldly — there was no doubt in his mind that Eastman was heading for a fall — one that would leave him in pieces. He picked up the phone on his desk and dialled Joe's number. It was time to step things up and put the next part of their plan into action.

Chapter Eight

Alistair lay on his hard, narrow bed and stared up at the ceiling of his tiny room. It was white, just like the walls and the tiled floor. A hairline crack in the plaster ran from one corner of the ceiling to the end of the fluorescent strip light, which, so far during his stay in this hellhole, had never been switched off. He wasn't sure how long he'd been at the clinic because his room didn't have a window and the light remained constantly bright. Whenever he tried to drop off to sleep, a shrill alarm sounded followed by loud Europop played through a speaker. If his exhaustion let him sleep through the racket then an orderly the size of a gorilla would drag him to the communal showers, strip him down and push him under the freezing cold spray until his teeth chattered and his toes turned blue. He'd gone past being exhausted days ago and had reached a state where he wasn't ever sure if he was awake or dreaming.

He was so confused that he couldn't remember if he was hungry. A tin tray of barely edible food was delivered to his room at intervals along with plastic utensils and a beaker of water. He forced himself to eat and drink everything, however disgusting. He was getting weaker anyway without starving himself too—they'd probably force-feed him and that was enough to ensure he shovelled lumpy mashed potatoes and over-boiled vegetables into his mouth as quickly as possible. His guts ached constantly, but he didn't think he was being poisoned—that would be far too easy—it was just the stress and the anxiety he always felt when he couldn't be with Carey.

When they took him to the viewing room it was only thoughts of Carey that kept him going. The same doctor who had been at his father's house was there, talking at him in low, patronising tones about how he only needed to recognise the error of his ways. He was young, easily manipulated, he'd been forced into a life that he didn't want or need. He could be normal again, but they had to cleanse him of any deviant thoughts or desires and that was what the clinic's treatments were about.

The viewing room was tiny and claustrophobic, the end wall taken up almost entirely by a large screen. In front of it was positioned a black leather recliner where Alistair was seated then tied down with wide leather straps that buckled around his wrists and ankles. Pads were fixed to his temples, then leads attached that connected to machinery with lots of flashing lights. The doctor explained, "This will measure your brain activity, specifically related to arousal. We can detect even the smallest differences in your reactions to images, however subliminal. This first session will be to set some base measures for comparison purposes so all you need to do is lie back and watch the screen."

Alistair hardly had a choice. The doctor left the room and the lights were switched off, leaving him in total darkness, then the film began. Image after image flashed up on the screen in rapid succession, almost too quick to process. There were pictures of everyday objects, animals, flowers, children playing and interspersed were images of gay couples kissing or holding hands. There were also brief flashes of images related to the lifestyle—bondage, submission... Everything blurred together until the film became one long sequence of light and colour. By the end of it Alistair's eyes felt grainy and sore, his head throbbed and there was a coppery taste in his mouth where he had bitten his tongue. His wrists and ankles ached where he'd unknowingly pulled on his bonds hard enough to bruise.

Back in his room, Alistair lost track of time again as day and night merged. He ate what was delivered, slept when he could and tried to hold onto his sanity. He guessed it had been a day or two since his first visit to the viewing room and he knew they would come for him soon. Alistair whimpered and curled onto his side. It was impossible to get comfortable on the thin, vinyl-covered mattress and there was no bedding at all. He was wearing thin white trousers and a dark grey T-shirt—he hadn't been given underwear or socks—and though the room was uncomfortably warm, his skin still felt chilly. He wondered vaguely if he were getting ill. That wouldn't be so bad—sneezing a few germs over his gaolers would provide a small measure of perverse satisfaction.

He didn't have time to contemplate any more options for bacteria-ridden revenge before the door opened and the orderly he'd christened King Kong loomed over him. The man must lace his cornflakes with steroids because his bulging muscles could not be natural. Alistair felt nauseated — either he really was ill or the sight of Kong's flexing biceps was turning his stomach.

"Up, pretty boy, time to visit the doctor." The words were grunted out.

"Sorry to disappoint you," Alistair slurred, "but I'm not gonna be able to get it up for you *or* the doctor. Not my type."

"Funny. Now get your arse out of bed."

Alistair giggled hysterically. "You shouldn't be looking at my arse... Hey! Are you gay too? I've got friends who would love to meet you..."

"There's no such thing as gay. Someone's been messing with your head and you need straightening out. Now get the hell up!"

Alistair felt dizzy — the whole situation had to be a joke or a bad dream. He retorted without thinking about the consequences, "You did not just say 'straightening out'! Really? Did they teach you that in bad pun school?"

The orderly growled and took a firm grip of Alistair's arm, yanking him to his feet. "Either move your feet or I carry you. Your choice."

The thought of being manhandled any more than was absolutely necessary was good motivation. Alistair forced his shaky legs into action and trailed his minder out of the room into the corridor. They followed the familiar route out of what Alistair was beginning to think of as the cell block, into an equally bleak series of passages lined with windowless doors marked only by numbers. Kong paused in front of one door and shoved it open to reveal a communal bathroom. "Use the toilet and take a shower. You've got ten minutes. There's a towel and a set of clothes in there for you."

Alistair sighed with relief as the door closed behind him and Kong remained outside. He looked around quickly for any possible escape routes, but there were no windows or any other doors. Even the ceiling was blank apart from the ubiquitous fluorescent light fitting and a vent for the extractor. He did the only thing he could do—he took a shower. It didn't make him feel any less ill, but at least he smelt better. He grabbed a thin grey towel from a hook and rubbed himself down briskly in the vague hope that the stimulation of the rough fabric against his skin might make him more alert. He felt like his head was stuffed with cotton wool and his thoughts were coming far too slowly to be of any use. There were no doors on the toilet stalls, but it didn't seem likely that anyone would be joining him so he used the facilities as quickly as he could.

He left his discarded clothes in a heap on the floor and pulled on the replacement set he found, which were virtually identical to those he'd just taken off. The T-shirt was at least a size too big and swamped his slender frame. The soft white trousers hung shapelessly from his hips. Both items smelt vaguely of bleach. Alistair fingered his chin and found a layer of fuzzy stubble. He laughed, then sounding a little hysterical said, "Give me another month and I might manage a beard." He examined the bruises on his arms, which were an interesting shade of green, fading to yellow. Both Kong and the thugs that had taken him from The Underground had grips like gorillas and he'd always marked easily. Carey wouldn't be happy—he was possessive about every inch of Alistair's pristine skin, treating him like a personal canvas that he loved to decorate. Alistair smiled—Carey was an artist when he wielded a crop or cane, laying stripes on Alistair's arse with creative precision.

Alistair bit back a sob as the bathroom door creaked open and Kong leaned in. "Shift your arse, pretty boy. Doc's waiting."

"You really must stop fixating on my backside," Alistair sneered, "or you may just find out what it's like on this side of the fence."

Kong just grunted and grabbed Alistair's arm hard enough to no doubt leave another ring of bruises. Two minutes later they were back in the viewing room and Alistair tried to control his shaking hands as he contemplated another session in front of the flashing images.

Dr McBride was waiting, clipboard in hand, looking impatient and officious. He gestured to Kong. "Strip him and get him into the chair, we're already running late."

Alistair struggled hard as the big orderly began to pull at clothes he'd only just put on. "Hey! Get your hands off me!" He fought desperately, but Kong ripped his T-shirt off and all but threw him into the reclining chair. Once his wrists had been buckled into restraints, there was nothing he could do to prevent the removal of his trousers. Straps went around his ankles next, fixing his legs wide apart, leaving him horribly exposed and vulnerable. He cursed and jerked in his bonds, but it was useless. A final buckled strap was passed around his neck and he had to take a few deep breaths to avoid panicking.

"Thank you, you may go." McBride ushered Kong from the room and locked the door. "Now, Mr Easton, a little cooperation would be much appreciated. This treatment is in your best interest."

Alistair wanted to scream, but managed to limit himself to a hoarse shout, "You fucking quack! Let me go!"

"I'm afraid that is not possible. Your father is very keen to see you get better and has paid a great deal of money to ensure you stay here and complete the course. The sooner you accept your illness, the quicker the cure will take hold." The doctor sounded like he was repeating a mantra he had used dozens of times before.

"You're the sick one, you bastard. You know damn well I'm here against my will." Alistair tried not to sound as scared as he felt.

McBride pulled on a pair of lurid purple surgical gloves and began to fiddle with a small metal box that had wires dangling from the side. Alistair couldn't see enough to work out what he was doing but then the doctor loomed into view.

"This"—he held up a thick metal ring, about an inch and a half across—"will teach you to think differently about the images you see on the screen." He unhinged the ring and positioned it around the base of Alistair's cock and balls, then he snapped it closed and connected two coloured wires to small terminals on its edge. "Each time you see a picture that relates to your deviance, you will experience pain. Over the coming weeks, as we repeat the treatment, your brain will learn to control any inappropriate impulses. It's a very effective method."

The doctor sounded coldly clinical. Sweat broke out on Alistair's skin and his strangled sob sounded loud in the tiny room. The doctor's latex-clad touch against his balls brought bile to his throat. He could feel the wires trailing across his thigh twitch as McBride connected them to the power source.

"This room is very well soundproofed, so don't worry about staying silent. I will be next door in the observation area, monitoring the equipment." The doctor dimmed the lights and left the room. Alistair heard the snick of a lock after the door had closed and for the first time felt real despair. He knew it wasn't logical and he hated himself for it, but in his head he was angry that Carey hadn't come for him. Where the hell was he? Didn't he care?

The screen in front of him glowed and a series of pictures began to flash up. They appeared much more slowly this time, remaining in view for several seconds. Children playing in a park, a man and a woman hugging, a squirrel eating an acorn, a hot air balloon drifting in a cloudless sky, two young men kissing... A sharp stab of pain shot through Alistair's balls and his hips jerked upwards involuntarily. "You fucking son of a bitch!" Alistair yelled at no one in particular. He closed his eyes, refusing to look at the screen. McBride's voice echoed through a speaker, "Keep your eyes open, Mr Easton, or I will be forced to conduct two of these sessions a day instead of one."

Alistair glared. His muscles ached with tension and he cursed his frustration at bland pictures of kittens, a bride and groom, suburban streets... Then there was a stark black and white shot of a naked man being whipped on a St Andrew's cross. Alistair anticipated the pain and held his breath as agony knifed through his cock. He took short, rapid breaths, trying to control his response to the shock of the pain. He refused to give McBride the satisfaction of hearing him scream.

It went on for what felt like hours. Alistair was utterly exhausted, his groin ached liked he'd been repeatedly kicked. The metallic taste of blood was sour on his tongue where he'd bitten the inside of his cheek. He had no idea how he was going to face another session without losing his mind, but then that was probably the whole idea. They wanted to drive him crazy, get him into such a state that he'd believe all the nonsense they were spouting. If it wasn't so painful it would be funny. Alistair had known without a doubt that he was gay from the time he'd reached puberty. It wasn't a state of mind, it wasn't delusion—it was fact. By the time he'd reached seventeen he'd begun to recognise his submissive tendencies for what they were. He was absolutely, unshakably comfortable with who and what he was. These people had chosen the worst possible person to try to convert because nothing they could say or do would shatter Alistair's acceptance of his sexuality. They could drive him mad—they'd just have a barmy gay guy on their hands!

Alistair was still chuckling to himself at that thought when Doctor McBride came back into the room and released him from the restraints. Having the doctor's hands on him as he removed the metal ring was worse than the shocks had been. His touch made Alistair's skin crawl.

"Get dressed. Cyril will take you for something to eat and then you will join a group session."

Alistair assumed that Cyril was Kong's real name. He sniggered—it was possibly the least apt name for the man that anyone could have come up with. Kong was far better. McBride handed over a fresh grey T-shirt to replace the ripped one and a pair of white canvas shoes. Alistair pulled the top on then slid off the chair to put on the trousers and shoes. His feet hit the floor and his knees buckled. He grabbed the edge of the chair and waited as his twitching muscles got used to his weight. He felt so weak and shaky, it was horrible. He watched as the doctor wiped the metal ring and connectors with sterilising gel and wound the wires around the power unit.

"How can you think that this is ethical? You should be struck off," Alistair challenged.

McBride looked back at him with mild curiosity. "In a few weeks, Mr Easton, you will be shaking my hand in gratitude. You'll be able to return home and have a normal life, free of the damaging proclivities that have warped your mind."

Alistair shook his head in disbelief. "You don't really believe that crap. I hope the money my father is paying you is enough to salve your conscience, because what you're doing is criminal."

"You are a very damaged young man." McBride flicked his fingers in a dismissive gesture as Kong pushed his bulk around the door. "Cyril, take Mr Easton to the cafeteria and make sure he eats. Then he'll be joining group therapy in the sun lounge."

Alistair didn't have the strength to resist as Kong ushered him from the room. He wanted out anyway. Every minute he spent in McBride's company was a minute too long. They made a brief bathroom stop, then he was escorted into a self-service restaurant that looked remarkably normal. After what he had just been through Alistair found 'normal' hard to process. Kong shoved a tray into his hands and he looked at it blankly until he was guided firmly towards a serving area. Just looking at the containers of steaming food made his stomach lurch, but he pointed randomly and a dish of pasta was placed on his tray. He took a small plate of salad and a carton of milk from a chiller cabinet and looked around, not knowing what to do next. Kong gripped his shoulder and steered him to an empty table, pulling out the plastic chair so that he could sit.

Alistair picked up a fork and prodded at the pasta disinterestedly. He knew he should eat if only to keep his energy levels up, but he was so exhausted that moving food from the plate to his mouth seemed like an insurmountable challenge. The chair opposite him scraped the floor and someone sat down with their own lunch. The newcomer leaned across the table, gently unwrapped Alistair's fingers from his fork and took it away. A tube of pasta was speared and held up in front of his mouth. "Here. Let me help."

Alistair looked at Kong who shrugged and ambled away to take a newspaper from a nearby shelf. The orderly parked himself at another table and settled down to read.

"Come on, eat for me, sweetie. You look like a light breeze could blow you over." Alistair recognised the gentle, teasing tones of his new friend's voice but didn't believe what he was hearing. He looked up nervously and took in enormous blue eyes and tumbling golden curls. It had to be a mirage. His mind was playing tricks on him. He opened his mouth and accepted a tube of sauce-covered pasta then chewed it slowly.

"That's right. Now how about another one?"

"Is it really you?" Alistair whispered.

Olly's grin lit up his whole face. "Eat up, gorgeous. Carey will be very unhappy if you don't keep your strength up. Don't let on you know me." Olly kept his voice very low then raised the volume a little to say, "My name's Olly. What's yours?"

Alistair took back his fork and mechanically shovelled food into his mouth. He chewed and swallowed. "Alistair. Why are you here, Olly?" He took in Olly's clothes and realised they were identical to his own.

"Well, I'd like to say it's to meet interesting new people, but so far you're the only person I've met who doesn't look at me like I'm a freak. My therapist has checked me in for some group sessions, lectures and stuff, because my parents think I'm conflicted about my sexuality."

"And are you?" Alistair asked.

"Oh yes." Olly tilted his head thoughtfully. "I'm undecided as to whether I prefer tall, dark and gorgeous or tall, blond and gorgeous. It's a conundrum. So many men, so little time... What's a boy to do?" He fluttered his eyelashes. "But dear old Dad is holding out for a radical change of direction. He's promised that if this doesn't do the trick, he'll subscribe to *Attitude* and start buying me clothes from Abercrombie."

Alistair almost choked on his pasta. "You don't seem to be taking this very seriously?"

Olly pasted a very prim expression on his face. "I have promised to listen, pay attention and keep an open mind. My therapist can be very...persuasive. Are you joining in with the happy-clappy tree hugging?"

Alistair dredged up a smile. "I think so. I just follow Kong over there"—he gestured in Cyril's direction—"or he drags me wherever I'm supposed to be."

Olly turned and gave the orderly a cheeky wink. "My, he's a big boy, isn't he?"

Alistair rubbed at the bruises on his arms. "He certainly is." He swallowed hard, fighting back the tears that threatened to overwhelm him.

"So why are you in here?" Olly's expression was full of sympathy.

"I..." Alistair didn't get a chance to say anything more as Kong jerked him from his chair.

"Time to go." Kong gripped his shoulder tightly and Alistair knew he was being warned. He lowered his eyes and didn't fight. He felt like a huge weight had lifted from his shoulders now that he knew he had a friend nearby. He just hoped that whatever plan had been hatched by his friends and Carey would swing into operation sooner rather than later.

Kong escorted him to a room that was laid out with a small circle of chairs. There was one large window looking out onto a garden and Alistair could see a few people strolling around or sitting on benches, mostly dressed as he was. A side table carried a selection of pamphlets that had titles like 'The Path to Success is Straight' and 'The Myth of Homosexuality'. Alistair wandered across to the chairs and took one where he could see out of the window. The room hardly qualified as sunny, but it was comforting to be able to see that the outside world still existed.

Kong hovered by the door and, when a few minutes later a man in a shirt and tie joined them, he left. More people arrived and the seats were gradually filled. Alistair looked around at his companions, suppressing a smile when he saw Olly opposite him. There were four other men dressed in grey and white. Two were older and seemed to know each other because they chatted quietly before sitting on adjoining seats. Alistair named them Tweedledum and Tweedledee. Another was a fierce-looking guy with a beard and a bulbous red nose and finally there was a boy who looked even younger than Olly. He was a pretty little thing, small and slim with shiny chestnut hair that fell into his eyes. He curled onto his chair looking absolutely terrified.

Alistair found himself between the course leader and the bearded guy who kept muttering to himself under his breath. He avoided making eye contact with Olly because he didn't trust himself not to betray that they knew each other. Olly would let him know what was going on when it was safe to do so—in the meantime he had to carry on with the charade. He was so tired he could barely keep his eyes open—that he didn't have to fake. He yawned and the course leader tutted impatiently then tapped his chair with a biro.

"Gentlemen, your attention please. My name is Mo and I'll be leading today's session. This is the first group for all of you, so we'll start with some introductions. Just first names, please, and then share a little about why you are here."

You have to be fucking kidding me! Alistair thought it, he didn't say it, but he had to dig his nails into his thigh to stop the words slipping from his lips.

Mo began on his left and Tweedle Dum started things off.

"Hi, I'm Saul. This is my third stay here and I come because I'm married with a couple of kids but thought I'd made a mistake. The courses help remind me that any feelings I have for men are all in my mind."

Tweedle Dee on the next chair nodded understandingly. "With you there, friend. I got a bit confused when I was younger and ended up with addiction issues. This place put me right but recently I've had warped thoughts in my head about men and I'm worried about getting back on the booze, so here I am. My name's Lee." Alistair was very satisfied that he could rename him Tweedle Lee.

"Thank you, Lee. We're here for you." Mo nodded at Olly to go next.

Olly grinned at everyone. "Hey! I'm Olly. I'm happily gay. I love men, they're yummy! My Dad reckons it's a phase so I'm humouring him." He put on a deep gruff voice, "'Son, I know you think you're gay, but a good woman would do you the world of good'." Olly giggled. "What's good is a nice meaty cock stuffed so far up my…"

"Thank you, Olly! Perhaps we could move on?" Mo's eyes might as well have been on stalks they popped out so far. Alistair bit his lip to avoid laughing. Olly was rocking his chair back on its legs and looked like he might overbalance at any moment. Tweedle Lee's mouth was hanging open and Saul had his hands crossed suspiciously in his lap. The boy sitting next to Olly looked mortified that he had to go next—he chewed on his lower lip and looked at the floor. When he plucked up the courage to speak Alistair could barely hear him.

"I'm Kai. I live with my uncle. He wanted to know why I never had a girlfriend so I told him I like boys. He sent me here."

Kai looked like he was about to burst into tears. Olly patted his knee and Alistair watched as Kai leaned towards him gratefully. The boy could have had 'sub' tattooed on his forehead and it wouldn't have been any more obvious that he needed to be taken care of. He was so pretty—Alistair knew that any number of members at The Underground would snap him up in an instant. How cruel and ignorant of his uncle to send him away when what he needed was love and support.

It was almost Alistair's turn and he hadn't decided what to say. The final member of the group was speaking, but he'd missed most of it. He caught the name Bryan, but that was about it and he didn't really care. The man's face was red and he was sweating profusely—he looked like he was experiencing severe withdrawal symptoms.

"Last but not least then." Mo turned to Alistair with a false smile.

Alistair lifted his head and locked gazes with Olly. "My name is Alistair. I'm here because I was taken by force, drugged and threatened. I'm proud to be gay and nothing anyone here says or does is going to change that. I'm here because my father values his reputation more than his son." His voice cracked and he clenched both hands into fists.

Olly clapped enthusiastically. "Go, Alistair! We can form the 'we will not be turned club'! Membership benefits include free samples of fruit-flavoured lube and a vibrating butt plug!"

Kai blushed prettily and whispered, "Can I join?"

Saul looked like he was in pain and muttered, "Don't let them talk about butt plugs, it's not fair!"

Mo's face turned an interesting shade of purple. "I will not tolerate this disruption! None of you are gay, there's no such state. You need to take this seriously in order to heal!" He was losing control, clearly not used to a group that contained less than compliant members.

Bryan caught Alistair's eye. "Is it true? Are you here against your will?"

Before Alistair could respond, the door slammed open and Dr McBride stormed in accompanied by a red-faced Cyril who grabbed Alistair and held his arms. McBride produced a syringe and plunged the needle into Alistair's biceps. "I'm sorry, Mo, it was clearly too early for Alistair to join the group. He's a very sick young man. I apologise for this interruption—he will be returned to isolation until he can be trusted in company."

Alistair felt heat seep into his muscles and his limbs began to feel heavy. He looked desperately at Olly and registered his brief, reassuring smile before everything faded to grey.

Chapter Nine

Aiden hunched over his computer and typed feverishly. His small, basement lair was dark, lit only by the glow of several monitors. He finished pounding the keyboard, punched the return key and waited. Rows and rows of code scrolled down in front of his eyes and his serious expression of concentration began to relax into a smile. He rolled his shoulders and winced as his joints creaked stiffly—he had no idea how many hours he'd been sat there working, but his body was starting to protest. The screen flashed to black and Aiden held his breath. He tapped the arm of his chair in agitation then he let his breath out in a whoosh as the screen cleared to reveal lines of accounting information.

"Yes!" He twirled his chair round in excitement. "Gotcha!" Quickly he shoved a data stick into a port and began to download information, watching nervously as the bar showing the activity gradually turned green. When it had filled and flashed to show the job was complete, Aiden rapidly shut down the system, eliminating all traces of his visit as he went.

"That'll fool them for a while…" He scrubbed both hands through his hair, which was already standing up in messy disarray. He rummaged for his mobile beneath an untidy mound of papers and dialled a number that he knew by heart.

Dave Becket answered in his usual deep, clipped tone. "Becket. Well?"

Aiden rolled his eyes. "It's a good job you're not a doctor, boss, 'cause your bedside manner needs some work."

"Aiden…" Becket's tone held a warning. "Do I need to speak to Heath about your attitude?"

"Probably." Aiden wandered around the small room as he talked, "You will anyway. The two of you are made from the same mould. One with a hell of a lot of rough edges."

"Cheeky brat."

Aiden chuckled. "This brat has just done what his soon-to-be-grateful boss demanded."

"You did it? That's excellent. Was it there?" Becket actually sounded excited.

"Yes. Three payments from the account number you gave me, routed via the Caymans." Aiden couldn't help but feel a little smug.

"I don't want to know how you did it, Aiden, but that account is linked to a known terrorist organisation. It's enough to bring Easton's firm to its knees. His customers may put up with religious fanatics and gangsters on the client list, but terrorists attract far too much attention." Becket let a little emotion creep into his voice.

"Good." Aiden asked, "What about Alistair? How's it going at the clinic?"

"It's up to Joe and Olly now," Becket replied. "They're inside the place. I imagine Olly's causing all kinds of chaos. Alistair will be safe soon, I'm sure. Take a few hours off — you've earned them."

"Your generosity knows no bounds, Becket. I'll call you tomorrow." Aiden switched off the phone. The adrenaline that had kept him going as he'd worked seeped away and left him feeling shaky. Several empty fizzy drink cans and chocolate wrappers littered his desk, attesting to the sugar rush that was now descending into a dramatic energy crash. The last few days had been intense and now he'd achieved his goal he needed something else to focus on or he was going to fall apart. "A run, that'll do it."

Aiden powered down his other equipment and grabbed his fleece with The Edge's logo emblazoned across it. He was about to return to the real world and needed to look like he belonged. The fleece made him look like just another staff member at The Edge, the corporate training company owned by Heath and Joe. It was a busy week with plenty of bookings and he had to remember that most of the people on the island knew absolutely nothing about The Edge's sidelines — either as a provider of courses for Dominant men or as a very small, discreet branch of the intelligence services. He chuckled at the thought. It was a very clever cover and its creator, Dave Becket, was very proud of his cunning.

Aiden left the room then pulled the door closed behind him, making sure the lock engaged. He walked along a narrow corridor, turned a corner and went through another door, which gave access to the main basement area of The Edge's headquarters building. Everything was quiet. The rooms along this passage were used mainly at the weekends unless the company was closed to their normal business during the week for special courses. Some were normal seminar rooms, but others were set up as themed playrooms—many of which he'd enjoyed using with Heath.

As he thought of his partner, Aiden smiled. Heath had been very patient for the last few days, leaving him alone to work because he knew it was for Alistair and Carey. Normally Heath insisted that Aiden restrict his working hours and spent time in the fresh air. He also made sure that Aiden ate a healthy diet. If he found out what Aiden had been consuming for the last few days, he'd throw a fit. Not such a bad thing, Aiden mused. Heath was very creative when it came to punishments and it had been a while since they had spent any length of time together. As he strolled along the corridor, he debated the best way to rile his dominant lover.

He climbed the stairs and let himself out of the basement area. The large entrance hall was quiet with just the mellow ticking of a grandfather clock to break the silence. Joe's office door was firmly shut and so was Heath's opposite. Aiden wasn't surprised. The Edge was busy and Heath was probably teaching. The ornate hands of the clock told him that it was a little after six. The early evening sun filtered through the windows, casting a warm glow across the parquet floor. To Aiden it felt excessively bright. He'd been working in the dark for far too long, a run was definitely a good idea. He headed to the apartment he shared with Heath, let himself in and went straight to their bedroom. He pulled out a pair of black shorts and an old corporate T-shirt from a drawer and changed his clothes. A shower would have been nice but pointless before a run—he could pamper himself a little when he got back. He sat on the edge of the bed and bent to put on his running shoes, wincing at the pop of joints in his back.

"You've been working too hard."

Aiden looked up and scowled at the owner of the voice. "How you manage to move so quietly is beyond me!"

All six feet five inches of his gorgeous lover were lounging against the doorframe. Aiden's breath caught in his throat as Heath advanced towards him. The man moved so gracefully, like a big cat on the hunt, and Aiden had no doubt that he was the prey. Heath leaned over him and cupped his neck, stroking the silver metal that sat snugly against Aiden's skin. He took hold of a few strands of hair and Aiden let his head tilt backwards at the pressure. Heath kissed him and he parted his lips willingly, letting Heath take control. As always he felt a little resistant before accepting that the submission made him feel good. More than good. As Heath held him, explored him...owned him with his kiss, Aiden felt the heat hit his groin in a rush. He moaned softly and hoped that Heath might throw him down on the bed and take him right there and then. When Heath moved away, it took Aiden a few seconds to realise that it wasn't going to happen.

Heath grinned in a way that said he knew exactly what was on Aiden's mind. "I'll run with you. Why don't you get some bottles of water from the fridge while I change?" He pulled off his shirt and it was all Aiden could do to stop himself drooling like an overexcited puppy. Heath raised one eyebrow slightly and in that tiny movement managed to convey the promise of serious displeasure if Aiden didn't do as he'd been told. Aiden dragged his gaze away from Heath's rippling muscles and went to get the water.

He took the bottles from the fridge and held one against his burning forehead. He was tempted to press it against his aching dick too but thought the shock might kill him. He set the drinks on the kitchen counter and did a few stretches to take his mind off the delights of Heath's bare flesh.

A couple of minutes later Heath joined him, also wearing black with The Edge emblazoned across his shirt. He put the water bottles into a small rucksack and slung it onto his back. Aiden wondered what else was in the bag but didn't get a chance to ask as he was ushered out of the door.

"Come on, brat, let's go. It'll be dark in an hour or so."

"Yes, Sir." Aiden allowed an edge of sarcasm to creep into his tone and was rewarded with a sharp slap on the arse.

"I can see that giving you a little freedom was a mistake." Heath jogged down the stairs, through the hall and out into the yard, where he turned and waited for Aiden to join him. "We'll head cross-country to the East beach then do the circuit training obstacles on the way back. Try to keep up." He smirked and set off at a pace that Aiden knew was a direct challenge. He cursed and sprinted to catch up. Heath had a smooth, easy gait as he ran. He loped along, making it look like a gentle jog when Aiden had to run hard to match him. As they ran away from The Edge, they passed quite a few course members, finished with their activities and returning to their accommodation before dinner and evening classes. Heath nodded and waved at the instructors and acknowledged a few people he recognised but Aiden had to focus on pumping his arms and ignoring the rapidly increasing burn in his thighs. It took them a good half an hour to reach the beach on the far side of the island with Heath choosing some narrow paths through the trees rather than the most direct route.

Aiden lurched to a halt on the pebbles, put his hands on his hips and bent at the waist, gasping for breath. When he finally decided that he wasn't going to die he looked up to find Heath smirking at him with amused satisfaction. "Bastard." Aiden didn't have the energy for anything more inventive—he plopped down on the pebbles and wriggled until his arse made a comfortable dent. He caught the bottle of water that flew in his direction, unscrewed the cap then took a long drink before tipping the rest over his head and shaking his hair like a dog. Water soaked his shoulders and chest making his shirt cling closely to his skin. He peeked from beneath dark lashes to see if his actions were having the desired effect. Heath's expression remained cool, but his body betrayed him. Aiden grinned at the sizeable erection tenting Heath's shorts. "Can I help you with anything...Sir?" Aiden cocked his head to one side and put on his best innocent expression.

Heath growled. He actually growled. "You've got ten minutes to get to the scramble nets in the woods or I'll put that tempting cock of yours into a cage tonight and it won't be eligible for parole for at least a week."

"You wouldn't."

"I would. Now move your arse."

Aiden scrambled to his feet and shot off towards the trees. He knew better than to disobey when Heath made promises like that. Of course, saving himself from chastity didn't mean that he wouldn't be punished in some other way. In fact, it was cast iron guaranteed.

Heath caught up with him just as he reached the nets and pushed him back against the vertical web of thick, knotted ropes. Aiden bounced and produced a world-class glare.

"Strip." Heath stood in front of him looking solid, implacable and devastatingly sexy.

"Fuck off!" Aiden glanced around. They were deep in the woods and it was unlikely that anyone would wander by, but it was possible.

"Sweetheart, either do as I say or I will rip your clothes off strip by strip. Choose the latter option and remember that you will be walking back to The Edge butt naked. Your decision." Heath's smile was wicked.

"That's not much of a choice, Sir." Aiden lowered his eyes, defiance draining from him to be replaced by an aching need to please Heath. He kicked off his running shoes and socks first, then peeled his soggy shirt over his head. His shorts went next, leaving him clad only in a black jockstrap. He hooked a thumb under the elastic.

"Wait. Leave that on." Heath rummaged in his rucksack and produced several coils of rope. Aiden swallowed hard and watched Heath's every move. His cock twitched and fought the confines of his underwear. He really wanted to touch himself but didn't dare. Instead he stood with his hands grasped behind his back to stop them shaking.

"Face the net." Heath spoke quietly but with authority. Aiden complied and shivered as Heath gently drew his hands apart and wrapped rope around each wrist. "Stretch up on your toes and hold onto the ropes." Aiden reached as high as he could and grabbed hold. It was good to have something to do with his hands as Heath climbed up the first few rungs and tied first one arm then the other in place.

Inevitably, the thrill of being restrained sent shivers of need down Aiden's spine. The net vibrated as Heath climbed down and stood behind him. Aiden felt a light tap to one ankle and spread his legs wider. Heath set about binding him in place until he was virtually immobile, and though he tested the strength of the ropes there was no give. He was completely at Heath's mercy and it was making him horny as hell.

Aiden jerked as Heath stroked his exposed arse cheeks. He was tied in such a way that his cock, still confined by fabric, jutted through a hole in the rope grid and he could get absolutely no friction. Heath kneaded his flesh and pulled his cheeks apart, exposing his hole to the cool air. Helpless to resist, Aiden pushed back towards him, desperate to be filled.

"Please! Heath... Sir!"

"Remembered your manners then? It's a shame you couldn't be more respectful earlier." Heath teased as he touched, "Because now I'm forced to discipline you. Of course, I realise that it's my fault—leaving you alone for so long was a mistake, and one that needs to be remedied. You understand that I need to remind you who's in charge, Aiden, don't you?"

Aiden gasped as his perineum was rubbed. "I'm sorry, Sir! It won't happen again. Please... I need you in me!"

"Really?" Heath did not sound convinced. "And how many times have you said the same thing? You're my submissive—you're supposed to be obedient and respectful."

Aiden moaned as Heath's touch disappeared. He could hear him rummaging in the back and seconds later he felt the drape of leather strands across the curve of his backside.

"You packed a flogger to go on a run? Jesus, Heath! What else have you got in that bag?"

"Wouldn't you like to know?" Heath's low chuckle gave Aiden goose pimples. The sound of footsteps told him that Heath was moving in front of him. He stared at his tormentor and sagged in his bonds. Heath had that look that Aiden had come to know and crave, a perfect combination of love and stubborn determination. That look meant that nothing Aiden could do or say would make the slightest jot of difference to what was going to happen next. He could beg until his throat was raw and Heath would still do whatever it was he had planned in that Dominant mind of his.

Heath placed the flogger on the ground then stretched out a hand and cupped Aiden's package, making him squirm as much as his restraints would allow, which wasn't much. "Perhaps you would be more comfortable if we gave your cock a little freedom? What do you think?"

Aiden could only moan his frustration as Heath stroked and squeezed with one hand and pulled a Swiss army knife from his pocket. He flicked out the shiny blade and slid it beneath the elastic that gripped Aiden's hips. A couple of quick slices and his jock fell away in tatters leaving him completely exposed. Heath took full advantage of his prize and continued to fondle Aiden's cock and balls, humming happily.

Aiden wanted to scream from frustration. If didn't seem possible for him to get any harder, but his cock felt achingly solid. Heath was rubbing a slick of pre-cm into Aiden's sensitive skin and he couldn't take much more. "Sir! Please... I'm going to come... I can't..." Aiden sobbed out the words.

"Oh no, we can't have that." Heath stopped touching, produced a leather strap and without ceremony, ringed Aiden's cock. "No coming until I say you can." He picked up the flogger and allowed the leather strands to drift across Aiden's straining erection. "How many strokes do you think you deserve, my love?"

Coherence was impossible given his situation. All Aiden's brain cells had morphed into lust-flavoured jelly. He managed a couple of unimaginative curses, but that was it.

"Oh well, seems I will just have to decide for you." There was a distinct swagger in Heath's step as he returned to his position on the other side of the net. Aiden tried not to tense his buttocks in anticipation, knowing that the strokes would hurt more if he did, but when the first blow landed every muscle in his body tensed. Heath didn't hold back. He placed lash after lash on the curve of Aiden's arse, across his shoulders and upper back and over his thighs. Endorphins flooded Aiden's system as heat and pain turned him into a quivering wreck. If Heath didn't fuck him soon he was going to explode, cock ring notwithstanding.

He barely registered that the flogging had stopped, but the first touch of lube-slicked fingers to his hole had him crying and begging for more. Heath stretched him gently but thoroughly and Aiden tried desperately to push back on the invading fingers.

"All in good time, gorgeous." Heath stepped away and Aiden heard the welcome rustling of clothing being removed.

"Damn it, Heath, fuck me already!" As he cried the words the blunt head of Heath's cock pressed against his entrance and immediately surged forwards, filling him completely. Even with the preparation it hurt a little, but the burn was worth it as Heath nailed his prostate with the first stroke then proceeded to do it again and again. The light was fading and the wind slipped through the trees with barely a rustle. Aiden's whimpers and cries sounded so loud, but he didn't even consider that somebody might hear and investigate.

"Please... Please, Sir, let me come!"

Heath punched his hips forwards a few more times before he relented and pulled the cock ring from Aiden's dick and jacked him roughly.

"Come for me, baby. Come. Now!"

For once Aiden obeyed gratefully, shooting in a graceful arc onto fallen leaves.

"Good boy!" Heath slammed into him hard and cried out his own release.

Aiden pushed back against him as heat flooded his channel in a rush. "Oh! Yes!" Every sense was heightened, every nerve bristling with sensation. Aiden's cock spasmed again, untouched this time and every last creamy drop found release.

For a few moments Aiden had the warm weight of Heath's body pressed to his back. He didn't want to lose the closeness, but it was almost dark and the air was rapidly cooling.

"All right, love?" Heath's whisper tickled Aiden's ear. "Let's get you home so I can see to your back."

Aiden sighed contentedly. He was tired and achy but in the best way, and he didn't fidget as Heath released his ankles and wrists. He couldn't help but laugh when Heath produced a packet of baby wipes from his rucksack and used them to clean them both up. He then produced a sandwich bag, popped the soiled wipes inside and sealed it neatly before dropping it back into the pack. Aiden leant back on the net and sniggered, "Were you ever a Boy Scout, 'cause you're certainly well prepared?"

Heath twitched an eyebrow. "Boy Scouts have lots of useful skills, brat. Perhaps later I'll demonstrate a few unusual knots on you." He packed his ropes and flogger neatly.

Aiden just watched and languished, naked, against the ropes. Heath had to help him dress because his legs were a bit shaky and during the walk back to The Edge Heath kept an arm around his shoulders to steady him. Normally Aiden would baulk at such protectiveness, but he felt so safe, so loved in Heath's embrace that he gave in and let Heath guide him.

Later that night, after food and a hot shower, Aiden lay face down on the bed and moaned his gratitude as Heath rubbed soothing balm into his back and arse. "Oh God that feels good!"

Heath patted him gently. "All done. There's no broken skin and the soreness should be gone by morning. I haven't lost my touch." He climbed onto the bed and stretched out next to Aiden who edged sideways until he could sprawl across Heath's chest. Aiden loved to wrap himself around his bigger lover and Heath wasn't averse to a bit of cuddling.

"Fuck! That's cold!" Heath cursed as the chain that secured Aiden to the bed dragged across his lower leg.

Aiden just grunted, "Serves you right. If you weren't such a caveman you wouldn't have to put up with metalwork in the bed!"

He jiggled the ankle that was wrapped in a padded cuff linked to the chain, making Heath curse again. "Cheeky little sod. I should really make you sleep on the floor and that ankle cuff isn't even locked. You're spoilt."

"I know. I'm very lucky." There wasn't a trace of sarcasm in Aiden's voice. "I hope Alistair is okay. He must be missing Carey terribly. I can't even begin to imagine what it would be like to be forced apart from you." He nuzzled into the curve of Heath's neck.

Heath stroked his hair. "Alistair's strong. One more night and he'll be out of that hellhole. He'll survive and, thanks to you, his future should be free of that bastard of a father of his."

"I know." Aiden twitched as Heath moved his hand down and began to fondle his arse. "But it makes me sad to think of what he must be going through."

"Spread your legs wider," Heath ordered gruffly. "I'll help you think about something else."

Aiden heard the snap of a lid, the squirt of lube then his hole was thoroughly probed. Within seconds Heath ensured that he wasn't able to think at all.

Chapter Ten

Joe sat across the desk from Dr McBride and schooled his expression into professional neutrality. It wasn't easy. The man he was talking to was an utter arsehole and Joe had very little patience for McBride's greed-fuelled bigotry.

I deserve a fucking BAFTA, was the thought that went through his head as he watched McBride's lips moving and tried to filter some sense from the huge amount of hot air the man was expelling.

"And so you see, Joe... May I call you Joe? Your patient is too disruptive to take part in the group therapy sessions. He caused a great deal of upset yesterday and I'm afraid he is damaging the progress that other patients have made."

Joe nodded sagely. "I do understand. Oliver is quite a trial and can be rather strong-willed. I will withdraw him from the clinic immediately and seek out a more...intensive programme for him. His parents are very happy to spend any amount of money in their search for a cure for him—I'm sure there are other facilities that are a little less comfortable than your own establishment." Joe half rose to his feet. "My apologies, Doctor, for the inconvenience."

McBride steepled his fingers and spoke quickly, "Wait, Joe, please. Perhaps there is something we can do for young Oliver."

Joe sat back down, feigning reluctance, and sounded doubtful as he spoke, "I would welcome any suggestions you might have."

"Well" — McBride's eyes narrowed — "it's an expensive programme, but if you were interested in a slightly more radical therapy..."

Joe tried to appear keen. "I would definitely be interested."

McBride nodded. "I sympathise, believe me. Well. We do conduct electro therapy here — just in the most difficult cases you understand, and only with consent from the patient or their appointed guardian."

Joe leant back in his chair and looked thoughtful. "I do have power of attorney when it comes to Oliver's treatment. It does sound like a very interesting possibility. I wonder, though, would it be possible for me to witness the therapy in action? I don't think I could sanction it unless I was content about the way in which it is carried out."

"Well" — McBride appeared to hesitate — "we do have one client undergoing electro shock at the moment and he is due for another session this morning." He sighed melodramatically. "A very difficult case. The young man has been traumatised by a Dominant/submissive relationship. Very sad. He has already been assessed and had the first treatment. I wouldn't normally permit observers, but as you are a fellow professional it wouldn't be inappropriate."

Joe had to fight to stay in control of his emotions. If Alistair had already experienced the torture once, God knows what kind of mental state he was in. Olly had told him how bad Alistair looked and how scared he'd seemed. Now Joe could understand why.

"That would be most kind. I think Oliver is likely to be a perfect candidate for a similar process and, as I say, money is no object." Joe fought down nausea — the thought of Olly ever being subjected to such torment was enough to make his blood boil and Alistair had done nothing to deserve what he was going through. Carey would go ballistic when he found out.

McBride looked at his watch and pushed his chair back from the desk. "There's no time like the present. My patient should be prepped and ready by now, so if you would care to join me?"

Joe stood. It was a little earlier than he had hoped, but he had to trust that Olly would obey his instructions and be ready. He didn't want to leave Alistair suffering for a second longer than necessary. "After you, Doctor." He followed McBride, tuning out the sales pitch that he was given as they walked. McBride stopped outside an anonymous door and paused. "Now, you should know that the young man can be resistant, as you might expect, but he will be restrained so there's nothing to worry about."

Joe clenched a fist, holding back his fury. He was icily calm, focused on what he needed to do, but this was harder than he'd thought it would be. This so-called medical professional was nothing more than a greedy charlatan who had no business being near vulnerable people. He was a leech, feeding off ignorance and bigotry, and he needed to be stopped.

McBride opened the door and Joe followed him into the small, dimly lit room. He held back a gasp when he saw Alistair, naked and strapped to a reclining chair. Joe blanked his face and looked disinterested in the state of the patient, focusing his attention on McBride as he took out the equipment and unrolled some wires. Joe took a surreptitious glance at Alistair whose eyes were wide with surprise. He gave a minute shake of his head, hoping that Alistair would understand and not betray that he knew Joe. Alistair closed his eyes and sagged back in the chair, his body less tense than before.

Joe played his part and asked for an explanation of the equipment and how brain activity was measured. McBride rambled on with words that were plausible but lacking in any kind of scientific substance.

"So now we attach the leads to the base of the genitals using this ring." He held the metal ring up for Joe to see.

"Is the process painful?" Joe asked as he examined it.

"Yes, somewhat. The pain is necessary in educating the brain's responses to the stimuli on the screen."

Utter bullshit. Joe resisted the urge to dispute everything the doctor was saying. McBride leant forward to fasten the ring around the base of Alistair's cock. As soon as he was out of eye line, Joe pulled a syringe from his pocket, flipped off the protective cover on the needle and sank it into the doctor's neck. The doctor slapped at his skin, started to turn towards Joe, then collapsed sideways into an unconscious heap on the floor. Joe nudged him with a booted foot to make sure he was out. "Better than you deserve, you bastard. Alistair... Sweetie, you can open your eyes now." Joe began unfastening restraints as quickly as he could, wincing at the bruises that ringed Alistair's slender wrists and ankles. He kept murmuring reassurance to Alistair who blinked up at him nervously.

"Joe! I knew you had to be here somewhere when I saw Olly yesterday. Thank you! Thank you for coming to get me!"

"It's nothing, sweetheart. Now let's find you some clothes so that we can get you out of here. Carey is absolutely frantic with worry about you."

"Where is he, Joe?" Alistair swung his legs off the recliner. "Why didn't he come himself?"

Joe stroked a few blond strands away from Alistair's eyes. "He wanted to. Dave Becket was worried that people here might know his face, that they might have been briefed to look out for him. Nobody was willing to risk your safety in that way, but believe me—Carey took some convincing."

Alistair's smile lit his pale face. "I can't wait to see him. McBride got spare clothes from that cupboard last time I was in here." He pointed to a corner and Joe rummaged around and produced the usual grey T-shirt and white trousers.

"There aren't any shoes in here—you'll have to go barefoot. I can carry you if it gets rough."

"I'll be fine, Joe. I'll walk over broken glass if it means getting out of here. But what about Olly? We can't leave without him." Alistair yanked on the clothes as quickly as he could.

Joe opened the door a crack and took a peek outside. "The coast is clear. Olly will meet us by the gate if he does what he's been told for once." Alistair giggled and Joe enjoyed the sound. Alistair's resilience was remarkable.

"Olly was very naughty in the group session yesterday. He nearly caused a riot!" Alistair grinned happily.

"And he loved every minute of it." Joe took Alistair's hand and had another quick look down the corridor. "He'll be unbearable when we get home."

"I'm sure you'll soon have him under control, Sir." Alistair slipped back into his usual address with ease. "And have fun doing it!"

Joe grinned. "You know us too well. Now—no more talking. We need to be quick and quiet. Do you know where the orderly is that's been escorting you?"

Alistair shuddered. "Kong? He won't be back yet. This session was due to take two hours. McBride sent him away and told him to come back at eleven."

Joe let go of Alistair's hand while he pulled McBride's body across the floor and settled him into a corner, checking his breathing. "He'll be fine. Should be out for three or four hours. Let's go. If anyone tries to stop us, let me do the talking, okay?"

Joe closed the door firmly behind them and set off down the corridor at a steady pace. He knew that if he looked like he knew what he was doing and where he was going they were less likely to be questioned. They passed a few patients and a couple of staff without incident and took a side door out into the garden. This was where it got more risky because, with Alistair's bare feet, it was pretty obvious to anyone looking closely enough that he wasn't supposed to be outside. Alistair pulled his trousers down so that the waistband sat on his hips and the bottoms of his white trousers brushed the grass. Joe was amazed that Alistair could think quickly enough to anticipate the danger, given what he'd been through—he really was incredibly brave. Joe slowed his pace a little and put a hand on Alistair's shoulder. "We're taking a stroll in the grounds if anyone sees us. We'll head for the flowerbeds then disappear behind the shrubbery.

Once we're out of sight of the buildings, run through the trees towards the gate. With a bit of luck we'll make it unobserved. The car's parked just down the road and then we're free and clear."

Alistair nodded and wandered over to sniff at some blood-red roses before stepping quickly behind a huge buddleia. Joe looked casually around and swore. "Fuck! Alistair, run for the gates, we've been spotted. Don't stop for anything and if I don't join you, tell Olly to drive to London, no hanging around."

Joe was grateful that Alistair was a well-trained submissive used to taking orders because the boy immediately sprinted for the trees.

"Oi! You! Stay right where you are!" The shout came from a huge man dressed in an orderly's uniform who was thundering across the grass towards them. Joe slipped behind the bushes but didn't run. He waited, poised and ready. As Kong rounded the bush, his face red and perspiring, Joe employed his kickboxing skills to great effect. Kong went down like a felled tree, but it wasn't enough. He surged back to his feet and caught Joe with a glancing blow to the face. Joe tasted the warm metallic flavour of his own blood and grinned, relishing the prospect of a fight. He matched Kong in height—though not bulk—and was confident in his own skills. Kong was too big to move quickly and he was more flab than muscle. Joe whirled around and kicked high, making contact with a satisfying crunch. Kong went down again and this time he stayed down, clutching his nose through bloody fingers and moaning theatrically.

"Big baby," Joe muttered before he turned and ran towards the trees, adrenaline surging through his veins. It wasn't often he got the chance to use his martial arts abilities for anything more than fun. As he neared the gate he started to worry. There was no sign of Alistair or Olly and he didn't think that he'd been that far behind. He skidded to a halt on the gravel drive and looked around frantically. "Olly! Where are you?" he shouted impatiently.

"Here!" There was a flash of gold from Olly's curls as he hurtled from behind the wall and threw himself into Joe's arms. "Oh my God! You're bleeding and Alistair got here and you weren't with him and I was so scared and how could you think I'd leave without you and you're bleeding, are you all right?" Olly took a breath.

Joe took advantage of the pause and managed to get a word in edgeways. "Car, Olly. We'll discuss the fact that you disobeyed my orders later." Olly pouted but jogged towards the road where Alistair and another boy were waiting.

"Joe, this is Kai. He's here because his mean uncle sent him and he doesn't want to be here either. We can't leave him. Can we take him with us... Pleeeeease?" Olly begged with his big blue eyes.

Joe knew that refusal was futile. He shook his head in exasperation but decided that discussions could wait. "All of you, in the car!" He herded the three of them towards a black BMW with dark-tinted windows that was parked a few yards down the road. Alistair was limping a bit and Joe guessed that his feet were probably cut and bruised. Everything could wait until they were safely clear of the clinic.

As soon as they were on the road, Joe started to relax. The powerful car purred along, eating up the miles, taking them farther and farther away from Alistair's nightmare. All three boys had piled into the back seat and were wrapped around each other in a chattering, excited tangle of limbs. It was like chauffeuring a car full of chimpanzees after a Red Bull binge-drinking session, but Joe recognised hysterical shock when he saw it.

"Belt up, you three!" There was immediate, shocked silence and Joe grinned at them in the rear-view mirror. "I meant put your seatbelts on, but the silence works for me too." That set off the giggles then lots of whispered conversation. Joe listened in shamelessly.

"Joe's gorgeous, Olly, you're sooo lucky!" That was Kai.

"He's a really strict Dom, Kai. Olly gets his arse spanked a lot!" That was Alistair.

Olly's giggle came next. "Mmm. He is and I do. Scrummy!"

"He s-s-s-spanks you?" Kai stuttered.

"Uh-huh. And he ties me up and fucks me senseless. Lots. I am a very lucky boy."

Joe smirked at the sound of satisfaction in Olly's voice.

"So you're a submissive?" Kai sounded really curious.

"We both are." It was Alistair that replied. "My partner Carey is almost as big and bad as Joe."

"I have dreams…about being…being…" Kai stopped talking and sighed.

"Dominated?" Olly filled in the gap. "I like those kind of dreams, though they can get kind of soggy! But you should make it a reality."

"What do you mean? Why would anyone want me?"

Alistair and Olly both dissolved into laughter. "Oh, sweetie, you have no idea! You're cute and shy and innocent. You'll have those big bad Doms fighting over you like Rottweilers over a chew toy!"

"But I don't want to be a chew toy!" Kai protested.

"Poor turn of phrase." Alistair chuckled. "We just mean that you have nothing to worry about. You need to come back to The Underground with us and meet some of our friends."

Joe pulled into a lay-by and the whispers stopped. "Alistair, here's a phone." He tossed a mobile into the back seat. "Call Carey. Let him know you're safe and that we are on our way back to London. Better tell him to expect a house guest too." He climbed out of the car and fetched a small cooler from the boot. He opened the back door and gestured at Olly. "Move to the front, love, then this will fit between Kai and Alistair." Olly clambered out and Joe manoeuvred the cooler into the middle of the seat. "There are drinks and snacks in there. Help yourselves. We won't be stopping again."

Joe got back into the driver's seat and rolled his shoulders. Nobody was likely to be after them now. McBride was probably still unconscious, then he'd have to think up a few excuses for Alistair's father. Joe just hoped that the other elements of the plan were also underway. Rescuing Alistair was one thing. Keeping him safe was another thing entirely.

Olly leaned across him and delved in the door pocket, feeling up Joe's thighs as he went. "Olly, what the hell are you doing?" Joe did not find the idea of driving all the way back to London with a hard-on particularly appealing and a lap full of squirming Olly would have an inevitable effect. "First aid kit." Olly sat up and shuffled back to his own seat. "You have blood on your face."

Joe sat passively and let Olly clean his face with an antiseptic wipe. There was a lot of touching and kissing involved that wasn't strictly necessary. "Olly, I hope you don't treat all your patients this way." Olly kissed him again. "Oh no, Sir, you're a special case. In my professional opinion as a registered nurse, your bruising will be radically reduced by the application of kisses."

"Oh, is that so?" Joe grabbed a handful of blond hair and pulled Olly closer, taking control. Olly melted against him and opened for a deeper kiss. They separated reluctantly. "I feel much better, love, but keep that up and I won't be able to drive. If we delay Alistair's return then Carey will have both our hides and that man is pretty handy with a bullwhip."

Olly giggled at Joe's dour tone and put on his seatbelt. "Let's go then! The sooner we get home, the sooner I can administer more treatment."

The rest of the drive was uneventful. Alistair spent twenty minutes on the phone to Carey but did very little talking. Joe could see the soppy smile on his face in the rear-view mirror and assumed that all was well. After that, with the cool box relegated to the floor, Alistair crashed hard into sleep—the adrenaline that had been sustaining him gone. Kai slept too, his head resting in Alistair's lap. Olly dozed, making little muttering noises and occasionally humming to himself. Joe turned the radio on low and enjoyed the lack of excitement. Apart from a small cut to his face and some bruises, everything had gone remarkably well. It remained to be seen how Alistair would recover from his mistreatment and Kai was going to need a lot of care, but both boys were much stronger than they looked.

Joe pulled up outside The Underground shortly after one o'clock. He switched off the engine and laughed as Olly jerked awake with a plaintive, "Are we there yet?"

"What are you, six years old? Yes, we are here, and if you can rouse the two sleeping beauties in the back, we can go inside."

Olly pouted prettily. "I'm just excited!" He clicked open his seatbelt and swivelled round to kneel on his seat. "Oh look at them! Aren't they just the sweetest things?"

Joe rolled his eyes. "Adorable. Now wake them up, Olly!"

"Did you just use the word adorable? That's a first!" Olly leaned so far over his seat that Joe thought he might tumble head first into the back. He grabbed the back of Olly's trousers to stop him falling and they slipped down revealing a very bare arse. "Olly! Where's your underwear?"

"Lost them." Olly squirmed and reached out to tap Alistair's knee.

"Lost—? Oh never mind, I don't want to know!" Joe pulled Olly back into his seat.

"Oh! We're here! Wake up, Kai!" Alistair jiggled his knees until a sleepy Kai opened his eyes and stared around owlishly. "We're home! Quick, I can't wait to get inside!" Alistair said excitedly. He scrambled out of the car and nearly fell onto the pavement in his hurry. He shot past two very bemused security staff and punched the lift button impatiently. They all spilled out into the reception area where Christian gave a whoop of delight and held out his arms for a hug. Joe, Olly and Kai followed close behind and waited while Alistair mauled Christian and brushed off his worried apologies. "I'm fine! We're all fine! I'll tell you all about it later. Gotta find Carey!"

Christian let them through into the lounge and Alistair went for the stairs down to the bar level, too impatient to wait for the others. Joe followed at a pace that didn't risk life and limb with Olly behind, holding Kai's hand. When they emerged into the club there was bedlam. Over a sea of people Joe could just see Alistair clinging to Carey like a limpet. There were shouts of welcome, demands for information and drinks being raised all around. Carey managed a wave in his direction and Joe gently, but persistently, pushed a path through the crowd.

Carey kept Alistair held tight to his body and thrust out a hand. "I'll never be able to thank you enough, Joe. Or you, Olly. I owe you everything." His eyes glistened with emotion.

Joe patted his shoulder. "We're your friends, Carey, you don't owe us anything."

"Cut the crowding, people!" Joe looked up at Harry who was standing on the bar yelling. "Give them some space. You'll hear all about it soon enough." He hopped down and grinned at Joe. "Welcome back, mate. Good job."

The crowd thinned as people went back to their tables and settled down, though the level of chatter remained high. Olly and Kai were both holding onto Joe to avoid getting swept away by the crowd.

"Why don't we let Carey and Alistair get reacquainted and I'll get you some drinks?" Harry suggested and, though he was talking to Joe, his line of sight was firmly fixed on Kai.

Joe nodded. "Sounds good. It was a long drive. Fresh orange juice for all of us."

Joe took a seat at a table next to the bar. Olly immediately clambered onto his lap while Kai stood, nervously looking around the club. "I've never seen so much leather in one place before," Kai whispered.

Olly grabbed his hand and tugged him to a chair. "You should be here in the evenings. There's a lot more bare flesh to ogle then! Though it's hard to beat hot men in tight leather."

Joe tightened his grip around Olly's waist, painfully aware that his brat was bare beneath those soft white trousers. "You shouldn't be looking at other men," he snapped, "and they shouldn't be looking at you. You're mine."

Olly chewed his lower lip and looked back at him adoringly. "You'll just have to punish me, Sir."

Joe realised that he'd just been played.

Kai giggled and sat cross-legged in a chair, watching them with open curiosity. Joe was relieved when Harry arrived with a tray of drinks—he was starting to feel outnumbered! He felt a tap on his shoulder and turned to see Carey and Alistair. Carey looked exhausted, but happier than Joe had ever seen him. "Alistair and I have some catching up to do, but we'll see you back here this evening? Celebratory dinner on me."

Olly bounced in Joe's lap. "Yes! Can we, Sir?"

Joe grinned at Carey. "Of course we can. See you later."

Harry sat down with them and handed out their drinks. "It's great to have Alistair back. I don't think Carey could have lasted without him much longer." Joe quirked his lips in amusement. Harry was talking, but his attention was completely focused on Kai who was staring back at him like he was a giant ice cream sundae that needed a good licking. Joe was about to make introductions when Kai beat him to it.

"Hi, I'm Kai. You're gorgeous."

Olly dissolved into laughter. "Don't think Kai's as shy as we thought, Sir!"

Joe was lost for words. Harry's face was pink. Kai already had him wrapped around his little finger and it had only taken one sentence.

"Harry. I'm the bar manager here."

Kai chewed on his lip. "Are you a Dom?"

"Would that scare you?" Harry shuffled his chair a little closer to Kai.

Kai reached out and stroked the leather that was stretched taut over Harry's knees. "That feels nice," he purred.

"Oh God!" Harry looked like he might explode. "Joe, I wonder if I might take Kai back to my place, get him cleaned up and out of those clothes. I mean into some clean clothes. I mean—"

"Oh, I think I know *exactly* what you mean, Harry. If Kai wants to, then of course. He's supposed to be staying with Carey, but I imagine your boss has his mind on other things at the moment. I need to get Olly home too." Joe had quite a few ideas about what he wanted to do with his squirming, giggling sub when he got Olly back to the house.

Kai was standing up and tugging on Harry's hand. "Let's go. I'm really dirty and I love having my back scrubbed. Do you have a loofah?"

Harry let himself be pulled away.

"I'll let Goran know you're taking a few hours off, Harry!" Joe shouted after him. He swivelled Olly around in his lap. "You little brat, you've managed to corrupt that sweet, innocent boy already. He's going to be as much of a handful as you are."

"When are you going to get your hands full of me, Sir?" Olly managed to look innocent even though Joe knew he was anything but.

Joe shook his head. "What am I going to do with you?"

"Show me who's in charge, Sir?" Olly sounded hopeful.

"Sometimes I'm not sure I know the answer to that question, Olly. But we do need to discuss how careless you've been with your underwear..." Joe lifted Olly off his lap, took tight hold of a wrist and pulled him towards the exit.

Chapter Eleven

Carey picked up the newspaper that had just thudded onto his doormat and padded quietly back to the kitchen. Alistair was still sleeping and he didn't want to disturb him. Three weeks had passed since Alistair's dramatic rescue from the clinic, but he was still recovering. The bruises had faded, but nightmares disturbed his sleep and as a result he was still very tired. Carey smiled—he'd never had so much vanilla sex in his life, but he didn't want to push Alistair too soon. His young lover just wanted to be held, touched and reassured, and Carey was more than happy to oblige. His urge to protect was overwhelming and he didn't want to let Alistair out of his sight for a minute. He'd hardly spent any time at the club in the last weeks—just bringing paperwork home and letting Harry get on with the job of running the place. He had Alistair back and that was all that mattered.

He put the paper down on the kitchen counter then scooped coffee from a fresh packet into the percolator. Soon a tantalising aroma filled the kitchen, accompanied by the comfortingly familiar gurgling sounds of the machine at work. Carey gave silent thanks that he kept a basic perc at home rather than the insanely complicated machine that resided in the flat above the club. He poured himself a large mug and blew a stream of air over the surface, trying to cool it a little. The first sip, as always, was heavenly, awakening his taste buds with a burst of bitter flavour.

Carey sighed contentedly and pulled a stool up to the counter. He smoothed out the paper and stared at the headlines in delight, 'Easton Fisher Weston Linked to Terror Plot'. He put his mug down carefully and read the article from end to end. There was a small picture of Edward Easton as he left his office, trying to hide his face. Carey was clenching his teeth so hard his jaw was cramping. He forced himself to relax, sipped more coffee then read the article again. It was all a bit vague, there wasn't much that could be considered fact, but the article talked about the discovery of accounts linked to an active terrorist organisation. "Nice work, Aiden," Carey muttered. The piece went on to describe the propensity for EFW to deal with less than mainstream clients and talked about a number of shady organisations that had the firm on retainer. Carey snarled. No doubt there would be denials and counter-accusations. The disclosure was going to incite a feeding frenzy in the press and Edward Easton's firm was at the heart of it. Carey doubted that EFW would recover, but even if the firm survived Carey had plans in place to ensure that Edward Easton would not. He took a long swallow of coffee and realised that he was tasting it anew. A huge weight had lifted from his shoulders and everything felt, tasted and smelt better.

Carey sensed rather than heard Alistair come up behind him. He turned and watched as Alistair peered anxiously at the article, his forehead creased with worry. Carey waited patiently, then, when Alistair leaned in to him, Carey encircled his waist and pulled him closer. "Are you okay, sweetheart? This is really good news, you do realise that?"

Alistair nuzzled into his neck and Carey felt the dampness of tears against his skin. Through a few snuffles, Alistair managed to speak, "I know. It's just... It brings it all back, Carey. My father cares more about his reputation and his company than he does his own son. I hate him, but it still hurts."

"I know it's easy for me to say, love, but you mustn't let it get to you. Every tear you shed is a victory for that bastard, who doesn't deserve to be called a father." Carey's voice cracked a little.

Alistair hugged him tightly. "Make me forget, Sir. Give me something else to think about." Alistair took a step back. "I want us to get back to normal. You've been sweet and kind and gentle and I really love you for it, but that's not us. It's definitely not you!" He chuckled and wiped his eyes with the back of a hand. "I can't remember a time when you've gone more than a week without spanking me."

Carey's dick twitched into life and he took a moment to consider Alistair's appearance. The boy's blond hair was tousled from sleep and he was wearing a pair of pale blue cotton boxers and a loose, plain white T-shirt. The dark circles beneath his eyes had faded and some of the old sparkle had returned to his eyes.

"Are you sure?" Carey held himself back with a huge effort.

Alistair sank to his knees and looked up, fluttering his eyelashes shamelessly. "I'm sure, Sir. If you don't take me in hand again soon, I'll probably turn into Olly."

That did the trick. Carey slipped off his stool and tightened the belt on his robe. "Back to the bedroom. You've got one minute to get naked." Alistair jumped up like he'd knelt in a patch of stinging nettles and ran for the bedroom. Carey gave him a couple of minutes then followed.

Carey shut the bedroom door firmly and looked towards the bed. The vision that met his eyes hardened his cock to steel. Alistair had shed his clothes and was kneeling on the bed facing away from Carey. His forehead was pressed to the covers and his perfect, creamy smooth arse was presented in the ideal position for fucking. Carey swallowed hard. It was tempting to just remove his robe, step forward and claim what was offered so willingly, but that wasn't what either of them needed. He was the Dominant. It was his responsibility to control the scene and himself.

A little flattery wasn't out of order. "You are stunning, Alistair, quite stunning." Carey turned on his sound system and filled the room with classical music. Then he rummaged in a small chest under the window and pulled out his favourite butt plug. It was a solid steel sphere on a slim metal column with a useful handle on the end. It penetrated nice and deeply, applied the perfect amount of pressure to the prostate but didn't overstretch Alistair's channel. Carey liked him to stay nice and tight, but this plug turned him into a quivering wreck. Perfect.

Carey opened a pot of extra thick lubricant and smeared a big dollop of the stuff over the metal ball. He indulged himself and stroked Alistair's arse a few times, enjoying the sensation of silky skin beneath his fingers. Alistair kept still and quiet until Carey pushed the lubed ball against his hole, demanding entry. Carey loved the initial resistance but even more, the moment when Alistair surrendered his body and let him in. The ball slid past the protective outer ring of muscle then smoothly into Alistair's channel. Carey manipulated the handle until he got the gasp he was waiting for, then settled the plug in place. The hinged handle twisted and lay neatly along the crease between Alistair's buttocks, satisfying Carey's desire for order.

"Hmm. Now then, I feel a need to lay some pretty stripes on that pristine skin. But what to use? So many choices..." Carey smiled as Alistair twitched fractionally, betraying his nerves. Carey threw off his robe and went to the wardrobe. He selected a pair of battered leather chaps that Alistair loved and pulled them on. They framed his groin with satisfying symmetry and Carey loved the grip of leather on his thighs whilst his cock and balls were nicely accessible. He jacked himself a couple of times, getting just close enough to the edge that a little urgency would be added to his strokes.

Carey returned to the toy drawer and selected a springy cane. Alistair preferred a flogger or paddle, but Carey wanted to be more precise with the marks he left. He returned to the end of the bed, pleased to see that Alistair hadn't moved. "Six strokes, boy. Let's see how well you take them for me. You are not to come." Carey whipped the cane through the air a couple of times, testing its weight. It made a lovely whistling noise and was loud enough that Alistair would know what was coming. Tiny whimpers betrayed his understanding. Carey debated giving him a cock ring but decided that was too lenient. If

Alistair came without permission, he would be punished.

Carey laid two slim horizontal lines onto Alistair's left buttock, about four inches apart, then he joined them on one side with a vertical stroke that was harder to accomplish. He smiled at the results. A squared C decorated Alistair's arse in raised red welts that Carey knew would feel like they were on fire. Alistair moaned and shuffled his knees apart a little. Carey could see that his dick jutted hard and stiff from his body, curving towards his flat stomach.

Without giving any warning, Carey placed two vertical stripes, this time about three inches apart, on Alistair's right cheek and watched the colour bloom. He hummed along to the background music and flexed the cane. "Last one, love. You're doing incredibly well. You should see how amazing your arse looks."

Alistair whimpered, "I'm close, Sir. So hard. Hurts."

Carey silenced him with his final stroke, joined the vertical lines with a horizontal one, forming a perfect H. Carey nearly came as he admired his handiwork. His initials adorned Alistair's skin beautifully. He stepped forwards and grasped the handle of the plug, jiggling it enough to make Alistair yelp before slowly removing it. Carey dropped the metal ball on the bed, lubed his cock quickly and grasped Alistair's hips tightly. He couldn't wait to drive home his claim, to fill Alistair's slick channel with his seed. He loved that they could bareback without fear. He jerked his hips forwards and watched Alistair's hole swallow his cock greedily. His lover's channel was hot and tight and gripped him jealously. Alistair's desperate sob prompted him into action and he began to move, slowly at first, then faster and faster until the slap of flesh on flesh echoed the beat of the music.

"Sir! Please!" Alistair begged and sobbed.

Carey relented as he pounded Alistair's arse, "Come for me, boy!"

Alistair shot hard and fast without having his dick touched at all. It was so hot hearing the noises he made that Carey immediately followed, coming hard as he flexed his hips one final time. After a few moments of synchronised panting, Alistair collapsed forwards onto the bed and Carey slipped from his body. Cum oozed from Alistair's hole and dripped lazily down his thigh. Carey chuckled and fetched a cloth from the bathroom. He wiped Alistair's arse gently then fetched some salve to spread on the welts that felt hot beneath his touch. He cleaned up the mess left on the bed covers as best he could then stretched out next to Alistair. Alistair immediately shifted so that he could spread himself across Carey's chest. Carey sighed contently and stroked Alistair's hair. "I love you, Alistair."

"Love you too, Sir." Alistair snuggled against him sleepily. "You're wearing your chaps. Yummy."

"And you're wearing my initials. Are you sore?"

"Burns, Sir, but it's nice. You made me yours again."

Carey listened to Alistair's breathing until it evened out. When he was sure that Alistair was deeply asleep he slid from beneath him and left the bed. He pulled the covers up over his sleeping lover then grabbed a pair of old jeans, underwear and a sweatshirt. He turned the volume down low on the stereo, crept from the room then used the shower in the guest bathroom before he dressed and headed for the kitchen. They had missed breakfast and it was almost lunchtime so he threw together a salad and put potatoes in the oven to bake. They could have them with cheese or tuna and eat at the club later.

With food underway Carey went to his office and made a few phone calls. He had planned a big surprise for Alistair and wanted to make sure that all the final arrangements were in place. His job was to keep Alistair away from the club until seven. It wouldn't be difficult. After lunch he intended taking a trip to his favourite leather shop and treating them to a few new toys. Some new underwear for Alistair too. He'd seen an amazing pair of backless leather shorts that had a chastity tube sewn into the front of them. The thought of Alistair's cock imprisoned while his arse was exposed and accessible made Carey's world a very happy place. He allowed himself an evil chuckle and went to see if Alistair was awake.

* * * *

The day passed quickly. They came back from their shopping trip laden with bags, Alistair's face still pink from endless blushing. Carey had had great fun watching as Alistair had tried on various garments and harnesses in latex, leather and even lace. Fortunately the shop owner had been a tolerant man and a long-term friend of Carey's. He had smirked and turned a blind eye as Carey had had Alistair try out a sling suspended from the ceiling in the storeroom. Alistair's cries as Carey had fucked him hard had obviously been able to be heard in the shop because when they'd eventually emerged, looking rather dishevelled, they'd got a round of applause from several delighted customers.

Carey put the bags in the bedroom and sent Alistair off for a shower. He laid out the clothes he wanted him to wear and chose his own outfit. Alistair wandered out of the en suite with a tiny towel around his hips, rubbing his hair with another one. Carey waited for him to spot the clothes and grinned at Alistair's expression.

"I thought those were only for wearing in private, Sir?" Alistair gestured at a black leather thong where the front panel was missing and the two sides were held together with six short chains.

"We *are* in private, sweetheart, so indulge me. I want you to wear your leather trousers and a plain black T-shirt. Nobody will know what's underneath except us. You've worn less under that skimpy kilt for the last three years."

Alistair looked sceptical. "You won't order me to undress later in the evening?"

Carey licked his lips. "Well, now you've put the idea in my head…" He laughed at Alistair's indignant expression. "I promise. Of course, if you decide you want to, I won't stop you."

Carey went to take a shower while Alistair dressed. He washed and shampooed distractedly, visualising Alistair wearing just the thong. By the time he was done, his cock was hard and aching. He contemplated a hand job but instead dried off and strode naked back into the bedroom. He stood with his hands on his hips. "Look what you've done to me!"

Alistair grinned. "I've got it on. The little chains rub against my dick when I move."

Carey sighed as his cock jerked excitedly. He pointed to the floor at his feet. Alistair came to him, sank gracefully to his knees and kissed Carey's swollen tip. Then he took him into his mouth and sucked hard. Carey moaned. He was going to come embarrassingly fast. Alistair changed tack and began to mouth his balls, licking gently.

"Oh Christ!" Carey grabbed Alistair's hair and pulled him closer. Alistair took the hint and opened for him. Carey fucked his mouth, pausing as Alistair's throat constricted around his shaft. A couple more jerks of his hips and he came hard. Alistair swallowed every drop and licked his lips happily. "Better, Sir?"

Carey collapsed on to the end of the bed and wondered if he could summon up the energy to dress. "Much. Thank you, Alistair. Perhaps you could pass me my shirt? It's hanging on the wardrobe door handle." Alistair handed him his clothes piece by piece, smiling constantly. He seemed to find it necessary to bend over rather a lot, stretching black leather tightly across his arse. Carey growled, "More punishment for you tonight, boy."

Alistair looked at him innocently. "Of course, Sir. As you wish."

Eventually they got out of the house. Carey resigned himself to spending the evening with a hard-on because Alistair in leather and a very tight T-shirt was a recipe for frustration. He drove to The Underground thinking about his accountant who was the scariest, least appealing woman he'd ever come across. It didn't help much because he kept catching tantalising glimpses of leather stretched across Alistair's thighs as he sat quietly in the passenger seat.

When they parked down the road from the club Alistair peered out of the window curiously. "What's going on, Sir? There's a huge queue to get in!"

"Never mind them. Open the glove compartment, there's something in there for you."

Alistair did as he'd been told and pulled out a flat, square box.

"Open it, love." Carey watched as Alistair took the lid off with trembling fingers.

"Oh! Oh, Sir! It's beautiful!"

Carey took the slim leather collar from the box and fastened it carefully around Alistair's neck. "I wish this was a more romantic moment, but I want everyone in that club to know that you're mine."

Alistair's eyes glistened. "I love you so much, Carey." He touched the collar reverently, "This is perfect."

Carey felt himself welling up and coughed gruffly. "Let's get inside. There are a lot of people waiting for you."

Alistair clambered out of the car. "There are? Why?"

"Come inside and you'll see." Carey took Alistair's hand and held it tight. They walked along the pavement to The Underground's street level entrance and there was a smattering of applause from the line of waiting people.

"Carey, there are lots of girls here. These people aren't our members."

Carey chuckled and pulled him inside. They took the lift down to the reception area where Christian was in his usual spot. His face lit up as they approached. "Good evening, Sir, Alistair. It looks like this evening's going to be a huge success."

"I hope so, Christian. Do you have some help lined up for when the doors open?"

Christian nodded. "Goran's coming up for the first hour and we're going to bring people down the back stairs rather than use the lift. We'll be fine. I'll see you downstairs later. That's a beautiful collar, Alistair," he added shyly.

Carey and Alistair crossed the lounge and took the stairs down to the bar. Carey held the door open and let Alistair step out first. He froze, taking in the scene in front of him. The club had been cleared of furniture and everywhere there were freestanding black panels displaying his photographs, all mounted beautifully. Images of urban wildlife and London nightscapes were interspersed with his pictures of the BDSM scene. The effect was spectacular.

Carey drew Alistair into a hug and kissed him. "What do you think?"

Alistair looked stunned. "It's amazing, but why? I don't understand?"

Carey led him behind the screens to the bar where a small group of people were waiting. "Alistair!" Olly wrapped himself around his friend until Joe stepped forwards and detached him. Heath and Aiden were there, Heath cupping Aiden's neck possessively—Kai was perched on a stool at the bar where Harry was popping the corks on bottles of non-alcoholic bucks fizz. Dave Becket was actually smiling for once. All the serving staff were crowded round and everyone was talking at once.

Carey hushed them. "It's wonderful to have so many friends here and as you may have guessed, this is a complete surprise for Alistair." Someone handed out drinks and Carey held his glass up for a toast. "To The Nightlife Exhibition, may it be a great success!"

Alistair looked completely bewildered so Carey drew him to one side and pushed a glossy flyer into his hand for him to read. "While you were gone, your friends put this together. It's been promoted all over the London scene and you have a lot of friends, love. That's what the queue's about. They are all here to see your pictures. You deserve this, you're a brilliant photographer."

Alistair gulped his fizz and put the glass down. He looked around. "I can't really believe it. You did all this for me?"

"You're not going to cry on me, are you?" Carey sounded wary. "There's something else I need to show you, before the press arrive." He strolled across the room to a prominent display.

"Press? Oh... I don't know if I can— Oh. Oh!" Alistair's last exclamation was less about nerves and more about the photograph facing him. An older man, his skin sagging and wrinkled, knelt naked and blindfolded in front of a whip wielding Dominatrix. Except it wasn't a woman. On closer inspection and despite the high heels, corset and lacy underwear, it was very apparent that the person brandishing the whip was a man. A man whose wig had slipped just enough to reveal cropped hair. A man whose lace shorts bulged around an ample package. "Oh my God! That man on his knees is my father!" Alistair exclaimed, pointing at the kneeling figure. "Holy fuck!"

"One final nail in the bastard's coffin," Carey stated coldly. He wrapped his arms around his shaking lover from behind. "Even if he manages to worm his way out of terrorism charges, this isn't going to go away. By tomorrow it'll be on the front page of every tabloid newspaper in this country, and you'll be safe."

Alistair turned into his hold and looked up, tears running down his face. "Is it wrong to feel nothing but relief?"

"No, love. That is the man that had you kidnapped, held against your will and tortured. He has no right to call himself your father anymore. All the family you need is right here. Later I'll introduce you to Alan— he's the other man in the picture. He's risked a great deal going public with this, but he wanted to help you."

"But he doesn't even know me!" Alistair exclaimed.

"He knows how much I love you and that was enough for him. When you meet him, you'll understand."

"Okay, this is all so much to take in. You won't leave me tonight, will you? Stay with me?"

Carey kissed him gently. "I'll never leave you, sweetheart. You're mine remember?" He stroked Alistair's new collar. "Now, time to let the hordes in!"

Carey kept his promise, never straying from Alistair's side as crowds of people viewed the exhibition. Gradually, little gold dots appeared next to the pictures, indicating that they had been sold. Alistair lost some of his shyness when he talked about his work and Carey loved seeing him so animated. Reviewers showed up from several magazines and papers, drawn by the controversial subject matter, and seemed entranced both by the work and by Alistair himself. It didn't take long before someone spotted the only picture that wasn't Alistair's. The excited arts correspondent probably thought he'd got the scoop of his life as he snapped away and phoned in his story.

Gradually the crowd filtered away. Staff moved the exhibition boards to the walls and brought the furniture back into the club. Music started up and the dance floor filled rapidly. Carey and Alistair's closest friends gathered around them at the bar, laughing and joking. Dave Becket tapped his glass on the bar and waited for everyone to quiet down. He looked around, meeting everyone's gaze individually before he spoke. "I wanted to give you all some news before the party really gets started. EFW is now the subject of an official counter terrorism investigation. Their assets have been frozen and passports withdrawn from all the partners. Aiden's little hacking expedition has set off an avalanche that's going to wipe them out."

Aiden smiled shyly and moved a little closer to Heath who put a proprietary hand on his arse. Becket carried on, "You've all been introduced to Alan" — he pulled Alan forwards and there was a spontaneous round of applause. "Alan's selfless act in providing us with a unique photo opportunity means that if Edward Easton somehow avoids a prison sentence, which I doubt, his reputation will still be destroyed. Alistair will be safe from his hatred from now on."

"And strangely," Alan said modestly, "business is booming at Severin's Muse. I may lose some clients when the pictures are published, but I have a waiting list. Someone" — he smiled warmly at Carey — "has been recommending my services across the London scene."

"Thank you, Alan." Alistair stepped forwards and gave him a hug. "I can't believe what you did for me."

Alan shrugged. "I'm a sucker for true love, what can I say?"

Becket scowled before he spoke again, "I am really pleased to report that thanks to testimony from Alistair, and from Kai, Doctor McBride's clinic in Cornwall has been shut down. He's a wanted man. We haven't got the bastard yet, but we will."

Carey snarled, "If I ever set eyes on that evil son of a bitch..."

Alistair patted his arm. "You won't. He's a greedy coward and he'll never be able to peddle his corrupt practices ever again."

"So I think that's all the loose ends tied up. We can all get back to normal." Dave sounded very pleased with himself.

Joe interrupted, "I think there are a couple more things to clear up — Aiden, do you want tell them?"

Aiden shook his head. "No, you do it, Sir."

Joe nodded. "Okay. You remember the shift Aiden did while Alistair was gone?"

"How could anyone forget?" That was Harry, piping up from behind the bar.

Heath bridled, "Yes, well... He did manage to get some information while he was flaunting his arse."

"Hey!" Aiden exclaimed indignantly, "You don't seem to object to me wearing that fucking kilt at home!"

Olly collapsed in a giggling heap at Joe's feet while Heath looked like he didn't know where to put himself. "I should gag you, brat." He took a deep breath. "Carey suspected that there was someone on the inside feeding information to Alistair's father. A couple of the Doms told Aiden that a new member had been asking a lot of questions about Alistair and Carey — not suspicious in itself, but then the same man was spotted near the lights on the day of the fire. Harry had Goran ask Jonah Salter a few questions and he confessed to starting the fire. He spilled his guts to the police just to get away from Goran! Easton had paid him to get his goons into the club so that they could take Alistair."

"So that only leaves one mystery unsolved." Joe patted Olly's curls, prompting him to look up. "Just how did you manage to lose your underwear at the clinic, Olly?"

Kai nearly fell off his stool laughing. Olly chewed on his lip and looked around the group.

Carey chuckled. "Olly! You're the most devilish angel I've ever met. What did you do?"

"Why do you all assume I did something?" Olly sounded so affronted but then looked guilty as sin when everyone fell about laughing. "Fine. I'm not admitting to anything, but the course leader at the clinic, Mo, was such an obnoxious toad, I may have sneaked into his room that night and hidden a few extras in his suitcase."

"You put your underwear in his suitcase?" Joe stuttered.

"Actually, I used my thong as an elastic band to tie up a love note and a couple of flavoured condoms. I'm sure Mo's wife will be very interested to read about Big Cyril the orderly and where he likes to put his Kong-sized dick when she unpacks that case."

Joe was speechless. Kai who had obviously been in on the secret was howling with laughter and Alistair had tears running down his face. Carey looked at the other Doms, then at Joe. "You have a professional brat on your hands there, Joe."

"Don't I know it."

It was nearing midnight and the post-exhibition party was in full swing when Carey, with Alistair safe in his arms, found time to look for his friends and make sure they were all enjoying themselves. Kai was still glued to his bar stool, following Harry's every move. Every now and again Harry would ruffle Kai's hair affectionately or pull him forward for a kiss. Dave Becket was slow dancing with Christian even though the music was loud and fast. He had both hands on Christian's arse and they were pressed so closely together that Carey thought he wouldn't be able to force them apart with a crowbar. Olly had shed his conservative dress from earlier and was wearing a tiny pair of leather shorts and big work boots. Joe had his blond bundle of energy on a lead, but that wasn't stopping him dancing wildly.

Carey pulled Alistair's T-shirt from his head and threw it over the bar with a grin. He grabbed his wrist and pulled him onto the dance floor where he groped him shamelessly to the accompaniment of a lot of lewd comments and whistles. Alistair blushed beautifully and Carey felt his cock harden. "We've been dancing on the edge for far too long, love. The future's all ours." Alistair's smile and the love in his eyes warmed Carey's heart.

Alistair gave him a wickedly sexy look. "I'd prefer to be dancing horizontally." He licked his lips provocatively. Carey swallowed hard and dragged his unresisting lover away from the party.

A DOUBLE-
EDGED SWORD

Dedication

To unconditional love.

Chapter One

The Underground's stage was cleverly lit to highlight the chair set at its center. Almost throne-like, the bespoke piece of furniture was made from polished oak and upholstered with padded green leather. The back had a cushioned middle panel and intricately carved side pieces, so it looked impressively regal without sacrificing comfort. The arms were wide and flat, lightly padded as well. At first glance it could have been an antique piece from a stately home, but closer inspection showed how it earned its place on the stage of a BDSM club. At the top of the backrest, a curved leather neck support and headrest stood proud from the wood. The seat was significantly wider at the front than the rear and subtly concealed within the leather was a circular section that could be removed. Brass eyelets were set at regular intervals down each of the chair legs, the sides of the seat and in the vertical wooden panels of the back. It was a chair made for display, for restraint and for some very kinky play.

Dave Becket leaned back in his seat and watched disinterestedly as a blindfolded, naked man was led out onto the stage and positioned in the chair so that his arse, cock and balls were accessible. The Dom with him proceeded to fasten narrow leather straps around his sub's limbs until he was secured in position, legs spread wide.

"The show doesn't inspire you, Dave?"

Becket turned to his companion and shook his head. "Public displays don't do much for me, I'm afraid. Any sub of mine will be kept for my pleasure, not the titillation of others."

Carey Hoffman nodded his agreement. "I would never put Alistair up there, certainly. We seem to be in the minority, however." He gestured at the crowded tables that surrounded the stage. "The shows are very good for business."

Becket grunted and cast a glance around the room. The Underground was a popular venue. Membership was expensive and the serving staff attentive and pretty. For anyone seriously into the scene, it was the place to be. Becket attended when he could, though the demands of his job meant that his visits were sporadic at best. He enjoyed the atmosphere and Carey had become a good friend. There were advantages to being close to the club's owner, including the prime position of the table the two of them currently occupied.

"Will Alistair be joining you tonight, Carey?" Becket grinned as a soppy smile fixed itself onto Carey's handsome face.

"Yes, he will." Carey glanced at his watch. "In fact, he should be here any minute. He had to go over to a gallery in the West End and check on the hanging of some of his work but he should be back by now. He's probably upstairs changing."

"He's doing incredibly well with his photography, isn't he?"

Carey nodded, his expression full of pride. "Since he won the Forbes prize, he's been in great demand."

"I read about that," Becket said. "The youngest ever winner, I understand?"

"That's right. It was an amazing achievement even though he tries to play it down. Alistair is very shy about his success."

"That's because you keep him so well grounded, my friend." Becket took a sip from his glass of iced water and prodded at the slice of lime floating in the top. "What's your secret? The two of you always seems so…content."

Carey's forehead wrinkled in thought. "It's no secret and no mystery really. We're compatible. We give each other what we need."

Becket frowned. "But how did you know? I mean, was it love at first sight or did you grow together?"

Carey gave a short chuckle. "Fuck, Dave, your reputation would be shot if it ever got out that you were asking questions about feelings."

"And what about you?" Becket retorted. "You're supposed to be a big bad Dom but one mention of Alistair and you go all smooshy."

Carey choked on his drink. "Smooshy? There's a word I never thought I'd hear coming out of your mouth, Agent Becket. What's this really about, as if I couldn't guess?"

Becket's face heated. He shouldn't have started this conversation. Better to focus on the sub getting his arse whipped up on the stage. He was saved by

Alistair's arrival, the pretty blond immediately commanding all of Carey's attention.

"Good evening, Sir. Good evening, Mr Becket." Alistair leaned over to kiss his master then sank gracefully to his knees in front of Carey, head demurely bowed.

"I'm glad you're here, Alistair, I missed you." Carey ruffled Alistair's hair gently. "You look beautiful."

"Thank you, Sir."

Becket smiled as a delicate blush crept across Alistair's cheeks. Carey wasn't exaggerating—Alistair did look gorgeous. He wore skin-tight leather trousers in a shade of deep burgundy and nothing else, apart from the slim collar encircling his throat. He was slender and toned but not overly defined. Becket approved—he wasn't into men who spent more time in the gym than they did in the real world. Cut abs were great to look at but Alistair's sleek muscles were just as pretty.

Alistair looked up at his Master. "Is it all right if I get myself a drink, Sir?"

Carey immediately nodded. "Of course. Dave, would you like anything while Alistair is at the bar?"

"Another glass of mineral water would be welcome, thanks."

"And I'll have the same please, sweetheart."

Alistair practically glowed at the simple endearment. Becket snuck a sideways glance at Carey whose gaze was firmly fixed on Alistair's neat, leather-clad arse as he picked his way through the tables to the bar.

"You're a lucky bastard, Carey." Becket wasn't jealous. He could admire Alistair as a beautiful young man and a well-trained submissive, but Alistair wasn't his type. Becket liked an edgier look than the boy-next-door wholesomeness that Alistair effortlessly exuded.

"I know it." Carey's focus didn't leave Alistair until he returned with their drinks. "Thank you, love. Sit here please." Carey gestured to a spot on the floor between his legs.

Alistair wriggled into position and leaned back against Carey's chair with a contented sigh. "It's good to be off my feet, Sir."

"Relax and have your drink, love. Dave and I need to pick up the conversation we were having before you arrived. Don't think I've forgotten, Becket."

Becket groaned. "I should learn to keep my mouth shut."

Carey stroked Alistair's hair and quirked his lips. "Did you know that Christian hasn't played with anyone else but you since the day of the Nightlife exhibition?"

Becket thought back to the night when Alistair's photographs had been displayed around the club. The night that Alistair's bastard of a father had been put down for good. "That was months ago."

"It was. Have you seen anyone else since then?"

"No!" Becket felt strangely affronted, as if Carey was accusing him of betraying Christian's trust.

"Exactly. Christian needs a Dom. He needs you."

Alistair nodded his silent agreement.

"No one else has ever been able to give him what he needs, Dave," Carey continued. "The two of you were made for each other and I think you know it."

Becket relaxed his hunched shoulders. "We've played together a few times. It seems to work."

Carey sighed, sounding a little exasperated. "You've played with Christian every time you've been here over the last six months. I know you aren't here that often, Dave, but you've seen enough of the lad to know how well he responds to you."

Alistair tilted his head back to catch Carey's eye. "Sir... May I?"

"Of course, sweetheart. Perhaps you can talk some sense into this stubborn idiot."

Alistair giggled. "Christian's my friend, Mr Becket, he wouldn't scene with you if he didn't really, really like you. He talks about you all the time when you're not here. He misses you when you're away. You know Christian—he likes strict control. Now he's found someone who can give him what he needs, he's a bit lost when you're not around."

Becket frowned. "I didn't realize. We haven't even... I mean I haven't..." He stuttered to a stop.

"Fucked him. You haven't fucked him. You can say it, Dave, but I have to ask why the hell not? Jesus, he's gorgeous and he adores you. If you don't feel the same you need to let him know. After all this time, it's cruel to keep stringing him along." Carey sounded more than a little pissed off.

Becket groaned. "I've been such a fucking idiot. I've known since the first time I saw him that Christian was meant to be mine but I didn't think it was right to ask him for a commitment when I'm hardly ever here. He must think I'm a right callous bastard."

Alistair snuggled against Carey's thigh. "It's not too late, is it, Sir? Christian finishes his shift at eleven."

"It's not too late if my prize idiot of a friend here grows some balls and does what he should have done months ago. Have you got a private room booked for tonight, Dave?"

Becket shook his head. "No. I wasn't sure I would be able to get here and I didn't want to tie up a room for nothing. I didn't ask Christian to meet me either." He looked at the time. "It's gone eleven now—he's probably on his way home."

Carey petted Alistair a little. "Off you go, sweetheart. Go and see if Becket's surprise is ready."

Alistair got up and scampered away. Becket looked at Carey, feeling utterly ashamed of himself. "If I've left it too late and lost him, I don't know what I'll do. Some Dom I am. Fuck it, Carey, I feel like the worst kind of arsehole."

"Well, lucky for you you're the kind of arsehole that Christian wants. Don't fuck it up, I'm fond of him and I don't want to see him hurt."

Becket clenched a fist. "It sounds like you know where he is, Carey, are you up to something?"

Carey smirked. "When you arrived earlier I may have sent Sam upstairs with a note telling Christian he could finish early and to wait in the flat until you were ready for him."

Becket shook his head. "You're a devious bastard, Carey Hoffman. That's probably why I like you."

"Not the first time I've been called that and probably not the last. I reserved room eleven, will that suit you?"

Becket grinned. Room eleven was his favorite, kitted out like a medieval dungeon right down to the flagstone floor and stone clad walls.

"Perfect. Good job I came dressed for the occasion." He was wearing his battered black leather trousers, a charcoal gray T-shirt and heavy boots. The clothes were well worn and comfortable, marking him as an established Dom rather than some inexperienced newbie. He stood up and stretched, easing the kinks in his back.

On stage, the sub with the reddened arse was in the arms of his master being kissed stupid. Before the night was out, Dave decided he would be doing the same thing to Christian.

Alistair returned looking almost as smug as Carey. This time, Carey pulled his young lover into his lap and held him close.

"Christian's ready and waiting, Sir." Alistair snuggled against Carey's chest. "He looks amazing."

Becket turned and looked at them, raising an eyebrow. "Should I even ask?"

Carey shook his head. "Just enjoy the evening, Dave, you've got the room until closing. Call me tomorrow and let me know how it went, okay?"

"Sure." Becket knew that was Carey's way of warning him that he'd be checking up on him. "Just don't expect details."

As he walked away, Becket just caught Alistair's whisper, "Don't worry, Sir, Christian will tell me everything—he always does."

Becket rolled his eyes as he headed for the corridor that housed the private playrooms. No doubt Christian would be gossiping with Alistair by morning. They'd probably arrange a conference call with Olly and Aiden too and compare notes on his performance against Joe, Heath and Carey. Becket knew he had to redeem himself, he just hoped that he could meet Christian's exacting standards.

All the rooms available for private hire were well soundproofed. As Becket walked along the corridor the only noise was the slight squeak of the thick soles of his boots. He paused briefly outside the door to room eleven then grasped the handle firmly and opened it. For a moment, Becket forgot himself—he just stood and gaped. His heart pounded and his mouth went dry. Belatedly remembering that the door stood wide open, he hurriedly pulled it closed and took a couple of steps into the room.

Christian was displayed in front of him in a way that had his cock fighting to escape his leathers. *I'm being punished, that's what's going on here. This is some kind of penance for being a crappy Dom. I'm hard as fucking granite, trapped in a room with the most gorgeous sub ever created and I can't fuck him. Well, not yet anyway. Later. Definitely.* Becket pulled himself together with an effort and let his eyes feast on the vision in front of him.

Christian's arms were spread wide above his head, his wrists wrapped in leather cuffs attached to silver chains hanging from the ceiling. His legs were also spread wide, the short chains from his ankle cuffs linked to eyelets embedded in the stone floor. Every limb was stretched, every muscle defined. He was virtually naked – his only garment a snowy white G-string. His heels were off the floor and his arms took most of his weight. A strip of white silk was tied around his eyes, bright against the dark red of his hair.

Becket stepped forwards until he was within touching distance of Christian's body. "I hope for your sake, Christian, that the only other person who's seen you like this is Alistair."

Christian licked his lips. "Yes, Sir. No one else."

Becket clenched and unclenched his fist. He didn't even like the idea that Alistair had seen Christian this way. He would make sure that it never happened again. Christian's delectable body was for his eyes alone. He circled behind Christian and admired the rear view. A narrow strip of white silk separated buttocks that were firmly tensed. "Relax. You know I'm not going to hurt you."

On command, Christian's buttocks smoothed into shapely curves.

"Tell me your safe word." He already knew it, of course—the word was engraved on his mind even though Christian had never used it when they'd been together.

"Martini, Sir."

That always made Becket smile. It was Christian's oblique reference to Becket's job with the intelligence service. Shaken not stirred. If only his job were as glamorous as James Bond's. Unfortunately it was more about hard slog, long hours and sleep deprivation than fast cars and faster girls. Not that Becket would be interested in the girls, but he wouldn't turn down an Aston Martin as his company car.

"Good. Now, I think it would be better if you could see what I'm doing to you, don't you?" Becket unfastened Christian's blindfold then threw it to one side. Christian blinked and gazed at him with his clear green eyes.

"It's been three weeks since we were last together, Christian. Have you seen anyone else since then?" Becket knew he hadn't, he'd already heard it from Alistair and Carey, but he wanted Christian to confirm it.

"No, Sir. I wouldn't do that."

Becket ran his hand down Christian's smooth chest. "Why not? We don't have a contract."

Becket immediately regretted his words as hurt flashed in Christian's eyes. He hid it quickly but not fast enough for Becket's sharp observational skills to miss it. Christian trembled as Becket ghosted his fingers lower, tracing the ridge of Christian's cock through his skimpy underwear.

"No one else makes me feel the way you do, Sir. I'm happy to wait for you."

"And I'm pleased that you do. I don't want anyone else touching you, Christian, but it wouldn't be fair for me to demand exclusivity when I can't even tell you when I'm going to be here." He cupped Christian's balls and squeezed gently. "But maybe you don't care about fairness? Tell me what you want, Christian — you can speak freely."

Christian whimpered... It was the sweetest sound Becket had ever heard. He'd do anything to make Christian understand that he was valued and cherished, not just an occasional plaything.

"I *want* you to be demanding, Sir. Order me. Tell me what to do." Christian blushed and lowered his eyes.

"Even though I can't be here all the time?"

"Yes, Sir."

Becket's cock jerked. Christian enjoyed being controlled. Becket loved to do the controlling. Perhaps they did have as good a match as Alistair and Carey. He carried on fondling Christian's package. "We'll discuss this more at home."

"At home, Sir?"

"Yes, at home. That's where I intend to take you later so that I can fuck you hard enough that I'll be imprinted on your mind and your body while I'm away."

Christian's cock no longer fitted beneath the tiny scrap of silk he wore. Becket ripped the fabric away, exposing him, and took a hard grip. "Is that going to be a problem?"

"No, Sir," Christian gasped out the words and jerked his hips as much as he was able.

Becket slapped his arse lightly. "None of that now. You don't come until I say so."

Christian immediately stilled, though the almost imperceptible tremor in his arms revealed just how difficult it was for him to obey. Becket took a step back and admired his captive. "Fuck, you're beautiful."

Christian's body was sheened with perspiration, his cock jutted proud from his body, the tip gleaming with pre-cum. The faintest treasure trail ended in neatly trimmed hair the same color as that on Christian's head, a glorious dark red. Becket was tempted to taste. This was the first time he'd had Christian fully naked and for him it marked a significant turning point. On previous occasions when they'd played, he'd kept Christian covered because it helped him control his lust. Now, there was no need for that, and he feasted his eyes on Christian's delectable body. He resisted the urge to lick and bite — he wanted to keep Christian on the edge for as long as possible.

Becket bent and unfastened the links that held Christian's legs apart, leaving the leather ankle cuffs in place. Christian shuffled his feet together and stood, legs shaking.

"I'm going to let your arms down. It's going to hurt so take it slowly. I won't let you fall." He unlocked one wrist and supported Christian's arm as he lowered it to his side. He knew what the burn of lactic acid in muscles felt like and it wasn't pleasant. He released Christian's other arm and circled an arm around his waist, holding him steady as he shook. "All right?" Becket took Christian's chin in his hand and turned his head, looking into his eyes for any signs of distress.

"Burns, Sir, but I'm fine."

"Good. On your knees then."

Christian sank to the floor and rested his arse on his heels.

"Knees apart, hands behind your back."

Becket was pleased that Christian remained hard. He looked absolutely delicious and beautifully vulnerable. Becket stripped off his T-shirt and undid the button at his waistband. Christian was looking up from beneath his lashes, chewing on his lip. Becket smiled and for once was grateful for the demanding fitness regime his job required. His body was lean and hard, packed with muscle. He looked intimidating and he knew it. Christian didn't look scared — he looked...hungry.

"Don't fret, sweetheart, you'll have me in your mouth soon enough, but first I want to make sure you understand that your body now belongs to me." Becket walked to the back of the room and pulled a few things from hooks on the wall. He laid the items on top of a spanking bench and adjusted some fastenings. "Now, a few accessories to heighten your pleasure. Hold your arms out." Becket kept his voice low and firm. Christian trusted him and he didn't want that to change. "These are opera gloves. Have you worn them before?" He removed the wrist cuffs then slipped one long black leather glove up Christian's slender arm.

"No, Sir, I haven't." The glove was edged with D-rings. Its twin, which Becket pulled onto Christian's other arm, was edged with buckled leather straps.

"Now stand and put your arms behind your back again." As soon as Christian was upright, Becket started pushing straps through D-rings and buckling them tightly. He began at Christian's wrists and gradually worked his way up the length of his arms leaving the straps slightly longer the closer they were to Christian's shoulders. When he was done Christian's arms were locked tightly behind his back from wrist to shoulder.

"Perfect." Becket tested the fit carefully. "Anything pinching?"

"No, Sir, they feel…" Christian hesitated.

"Tell me, Christian, how do they make you feel?"

"I don't… Good, Sir," Christian admitted with a shy smile.

"You look spectacular. Now stand nice and still." Becket fetched another item and held it up so that Christian could see. "Pretty, isn't it?" The bulbous glass plug glimmered in the dim light. Becket loved the feel of it, cool, smooth and unyielding.

"It's big, Sir." Christian's eyes were wide and his expression anxious.

"It is, and that's why I'll be using plenty of lube. Come and bend over the bench."

Christian got into position, resting his chest on the bench, spreading his legs wide. Becket slicked his fingers and slipped one into Christian's hot passage, stretching him gently. "Fingers first, then the plug, okay?"

Christian nodded breathlessly and wiggled his arse a little.

"Cheeky brat." Becket added a second digit, then a third. He took his time even though he wanted to be rougher. When he was happy that Christian was ready he coated the plug with lube and pressed it gently against his entrance. "Relax for me."

Christian was so pliant and obedient, the plug penetrated smoothly and Becket pushed it into place, enjoying Christian's little gasps of pleasure. "Very good."

Christian vibrated at the slight praise and kept perfectly still as Becket bound a long leather thong around the base of his balls.

"I was going to put you in chastity but I'd have to let you come first and I'd rather keep you wanting for a while yet," Becket said softly. He tied off the leather and leaned back against the spanking bench, admiring his handiwork. With his gaze fixed on Christian's body, Becket lowered his zip and allowed his engorged cock to spring free. He sighed with relief.

Without being asked, Christian dropped to his knees in front of him and looked up hopefully.

"Please, Sir?"

Becket stroked himself a couple of times, teasing Christian shamelessly. "I'm clean. My certificate is registered with the club, but we can use a condom if you'd prefer?"

Christian's answer was to shuffle forwards and take Becket's leaking dick into his mouth.

"Oh fuck!" Becket grabbed a handful of Christian's hair like a lifeline. The man should win an award for the way he sucked cock. Becket knew he wouldn't last long. Christian didn't tease, he sucked hard, taking him deep. It felt like he was on some kind of mission to make Becket come in record time.

"Be still!" Becket snapped out the order.

Christian instantly stopped moving, swollen lips still wrapped around Becket's dick. "My turn." Becket began to move, slowly at first, then quicker, fucking Christian's mouth relentlessly. He tugged silky strands of hair the color of burnished copper and drove his shaft deep into Christian's throat.

Christian relaxed and took him. He didn't gag. He didn't move an inch. He just knelt there and let Becket possess him.

With a feral growl, Becket shot deep into Christian's throat. Christian was his, his alone and he needed to mark him. Christian looked stunned. He licked at a dribble of cum that slipped from his mouth then leaned forward and sucked Becket clean. As soon as he'd finished, Becket zipped up and pulled Christian to his feet. "Over the bench. Now." He pushed Christian over the padded spanking bench, making sure his body was properly supported and his legs braced, then went to find a flogger. There was a wide selection hanging on the wall and he picked one made up of soft, suede strands. It would do to warm Christian's skin before he used the cane on him.

Christian had his safe word and Becket was confident that the sub would use it if he needed to, but he still checked for any signs that Christian was frightened. He seemed completely the opposite, looking blissed out and wide-eyed. Becket debated releasing Christian's arms from the bondage gloves but decided against it. His position wasn't comfortable but his arse was still nicely exposed and available for the flogger.

Becket widened his stance and began to rotate the flogger in a figure of eight. He let the tips of the strands brush Christian's skin lightly before moving closer and increasing the strength of his strokes. Christian moaned as his arse and thighs were flogged. Becket didn't hit him hard. Christian wasn't such a masochist that he enjoyed severe pain. Becket respected the fact that Christian trusted him not to go too far and settled for creating a nice rosy blush. He made sure the flogger caught the end of the glass plug in Christian's arse a few times too. From the way the sub was twitching he must be absolutely desperate to come.

Becket put the flogger away and picked a slender black cane to replace it. Now he would leave his mark. He wanted Christian to be reminded of him every time he sat down for the next few days. He tapped Christian's arse lightly, warning him of what was coming. He waited long enough that Christian would be able to use his safe word if he wanted to then swung the cane.

He flicked his wrist at the last possible moment, reducing the weight of the blow but ensuring that a neat, red welt appeared on Christian's pink skin, then swung again to create a matching pair. Christian sobbed and pleaded for release, "Please, Sir... Please let me come. It hurts..."

Slowly and deliberately, Becket unstrapped the gloves that held Christian's arms together then turned him around so that he could undo the leather ties that denied him relief. Christian panted, but he didn't come. Becket was impressed by Christian's control — it was remarkable after being held on the edge for so long. He tapped the underside of Christian's rigid dick with the cane. "Come."

One word was all that it took. Christian jerked and spilled over the stone flags, his chest heaving and neck corded as his head fell back.

"Stunning. Just stunning." Becket took Christian into his arms, holding him firmly while he recovered his composure.

Gradually, Christian stopped shaking and relaxed into his hold, nuzzling into the curve of Becket's neck with a small sigh.

"There now, you're safe. I've got you." Becket enjoyed the feeling of Christian's naked body pressed against him but he didn't want Christian getting cold or stiff. He'd salve the cane welts as soon as they got home, maybe after a warm bath. "Come on. Let's get you dressed. I have plans that require a bed."

Christian let his breath out in a rush of warmth against Becket's neck. "The plug, Sir?"

"Stays." Becket knew that he wasn't going to be restrained once Christian was in his bed. He needed him stretched and ready, and besides, the glass base of the plug looked almost jewel-like—a precious gem, just like Christian.

Chapter Two

Christian was grateful that Becket's home was toasty warm. The moment the two of them set foot inside the door Becket had ordered him to strip. His clothes had been stored in a hall cupboard and he'd been naked ever since. There had been no preamble, no tour of the apartment, just nice clear orders to follow. So now he did precisely as he had been told. He lay face down on Becket's very comfortable bed with his hands stretched above his head and legs spread wide. A big, feathery pillow was wedged beneath his hips, raising his arse in the air, and he was painfully aware of the aftermath of the flogging he had received earlier. He could only imagine how pink his backside must be and he'd be feeling those two strokes of the cane for days.

Becket puttered quietly around the room. For such a big man, he moved gracefully and made little sound. Christian assumed that it was a skill essential to Becket's job—the ability to blend in—to remain unnoticed might be the difference between life and death. Christian shivered. He didn't like to think about how dangerous Becket's life was. They had played together a handful of times, but Christian knew very little about the man he allowed to take whips and floggers to his skin. All he was certain of was that Becket appealed to him in a way that no other Dom ever had. He wasn't devastatingly handsome like Joe, he didn't have the air of sheer power that Heath possessed or Carey's charisma, but he exuded an aura of absolute control and that pressed all Christian's buttons.

Christian shifted fractionally, attempting to ease the pressure on his rigid cock, which was trapped beneath him. Even with his hips raised it was uncomfortable. The instant he moved, the glass plug stuffing his arse reminded him of its presence. The plug was the biggest he had ever taken and pressed relentlessly against his gland. *Don't come, don't come, don't come.* The mantra cycled over and over in his head. Much longer and he wouldn't have any choice because his cock would overrule his brain.

A little tug on his hair was followed by soothing strokes and the bed dipped as Becket sat next to him. Christian was acutely aware of being naked and vulnerable while Becket was still fully dressed. It wasn't fair—he wanted to see Becket's muscular body in all its glory. Doms didn't do 'fair', though. That was a fact of life.

"How much do you want me inside you, Christian?"

Bloody stupid question! More than anything, of course. Becket jiggled the plug and smoothed the warm skin of Christian's arse making him jerk and moan. It was impossible to string words together into coherent sentences.

Christian managed a desperate "Please! Now! Sir!" and hoped that he was getting his point across.

"Hmm. That's what I thought, but you can wait a little bit longer, I'm sure?"

Christian knew he wasn't really being asked for an opinion. His need for Becket to be inside him was all consuming. He couldn't wait a second longer, but Becket was going to make him. It had to be against the Geneva convention, or some other international treaty, for Becket to torment him this way.

Something soft brushed across Christian's wrists and he looked up to see a loop of silken rope encircling them. The loop cinched tight, then Becket tied the ends off around the headboard.

"There. That's much better. Nice and safe." He sounded unbelievably smug.

Christian wanted to howl his frustration. He tugged on the ropes hoping that the pain of the cord digging into his flesh would provide a distraction, but Becket had anticipated him. The ropes were snug and secure, but soft, and the tugging did nothing but reinforce how helpless he was. Christian ground his teeth and suppressed a curse as Becket used another piece of soft rope to bind his ankles tightly together.

"Now your tight little hole will be even tighter." Becket sounded deeply satisfied. He sounded like a Dom whose sub was pleasing him.

That gave Christian the strength to be still and not whine about how much his dick was aching.

"Very good." Becket stood where Christian could see him and stripped off his shirt.

Christian took in the expanse of hard muscle and this time couldn't keep quiet. "Oh God! Sir, please!"

Becket nodded briefly and unbuttoned his fly. Before Christian could catch sight of anything interesting, Becket disappeared from view, then climbed onto the bed, straddling Christian's legs. Christian imagined what Becket must look like with his cock jutting from well-worn leather, thigh muscles tensed. As the glass plug was pulled slowly from Christian's arse, he almost came. Becket plumped the pillows under Christian's hips, shifting his arse higher into the air. The cool slick of lube was pushed between his arse cheeks and pressed into his empty hole.

Unable to spread his legs, Christian felt as if every touch was magnified as Becket finger-fucked him steadily. Then the fingers were replaced with the blunt, slick head of Becket's cock. Christian wasn't sure if Becket was bigger than the glass plug, but with his legs pressed together it definitely felt that way as Becket pushed home.

Christian's movements were so restricted he was utterly reliant on Becket for pleasure. It was an amazing feeling to be controlled emotionally and physically. Becket's repeated penetration was deep but agonizingly slow. Christian wanted to urge him to go faster, harder, but he resisted and kept as quiet as he was able.

He lifted a little farther as Becket grabbed his hips and pulled him back against every thrust. He would have bruises, he was sure. Blue-black reminders of an amazing night. It was a shame they would fade. Christian liked the idea of Becket's marks permanently etched on his skin. Christian was going to feel Becket inside him for days. With every forward thrust, Becket grunted. It was a raw, animalistic sound that made Christian shiver with delight. He was losing control of his body, shaking with the need to come yet somehow resisting. Without any barrier between them, it felt amazing, and when Becket gave a final, powerful thrust and came hard, Christian felt the hot rush of fluid coating his channel. "Sir! Oh! Thank you, Sir."

"Not done yet," Becket growled and lifted Christian onto his knees as if he weighed nothing. He was still bent forwards, his weight on his forearms, but now his arse was high in the air. Becket untied the rope around his ankles and nudged his damp, sweat-slicked thighs apart. His arms were trembling, every muscle tensed, his skin glistening. He felt feverishly hot. Christian held his breath, praying that Becket would allow him release. The moment Becket reached between Christian's legs and grasped his cock, Christian came with a shuddering gasp of pleasure.

Becket leaned over him to untie the rope holding his wrists and as the tension disappeared, Christian fell against him. He stiffened, wondering if Becket would shy away from the contact, but Becket wrapped him in a hug and lowered him to the bed.

"Tell anyone that I like to cuddle and you won't sit down for a week," Becket muttered.

Christian smiled sleepily and ignored the sticky cum trickling from his arse and dampening the covers beneath him. "No, Sir," he murmured. Becket left him briefly then came back with fresh sheets. "Go and take a quick shower—I've left it running for you. Don't be long."

Christian did as he'd been told. After a cursory scrub down he toweled off and returned to the bedroom where Becket was tucking the last corner of a clean sheet under the mattress.

"Bed's ready, you can lie down."

Christian scrambled onto the bed, then he was surrounded by heat. The cozy duvet was pulled over him and Becket's body pressed to his back. Christian wriggled until he was as close to Becket as he could get, his arse pressing against Becket's soft cock, encouraging it to harden again.

"Thank you for letting me stay, Sir."

Becket kissed his neck. "If I had my way you'd never leave this bed again. I'd keep you here, naked and chained, always ready for my pleasure."

Christian squirmed at the thought. "Sounds lovely, Sir, if not very practical."

Becket laughed, a deep rumbling sound that made Christian feel warm inside.

"Did you think I'd kick you out?" Becket tightened his hold.

"I didn't know what to expect, Sir. You're a very private person."

"Some guys screw and run. Some masters like their subs to sleep on the floor in chains. I like to cuddle. Now, go to sleep."

"Yes, Sir." It was easy to be obedient when he was safe and content and thoroughly sated.

* * * *

Waking up barely five hours later was a great deal harder, though Christian's pain eased considerably at the sight of Becket, naked and sweaty, pumping his way through dozens of press-ups right next to the bed. Christian's cock woke up faster than the rest of him, springing to attention in appreciation of muscles working overtime. He bit back a moan, but Becket seemed to sense him watching and turned his head, still pushing up and down.

"Good morning."

"Yes, Sir, it is!" Christian couldn't think of many sights he'd rather wake up to.

"If I didn't have to get to work, I'd drag you down here and fuck you stupid, but unfortunately, duty calls."

It's the thought that counts. "Oh, I'll grab my clothes and..."

"Relax." Becket stood with his hands on his hips, his gorgeous cock stiff and enticing. "There's no hurry. You can leave when you're ready, just be sure to close the door on your way out."

Christian couldn't stop himself. He slipped out of bed and dropped to his knees in front of Becket. He didn't wait for permission, just parted his lips and claimed his prize. Becket's dick tasted deliciously salty as Christian bathed it with his tongue, then sucked vigorously.

"Holy fuck!"

Christian smiled as Becket held him in place. It didn't take long. Christian relaxed his throat, swallowed Becket down and welcomed the hot spurts of cum that followed. Once he was sure that Becket was completely sated, he let Becket's cock slip from his lips and licked them slowly, savoring the taste. Becket pulled him up by his hair, firmly but not roughly.

"You realize I'll have to punish you for taking liberties?"

"Of course, Sir."

Christian gasped as Becket squeezed his cock and jacked him slowly, still holding him with a firm grip on his hair.

"Next time we meet."

Christian couldn't respond. Just the thought of Becket's rough hands on his cock was usually enough to get him off — the reality of it was overwhelming. He shot hard, knees trembling with reaction.

Becket scooped him up with little effort and deposited him on the bed. "In my line of work, taking a sickie is not an option. If it was, I would be developing a sudden case of man flu."

Becket disappeared toward the shower and Christian cuddled under the duvet, breathing in Becket's scent. He had so many questions that he wanted to ask, but didn't dare. He didn't want to spoil the moment.

Brushed and polished, Becket reappeared in the bedroom and stared hard at Christian as he knotted his tie. "Are you working today?"

"Yes, Sir. Saturdays are really busy—I'm covering reception at lunchtime and then again this evening until eleven. The security guys take over the desk for anyone who arrives after that." He didn't mention the second job that he would be leaving for as soon as Becket was on his way to work.

"I'll try to get to the club tonight, but I can't promise," Becket said.

"I know that, Sir, and I understand."

"Understand that I don't want you with anyone else. I know it's not fair but I don't care. I'm a selfish bastard and I don't share."

"Yes, Sir. I mean no, Sir. Oh...for pity's sake!" Christian took a deep breath and tried to forget that he was naked, in Becket's bed and the man was standing over him, all blond and gorgeous and possessive. "What I meant to say, Sir, is that I have no intention of being with anyone else."

Becket didn't smile, but he did look satisfied. "I'd really like to put you in chastity—a nice shiny steel tube maybe. Those trousers that Carey makes you wear are so fucking tight that everyone would know that you were off limits."

Christian swallowed and felt his face heat.

"Unfortunately, with my unpredictable schedule, you might end up being locked up for weeks."

Christian looked down, avoiding eye contact. He didn't want to give away that he was turned on by the idea that Becket could control a part of him even when they were separated.

Becket chuckled softly. "You can't hide from me, Christian. I know exactly what's going on inside that pretty head. If I get time today I'll go shopping for something suitably cruel."

Christian whimpered and resisted the urge to wrap his hand protectively around his cock.

"I have to go. I'd kiss you, but then I'd have to fuck you and that would make me late. My boss could make the hardest Dom quake in his leathers, so I'm not setting myself up for target practice."

Christian winced. "I don't think I'd want to work for him. Carey's a good boss. Strict but kind."

"He is a she and an example of the kind of female that makes me glad I'm not bi, let alone straight. I value my balls."

Christian snickered. "Have a good day, Sir."

Becket raised one blond eyebrow then turned on his heel and left. The front door latch clicked and Christian instantly felt lonely. Becket had the type of presence that filled a room and now he was gone there was too much space. Christian hugged his knees and smiled as he recalled the previous night. He'd waited a long time to feel Becket inside him and the experience had exceeded all his dreams, but now he couldn't wait for the next time. He squirmed at the thought of being put in chastity and winced as his sore arse reminded him that Becket had a very firm hand.

He sighed and swung his legs out of bed, reluctant to leave its warmth. He'd just have time to get home and change before heading for the Arc en Ciel, the little French coffee house where he waited tables in the mornings and on his days off. He wandered to the bathroom and took a quick shower, careful to leave the room pristine afterwards. Shaving and brushing his teeth would have to wait until he got home.

He went to retrieve his clothes from the hall cupboard and took in his surroundings for the first time. The décor had not really been on his mind the previous evening but now he became aware of just how austere the flat was. Everything was very modern and tastefully decorated, but there was no sign of anything personal that could be linked to Dave Becket, or give a hint about the man's personality. No photographs, no personal knick-knacks, not even a shelf of books. The place reminded Christian of a show home on a new housing development, designed to make an impression, but not one that needed to last. He dressed, made the bed neatly, then let himself out.

In the lobby of the building—all marble and mirrors—the security guard gave him a nod of recognition. Christian smiled back, wondering how the man apparently knew who he was when someone else had been on duty the previous night. Actually, it had been the early hours of the morning. Christian yawned as his brain registered just how little sleep he'd had and wandered out into a drizzly, gray London morning.

A twenty-minute walk took him across the Thames and through a tunnel beneath the railway to a small Victorian street tucked behind Waterloo Station. On the surface it looked a bit tatty, but the road teemed with life. A couple of fruit and vegetable stalls were set up at one end, the traders shouting their wares with gusto. The tiny newsagent's was already open and Hollis, the owner, was leaning in the doorway beaming out at the world and shouting greetings to passers-by in his mellow Jamaican accent.

A couple of the shops were boarded up and daubed with colorful graffiti, but most of the premises were occupied. A dry-cleaner's rubbed soot-tinged shoulders with a hardware store, while a charity shop shared pavement space with a shoe shop—baskets of cheap trainers jostling with crates of dog-eared paperbacks. Christian jogged across the road and headed for a green door, half hidden behind a bottle bank. The door separated a Chinese grocery store and an off-license, neither of which was yet open.

Christian groped in his pocket for his keys then opened the door, which swung outwards to reveal a scruffy staircase. He trotted up the short flight to another door that granted access to the flat over the grocer's. Christian let himself in and sighed softly. Since his friend Emily had moved out to live with her boyfriend, the place seemed so empty. So far his attempts to find someone new to share the rent had failed miserably and that was why he now had to rush off to the small café at the other end of the road. His second job was the only thing keeping him off the streets.

Christian had a quick shave. He scrubbed his teeth and tamed his hair then changed into a pair of clean black jeans and a black T-shirt with *Arc en Ciel* printed across it in rainbow colored letters. The timing of his shifts was carefully calculated to allow just enough time for him to finish at the café and get back across the river to The Underground. He covered the breakfast shift at the café, then lunch at The

Underground from eleven until three. Then he had four hours off until his evening shift at The Underground, which finished at eleven. In-between, Carey let him use the office or his flat to study. By the time he'd finished at night and gotten home, Christian usually managed to grab a few hours' sleep before starting all over again. It was exhausting and juggling his time was starting to take its toll. Christian didn't regret a minute spent with Becket, but after the preceding evening's exertions, he could have done with a full day in bed to recover.

He grabbed his battered leather satchel and shoved in the two textbooks he was reading. He kept a small wash bag with him, so that went in too alongside his wallet and cheap mobile phone. Knowing that he would be on his feet for the next few hours, he pulled on comfortable black trainers that looked reasonably smart and headed for the door.

The advantage of his café job was that it came with free food and coffee, which meant he got some kind of breakfast in the mornings. He got lunch and supper at The Underground, so he didn't starve, and Carey provided staff uniform, so his clothing expenses were low. Christian could manage and he didn't complain. He knew lots of people who were much worse off than he was. He, at least, had a roof over his head, even if it was a little precariously balanced.

He walked to work with more bounce in his step than he'd had in a long time. Becket filled his thoughts and the slight ache in his arse was a delicious reminder of the previous night. Christian whistled cheerfully and hoped that Becket would make it to The Underground again that night. His shift would certainly pass more quickly while he daydreamed about what they might get up to if he did.

Chapter Three

It was a chilly morning and wisps of mist swirled above the Thames like steam over coffee. Small boats and barges chugged their way up and down the busy waterway, inhabiting their own special world, separated from the bustle of the city by the riverbanks. Becket couldn't help feeling a little smug as he strolled along the embankment toward his office. He sank his hands deeper into his pockets and picked up his pace, enjoying the stretch in his muscles. He was feeling the effects of the strenuous night and that broadened his smile even more as he imagined how much more Christian would be feeling it.

Becket couldn't believe his luck that Christian wanted to spend time with him, let alone offer such perfect, willing submission. He had an amazing visual stuck in his head of Christian stretched and spread out on his bed. He loved how the young man's lithe body was so responsive to bondage, and couldn't wait to put him in strict chastity. Christian had tried to hide it but Becket was tuned in to noticing the slightest indications of emotion from his sub and Christian had definitely been aroused by the thought of being denied control of his cock. Becket was all for giving him what he wanted. Maybe it was time to consider a change of career direction, preferably one that would allow him to forge a proper relationship with Christian. Becket had given the best part of eleven years to a demanding, dangerous job and as much as he loved the thrill of fieldwork, there were plenty of other ways he could make a contribution that didn't have quite such a negative effect on his private life. He wanted a full-time sub. He wanted Christian.

Becket didn't even notice that he was almost at work until he looked up and realized that he'd nearly missed the turning he needed to take. *Idiot, get your head out of the clouds.* He gave himself a mental shake. In his line of work he needed to be alert to his surroundings at all times—being this careless could get him killed. He looked around, taking in all the little things that years of observation training had made him notice. Reflections in shop windows, flashes of light in the corner of his eye, a shadow where one had no right to be. He watched the people around him, giving just as much attention to businessmen in smart suits chatting on their phones as to street sweepers and the postman. Everything seemed in order as he used the card reader that granted him access to his building. When the door clicked shut behind him he glanced up at the security camera then waited for the inner door to open.

The morning routine of passing through security was comforting. Once he'd negotiated the bombproof doors, scanners and cameras, Becket reached reception. He looked forward to his daily banter with the receptionist. She looked like a middle-aged librarian but had a tongue that could cut steel. It was a great way to warm up his brain for the day ahead.

"Morning, gorgeous."

"Someone looks like the cat who got the mouse."

"Shouldn't that be cream?" Becket licked his lips suggestively.

"Not in your case, Mr Becket. Did you at least leave your victim conscious?"

"Conscious and tingling in all the right places."

The receptionist shook her head. Her bun didn't move—even a fraction—and Becket was sure it was cemented in place.

"Well, I hope the poor young man sees sense and finds himself someone more…more…stable."

"For a moment there, I thought you might be lost for words." Becket grinned, delighted at having flummoxed his sparring partner if only briefly.

"Temporarily stunned by the shock of seeing you happy. I will be back on form tomorrow, I can assure you."

Becket knew he was dismissed when she bent over her keyboard and started tapping furiously.

He headed off to the large open plan office where he and about a hundred other agents plied their trade. The place was already buzzing with activity, and Becket immediately sensed an urgency and agitation that was more pronounced than usual. He turned to his closest colleague, "What's up?"

"Becket! About bloody time you got here. One of your tame geeks has set a few hares running and the boss has been looking for you for the past half an hour."

"Shit! Which one?"

"You know—short, blonde, temper like a charging rhino."

"Not which boss, you idiot, which geek?"

"Oh, right." His colleague grinned. "Anders. North Yorkshire."

"Aiden," Becket muttered under his breath as he headed toward his boss's office at the end of the room. He could see her glaring at him through the glass and got plenty of sympathetic comments as he wended his way through the office. Even though she was staring right at him, Becket still knocked at his superior's door before he went in. He didn't want to reduce his life expectancy any further.

"Sit."

"Yes, ma'am."

Becket thought that Josephine Cornish would make an excellent Domme. If he didn't already know that she was happily married with three grown-up children, two elephant-sized Bernese mountain dogs and a foul-mouthed gray parrot at home, he could almost visualize her brandishing a whip. He shuddered and folded his hands instinctively across his lap.

"So, Mr Becket, I knew there was a good reason for letting you get away with murder. Setting up your little outpost in the north was unconventional to say the least, but Mr Anders seems to have hit the jackpot once again."

Becket started to speak but a raised finger silenced him.

"I realize that you have not caught up as of yet and I'm not criticizing the fact that you were out of contact last night—we all need some downtime, though your nocturnal activities are something that you and I need to discuss very soon." She paused. "Your young man in Yorkshire is a valuable asset and extremely bright, isn't he? Why isn't he working in London?"

"Because his cover is more effective where he is, and yes, Aiden is frighteningly intelligent." Becket leaned back a little. "If you tried to relocate him, he'd leave. He has other ties in the north."

"Indeed he does. I've read his file. Intriguing. But regardless, he's come up with something that might be significant, hence the rumpus going on out there." She gestured toward the office.

Becket didn't even glance behind him. It was always the same with a new lead as people scrambled to set up communications systems, data logs and security protocols in advance of an operation. He kept his attention focused on the deceptively mild expression on his boss's face.

"I'm giving you the lead on this one, Becket. Here's a brief summary of what we know so far."

Becket leaned forward, listening attentively.

"Young Aiden spends his time in some pretty dark places, doesn't he? He was skulking around a particularly nasty online chat room, listening in to some very private conversations. I like him, he's my kind of delinquent."

Becket snorted. "He's supposed to be hacking terrorist bank accounts, not cruising black sites."

Cornish raised a neatly penciled eyebrow. "I get the impression that Aiden is not particularly good at following orders."

Becket smirked. "Oh, he has his moments, if they're issued by the right person."

"Regardless, his illicit snooping has turned up something intriguing." Cornish tapped a pencil on the edge of her desk. "Your young man was earwigging some chat, which, on the surface, was about a role-playing game called The Crucifix. I dread to think how his brain works but from fairly random statements about" — she looked down at a piece of paper and frowned — "Vampiric monks and locations linked to the Knights Templar in the thirteenth century... Jesus... He managed to come up with an algorithm that translated it from a code to the location of a possible bomb attack."

"Vampiric monks?" Those were not words Becket had ever expected to hear coming from his hardass boss.

"Do you have a hearing problem, Mr Becket? Perhaps it's time I booked you in for another physical?"

"No, ma'am. Monks. Knights. Code. Bomb threat. Got it."

"You wouldn't be cheeking me, would you, Agent Becket? There are plenty of truly unpleasant jobs I can have you doing before this day's out."

"Wouldn't dream of it, ma'am." Becket tried to look innocent, not easy for somebody whose appearance leaned toward intimidating at the best of times.

He was pretty certain he could detect a tiny twinkle of amusement in Josephine's eyes. She liked him and he knew it. Unfortunately that didn't mean she let him get away with anything at all.

"Why are you still sitting here, Becket? You have work to do. Try not to make a pig's breakfast of it." She glared at him. "And make sure you keep me informed. Despite what you may have heard, I'm not a mind reader."

Becket got to his feet and headed for the door. He needed to talk to Aiden first, then catch up with what the hell his colleagues were doing. As he made his way to his desk, various people shouted updates in his direction and by the time he sat down he felt a bit more oriented.

He grabbed the nearest junior agent by the collar and steered him to a chair. "Sit. Don't speak. You've been commandeered. Your job today is to do what I tell you to do and make sure other people do what I tell them to do. You can write, I assume?"

Anxious, bespectacled eyes widened, but their owner nodded and kept his mouth shut.

Becket was pleased—he'd picked a good one. He took a closer look and grinned. The slight young man looked more like a graduate student than an intelligence agent. He had floppy brown hair that fell into his eyes, tangling with wire-rimmed glasses.

"Name?"

"Martyn, sir. Everyone calls me Marty."

"You don't have to 'sir' me, Marty. I'm a senior field agent not management. Call me Becket."

"Yes, sir."

Becket chuckled as Marty blushed to the roots of his hair. "Whatever. Now relax, I'm not going to eat you. Here's what I need you to do..." He began to reel off a long list of tasks that Marty jotted down quickly and efficiently.

Becket was impressed. He didn't have to slow down or repeat anything. Marty asked a couple of succinct, pertinent questions but that was it. "Okay, Marty, that's it for now. Take the desk opposite mine and get on with it."

"Yes, sir."

Becket listened in for a couple of minutes as Marty got to work but soon realized that he had nothing to worry about. Marty knew exactly what he was doing and he did it well. Becket plotted to steal him from whoever he currently worked for and adopt him as a permanent assistant. He picked up the secure phone and dialed Aiden's number.

"Morning, boss," Aiden answered instantly. His voice sounded a bit rough.

"Morning, sunshine. You've managed to put a big hairy cat amongst the pigeons again, haven't you?"

"Sorry. Yes. I got so bored with that other job that I did a little mooching around the net and this caught my eye. These idiots aren't very good—the code was obvious."

"Obvious to you maybe, genius boy. The rest of us mere mortals would have put it down to gamer-speak and ignored it. Have you been up all night?"

"Yep. Red Bull is a wondrous invention, but Heath's really pissed off. He's going to tan my hide when I get out of here."

Becket snorted. "He'll do more than that and you'll love it. Now give me chapter and verse. I've heard the edited version but I want to hear what you really think, not just the facts."

Becket listened intently as Aiden summarized his nocturnal online activities, then frowned. "So you don't think it's a hoax or just a bunch of wannabes showing off to their mates?"

"No. It's real." Aiden sounded absolutely confident. "It's going to happen today, in London. I just don't know exactly where or when. The why seems to be related to a controversial religious sect that believes Christianity is a dumbing down of true faith. They take the eye for an eye idea absolutely literally. I think the general idea is to wipe out as many non-conservative faiths as possible or at the very least discredit them or discourage their followers."

"Do you have any sense of where they might strike?"

"I would guess at a church. That would cause the most public outcry and these idiots will be seeking publicity. But any organization linked to moderate religion might be a possibility. I'm going back to the chat room under different aliases but there hasn't been anything new. I'll call you as soon as anything comes up, but for Christ's sake don't let anyone else try to access it. It's taken me a long time to establish my characters there. Anyone new arriving now would drive our suspects elsewhere."

"Done. Check in with me in an hour regardless."

Becket replaced the receiver and dialed again. "Heath?"

"Becket. You are not my favorite person at the moment." Heath's gruff tones came back at him.

"I know. Sorry. Aiden's a bit too clever for his own good."

"Tell me about it."

Becket chuckled at Heath's pained sigh. "I just wanted to let you know that he's on to something very important. When it's over he can have a few days off, but I need him focused until then."

"You know I don't interfere with his work, Becket."

"I do. And I know you'll keep him nicely grounded when this is done."

"He always comes out of a mission in need of a bloody good spanking. At least I have that to look forward to. You should visit soon. Joe and Olly would love to see you."

"I'll see what I can do. Talk to you soon."

Becket rang off again, confident that his best asset would not be allowed to burn himself out. A large cup of coffee appeared at his elbow.

"Skinny latte, no sugar, sir." Marty began to list the actions he'd already undertaken while Becket had been making his calls.

Becket nodded—everything that could be done was being done. Now they had to play a waiting game and pray that Aiden's online friends gave away some more information. Becket sipped his coffee. "Oh, that's good! How did you know what I liked, Marty?"

His new assistant looked at him as if he were a prize idiot. "Sir, I have a PhD from Cambridge. I'm quite capable of asking the right questions to find out how you like your coffee."

Becket grinned—there was a bit of brat behind Marty's intellectual façade.

"Do they ever let you out of the office, Marty?"

"No, sir. I'm an analyst, not a field agent."

"Well, I might need you to venture out with me today. Is that okay with you?"

"Yes, sir!"

"Call me Becket, Marty."

"Yes, sir."

* * * *

Aiden stretched and winced as every vertebra in his spine either cracked or popped. He'd been hunched over his computer for far too long and he was going to pay the price in chiropractic fees. He needed a shower and proper food. He turned on his iPod, stuffed the buds in his ears and jigged around the room, thankful that nobody could see him. He would never be a contestant on *Strictly* that was for sure. The only dancing he could manage with any kind of grace was when he was tightly pressed against Heath's hard body and how he looked was generally the last thing on his mind.

He didn't get any opportunities to practice his moves either because Heath wouldn't let him onto the dance floor alone. The one and only time that Olly had suggested they dance together had resulted in Aiden spending the entire night at the end of a chain fastened to Heath's chair. Olly, needless to say, had thought that was hysterical.

Aiden couldn't help but smile as he recalled his little blond friend's antics. With Joe's help, Olly had recovered from a traumatic past and had become a bubbly, irrepressibly naughty sub that everyone loved. Where Olly was outgoing and demonstrative, Aiden was introverted and reserved. Strangely, they made a good pair. Aiden sighed and rolled his shoulders. He needed to get back to work. He checked his email and text messages to make sure there were no further instructions from Becket, then signed into The Crucifix. He'd already done a lot of digging into the game, which was well hidden, though not well enough for someone like him who knew where to look. It was a genuine game, if somewhat subversive. A reasonably good knowledge of hacking was needed to be able to crack most of the level codes and he could imagine the kind of gamers—buried in their bedrooms and basements—who would be intensely involved in the various scenarios.

Aiden activated his avatar, a knight called Sir Hugh de Paduinan, named after a real Templar who had lived between 1140 and 1189. He signed into the chat room and indicated his availability to converse with fellow players, then sat back and waited. He never instigated conversations and he had to be careful not to change his behavior patterns. He took his avatar off to a tavern, avoided a brawl, then visited a blacksmith to get his sword sharpened. He'd been online for almost forty-five minutes before the chat room became active and at first it was just banter between a couple of the regular players he often teamed up with.

He listened in to a few more conversations and was on the brink of giving up when a couple of avatars he recognized started talking. On the surface it seemed like a discussion about a planned expedition to a new level of the game, but Aiden began to spot some of the key words that he had identified as being part of a code. The trigger word was Montgisard, a famous Templar victory, but the conversation that followed seemed nonsensical on the surface. Aiden started tapping the words into a second computer, working feverishly to keep up with the dialog. As suddenly as it had begun, the participants disappeared from the chat room and the conversation ended. Aiden stabbed the final words into his program and activated it. He twirled on his chair as the words were decoded.

"Fuck! So frigging obvious! I should have known they wouldn't be subtle!" Aiden grabbed the phone and pressed speed dial number two. The three rings seemed to take forever. He checked his watch. There was still time, but it would be close. "Pick up, pick up, pick up!" Aiden drummed his fingers on the desk until, finally, Becket picked up his phone.

"What the fuck, Becket? Do you have more important things to do than answer my calls?"

"What have you got for me, brat?"

"Temple Church, midday. You have ninety minutes, and I think you'll need the bomb squad."

"Temple Church near Fleet Street?"

"Yes! Stop asking me stupid questions and go!"

When Becket slammed the phone down, Aiden breathed a huge sigh of relief. He'd done his part but now came the bit he hated about every mission, the bit when he had to sit and wait and hope. Sending his colleagues toward danger gave him no pleasure—it made him feel sick and anxious. He needed a distraction while Becket did what he was good at. Aiden called the only person who could get him through the guilt of being at a safe distance from the action. Aiden called Heath.

Chapter Four

Heath wasn't sure whether to frown or grin. Aiden rarely called him when he was working so when he did, it meant that something serious was going on. Aiden could get so intensely focused on his work that he'd forget to eat or sleep. His brain worked in ways that Heath didn't attempt to understand. His intelligence was sexy but it also made him think too much, and for Aiden, that meant spending too long thinking about why he shouldn't be submitting to his master. Heath's lips quirked — Aiden's resistance was half the fun and when he did stop fighting his desires, he gave up everything. That level of trust was something that Heath had only dreamt about before he'd met Aiden.

He punched the code that only a very select number of people knew into a security pad and pushed open the door into Aiden's domain. Despite all the high-tech gadgetry that surrounded Aiden, Heath felt comfortable in the room. It was dark, gloomy and had bare stone walls. It made a fine temporary dungeon.

Aiden whirled around in his chair, and Heath felt the jolt to his heart that always came whenever he met Aiden's pretty eyes. His man was gorgeous, but his face looked tense, the little frown lines above the bridge of his nose deeper than usual. Heath pushed his shoulders back and took advantage of his six-foot-five frame to glare down at his sub. Aiden paled a little and slid from his chair onto his knees.

"Better. Now, what's going on, sweetheart?" Heath resisted the urge to take Aiden into his arms and hug the worry out of him. That wasn't what he needed.

Aiden looked at the floor. "There's a bomb. In London. I just sent Becket straight to it, Sir."

"And I suppose you intend to sit there, worrying yourself half to death, until Becket calls you to tell you it's over?"

Aiden worried at his bottom lip with even teeth. "What if he gets hurt? What if I was too slow?"

"Take your clothes off, Aiden." Heath waited for the explosion and wasn't disappointed.

"You can't possibly expect me to get into a scene with you now... Sir." The Sir was definitely an afterthought and that would have to be punished, but for now Heath was intent on distraction. Aiden had called him. He needed this.

"This is your life, Aiden, not a scene. That leather around your neck says so."

Aiden's fingers strayed toward his collar as if he had forgotten it was there. He looked stubbornly resistant. "I don't want to do this now."

"Yes. You do. Now either undress or I will do it for you."

Aiden shook his dark head stubbornly and Heath growled. His sweet man really was suffering if he needed to play this hard. Aiden was clambering to his feet when Heath pounced, tackling him from behind and pinning both arms to his sides. He shoved a hand inside Aiden's black cargoes and took a firm hold of his dick. "This is mine. You are mine. You belong to me body and soul, Aiden, so do what the fuck I say or you'll find your balls in a press quicker than you can say hard drive."

"Did you just come up with a geek innuendo, Sir? I'm impressed." Aiden's voice was a fraction higher than normal.

"I could always just plug and play... See I have an endless supply." Heath yanked Aiden's trousers down to thigh level and rubbed the edge of his hole. "Of course, if you decide to play nice, I'll revert to the hard drive."

Aiden yanked his black polo shirt over his head and wiggled his hips so that his trousers fell to his ankles. He hopped clumsily until he could kick them off and toed off his shoes and socks. Heath gave him just enough freedom to strip but didn't let go of him entirely. He looked around the room for a flat surface and maneuvered his prisoner toward a spare desk, groping in his pocket for the sachet of lube he'd put there earlier. He bent Aiden over the table and tapped his ankles with a booted foot making Aiden widen his stance.

"Being under pressure is no excuse for disrespecting your master. You know you have to be punished, Aiden." That got his pretty sub squirming and fighting again, just the way Heath liked him.

"No! You are not doing this to me now!"

"Be still." Heath planted a heavy smack across Aiden's firm buttock.

"Bastard! Stop. I can't..."

Heath pushed him down hard. "Behave."

"Let go of me, Heath!" Aiden fought hard.

"The only person giving orders around here is me, and with your attitude I'm tempted to put you in chastity and then screw you." Heath was used to Aiden's belligerence. His sub enjoyed a firm hand. He had a safe word and was quite capable of using it. Heath was tuned in to his moods and knew exactly how to treat him. He pushed Aiden over the table again using his heavier frame to keep him in place and grabbed two slender wrists in one hand. With the other he released his own belt buckle and slipped the belt from its loops. He used it to strap Aiden's wrists tightly together.

"You're lucky I'm such a kind, understanding Master. I should be using the belt on your disobedient, disrespectful arse."

Aiden cursed and fought. Heath just shoved him down harder. "You want it rough, sweetheart? Then that's what you're going to get." With his belt being used to better purpose than holding his jeans up, Heath didn't have a problem slipping the studs at his fly from their holes and releasing his straining cock.

He only needed one hand and his teeth to rip open the little foil packet of lube, which contained more than enough to slick his shaft and give Aiden's hole a nice glossy sheen. It took all of Heath's restraint to prepare Aiden before pounding into him. He realized he was being rough as he shoved two fingers into Aiden's tight channel, but Aiden's gasp was of pleasure not pain.

"Sir! Please… I'm ready! I need you!"

"Pushy brat." Heath lined up his cock and penetrated the warmth of Aiden's body steadily. He hadn't really prepared him enough and there was no way he was going to risk damaging him. Aiden wasn't interested in taking care of himself — he pushed back hard, taking Heath by surprise.

"Oh, you little..."

"Stop talking and fuck me, Heath. You can punish me later!" Aiden wiggled his arse and clenched his inner muscles.

Heath hissed and pressed Aiden down onto the desk. He snapped his hips, pushing deep inside Aiden's channel, then let go of his restraint. Aiden was going to be sore but Heath knew that the feeling would keep him focused for the rest of the day. Heath gripped Aiden's hips with both hands and gave him a thorough pounding. His own orgasm was building fast and he wasn't going to last long. He slowed his movements, savoring the sensation of the tingle rolling the length of his spine and igniting a fire in his balls.

"Come, love!"

Beneath him, Aiden gasped his release, and Heath let himself follow with a profoundly satisfied grunt. It took a few deep, heaving breaths before Heath was able to stand and step back from Aiden's prone form. He spotted an open box of tissues and grabbed a couple to clean himself up, then tucked his softening cock back inside his trousers and buttoned up. Aiden's sweat-slicked skin shined in the dim light and his arse was rosy from Heath's hand. He looked good enough to eat. When he moaned, Heath stepped forwards and cleaned him up before releasing his wrists and pulling him into a tight hug.

"Better?"

"Always. You know me too well."

Aiden nuzzled into Heath's neck, and Heath stroked his hot skin. He loved having Aiden naked in his arms, needing the security of his hold. He shuffled them across to Aiden's swivel chair and sat down, pulling Aiden onto his lap.

"I'll wait with you until Becket calls back, okay?"

Aiden melted against him. "Can I get dressed?"

"No." For a few minutes at least Heath was going to take full advantage of being able to stroke and kiss Aiden's bare skin.

In Heath's opinion, covering up Aiden's gorgeous body was nothing short of sinful and ought to be against the law. He took hold of Aiden's soft cock and began to fondle the silky skin. "Maybe later. If you're good." Post sex pliability never lasted long with Aiden—it was unlikely that he would behave. Heath could look forward to a good few hours of playtime. Life was good.

* * * *

L'Arc en Ciel was hellishly busy. As fast as Christian cleared tables they filled again with drained cups and crumb-filled, sticky plates. The queue at the counter stretched toward the door and never seemed to get any shorter. Even the three small pavement tables were constantly occupied despite a light drizzle. A stripy awning protected them, but it was still chilly. Christian didn't mind. Clearing outside gave him some respite from the heat in the café, which was nice and cozy for the customers but far too hot for a busy waiter. He checked his watch, swore and dashed inside. It was already five minutes past when he should have left for The Underground. He threw his apron behind the counter, grabbed his satchel and shot out of the door, already running as he waved goodbye to his harried colleagues.

Being able to wear trainers to his morning job was a big advantage when it came to sprinting across London. Buses and Tubes cost money and actually it was quicker to jog across Waterloo Bridge and negotiate the warren of alleys and passages that were great shortcuts. Christian hated to be late—he loved his job at The Underground and Carey didn't deserve to be put out by his receptionist showing up looking like he'd just run a marathon.

Christian shot past the bouncers, who were already manning the door at the club, took the lift and headed straight to the staff changing room. He shed his shoes, socks and shirt before he was halfway across the changing room and got himself several wolf whistles from the half dozen staff already changing. The uniform for the waiting staff at The Underground was so skimpy that there was no possibility of staying bashful for long. Christian threw his jeans out of the shower room, tore off his underwear and skidded into the cubicle, barely avoiding an abrupt meeting with the tiled wall.

He took a shower at record-breaking speed then realized that he'd forgotten a towel.

"Shit! Guys! Someone toss me a towel." All he got was a chorus of delighted laughter. Christian shook his head like a damp dog, spraying droplets everywhere. He walked out into the changing area buck naked, to catcalls and lewd comments.

"Ha bloody ha. Thanks for your support, boys."

He grinned as five towels flew in his direction. He dried off quickly and pulled his uniform from his locker. He shimmied into the tiny net thong that Carey insisted the staff wore. Christian was grateful that he got to wear leather trousers over his rather than the short leather kilt that the waiting staff wore. Not that the trousers were much less revealing. They were so tight that the ridge of his cock was clearly outlined beneath the soft fabric. He yanked them up then sat on a bench to pull on his socks and boots.

"Hey, Christian!"

Christian looked up to see his friend Alistair holding out his T-shirt.

"Don't forget this. Though I'm sure the members would love it if you did."

Christian snorted and took in the fact that Alistair was wearing the waiters' uniform. "Are you working today? I didn't think Carey let you wait tables anymore?"

"He doesn't usually, but there's a bug going round and we're a bit short staffed. I volunteered to fill in and he didn't have a lot of choice."

Christian shrugged into his shirt and chuckled. "He'll be watching you like a hawk."

"No doubt." Alistair touched his collar and smiled serenely. "This outfit really turns him on. I'm sure I'll manage to do something that requires discipline later."

Christian tried not to feel too jealous. Alistair and Carey made a great couple, and he didn't begrudge them a moment's happiness. It would be nice to have the same thing for himself, though. His thoughts strayed to Becket and he had to force himself to think about something else. Sporting a hard-on in tight leather trousers was not a comfortable experience, though they felt a little looser than normal. He must have lost a couple of pounds.

"Will Becket be coming by later?" Alistair asked—all innocence.

"I hope so. It's hard for him to say… You know."

Alistair looked sympathetic. "Sure. You really like him, don't you?"

Christian nodded, feeling shy.

"Are you okay? You look tired."

Alistair looked so concerned that Christian nearly welled up. Alistair always had everyone else's welfare on his mind and it was the first time in an age that anyone had asked Christian how he was doing. The strain of keeping up with two jobs and covering his rent, studying and pining for Becket was beginning to take its toll. He'd pushed aside the tiredness and avoided admitting that he was barely coping. If Alistair pressed him on it, he'd probably have a mini breakdown.

"I'd better get upstairs or Carey will be docking my pay." He evaded Alistair's clear blue gaze and scurried away. At least at the reception desk he could take the weight off his feet during quiet spells and daydream about Becket.

Anyone who came into The Underground had first to get past the bouncers on the door, then use a security code that granted access to a bland hallway containing a lift door. The lift descended to a plushly carpeted corridor that housed Christian's desk. Once the member's details had been logged on the computer system, Christian allowed them to use the lift to the club levels below. There was a staircase as well, which the staff used, but most members preferred to descend in style.

Christian prided himself in knowing all the club members by sight and the vast majority by name. The computerized database told him whether Doms preferred to be addressed by their name or by an honorific. Attached subs also had notes—whether or not it was permissible to address them directly, for example. Unattached subs could be members in their own right, or sponsored, and were then addressed by their first name. All guest Doms required a minimum of two references on record before they were granted entry and those references were stringently checked.

On the very rare occasion that someone caused Christian a problem, he had a panic button hidden beneath his desk—something that had been installed after Alistair's abduction, along with additional security cameras. At his desk, Christian felt perfectly safe. It had taken him a while to get over the attack he'd experienced when Alistair had been taken, but Carey had done everything he could to make Christian feel comfortable. The vast majority of Doms were very protective toward him and he'd had his share of offers to play. Since meeting Becket, though, he hadn't been interested in anyone else and his gentle rebuttals were always met with good grace.

He trotted up the stairs, got settled and turned on the computer. He checked his watch—ten fifty-eight— he really had cut it fine. He'd bet money that there would be members coming through the door as soon as the club opened. There was often a dignified stampede for the best tables at lunchtime. The Underground had a reputation for excellent food and members that worked in central London often dropped by for an hour to eat and catch up with friends. At weekends, there was a different crowd, often traveling from farther away and spending the entire afternoon and evening enjoying the facilities.

Sure enough, Christian's first customers appeared at one minute past eleven. Two Saturday regulars, dressed to play with a couple of giggling subs in tow. Christian booked them all in and got a couple of rough hugs for his trouble. After them, there was a steady stream of arrivals. Christian never failed to marvel at the variety of men that were into the scene. They came in all shapes, colors and sizes. Between them they probably kept the leather clothing industry in business. At five past twelve, Christian finally got the chance to sit down. He started updating some guest records on the computer then paused as he felt a slight vibration beneath his fingertips. He looked up, but everything seemed normal. The club was too far from the Tube lines to feel the rumble of trains, but sometimes a very heavy lorry rolling past shook the building. The sensation was soon forgotten as the slight lull in arrivals ended and the usual Saturday rush resumed.

Christian was chatting away to a couple of unaccompanied subs he knew when Carey Hoffman pushed his way through the door from the stairs, accompanied by Goran, one of the bar staff. Christian bit his lip to stop his smile as the two subs went silent and looked up at Goran in awe. The man was pretty awe-inspiring. He was huge—tall, heavily muscled and powerful—and he could scowl for England. He was a sub's dream.

"Christian, you can take a break." Carey smiled gently. "Goran will watch the desk for you. Come down to the office, there's something I need to tell you."

Christian's immediate anxiety that he had done something wrong must have shown on his face because Carey squeezed his shoulder reassuringly. "It's all right. I have coffee waiting."

Christian left his two friends to Goran's tender mercies and followed Carey downstairs to his office at the back of the club. Two cups of coffee were waiting on the desk.

"Take a seat, Christian."

Instead of taking his chair behind the desk, Carey pulled it around and sat next to Christian. The office door opened and Alistair came in, his eyes looking a little red as though he'd been crying.

Christian started to panic. He looked from Alistair to Carey. "What's going on, Alistair? Sir?"

"Now don't panic, try to stay calm." That did no good at all. Alistair dropped to his knees and took a tight hold of Christian's hand.

"Tell him, Sir."

Carey sighed. "About half an hour ago there was an explosion... A bomb... In a church near Fleet Street."

Realization dawned and Christian muttered, "I felt it. Well, I felt a vibration."

"That was it. It was a significant explosion."

"How... How do you know anything about it, Sir?"

"Heath rang. Aiden knew what was going to happen. He alerted his secret service colleagues and they went to clear the location."

Christian felt sick. "Becket. Was he there? Is he okay?"

Carey frowned. "All Aiden had been told was that Becket and one of his colleagues were still in the church when the device went off."

"Oh God!" Christian began to tremble. He felt cold even though the office was warm.

"They're looking for him, Christian. I'm sure he'll be fine—he's as tough as an old boot."

Christian nodded automatically. "Of course. He'll be fine. He has to be..." His voice trailed off into a whimper.

"As soon as Aiden hears anything new, Heath will call. Sam has run up to Fleet Street to see if he can find out anything more, but I doubt he'll be allowed anywhere near. Does Becket have any close family? His next of kin will be contacted first."

"I... I... Just a younger brother, I think. His name's Gideon. Becket calls him Giddy. Their father brought them up because their mother died when they were very young. Complications from Gideon's birth, I think. Their father died from lung cancer about five years ago. I don't know of anyone else."

Alistair stroked Christian's knee. "Sweetie, do you have Gideon's number?"

Christian shook his head numbly. "No. I only met him once. He was fun — reminded me of Olly."

"Well, it can't be that difficult to track down a Gideon Becket. I'll call Heath and see if Aiden can get to work on it. Aiden probably needs a distraction as much as you do, Christian. Heath said he feels terribly guilty."

"That's ridiculous. He didn't plant the bomb." Christian's lip quivered. He was only holding back tears with an effort. He knew it was ridiculous — Becket was away a lot and he'd never felt this vulnerable before. He'd missed him, of course he had, but the feeling had always been counteracted by the delicious anticipation of his return. That anticipation had just been ripped away from him and it was as if the ground had been torn from beneath his feet at the same time. "I should get back to work..." He looked helplessly around the office.

"You should do no such thing!" Alistair jumped to his feet. "You can come upstairs to the flat with me. We'll make something to eat and put some fresh coffee on." He looked pointedly at the mug Christian had ignored.

Christian looked at Carey, who nodded his agreement. "Goran will be fine upstairs so long as he can extract himself from the pile of fawning subs that I know will be climbing all over him by now."

Christian managed a brief laugh. He let Alistair tug him to his feet. "Thanks, Carey... You will tell me...if you hear anything at all?"

"Of course. Try not to worry."

Christian was grateful for the reassurance but it was ruined by the worry that clouded Carey's eyes. He fought down his fear and prepared for an anxious wait.

Chapter Five

Becket opened his eyes slowly. His eyelids were as heavy as lead and it took a huge effort of will to make them rise. The next thing he managed was a weak cough. The immediate catch of dust in his throat turned it into a choking gasp for air. Pain blossomed across his chest, deep and aching. Becket's grainy vision swam into focus and he found himself staring at a pair of dead eyes, cold as stone. It took a few moments to realize that the eyes really were stone — part of the broken head of a piece of statuary from a tomb. Becket shifted carefully and pieces of rubble rolled from his body. There was a thick fog of dust and debris hanging in the air. He could not have been unconscious for that long or the air would have cleared a bit.

"Marty?" The name croaked from his lips. He gagged, spit out a mouthful of dust and tried again. "Marty?"

There was no response. Somewhere a cascade of falling stone hit the floor, and Becket wondered how unstable the building was, how much damage had been done. He shifted again, trying to gauge his position. He was lying face down, his back covered with debris. He'd obviously been thrown forwards by the blast. There was a ringing in his ears that wasn't in any way tuneful, and from the metallic coppery taste on his lips he guessed his nose or lip or both had been bleeding. Every inch of exposed skin that he could see was coated in a thick layer of dust. Blood mixed with the grime on his forearms but mercifully, neither seemed to be broken. His ribs hadn't gotten away so lightly. Becket wasn't sure whether they were bruised or cracked but he did know they bloody well hurt.

Moving seemed like a good plan but wasn't that easy to accomplish. Becket attempted to push up with his arms only to discover that his hips were firmly pinned by something solid and immovable. There was no pain. In fact there wasn't much of anything. He couldn't feel his legs at all. All kinds of instant, horrific scenarios flashed through his head until he was thankfully distracted by a low groan.

"Marty? Is that you? Are you okay?"

Coughing and spluttering followed.

"Mr Becket, sir? Is that you? Why do I feel like I just got blown up?"

"Because you did, Marty." Becket chuckled.

"But I'm an analyst. I don't think I'm allowed to get blown up. The biggest work-related injury I've ever had is a paper cut."

"Sorry to be the one responsible for taking you up a level." Becket shifted his head as far as he was able but he couldn't see Marty. "Where are you? Can you move?"

"I think so."

Becket registered the sounds of cursing mingled with the crunch of broken glass and the thump of something heavy hitting the floor. Footsteps shuffled toward him, then Marty's blood-streaked face appeared through the dust.

"Sir! You don't look so good." Marty brushed accumulated debris away from the area in front of Becket's head.

"Good to know, Marty, thanks. I can't move. Think something's pinning me down."

Marty picked his way carefully through the rubble. "It's part of the top slab of a tomb, it's resting on your hips. Sir Gerv...something or other."

"Marty."

"Yes, sir?"

"I'm not that bothered about who was buried under the slab that is now crushing my spine."

"No, sir. Sorry, sir."

"Call me Becket, Marty." Becket suppressed a moan.

"Yes, sir. I'm not going to be able to move this slab, it's too big and I don't want to cause any more damage. I'm going to try to find a way out. Don't die while I'm gone, okay?"

If Becket's eyes hadn't been full of grit he might have rolled them. "I'll try not to."

He listened to the noise of Marty stumbling through the darkness. For a committed geek, Marty had an interesting range of expletives. Becket took his mind off his situation by wondering again if Marty was gay. He'd make an interesting sub. That got him thinking about his red-haired beauty. Would Christian be worried about him? What would he think when Becket failed to show up at the club? Aiden would get a message to him but Becket didn't want Christian upset. As a Dom it was his natural instinct to protect and shelter his sub and Christian was his. Becket couldn't think of the younger man as anything but belonging to him. Just the idea that anyone else might lay a finger on Christian's creamy skin was enough to make him see red.

As he lay in the ruins of the church, waiting for rescue, Becket decided that he couldn't carry on as he had been. He couldn't keep leaving Christian alone and he wasn't prepared to give him up. He'd just had the most dramatic wake-up call and it would be bloody stupid to ignore it. If he survived. He felt cold and sleepy. It would be so easy to just drift into the darkness and let the fear dissipate, but Becket knew he had to stay awake.

He was in shock—well, who wouldn't be, for Christ's sake?—he had to try to stay conscious. Moving was not an option, even for those body parts that were not being compressed under a ton of stone. He knew the risks of moving when it was highly likely that he had a spinal injury. He'd just have to think about something that was guaranteed to keep him awake. He grinned and began to picture all the toys he would like to use on Christian, trying to think of something for every letter of the alphabet.

"'A' for anal beads... Arab strap... Hmm, both of those are very interesting possibilities. Bondage... Oh yes, lots of that... Blindfold, ball gag, ball splitter, bit gag, butt plug... Oh I think 'B' is my new favorite letter." Becket had to stop and cough up some dust. "Okay, 'C'. Let me think... Chastity, absolutely and as soon as possible. Clamps—always fun. Crop, cock ring, cock strap... Collar... Oh yes, that pretty neck needs to be wrapped in leather." Despite the horrendous position he was in, Becket was having fun and his list was working, he was still awake. Under normal circumstances his cock would also be getting lively. He sent a short prayer upstairs for the well-being of his cock. Well, he *was* in a church, or under it, depending on your point of view.

"'D' is for dildo and dumb-arse. Yep, that's me all right. Who the hell runs toward a ticking bomb instead of away from it? What a fucking idiot." Becket's thoughts drifted back to the phone call that had started him down the path to this mess.

Aiden had called. He'd been absolutely certain about the bomb, the location and the timing. Becket had no reason to doubt him because Aiden had an uncanny knack for digging secrets from some very shady places. Becket had worked on the assumption that Aiden's information was correct and therefore that lives were in danger. He'd made two calls in rapid succession, to the Metropolitan Police and the Army Bomb Disposal Unit. That had set evacuation procedures in motion. He'd then yelled an update in the general direction of his boss, grabbed Marty and headed for the door.

In the few minutes since Aiden had called, Marty had managed to acquire an instant knowledge of Temple Church and its environs. He'd reeled off a lesson in the car as they'd driven toward the church. "The Church was built by the Knights Templar, the order of crusading monks founded to protect pilgrims on their way to and from Jerusalem in the twelfth century. It's in two parts—the Round and the Chancel. The patriarch of Jerusalem consecrated the Round Church in 1185. It was designed to recall the holiest place in the Crusaders' world—the circular Church of the Holy Sepulchre in Jerusalem. It was refurbished after the Great Fire of London and then again by the Victorians. It's famous for its effigy tombs and nowadays attracts a lot of tourists."

"That's just wonderful, Marty. It's a Saturday lunchtime, which means that our bomber will have plenty of nice innocent people to kill. You've made me feel so much better."

"Sorry, sir."

When they'd reached the area around the church, several roads had already been cordoned off, and the police had been doing their best to clear streets and buildings, but it was a huge job and there hadn't nearly been enough time. Becket had abandoned the car, and he and Marty had flashed their identification badges before crossing the barriers and heading toward Temple Church.

"What do you think, sir? Will it be a vehicle or a suicide bomber or something else?" Marty had sounded almost excited as he'd scurried to keep up with Becket's long strides.

The doors of the imposing church had stood open and a steady stream of confused-looking people had been filing out, clutching bags and cameras. Becket had glanced around, assessing the situation as best he could, then headed toward the open doors. Outside, a uniformed policeman had ushered people away as quickly as he'd been able to. Becket had flashed his badge again and asked, "What's the situation with evacuation?"

"There's no Tannoy system in the church but we used the microphone on the pulpit to announce that the church was closing. Most people are out now, but there are several small anterooms and underground areas that haven't been checked. They're not open to the public, but there's no record of who has entered the building today."

"Okay. Marty, you take the basement area, I'll take the side rooms." He'd checked his watch. "We have ten minutes. Don't cut it too fine—clear where you can and then get out."

The two of them had run into the building and sprinted down the central aisle. Becket had turned toward the font and skirted some of the tombs that stuck up from the floor, barely glancing at the carved effigies. As he'd passed a larger tomb, he'd noticed out of the corner of his eye that the heavy stone lid was slightly out of line. It had clearly been moved, and not long ago.

He'd turned and shouted to Marty, "The bomb's already here! Get out!"

Following his own advice he'd turned and run. He'd registered Marty's startled face then the world had gone to hell in a moment of insanity. A wave of air pressure had thrown him off his feet as his ears had filled with an echoing boom. He'd just had time to think *Fuck—this is going to hurt* before everything had gone dark.

Becket drifted into unconsciousness for a while. Coming round again to increased pain was good. If he hurt, he was still alive, and it was something of a relief that he could feel some sensation in his legs even if the feeling was one of stabbing agony.

"Hey, he's back with us, guys!"

The cause of Becket's pain leaned over him, grinning.

"Get off me, you fucking oaf. Everything hurts."

"It's not me putting pressure on you, you're covered in stone."

"All the same. Who the hell are you anyway? I hope you're the cavalry."

"Sorry, no horse. Fire and Rescue. This is a first for us—man trapped by exploding tomb—how you feeling?"

"Why are all firemen fucking comedians?" Becket growled at his rescuer. "I feel like shit and apparently you're determined to make it worse."

Crinkles appeared at the corners of the fireman's twinkly eyes. "We aim to please. Now you clearly don't need mollycoddling, so here it is. We're about to lift the biggest piece of debris off your back, but we don't know what's going on under there. You could be bleeding and the release of the compression will make it worse. You could have broken bones or internal damage. It's probably going to hurt like a bastard, but I'd really appreciate it if you could keep still. Okay?"

Becket let his breath out in a whoosh. "Just so long as you lightweights don't drop the bloody slab back on me."

The fireman got closer to Becket's ear and whispered conspiratorially, "As a fellow member of The Underground, I swear to protect the good bits to the best of my ability."

Becket chuckled. "Well, well. We do get everywhere, don't we?" He didn't recognize the man, but he knew there were at least three firemen who were club members. All Doms. Two of them had helped out when a fire, arranged by Alistair's father, had started at the club. This one was hidden beneath his wide-brimmed helmet so Becket couldn't even tell what color his hair was.

"The paramedics are on standby in case you start spurting the red stuff. Ready?"

To Becket's surprise, the fireman grasped his hand and squeezed. It was comforting, if a little embarrassing.

"Ready." Becket held his breath and listened as the team of firemen got into position around him, counted down then heaved the slab away from him. His first reaction was utter relief that the crushing weight was gone, but then the pain stabbed through his back like a lightning bolt and he screamed. Through a white haze of agony he managed to keep still and gradually the pain lessened.

"Fuck, man, you nearly broke my fingers," the fireman complained. "This must be what it's like for straight blokes when their wives are giving birth. I have new respect."

"Well, pardon me for bruising your delicate digits," Becket retorted. "What's your name?"

"Salter Beauman. Everyone calls me Beau."

Becket groaned as his neck was immobilized in a surgical collar and a spinal board was belted to his back. His limbs were strapped down as well until his entire body was restrained.

"They're going to turn you over now," Beau commentated on the situation. "Bet you're not usually the one strapped down, are you?"

"I'm not taking that wager." Becket gasped as he was maneuvered over and placed on a wheeled stretcher. He ignored the manhandling as the paramedics checked him out. He felt a bit dizzy and he wasn't taking in what they were saying about his injuries.

"Marty—is he okay?"

Beau frowned. "Is that the guy that was with you? Short, specs, pretty?"

"Pretty?" Becket challenged.

"Oh, sorry—is he yours?"

Becket coughed dramatically. "Christ no. He's a colleague." Becket thought that Beau looked pleased at that.

"He's fine. A bit battered. He was the one who let us know that you were trapped in here. He managed to find his way out and practically gave us a grid reference for your location."

Becket closed his eyes and saw stars. "Feeling a bit lightheaded, Beau. Did they get the bombers yet?"

"We have to get him out of here now or he's going to bleed out on us."

That was a voice Becket didn't recognize.

"Go for it. Haven't heard about any arrests, sorry. I'll be at the hospital when you wake up, okay? I'm going off shift." Beau's voice faded away.

Becket felt warm and comfortable. A mask on his face was feeding him gas that made him really happy. He gave in to the urge to sleep and everything went dark.

* * * *

A cool hand on his forehead was the next sensation Becket felt. He thought he was moving and that was confusing until he realized that he was being wheeled along on a gurney. Fluorescent light strips merged together above him like illuminated rail tracks. There were people either side of him, some wearing pink and lilac. He didn't understand what was going on and the backwards motion made him feel sick. There was a brief jolt as his trolley was maneuvered through a pair of swing doors, then it finally came to rest against a wall.

People in surgical masks loomed over him, foreheads creased with worry, eyes anxious. Becket coughed and tried to speak but his mouth was so dry that the only sound he managed was a dry rasp.

"Nurse. Ice chips please."

One of the pink people held a plastic cup to his lips. Tiny chips of ice melted against them before Becket realized he needed to open his mouth. Cool meltwater trickled across his tongue. It was the most wonderful thing Becket had ever tasted.

"Can't move." He tried not to panic.

"You are strapped down, Mr Becket. We don't want you to move until all your injuries have been fully assessed. I'm Doctor Edwards. Are you in any pain?"

Becket couldn't shake his head. "No. Can't feel a thing."

"Good. We're pumping you full of morphine. You'll not be awake long and we may have to keep you sedated for a while."

"Is it bad?"

"Ah. Morbid curiosity is a good sign. I've not done more than a cursory exam so don't take any of this as gospel. You have deep lacerations on the backs of your legs, which may require surgery. You've also had a bang on the head and probably have concussion. You have bruises in places you'd probably rather not know about and may well have broken bones. You'll be scanned, X-rayed and prodded for the next few hours so settle back and enjoy. As soon as I have any more information for you, I'll let you know."

"My back...?"

"Best not to worry about that until we know more, and before you start complaining about me flannelling you, I'm not. You were hit hard, Mr Becket. Spinal damage is a possibility but I don't make guesses about things like that, even educated ones."

Becket licked his lips. "Need to let people know where..."

The doctor interrupted, "There is a very large, dirty fireman cluttering up my waiting area asking to see you. I'm sure he'll pass on any message to your friend who I understand is being dealt with in another ward." The doctor turned away and gestured at a colleague. "I'll let him in but only for a couple of minutes. You're stable so they'll be wheeling you off to radiography shortly."

Becket felt woozy. He wanted to close his eyes but needed to stay awake long enough to talk to the fireman, whom he assumed was Salter Beauman. He'd only seen Beau with a helmet on so he didn't know what to expect. Beau strolled into the room like he owned the place. There was no doubt that he was a good-looking man. Soot-streaked skin couldn't hide his chiseled jaw and sharp cheekbones. Dust and dirt made his hair look gray, but Becket could see that it was jet black underneath the grime. Slate gray eyes were shaded by black lashes and gleamed as Beau leaned over him.

"Hey. You still look like shit." Beau beamed.

Becket grunted. "Thanks."

"Doc says you'll live."

"Good to know. Look, could you do me a favor?" Talking hurt, Becket's throat was sore.

"Of course. Just tell me what you need."

"Can you get a message to Carey Hoffman for me? Let him know where I am?" If Beau was a member of The Underground then he would know Carey.

"No problem. I'll head straight down there. The nurses are giving me the evil eye anyway, I think they want me out of here."

"Well, you're not exactly hygienic, are you?" Becket coughed and pain racked his body. "Bloody hell, ribs are shot."

"You're as white as a sheet. Look, I'll leave you to the tender mercies of this lot, and don't worry. I'll make sure everyone who needs to know gets the details about where you are."

"Can you keep an eye on Marty, too. He's never been in the field before."

Beau pinked beneath the dirt. "If you insist."

Becket held back a chuckle—he wasn't that much of a masochist.

"I do. Be gentle with him, he's an innocent."

"Not for much longer, if I have anything to do with it." Beau winked. "I wonder what young Marty thinks about leather? I might just have to take him to lunch at The Underground and see what happens."

Becket groaned and not from pain. "Just try not to break him, okay."

"I promise."

Then the doctor was back and Beau was ejected from the room.

"We're going to put you under so that you're not jigging around while we do all the necessary tests. The anesthetist is here. It'll all be over before you know it."

It crossed Becket's mind that everything being over could be rather permanent. He blanked out the thought as quickly as it had popped into his head.

"Count backwards from twenty, Mr Becket."

Becket didn't get past eighteen before everything faded.

Chapter Six

It was like some weird merry-go-round of light and dark. Spinning flashes of awareness interspersed with comforting darkness. Becket laughed at the thought of rising and falling on a carousel—he was a bit old for fairground rides. The laughter jogged him into consciousness and awareness of a familiar voice.

"Becket. Wake up, Becket. Come on now, sleepy time is over."

Sleepy time? What the fu...? Becket's brain resisted the pull of the real world valiantly.

"Come on, Becket. I've got a lovely warm, wet sponge waiting for you... You don't want to miss another bed bath, do you?"

That shocked Becket's eyes wide open. His first view was of a pair of big blue eyes and a mop of golden curls.

"Olly. Fuck. I've died and gone to hell." Speaking felt like someone had a rusty hacksaw blade at his throat.

"Sorry to disappoint you, Dave, but I've got a sweet, fluffy cloud booked in heaven. You, I'm sure, will be taking the down escalator when the time comes. You'll like it... It'll be just like a dungeon." Eyelashes batted alarmingly.

"Let me crank you up a bit." Olly made that sound like the filthiest suggestion ever.

The bed began to move and Becket found himself propped in a more upright position. That was better — now he could see that he was in a small hospital ward. There was one other bed next to him, which was empty. From the color of the walls and the curtaining, he wasn't in a general hospital, it looked military.

"Any dizziness? Nausea?" Olly shoved an old-fashioned thermometer into Becket's mouth then felt for a pulse, looking intently at the pocket watch attached to his dark green scrub shirt. Becket rolled his eyes — how was he supposed to answer with his mouth full.

Olly removed the thermometer and glanced at it. "Normal. Well, as normal as you'll ever be, Becket." He grinned cheekily. "But seriously, how do you feel? Are you in any pain?"

Becket shook his head. "Thirsty."

Olly poured a plastic beaker of water from a covered jug on the stand next to the bed and held it to his lips. Becket sipped gratefully then leaned back against his pillows. Machinery next to the bed flashed and beeped. Becket was attached to it by a series of wires stuck to pads on his chest. There was a cannula in the back of his hand with a tube connected that led to a bag of clear fluid suspended above him.

Olly perched on the edge of the bed. "I'm sure you're wondering what in the hell is going on, so I'll give you the potted Olly version before the big bad military doctor gets here. I'm warning you now, she's scary as hell." Olly wriggled and made himself comfortable. "You have the great pleasure of being resident at Bourton Military Hospital and Convalescent Facility, North Yorkshire. You've been here for three days, since they patched you up in London after the explosion."

"Three days?"

"You've been sedated, probably to stop you complaining."

"Olly…"

"Fine. It was to stop you opening up any of your wounds or jiggling anything important." Olly winked.

"Jesus. Joe should keep you permanently gagged."

Olly attempted to look insulted. "This is my place of work, Agent Becket, and I'll have you know that I am a highly respected professional."

"Professional brat."

"Careful, Becket, you're being mean to the man in charge of your catheter."

"Oh God, what did I do to deserve this?" Becket closed his eyes and tried not to think about what Olly would have been touching in order to insert the catheter in the first place.

"Olly, can you please get to the important stuff. What exactly is wrong with me and is any of it likely to be permanent?"

"Miraculously, you're going to be just fine. You have a list of injuries as long as my arm—but then you did get yourself blown up, so that's not very surprising, is it?"

Becket debated whether or not he could get his hands anywhere near Olly's neck and decided that it wasn't worth the effort. He'd just have a few quiet words with Joe the next time he saw him.

"So, lots of cuts and bruises. The best bruise is right on your arse—you have a very nice one by the way, arse that is, not bruise—so sitting is not going to be comfortable for a while. There are some deep cuts on the backs of your legs, two of which have stitches in them. The amount of blood you lost was worrying, but they filled you up with the good stuff back at the hospital in London."

Becket tried not to think about Olly admiring his arse.

"To start with, there was some blood in your pee, but it's clear now. Big relief. They've also X-rayed every inch of you and the only fracture you have is a hairline crack on one side of your pelvis. Your ribs are bruised to hell, but amazingly not broken. It'll be a few weeks before you can run after me but your legs will be fine. There's no damage to your spine and no paralysis. Of course, after all those X-rays, parts of you will probably mutate and you'll have the biggest di…"

"Nurse Glenn, I hope you are not upsetting my patient."

Olly's mouth slammed shut quicker than if Joe was giving him a scolding, making Becket grin happily.

"No, Doctor. Just giving him a little TLC."

"Hmm. Well you can go and make yourself useful. Corporal Haines is having a nasty reaction to his medication again and needs a bit of a clean-up."

"Why can that man not puke into a bucket like everybody else? He's a trained soldier for goodness sake—he can hit a target on the rifle range, why not when he's vomiting his guts up?" Olly left the room muttering away to himself.

Becket looked at the doctor who was restraining her laughter with difficulty. "I can assure you, Mr Becket, that Nurse Glenn is the best we have, despite his…idiosyncrasies. Allow me to introduce myself—

Doctor Fiona Epstein. I'll be overseeing your care while you are with us here at Bourton."

"It's a pleasure, Doc. Olly's given me an update – in his own unique way. Is there anything I should be worried about?"

"We were all very concerned about you for a while. Blood loss was a problem and then we weren't certain about spinal injuries. The sedation was to keep you completely still while the swelling went down and we could take better X-rays. You have been incredibly lucky considering the circumstances. You're young and fit, so recovery should not be a problem."

"When can I get out of here?"

The doctor smiled. "You men are all the same, can't wait to get out of my nice, comfy hospital."

Becket grinned. "Feeling unloved, Doc?"

"Absolutely. Now, your pelvic fracture is minor and stable, so in your case I wouldn't encourage too long in bed anyway. You don't have to remain immobile. However, you have considerable bruising and you are going to be in some discomfort for a few weeks. You won't be going back to work for a while – six weeks probably. I'm arranging alternative accommodation for your recuperation where you'll be able to be more active."

Becket frowned – he didn't want to be farmed off to some remote corner of the country. "Where will that be, Doc?"

"Well, it's slightly unusual, but friends of yours have offered to put you up for a while. Their premises are close enough that you'll be able to come in here for check-ups and initial physiotherapy and they do have expert staff on hand. But I'll let them tell you themselves – I believe you have visitors waiting. Once they've gone I'll get Nurse Glenn to remove your catheter. Walking to the bathroom will be good exercise for you."

Becket groaned at the thought of the commentary he was likely to get from Olly during *that* procedure.

"I'll consider discharging you tomorrow morning once I've examined you. I'll let your visitors in, but they mustn't stay too long. You do still need to rest. If you need more pain relief, press the bell next to the bed."

"Thanks, Doc." Becket looked at the door curiously, waiting to see who would appear.

The doctor started scribbling some notes on the chart at the end of the bed and a couple of minutes later the door opened again and two familiar faces appeared.

Becket couldn't fail to notice the doctor's reaction to the new arrivals. She schooled her features quickly but not before the slight widening of eyes that betrayed her interest in the two tall, handsome men. Becket grinned. Joe and Heath certainly made an imposing pair and nobody could deny how good-looking they both were. Joe Dexter could be dressed in a sack and he'd still look like an Armani model and Heath had that whole tall, dark and broody thing going on that seemed to make most women go weak at the knees. The doctor made a hurried exit muttering about things she needed to do.

"Hey, guys, I wasn't expecting visitors. It's good to see you," Becket said.

Heath pulled up a chair and swung a leg over it so that he could lean against the backrest. "From what I hear, it's a miracle that we're not attending your funeral, you bloody idiot."

Joe's bedside manner was a little less antagonistic. "What Heath is trying to say, I assume, is that we're glad you're alive."

"Thanks. I think." Becket grinned. "I really am glad you are both here—Olly's my nurse and I'm seriously in need of some protection. You have no idea!"

Heath grunted. "Oh, I think we probably do."

Joe looked utterly serene. "Don't worry, Becket. I can assure you that Olly will confess everything to me this evening and be appropriately punished."

"I'm surprised the brat can ever sit down, he gets spanked that often." Heath rolled his eyes.

Becket chuckled. It made his ribs hurt but it was worth it. "How's Aiden? Not blaming himself for any of this, I hope?"

"You know Aiden. Far too many brain cells in that pretty head of his. He's frustrated that the bombers haven't been tracked down yet. Still, there are ways and means to take him out of himself. He's doing fine—probably a bit sore, but fine." Heath smiled wickedly.

"He saved a lot of lives. The bombers were idiots—they put the explosives in a tomb, which absorbed a lot of the explosion, but the church was packed with tourists. If Aiden hadn't worked out what was going on and where, there would certainly have been some fatalities and a lot of nasty injuries."

Joe leaned against the wall. "And instead the only one badly injured was you."

"I'm okay. Nothing that won't mend with a bit of R & R, from what the doc says."

"Indeed, and that's where we come in." Joe smiled lazily. "You are going to come and recuperate with us at The Edge. We've got plenty of room and Olly has arranged some time off so he'll be on hand to provide any medical care you need." Joe managed to make something that should have been Becket's choice into a non-negotiable fact, just by the tone of his voice.

Becket looked at both his friends. "Really? When the doc said she had made some arrangements I had no idea she was talking about The Edge. Are you sure? I mean, you have a business to run, won't I just be in the way?"

"It's all arranged. We just need the doc to sign your release papers."

"I don't know what to say…" Becket was touched by the offer.

"Hey! You two shouldn't be wearing out my patient." All three men looked toward the door where Olly had appeared. "He needs his rest and there's another visitor waiting to see him. Don't you have things to do?"

Becket watched with interest as Joe raised an eyebrow. It was all the signal Olly needed to fling himself across the room and into Joe's arms.

"Becket's a terrible patient, Sir, he keeps telling me off and I haven't done anything wrong, honestly. Well, maybe I was just a little bit cheeky, but he needs cheering up, doesn't he? So that's all right, and I've been looking after him really well and I only took a peek at his arse, which is delicious by the way, and I thought pure thoughts when I had my hands on his…"

"Olly!" Becket, Heath and Joe all felt the need to cut off the excited flow of words spilling from Olly's pretty pink lips.

Joe extricated himself from Olly's grip and gave his sub a stern look. "It sounds like you need a good deal more than a telling off, brat. You and I will be having a frank discussion when you get home later."

For all his angelic appearance, Olly might as well have had little horns poking out of his blond curls. His big blue eyes widened and his lower lip trembled just a little. Joe looked completely unaffected, while Heath smirked knowingly.

Joe turned to Becket. "We'll leave you in peace because there is a much more important visitor waiting for you. We'll be back tomorrow—the doc is going to ring us as soon as she's happy it's safe to move you."

Becket's heart leaped. Perhaps his new visitor might be Christian. "Thanks, Joe. I'll see you tomorrow, even if it means holding the doctor to ransom."

Olly sniggered but cast his eyes down when Joe gave him a pointed look. "You'll drive straight home after work, Olly, and present yourself in my office."

It was Heath's turn to snigger, and Olly glared at him before fixing the sweetest smile on his face and replying politely to Joe, "Yes, Sir."

Once Joe and Heath had left, Olly bustled around the room checking Becket's drip, taking his blood pressure and updating the chart that hung on the frame at the end of the bed yet again. He chattered away constantly, giving a running commentary on what he was doing and life in general.

Olly finally paused for breath and looked around the room as if checking that everything was in order. He frowned and straightened the bedding until he was satisfied with the level of order then attacked Becket's pillows.

"Can't have you slouching down and looking untidy, can we?"

Becket pitied the poor pillow that was getting quite a beating. When Olly had finished he was more comfortable, though.

"Perfect. Just give me a couple of minutes and I'll be back with your next visitor. You don't feel too tired, do you?"

"I've been asleep for three days, Olly, I think I can manage. Who is it anyway?"

"Can't tell you, it's a surprise."

Becket growled, "Be glad I'm stuck in bed, Olly."

Olly just grinned and scooted out of the door. Becket sighed and settled back against his very plump pillows. All his irritation was instantly forgotten when the door opened and Olly dragged Christian to the side of the bed. He looked even more beautiful than Becket remembered. He also looked exhausted. His face was pale and dark rings circled his eyes.

With a remarkably uncharacteristic display of diplomacy, Olly slipped quietly from the room and left them alone.

"Hello, Sir." Christian had his gaze fixed firmly on the floor. Becket patted the side of the bed.

"Come here, sweetheart."

"But you're... You're..." Christian started to cry.

Becket's heart broke in two. Knowing that Christian needed direction, Becket toughened his tone. "Sit here, Christian. I'm hurt but I'm mending. I'm not going to break if you do as you're told and sit on the bed next to me."

"Oh." Christian scrubbed an arm across his eyes and sat down.

"I need a kiss. It will make me feel better." Becket reached out and cupped Christian's neck so that he could pull him down to the right level. He made sure there was nothing weak about the kiss that followed. For just a second Christian resisted and held back. Becket pulled him close and probed at Christian's lips with his tongue, demanding entry. The resistance melted away and Christian opened for him, giving up any pretense that he wasn't enjoying every second of his master's kiss.

Eventually Becket moved back but he put a restraining hand on Christian's thigh to make sure he didn't try to edge away.

"Talk to me, sweetheart. How did you find out that I'd gotten myself into a bit of trouble?"

Christian looked satisfyingly shell-shocked. He touched a finger to his lips as if trying to feel the kiss again and smiled.

"I felt the bomb, Sir. Of course I didn't know what it was at the time, but I was working at the club and everything trembled for a second. A bit later, Carey and Alistair told me about the explosion and that you might be involved. Carey sent Sam up to the area of the church to investigate and then made a few calls. Carey sure does know a lot of important people because he managed to find out that you and a colleague had been trapped in the church. Then a fireman showed up and told us that you'd been pulled out of the rubble and taken to hospital."

Becket stroked Christian's thigh. "I don't remember the trip from the church to the hospital at all and I only remember coming round in the hospital briefly. There was a fireman... Beau... He's a club member. He was part of the rescue team and he was there again when I woke up."

"Yes, Beau's a really nice guy. He came down to The Underground and let Carey know where you were, but by the time we got to the hospital you were in surgery. They had to pull some bits of debris from your wounds and stitch you up. Everyone was really worried about your back. I was so scared."

"What do you mean he's a really nice guy? I don't want you looking at sexy firemen while I'm lying here in bed."

Christian's eyes went wide with shock. "Oh no, Sir…"

Becket couldn't stop himself laughing. "Sorry, love, couldn't resist teasing you."

"Sir! Don't do that!"

"Carry on. What happened next?"

"Carey and Alistair looked after me the whole time. I'd have been a complete mess without them, Sir. I don't know how I'll ever be able to thank them."

"They're our friends, Christian. That's what friends do and they won't be expecting any thanks for it."

"Well, anyway, I've never drunk so much coffee in my life waiting to find out what was going on. We were waiting in this little side room and eventually a doctor came out and told us that it wasn't worth waiting because they were going to keep you sedated until they could take more X-rays of your back. They wouldn't let anyone in to see you at all, and then your brother arrived."

"Giddy was here?"

"Not here. At the hospital in London. Carey tracked him down and he came as soon as he knew what had happened. He offered to stay at the hospital overnight and because he was a blood relative, they let him use a trolley bed in a side room. Carey took me back to his place. He wouldn't let me go home on my own."

Becket made a mental note to buy his friend a drink as soon as he was able.

"Alistair sat up with me until I was too tired to stay awake any longer and then I stayed in the spare room. Carey made me leave the door open in case I got scared or had bad dreams. I'm not a child, Becket, I could have looked after myself."

"I'm sure you could, darling, but you were in shock and that does peculiar things to a person. I'm really glad that Carey took care of you."

"I woke up really early and Alistair was already up too. Have you ever seen Carey's coffee machine? You need a degree in nuclear physics to work that thing. Alistair persuaded it to produce coffee and as soon as we'd had some breakfast, Carey took us both back to the hospital."

"And I still wasn't awake?"

"No. We saw Gideon and he said that they decided to keep you under while they transported you up here. The good news was that there were no spinal fractures but they couldn't be sure about nerve damage. There was so much bruising and swelling as well. They wanted you somewhere that was more familiar with dealing with injuries incurred through contact with explosives. I couldn't believe it when we found out they were sending you to the hospital that Olly worked at, or how close to the The Edge you were going to be. Alistair got back on the phone, spoke to Joe and Heath, and here we all are. Gideon sent his love. He should be here later. I stayed at The Edge last night and I slept a little better." Christian sounded a little guilty.

"There's no need to feel bad about sleeping, love. I'd rather you weren't having nightmares. I only want you tossing and turning when you're in bed with me. Preferably when you're under me."

Christian chuckled. "Yes, Sir. I can't wait. Do you know how long you're going to be out of action?"

"Well, the doc wants me up and around as soon as possible but it's going to be six weeks or so before I'm completely back to normal. Of course, that's only if I survive Olly's nursing."

That got a proper laugh out of Christian. "I'm told he's a brilliant nurse, Sir."

"Oh I don't doubt his medical skills—it's his mouth that's the problem."

Right on cue, Olly appeared at the door. "Sorry, Christian, time's up. Becket needs his beauty sleep, not that there's likely to be much improvement, and I have to change his drip over."

Becket had to admit that he felt like he'd run a marathon. He pulled Christian in for a soft, gentle kiss. "How are you getting back to The Edge, love?"

"Heath lent me his car, so I can drive back. I'll see you tomorrow, okay?"

"I'll look forward to it. Be good this evening. No letting Olly lead you astray." He spared a glare for Olly who was looking perfectly innocent.

"With any luck they'll let me transfer over to The Edge tomorrow." Christian walked to the door. He moved so gracefully, just the sway of his hips was enough to make Becket feel a bit hot and bothered. He wondered if it was even possible to get an erection with a catheter inserted, then the thought of Olly taking it out ensured that he wasn't going to find out any time soon. Christian gave a last wave and disappeared. Becket didn't feel anything that Olly did because he slipped instantly into sleep.

Chapter Seven

Christian made the short drive back to the island where The Edge was situated with a white-knuckled grip on the steering wheel. He sat bolt upright and let the cold breeze from the car's open window keep him awake. The last three days had been the longest of his life and though he'd slept it had been through exhaustion and he still wasn't rested. Only the thought of what Heath's reaction would be if Christian crashed his car kept him alert.

He crossed the causeway and stopped the car for a moment to look at the view. The North Yorkshire coast in all its rugged grandeur stretched into the distance, holding back a choppy, steel-gray sea. It was disturbingly beautiful. Compared to the London streets that Christian was used to, this view felt wild and untouched. He liked it — it made him feel free. He drove the rest of the way across the narrow bridge of land then pulled through the gates to The Edge. The main buildings loomed over him as he parked in Heath's reserved space and got out. For a moment he had to stand and hold onto the car door because he felt a little lightheaded. Once the world had settled back to being a more solid place, he locked the car and went inside.

The Edge's entrance hall was very grand but still managed to be welcoming with a large open fire burning in a huge stone fireplace. Heath's office door was open so Christian knocked, wanting to return Heath's car keys before he went to bed.

"Come in." Heath always managed to sound slightly taciturn, his voice was so low.

Christian pushed the door open a little nervously. Heath had a stack of books in his arms and was putting them back on a shelf. There was no sign of Aiden. Christian had half expected to find Heath's sub kneeling naked and chained in a corner. The thought made him smile.

"Christian, you're back. How's Becket doing?" Heath sounded concerned.

"He seemed tired when I left, but he was almost his usual self while I was there. Olly's looking after him well."

Heath rolled his eyes. "Much as I hate to admit it, the brat is a bloody good nurse. Mind you, I think most of the patients over there get better quicker just to get away from his sarcastic mouth. Becket will be no exception."

"I hope they let him out tomorrow, I hate seeing him in hospital. He seems so vulnerable."

Heath patted Christian's shoulder. "Sit down, Christian, before you fall down."

Gratefully, Christian sat in the chair in front of Heath's desk. "I'm a bit tired."

"You're exhausted. And feeling very insecure, I imagine. It's tough, isn't it, realizing that your Dom is only human?"

Christian nodded. "I'm just being stupid."

Heath went and sat behind his desk. Behind him on the windowsill sat a tray holding a decanter and two big tumblers. He poured a couple of fingers of golden liquid into one of the glasses and handed it over.

"Drink this. It'll do you good."

Christian didn't normally touch alcohol but the circumstances seemed to merit a stiff drink. He downed it in one go and fire streaked from his throat to his stomach.

"Oh… Wow!"

Heath smirked. "Brandy has great medicinal properties. Becket is still the same person he was before the explosion, Christian. I bet he was ordering you around from his hospital bed, wasn't he?"

Christian nodded.

"He won't stop being dominant because he's injured. It's not something that can be switched on and off. Becket's a Dom through and through. If he was a stick of rock and you cut him in half, 'Master' would probably be stamped right though him. He wouldn't want you to be worrying about him."

"I can't help it, Heath. All I can think about is what if he'd been killed? What would I do without him? I know we've not been a 'proper' couple like you and Aiden or Olly and Joe, but he's such an important part of my life. I think I'd fall apart if he was gone and that's so selfish."

"Just because you're not together twenty-four seven, doesn't make your relationship any less committed. And what you're feeling is completely normal. You're a submissive, Christian. You need your Master to be there for you and that doesn't make you selfish, so stop beating yourself up. Aiden gets edgy if I have to go away overnight and leave him here."

That surprised Christian no end. "Really? But Aiden's so...strong."

Heath chuckled. "He is strong, but he's also submissive. It may look like he fights it every inch of the way, but Aiden knows what he is. Of course, it works both ways. I get just as edgy when I can't be here to watch over him. All the good Doms I know have a tendency to be overprotective. It's just the way we are. Joe's like a bear with a sore head if he has to be apart from Olly for any length of time. I'd bet good money that Becket will be itching to be somewhere he can keep a closer eye on you. That's why you can both stay here for as long as it takes for him to recover properly."

"That's so kind, Sir." The honorific just slipped out and Christian immediately worried that Heath might think he'd spoken out of turn.

Heath just smiled. "It's all right, Christian, just call me what you feel comfortable with. The same goes for Joe. You call Becket Sir, don't you?"

Christian nodded. "Yes."

"Well then, don't think of Joe or me any differently. If you want to call us by our names, that's fine too."

"Thanks. I think I'm just going to go on to bed if that's okay?"

"Of course, oh wait—here's Aiden."

Christian turned toward the door. He hadn't heard it open, but Aiden was standing there, as gorgeous as always. He was wearing the all black uniform of The Edge, which suited his dark good looks. Christian got a shy smile but Aiden didn't speak. He walked across the room and sank gracefully to his knees in front of Heath. "Good evening, Sir."

Heath tousled Aiden's hair and pulled him to his feet for a kiss. Christian watched and to his dismay felt the tiniest spike of envy. Aiden appeared so perfectly serene as he turned in Heath's arms. With his back to Heath's chest, Aiden had Heath holding him close and Christian really, really wanted to be restrained by Becket's arms in just that way.

"Hey, Christian, how's Becket doing?"

Christian knew he wasn't imagining the hint of tension in Aiden's voice, much as he'd tried to disguise it.

"He's going to be absolutely fine," he said, with a lot more certainty than he felt, but Aiden's smile was reward enough. "Hopefully you'll see him yourself tomorrow. If the doctor doesn't sign his release papers, he'll probably dig his way out just to get away from Olly."

"Olly's like a sparkler, all energy and brightness. Without Joe around to control him he's like an explosion in a firework factory."

Christian laughed. "That sums him up perfectly! Everyone at the hospital says he's an amazing nurse."

"When he's working, Olly has a surprisingly wide authoritarian streak, it helps him fulfill his inner brat."

Christian yawned. "Sorry — haven't really slept enough in the last few days. I was just off to bed."

Heath stroked Aiden's cheek. "Why don't you walk Christian to his room, love. I've got some paperwork to catch up on but I shouldn't be more than an hour. I'll see you upstairs later."

"Yes, Sir." Aiden turned and tilted his head expectantly.

"Demanding brat." Heath didn't sound at all annoyed. He ravished Aiden's mouth with a fierce kiss then pulled away reluctantly. "Now go on, the pair of you, before Christian collapses."

Aiden led the way and Christian followed him through the hall and along a passage to the room that he had been given. It was more a small suite than just a room—a sitting area with a comfy couch and a brand new television was separate from the bedroom, which housed a king-sized bed. The bathroom was spacious enough for a wheelchair. The accommodation had been carefully designed with less abled people in mind, and Christian was grateful that it would allow Becket to be as independent as possible while he was recovering. He realized that he was standing stock still and shook himself into action.

"Sit down, Christian. I'll make you a mug of hot chocolate. It'll help you sleep," Aiden said gently.

Christian didn't have the energy to argue and a warm milky drink sounded very appealing. "Thanks, Aiden, that would be great." He collapsed onto the couch feeling far older than his twenty-five years.

Aiden puttered around filling the kettle and spooning chocolate powder into two mugs. Soon the aroma of warm chocolate filled the room and Aiden was pushing a mug into Christian's hands. He was so tired he could barely grip the handle. He took a cautious sip, but the drink wasn't too hot. Aiden must have added some cold milk to cool it a little. The taste of chocolate caressed Christian's tongue and he sighed happily. "Oh that's good."

Aiden took a seat next to him on the sofa. "You must be shattered. I think people have a tendency to focus solely on the patient in these situations and forget how hard it can be on their loved ones."

Christian shrugged. "I'm just tired. It's nothing compared to what Becket must be going through. Even though I know he's going to be fine, he hates being in the hospital."

"And you don't like seeing him hurt?"

"It scares me." There, it was out in the open. Christian felt a lot more comfortable confessing to Aiden than he would have to Heath or Joe.

"And Becket's not here to take your mind away from where it doesn't want to be. I understand, believe me. After the explosion, I felt so guilty. I sent Becket to that church. It was my fault."

"Of course it wasn't! You didn't put the bomb there." Christian wanted Aiden to understand that he didn't blame him at all.

"I know. But it took a couple of hours with Heath for me to be convinced." Aiden chuckled. "I'm sure you can imagine just how persuasive he can be."

Christian knew exactly what Aiden was talking about. Heath had a commanding presence that oozed authority. Christian was constantly amazed by the way Aiden seemed able to resist him.

"You're wondering why I fight him, aren't you?" Aiden asked.

"I'm sorry. Was it that obvious? It's really none of my business."

Aiden laughed and sipped his chocolate. "Christian, you are such a refreshing change from Olly. He has a double helping of the nosiness gene. I don't mind…really."

"It's just that you and Heath are so good together, but you still seem…resistant."

"The lifestyle isn't a one size fits all kind of thing, is it? Joe only has to look at Olly in a certain way and Olly turns into a pile of submissive goo. Alistair craves the peace that Carey's discipline brings him. I find submission more of a challenge."

Christian looked at Aiden and, just as he did every time he saw him, wondered at just how beautiful he was. "You mean you're not sure that it's what you want?"

"Not at all. I'm not in denial. I know I'm submissive and I'm not ashamed of it, but sometimes I have to remind myself that submission is not weakness. Fighting Heath is fun. Giving in to him is a hell of a lot more fun! Heath wouldn't do well with someone who was too compliant. He likes to conquer."

Christian leaned back against the sofa. "Becket and I seem to fit well but we haven't really had enough time together to test our compatibility. I'm sure for me, if you see what I mean... I don't have any doubts, but I can't say the same about Becket. He says all the right things but he knows I need more of a commitment and I'm not sure he wants to give me that. I thought I could be happy with playing together when he was available, but I'm falling in love with him, Aiden. I miss him so much when he's not around. He's going to end up thinking I'm just a needy, clingy... Oh I don't know." Christian sighed and put down his mug. "I'm just tired and it's making me overly emotional."

"I don't think you have anything to worry about, Christian. I'm sure the pair of you will find a way to make it work. Becket's a different man when he's with you. It's obvious to all of us how strongly he feels."

Aiden stood up. "I'll leave you be. Get some sleep and try not to worry too much. You'll have plenty of time over the next few weeks to get to know Becket better." He reached out and gave Christian's hand a squeeze.

Christian fancied that a little of Aiden's strength passed to him through that simple touch. "Thanks, Aiden, I know Heath will be waiting for you by now. I don't want you getting into any trouble because of me."

Aiden's eyes seemed to glitter in the low light. "Making him wait has its rewards, Christian. I'll see you at breakfast." With a final smile Aiden left, pulling the door softly closed behind him.

Christian paid a cursory visit to the bathroom. He tugged his clothes off then dropped them in a pile on the floor. Too tired to tidy them away, he climbed into bed. Whether it was Aiden's reassurance or sheer bloody exhaustion didn't matter — the moment his head hit the pillow, Christian was asleep.

* * * *

Waking up was a hell of a lot harder than falling asleep had been. Christian felt as if he was dragging his consciousness through sticky black treacle. His eyelids weighed at least twenty pounds. Each. He had the strange impression that he was at sea, the rise and fall of the waves lifting his body then dropping it. The sensation was slightly nauseating.

"Wake up, wake up, wake up!"

"Wha…" Christian opened his eyes to discover that his sailing partner was Olly, who was bouncing up and down on the edge of the mattress. Olly couldn't have looked more bright-eyed and bushy-tailed if he'd been dressed in a squirrel costume and sprayed with glitter. All Christian could manage was a groan.

Olly bounced some more. "Get your lazy arse out of bed, Christian, Becket's coming home today and we have to have breakfast and turn you back into a human being before he gets here. Breakfast first, though. I need energy if I'm going to tackle your appalling self-image issues and the staff restaurant here serves the most amazing waffles with syrup and syrup doesn't count as sugar does it so Joe won't stop me from having a few especially if I hide the syrup under some blueberries and they count as one of my five a day at least which is great because they're almost like sweets!"

Christian decided that he'd entered some kind of alternate dimension where his capacity to understand the English language had been severely curtailed. Olly talked without punctuation and it was challenging to the ears. He tried what he hoped was a pitiful moan, hoping to elicit some sympathy from his tormentor, but it didn't work. Olly tried to yank back the covers.

"Olly! I don't have anything on!" Christian suddenly felt a lot more awake.

"Oh don't tell me you're all coy and shy? Just like Aiden—he gets all bashful too, which is hysterical. If I had a body like his I'd be parading around in a thong, not hiding all those muscles away."

Christian held tight to the covers. "I can't imagine Heath letting Aiden parade around anywhere, and I'm pretty sure that Joe prefers to keep you under wraps as well."

Olly pouted. "That's not the point. I know you have a hot bod under there. You move like a dancer and I've seen you in those leather trousers Carey makes you wear at the club. They don't leave very much to the imagination, and believe me—I have a very active one of those."

Christian risked sitting up and took a proper look at Olly. He was wearing the black fleece and cargoes that made up the staff uniform at The Edge, but the corporate effect was ruined by a pair of sparkly pink baseball boots.

"Why aren't you working? Shouldn't you be looking after Becket?" Christian felt a bit panicky.

"I only work part-time at the hospital and I've taken a few days off to look after Becket here. I've left the lovely Becket in good hands—he is rather a dish, isn't he? Though a complete wimp. Considering he's a super-spy or whatever, you'd have thought he'd be glad to get rid of a catheter, wouldn't you? But oh no, what a fuss. Anyone would think I'd never seen a dick before."

"Olly!"

"Oh my God! You, Aiden and Alistair are all from the same mold, I swear. Fine. I'll leave you to get up in peace. You've got fifteen minutes to shower, shave and dress. In sixteen minutes I'll be back to retrieve you. My stomach will not wait a minute longer."

Christian relaxed and let down his guard along with his hold on the bed clothes. In a very impressive display of dexterity, Olly hopped off the bed, twisted around and yanked the covers off with a gleeful giggle. "Very nice, Christian!"

He ran for the door before Christian could react. The door slammed and Christian flopped back on the bed. He'd only been awake for ten minutes and Olly had already managed to wear him out.

Deciding that risking a return visit from Olly was not worth the hassle, Christian got up, had the quickest shower in history, dried off and dressed. He rubbed at his hair until it was damp rather than sopping wet. It had gotten too long to be combed into submission, so he had to settle for tousled. He glared at the mirror and cursed whatever heritage had gifted him with untamable dark red waves. He'd only brought a small bag of clothes with him so choosing jeans and his favorite soft black pullover didn't take long, then he sat on the edge of the bed to deal with socks and trainers. He was as ready as he was ever going to be. Olly must have been waiting right outside the door because the moment Christian pushed it open Olly was there, grabbing his hand and dragging him along to the dining room, chattering away continually as they went.

"Do you know how they get those cute little square patterns in the waffles? They're good aren't they because all the syrup makes little pools in them? I look at them and think they'd make good swimming pools for something really tiny, but I got Emile to show me and they don't come out of a packet he gets the cooks to make them from scratch and they make this special batter and pour it into a waffle iron—sounds like something Joe might use to tie me up but it isn't, he likes to do that you know and I like him to as well but waffles are really yummy and Emile let me have a fresh one right out of the pan and then he let me pour the batter and make one myself and that's why I'm addicted to them it's all his fault."

Christian didn't even attempt to get a word in edge-ways—his brain was having a hard enough time just keeping up. It was a relief when they reached the staff dining room and Olly had the distraction of his friends and colleagues shouting greetings to him. Everyone knew Olly and he seemed to know everything about everyone. Before he knew it Christian was sitting at a table opposite Olly with a tray in front of him. It was laden with food he didn't even remember choosing, but it all looked good and his stomach was growling eagerly. He took a long drink of freshly squeezed orange juice first, just to confirm that his taste buds were still alive. The fresh flavor burst over his tongue and he gave a deep, satisfied sigh.

"The food here is brilliant, isn't it?" Olly was munching his way through a stack of waffles that were drowning in warm syrup and piled with blueberries. "I'll have to introduce you to Emile—he's nearly as scary as Heath, but anyone who can cook like he can can't be all bad."

Christian started on his bowl of fruit and yoghurt. "Where are the others?" He looked around at the half dozen or so other people enjoying a late breakfast. There was no sign of Heath, Joe or Aiden.

"All working. We have a big group of trainees in this week from Becket's place. Baby spies. So Joe is teaching, and Heath will be up to his neck in paperwork. He'll be nice and grumpy later." Olly grinned. "Aiden will be in his lair in the basement. I'm not allowed in there. Not that that has ever stopped me!" Another huge fork-full of waffle disappeared. "Aiden's really, really clever. He thinks too much. It's not good for him. Brains and beauty, I'm amazed he's not some arrogant pain in the arse."

"I like him." Christian sliced into a juicy grilled tomato.

"You like me too, though, don't you?" Olly made huge puppy eyes and let his bottom lip quiver.

"Of course I do! You're irresistible, Olly."

Olly beamed. "I know. It's a gift."

The chatter around them quietened a little making Christian look up. Joe was making his way across the room, stopping for a quick word with each of his staff. Joe made all his interactions look effortless. His light blue eyes had a mesmerizing quality that held people's attention and, though he was quietly spoken, nobody ever talked over him or interrupted.

"Um, Olly?"

Olly licked syrup from the back of his spoon. "Yes?"

Christian pointed with his fork and Olly turned around. "Uh-oh."

Joe walked over and stood behind Olly's chair, which Olly tipped back until his feet were dangling off the ground and he was leaning against his master. "Hello, Sir."

"How many waffles did you have with your syrup, Oliver?" Joe sounded stern but Christian detected a twinkle in his pale eyes.

"I had lots of blueberries too, Sir."

"Does that excuse you? You thought you could get away with disobedience because I wasn't around, didn't you?"

Olly rocked his chair back to the floor and hung his head. Blond curls fell over his face, hiding his grin from Joe.

"I know you're smiling, brat. You can look after Christian this morning, but after Becket gets here, you and I have an appointment with the spanking bench."

"As you wish, Sir." Olly didn't sound at all upset.

"I think an hour or so in the cockhead gag this evening would do you some good too."

"Oh."

"Yes, oh."

Joe smiled at Christian as if he hadn't just been promising punishment to his sub. "I hope you slept well, Christian. The hospital administrator rang and confirmed that we can collect Becket this afternoon."

"That's wonderful, Sir, thank you!"

"No problem. I have to get back to work. Don't let Olly lead you too far astray this morning."

Olly sputtered into his juice. "That's so unfair! I'm a very trustworthy individual."

Joe stroked Olly's hair. "Of course you are, love, when it suits you." Joe kissed the top of Olly's head and winked at Christian before walking away.

Christian laughed, "He knows you so well, Olly!"

Olly scowled. "I hate that gag."

"You hate anything that stops you speaking!"

"True, but this one has a silicon cock that fills your mouth right up and then a wide leather strap that covers half your face. It buckles up so tight that you can't say a word." Olly scraped the last of the syrup from his plate and grinned. "I'd wear it for three hours if it meant more waffles, though!"

Chapter Eight

Deciding that he couldn't be punished any more, Olly had a second helping of waffles while Christian finished up with a plate of crispy bacon and poached eggs. He felt comfortably full and was really looking forward to Becket's arrival. Instead of traveling to the hospital, it had been decided that Christian and Olly would make sure everything was ready for Becket to settle in while Heath and Aiden provided the taxi service for the short trip.

Olly patted his stomach. "Now I'm suitably fueled, I'm ready to give you your makeover."

Christian blinked. "What do you mean, makeover?"

"I'm going to make sure you look like the sweet little sub you are. It's my welcome home present for Becket."

"I'm not sure, Olly. I don't think I really need…"

"Oh you do. Really you do. We're going to start with that mop on the top of your head and work down. You need a full service."

Christian wondered if he should make a run for it.

"Don't even think about it, sweetie. I'll chase you down and catch you in no time. Cooperation is your best and least painful option."

How the hell did he read my mind?

"First stop is the hairdresser." Olly made snipping motions with his fingers and pushed his chair back. "Come on."

"You're not going to cut it, are you, Olly?"

Olly looked hurt. "Don't you trust me?" He batted his eyelashes alarmingly. "Oh, don't panic. One of the pastry chefs was a trainee hairdresser before he was imprisoned in Emile's kitchen and he likes to keep his hand in. He's straight but don't hold that against him. He cuts Joe's hair and Heath's so he must be good. If he mucked it up on either of them he'd probably be the ingredients in one of Emile's stews by now."

Christian felt a little reassured. He'd been picturing Olly brandishing a set of garden shears up until then. He wasn't vain but he didn't want to look like a recently shorn sheep.

Olly dragged the cook, whose name was Hugh, out of the kitchen and into the staff restaurant where he produced a spray bottle of water and a pair of scissors. Christian tried not to make it obvious that he was gripping the sides of his chair as Hugh snipped away and chatted with Olly, seemingly paying scant attention to what he was doing.

"Hugh, get your useless English arse back in this kitchen before I flambé your balls! *Immédiatement!*"

Hugh sighed. "There you go, Olly, Christian's all done and I've done a fine job even if I do say so myself. Those were the dulcet tones of the boss, so I'd better go. I value my dangly bits."

"Thanks, Hugh. We'll sweep up."

Hugh disappeared back into the kitchen, and Olly fetched a soft broom from a store cupboard. "Don't look so worried, you look great."

Christian felt around his neck, wishing for a mirror. "It did need a trim. What's with Emile? He sounded furious."

"He always sounds like that and despite the way it sounded, he doesn't hate the English. He thinks that *anyone* who isn't French is an inferior species. Emile does discrimination on a global scale. He makes all the kitchen staff learn French."

Christian brushed some bits of hair from his neck. "Okay, what's next?"

"We're going over to my place to indulge in a little manscaping. Then we're going to tackle your wardrobe. I know you haven't got many clothes with you so I raided Aiden's cupboards. You and he are about the same size, and before you ask, yes I did talk to him about it first."

Olly led the way through the main building and across the courtyard to the house that he and Joe shared. Christian felt nervous but the idea of preparing himself specifically for Becket was exciting as well. He'd packed in such a hurry for the trip to Yorkshire that he'd not put any thought into it. He didn't own very many smart clothes anyway, and nothing that might be appealing to Becket. The only leather Christian owned were the trousers he wore at The Underground.

Olly and Joe lived in a converted carriage house at the rear of The Edge. As Christian looked around the bedroom curiously, Olly sat on the edge of the bed and bounced. "The bathroom's just through there. I've left you everything you'll need. Take your time and when you're all done we'll decide on the best outfit.

I've put the clothes in the wardrobe in your room in the main house. Heath and Aiden live over there so it was easier than carrying it all over here."

Christian ventured into the bathroom, which was a decent size. There was a double-width shower cubicle with a modern powerful shower installed. Christian's attention was drawn to the collection of items laid out by the sink. There was a neatly packaged enema kit, a couple of fresh razors, a can of expensive shaving gel and a tube of depilatory cream. There was also a tub of lube and a fat little butt plug in its own blister pack. "Oh my God!"

"I thought of everything, didn't I?" The sound of Olly's voice behind him made Christian jump. He turned to see his friend lounging in the doorway with a grin fixed to his pretty face. "Do you need instructions for any of that?"

Christian shook his head slowly. "No...but..."

"You need to be prepared for anything, don't you? Becket's injured. He's not ill and he's not dead. All his important bits are fully functioning. He's a Dom, Christian, remember? Even if he can't be fully involved in the process, he'll almost certainly have plans for your arse later."

Christian swallowed. "I hadn't thought that far ahead."

"That's why you have me to look after you." Olly giggled. "I've thought of all eventualities. I didn't think you'd be up for me shaving you down below, so I got the cream for that. Maneuvering a razor round your danglies is bloody difficult on your own. Of course, Joe always insists on doing that for me and he likes to tie me down while he's doing it, which is soooooooooo good! But I thought it would be a nice surprise for Becket. Of course, that's assuming that you aren't already..."

"None of your business, Olly."

"You'll love it. You won't believe how sensitive it makes the skin, trust me."

To his surprise, Christian found that he was half-hard just thinking about getting prepared for Becket. The idea of doing things to his body just to please his Dom made him feel good inside. He decided to stop thinking and start doing. He'd pretend that he was following Becket's orders and it would all be easy. "I'm not doing this with you standing there watching, Olly, and there's no lock on this door so you have to promise to stay out until I've finished, okay?"

Olly rolled his eyes. "I can never understand how people with such kinky sex lives can be so shy. Sure, I promise, but don't take all day. Joe's always telling me I have the attention span of a goldfish so it's quite likely that I'll forget I promised anything if you make me wait too long."

Christian gave him a gentle shove and shut the door. No matter what Olly said, this was going to take a while.

An hour later he emerged, clean, scrubbed and shaved. Hugh had made a nice job of his hair, which now sat in neat waves rather than a rebellious tangle. As he walked, his underwear rubbed against his newly shaven groin, giving credence to Olly's statement about sensitivity. Christian was hyper-aware of every movement, even though the shorts he had on under his jeans were made of nice soft cotton.

Olly was sprawled across the bed, glued to his Kindle, but looked up straight away. "Wow! Look at you! You're nearly as pretty as Aiden."

Christian felt his face heat. "Don't exaggerate, Olly, Aiden's gorgeous. I'm just...ordinary."

Olly tossed his Kindle onto the pillow then crawled to the edge of the bed. "You're kidding, right? Did you even look in the mirror in there? It's the shiny thing on the wall."

"You're just being nice." Christian threw the plug and lube onto the bed. "These can wait until later. I am not walking around with that thing stuffed up my arse until I know what time Becket's coming back."

Olly sat cross-legged. "Your self-confidence really has taken a battering, hasn't it? Take it from me, Christian, when Becket looks at you he doesn't see 'ordinary' he sees extraordinary. Subs at The Underground have always thrown themselves at Becket, Joe's told me, and yet he only ever plays with you. Doesn't that tell you something?" He jumped off the bed. "Still, it's not me who should be convincing you, and you're missing out not using that plug yet. There's nothing quite like the feeling of being stuffed nice and full." He wiggled his arse provocatively. "And I should know! Let's go and get you all tarted up — you can't welcome Becket dressed like that!"

"Like what?" Christian protested as Olly grabbed his hand and towed him toward the stairs. "These are my favorite jeans."

"And they look really...comfortable."

"You make that sound like a crime, Olly."

"It is. You're a sub. You're not supposed to be comfortable, you're supposed to be absolutely irresistible to your Dom. The two things are not compatible."

"But you're..."

"Wearing staff uniform. That doesn't count. Anyway, you haven't seen what I've got on underneath." Olly giggled all the way across the courtyard.

"I don't think I want to know." Christian followed Olly along the corridor to his room. "And you can't tell me that those boots are regulation."

Olly held out a pink glittery foot. "No, but they should be." He pushed open the door and looked around. "Hmm. Not bad. It needs the Olly touch really. I haven't been in here for a while."

"It's fine, Olly. I can't believe how generous everyone's being."

"That's what friends are for." Olly started rummaging in the wardrobe and his voice became muffled. "I brought down a few outfits so that you could choose." He emerged with an armful of clothes and tossed the pile onto the bed. "I also took the liberty of doing a bit of online shopping on your behalf. It's amazing what you can get with express delivery nowadays."

Christian fingered the soft leather of the first garment on the pile appreciatively. "Wow, this is so supple."

Olly rooted in a drawer then launched a small packet onto the bed. "Heath only wants Aiden wrapped in the best."

"Are you sure Aiden doesn't mind lending me his things? This is all so expensive." Christian picked up a pair of black leather trousers and held them up against himself.

"Stop worrying. He said, and I quote, 'He can borrow anything he likes'."

"But I like it all!"

"Well, it's my job to decide what you look best in. Underwear first."

Christian picked up the packets from the bed and looked at the pictures on the front. "You've made a mistake, Olly, this isn't underwear, it's a few bits of string." He turned the packet upside down in the hope that the picture might make more sense.

Olly sniggered. "Aren't they great? I got three colors. Personally I like the red, but black might suit you better."

Christian opened the packet dubiously. He didn't recognize the brand, GoodDevil, but it sounded like the kind of thing Olly would like.

"That style is called a matrix thong."

"Olly, there's nothing to cover my dick. Or my balls." Christian held up the tiny article.

"Of course not. The straps are designed to frame and show off your bits not hide them! Now put one on so we can get on with the fashion show."

"I am not parading around in front of you wearing this, Olly."

"Don't be such a wuss. I'm a nurse. I've seen more danglies in the last week than you're likely to see in a lifetime. Including Becket's!"

"Oh for pity's sake!" Christian gave up the fight and stripped off his clothes. He spent the next few minutes working out how to put on his new underwear then grabbed the first pair of trousers from the pile. The black leather clung to his legs like a second skin. There was a short exposed zipper at the front, another at the rear and the garment rode low on his hips.

"Oh yes! They look fabulous." Olly walked up and down, viewing from every angle. "Easy access, too. Okay. Next." He handed over a pair in a gorgeous shade of bitter chocolate.

"This color is gorgeous." Christian stroked the leather. "But I'm not sure it's going to go with my hair."

"You're probably right, but I wanted to see you in them anyway."

Christian squirmed out of the first pair of trousers and into the second. They weren't quite so tight and they rode a little higher. They felt great and he was less self-conscious with them on.

"Hmm." Olly looked thoughtful. "You definitely can't do that color. It's a shame 'cause they look great, though they could do with being a bit tighter. Whip 'em off. There's one more pair for you to try."

The last pair was black again with stud fastenings at the front and buckle trims around each thigh.

"These aren't as comfortable as the first pair, Olly."

Olly walked around him. "The simpler style suits you better anyway. You'd better put the first ones back on again and we'll sort out an appropriate top."

Christian was thankful that Olly was distracted by the selection of the rest of his outfit. He yanked off the trousers and pulled the first pair back on, zipping up very carefully.

"Okay, what's your preference? I have fishnet, PVC, silk…" Olly held up one garment after another.

"They're all so revealing! Don't you have anything plain? Wait… The green one's nice." Christian caught sight of a forest green top.

"Oh you have good taste… It's silk. The color will be perfect for you too. Put it on 'cause if it's too loose you're not having it."

The silk felt whisper soft against his skin, it was almost as if he wasn't wearing anything at all. Olly cooed appreciatively, "Oh yes, that's the one. God only knows how Aiden squeezed into it, he's a bit broader across the chest than you are and it's nice and snug on you."

"I don't know, Olly, it's a bit clingy." Christian looked in the mirror and hardly recognized himself. His uniform at The Underground was conservative in comparison to this.

"Don't be daft—you look stunning. You just need a bit of eyeliner and some clear gloss on your lips."

"I don't have any makeup… I'm not sure, won't it make me look like a girl?"

"Do you think I look like a girl? Or Aiden? We both wear makeup."

Christian stared at Olly's blond curls and Cupid's bow lips and was very tempted to make a sarcastic remark. He didn't. Olly was pretty but he still looked masculine in his own unique way. He couldn't recall noticing that Aiden used cosmetics, but maybe he did at the club. Lots of the subs and some of the Doms did. Christian had a sudden image of Becket wearing eyeliner and choked back laughter. Becket was one man who wouldn't be caught dead near a stick of kohl.

"All right. Just a little, though, if you can lend me something?"

"Of course. That just leaves footwear and that won't be an issue. You should go barefoot. Doms love that, it increases your vulnerability."

"Vulnerable is right, especially when they're stomping around in bloody great boots. I've always wondered how the waiting staff at The Underground don't get their toes squished more."

Olly giggled. "They learn to move fast." He checked his watch. "Wow, it's lunchtime. You'd better take that lot off—there are quite a lot of clients in this week and they're not used to the more alternative side of our business! With any luck Aiden might poke his head above ground and join us for lunch. I expect Joe and Heath will be schmoozing with the guests but we don't have to sit with them."

"Okay." Christian had forgotten all about being bashful and stripped off his clothes. Dressing in his comfortable jeans again was something of a relief even if he did catch Olly sniggering as he did up the fly with a lot of care. "Hey! If you're going to make me wear non-existent underwear, what do you expect?"

Olly skipped toward the door. "I suggest you invest in more button-fly jeans. Much safer."

Christian followed Olly to the busy staff dining room, where Aiden had snagged a small table in a corner. He waved at Christian and Olly when they joined the queue for food. Christian was too excited to be very hungry but he chose a salad and a bottle of juice then took his tray across to join Aiden. Olly wasn't far behind, balancing a bowl of vegetable soup, a hunk of granary bread and a smoothie.

Aiden raised a dark eyebrow and smirked. Olly scowled. "What? I like to eat healthily sometimes."

"Liar. You'd exist on sugar if Joe let you and you turn into a master criminal when it comes to getting your mitts on sweet things."

Olly dunked bread in his soup. "Don't listen to him, Christian, he's a spy-geek. He sees evil in everyone. Even little old me."

Aiden snorted. "How was your morning, Christian? Did you find something to wear?"

"I did. Thanks so much for lending me your stuff."

"My pleasure. I'll bet you're really looking forward to Becket getting here, aren't you?"

Christian nodded. "I am, but I'm a bit nervous too. It hasn't even been a week since he was hurt. I'm worried that he's leaving the hospital too soon."

Olly waved a spoon at him. "You don't need to worry, Becket's tough. It took a few days to rule out serious damage, but most of his injuries are relatively superficial. He'll heal quickly and I'm here if there are any problems. He has great pain medication — he'll be a happy bunny for the next few days until I wean him off the good stuff."

Christian looked at his plate and realized his salad had disappeared. He must have been hungrier than he had thought. "The worst thing about him getting better is knowing he's going back to such a dangerous job. Oh… That sounds like I don't want him well and I do, but I can't help but worry."

"You shouldn't, you know." Aiden smiled reassuringly. "Ninety-nine percent of the time Becket's job is a million miles away from danger. Talk to him. Let him know how you feel."

Olly's blond head bobbed. "Talking's good. Becket can't help you if you don't let him know what you're worrying about. If he finds out from someone else that you're fretting he'll probably give you a good spanking. Of course, that isn't much of an incentive to be more communicative…"

Aiden sighed. "Not helping, Olly. Not all of us like to have permanently glowing arses, you know."

"You don't?" Olly looked from Aiden to Christian as if he'd just been told the world was about to end.

Christian burst out laughing. "Oh, Olly, you're adorable. You're better than any medicine!"

Olly preened. "Adorable, huh?"

Aiden pushed his chair back. "I hate to break up this meeting of the Olly Appreciation Society but I have to meet Heath and head for the hospital."

"And my arse has a date with Joe's hand...or his flogger...or his cane...or maybe all three if I'm a really lucky boy!" Olly stood up eagerly. "You should go and get yourself ready, Christian. Becket will be back before you know it."

As Christian strolled back toward his room, he wondered just how much he should share with Becket. Christian had enough worries to keep a counsellor in business for weeks. He took a deep breath. Nothing was as important as Becket getting well. Everything else could wait, for a little while at least.

Chapter Nine

As Heath pulled into The Edge and parked as close to the door as he was able, Becket heaved a sigh of relief. Everyone at the hospital had been incredibly kind but that didn't stop him feeling like he'd just escaped from prison. He'd be eternally grateful to his brother. Gideon had visited Becket's flat and delivered a bag of clothes so that he could make a run for it in his own clothes rather than hospital scrubs.

Lying in his hospital bed, Becket had made a few decisions. It was amazing what clarity of thought could be brought on by close proximity to an exploding bomb. Now all he had to do was hope that those people affected by his choices would agree with his thinking.

He climbed out of the car and smiled at Aiden who was hovering close by. "I'm not going to fall over in a heap, Aiden, I promise."

Aiden looked a bit sheepish. "I was trying not to be too obvious."

Heath joined them, hefting Becket's bag onto his shoulder. "If this ugly lug fell on you, sweetheart, you'd be squashed. Stay away from him."

Becket tried not to laugh because he knew it would hurt, but it felt good to be treated normally. He could always rely on Heath to keep him firmly in the real world.

"We'll get you settled in your room and leave you be for a while." Heath didn't say 'to rest' but Becket knew it was implied. The after-effects of the trauma and the sedation had left him feeling constantly tired and even the short journey from the hospital had been wearing. He looked around, wondering where Christian was, and caught Aiden's eye.

"He's waiting for you inside."

Becket sighed. "Seems I'm another one not able to disguise what I'm up to, Aiden. I must be losing my touch."

Heath draped his arm possessively around Aiden's shoulders. "Could we not stand around out here yapping? If I don't get coffee soon things are going to get nasty."

Becket grinned. "Lead the way. I'd hate to be the cause of your deprivation."

Becket followed Heath and Aiden through the main hall and along a corridor. He'd been to The Edge many times in his capacity as Aiden's boss, but he'd always used one of the rooms reserved for course members when he'd stayed over. He wasn't familiar with this part of the building and he only noticed his surroundings out of habit. Deeply engrained training had him checking for exits and escape routes as automatically as he breathed. He tried to ignore the knot in his stomach as Heath dumped his bag outside an anonymous door.

"This is you. You'll want some privacy, so we'll leave you to it." Heath squeezed Becket's shoulder in a show of solidarity. "Enjoy. Oh, be warned. Joe is keeping Olly busy at the moment but he will be by for a visit later to check up on you and your medication."

Aiden choked back his laughter. "And he'll no doubt choose the least convenient moment to arrive. Make sure you lock the door!"

Heath towed Aiden away but shouted back over his shoulder, "Oh and get some rest because Joe is organizing dinner for the six of us. Seven o'clock at Joe and Olly's place. Christian will show you where."

Becket almost knocked on the door. He chuckled to himself. "Jesus, Becket, you're not a kid on his first date, you're a Dom with a beautiful sub waiting for you. Stop bloody talking to yourself and open the damn door!" He left his bag where it sat and turned the knob. He managed one step inside the room before he forgot how to breathe.

"Holy fuck!" For the first time since the explosion Becket had rock solid proof that all his important parts were in full working order. His cock jerked to attention and his mouth went dry. Christian looked... He looked...ravishable. Becket tried to get his mind around what he was seeing. Christian was barefoot— wearing a pair of leather trousers that were barely resisting gravity they sat so low. Front and center, a short zip begged to be lowered. Christian's shirt appeared to be painted on and it was in a beautiful shade of green that served to highlight the clear, lighter green of Christian's eyes, eyes accentuated by a smudge of dark liner. Burnished red hair shined and was the perfect length to be grabbed and pulled.

Becket was experiencing visual overload and it took a while before he realized that Christian was starting to look anxious.

Becket took a step forwards. "Mine." He pulled Christian into an unashamedly possessive kiss. He didn't want to be gentle or tender—he wanted to make sure that anyone who saw Christian later on that day would know he'd been kissed stupid. Becket dropped his hands from where they cupped the nape of Christian's neck, to his arse. He immediately found the zip that followed the line separating Christian's arse cheeks. Becket moaned into his sub's mouth before pulling away. "Fuck, Christian, are you trying to give me a relapse?"

"Sorry, Sir. Olly had a few suggestions for your welcome home. These are Aiden's clothes, not mine."

"Don't be sorry. You look perfect. We'll need to add a few things like these to your wardrobe as soon as possible."

Christian blushed prettily. "You really like them?"

"I love it. Of course, there is one problem."

"There is?"

"Yes. I need you to take the clothes off."

"Oh." Christian sounded a little disappointed.

"Because you've made me so horny I need instant access to your arse."

"Oh!" Christian became even pinker.

Becket eased toward the bed. He gathered the pillows and plumped them into a nice soft pile. "There. Now I can sit and enjoy the view while you undress." He sat on the edge of the bed and bent awkwardly, intending to take off his boots.

"Wait, Sir, let me do that." Christian sank to his knees and began to undo Becket's laces.

All Becket could see was leather pulling tight across Christian's thighs. He was feeling very warm and it had nothing to do with fever. Once his boots and socks had been dealt with, Becket swiveled around and settled into his nest of pillows. "Lock the door, Christian, I don't want any interruptions. Oh—I left my bag in the corridor."

Christian fetched the holdall and put it at the foot of the bed, then closed and locked the door.

"You look nervous, sweetheart. Don't be."

Christian shuffled his feet and examined the carpet. "I just... Shouldn't you be resting?"

"Who makes the decisions in this relationship, Christian?"

"You do, Sir."

"Then trust me. I promise I'll let you know if I get tired, okay?"

"Yes, Sir."

"Good. Now come and stand where I can see you properly. Calm down. All you have to do is follow my orders."

Christian visibly relaxed as soon as all the weight of responsibility left him. He stood straight, hands clasped loosely behind his back, eyes cast down.

"I want you to look at me, Christian, can you do that?" Becket wanted to watch Christian's expression as he submitted.

Christian met his gaze, unflinching. Becket undid the button at his waistband and lowered his fly. His aching cock needed a bit of space but he left his underwear in place. The boxers he had on were loose enough to allow tenting and he liked the feeling of silk against his hot skin. Becket didn't betray his pleasure with a smile—he schooled his features into a stern mask. "Take your top off."

Christian pulled the fabric over his head, tousling his hair nicely, then put it to one side. Becket itched to stroke the dark red strands back into place but settled for admiring Christian's toned physique. "You've lost a little weight."

"Yes, Sir. I haven't had much appetite."

"I worried you." Becket pushed down the guilt. He was around to look after his sub properly now. Christian wouldn't be missing any more meals. "You'll eat healthily from now on, Christian. That's an order."

"Yes, Sir."

"You still look stunning. I just wish I had a couple of clamps to decorate you with."

"Um, Sir?"

Becket raised an eyebrow.

"If you look in the drawer next to you, I think Heath left some things he thought you might need."

Becket pulled open the small drawer in the bedside cabinet and grinned. "Heath's been very thoughtful." He pulled out lube, a set of clamps and a heavy locking steel cock ring. He laid them neatly on the bed and glanced at Christian. "Time to get you bare. Trousers off."

Christian's hands were noticeably trembling as he lowered the short zip at the front of his trousers. Becket enjoyed the squirming and wriggling very much as Christian divested himself of the clinging leather. The discarded garment was pushed away with a bare foot, then Christian straightened. Becket swallowed and tried to find appropriate words. He came up short. "You shaved."

Christian's cock jutted proudly forwards supported by what appeared to be a piece of black string. His balls were circled by another black strip. Narrow straps rested on his hips.

"Is that supposed to be underwear? No, don't answer that. Whatever it is, I like it." Becket moistened his lips. "Turn around."

Christian pirouetted gracefully. Becket sucked in his breath. He was dangerously close to coming there and then.

"You're plugged?" He could clearly see that Christian was. "Bend over."

Christian spread his legs a little, bent at the waist and pushed his arse out. Becket had an overwhelming desire to leave his mark on the pristine skin.

"Take that piece of string off and come here. Straddle my thighs."

"Yes, Sir." Christian pulled off the skimpy thong and clambered onto the bed, settling into position with his legs spread wide across Becket's thighs.

It's a good job I'm not still attached to a heart rate monitor because the bloody thing would have blown a fuse by now. "You did all this for me?"

Christian rested a hand on each thigh. "Yes, Sir."

Becket shook his head in disbelief. "I don't deserve you. I've left you alone, failed to look after you, frightened you half to death and still you give yourself to me without reservation."

"I'm yours, Sir. Whatever that means is fine with me."

"Things are going to change, Christian. We have a lot to discuss. But first I intend to take full advantage of all your preparations."

Becket picked up the cock ring and warmed the metal in his hand before putting it carefully in place. Christian twitched as the thick steel band clicked shut.

"Oh that looks pretty. Move a bit nearer so I can get these clamps on." They were the type that screwed closed. Becket pinched one of Christian's nipples gently until it hardened. He seated a clamp and fixed it on tightly. A little hiss of air escaped Christian's lips, but that was the only thing that betrayed what he was feeling.

"How's that? Too tight?"

"Aches, Sir."

"Good, it's meant to." Becket got the second clamp into place. "Perfect." He lifted his hips and shoved his trousers and underwear down enough to release his cock. "Get me ready." He handed Christian the lube even though he wasn't sure if he could bear his lover's touch. *Perhaps I'd have been better off putting that cock ring on me.* He drew on every ounce of his self-control as Christian smoothed lube onto Becket's rigid shaft. Holding his breath helped.

"Take the plug out and slick yourself, Christian. This is going to be fast and hard, and I don't want to hurt you."

Watching Christian thrust two fingers into his own passage was too much. Becket had to close his eyes. When he thought enough time had passed he lifted one eyelid carefully. Christian was smiling at him.

"Thank God. I can't wait a second longer. Come here."

Christian shuffled forwards on his knees until he was lined up perfectly. Becket grabbed his hips and applied pressure so that Christian sank onto him. There was only a little resistance as Becket penetrated his lover. Christian still felt tight even though the plug had stretched him. The heat and closeness was glorious. Much as he wanted to jerk his hips, Becket was realistic. This time, he would have to allow Christian to do the work.

"Fuck yourself on me, sweetheart. Keep your eyes on mine." Becket kept his hands on Christian's hips as his sub lifted and dropped rapidly, over and over again. Christian's lips twisted into a grimace.

"You want to come, Christian? I need to hear you beg."

"It hurts, Sir, my cock aches. Please... Please let me come."

Becket concentrated on holding himself back. It was impossible. The perfect heat of Christian's passage, the grip of his inner muscles, the teeth worrying his swollen lower lip, the delicious whimpering... Becket came hard.

Christian's eyes widened as Becket shot deep inside him. "Oh, Sir... Thank you. Yes... Fill me so full... Love you inside me..."

Becket pulled Christian in for a kiss, his body still shuddering with the aftershock of orgasm. His lover tasted so sweet, so perfect and he'd gone to so much trouble. Becket would love to keep him wanting and needy but he couldn't be that evil, not on their first day back together.

"Would you like my mouth, beautiful?"

Christian froze. "Sir?"

Becket chuckled. "Put that gorgeous dick of yours in my mouth."

"But you're... I'm... You don't..."

"Christian, stop talking and do as you're told."

That got through. Christian went up on his knees so that his cock was level with Becket's mouth.

"Brace yourself on the wall and don't move." Becket left the cock ring in place and lapped at the leaking tip presented to his lips. "Mmm. You taste like salted caramel." He licked again then took Christian's full length into his mouth. Well, until his teeth clicked on metal. He savored the taste and withdrew slowly, dragging his teeth lightly.

Christian gasped. "Sir! It's too good. Please."

Becket leaned back. He undid the steel ring that was the only thing preventing Christian from coming then took his sub's hot shaft back into his mouth. Apart from a slight tremble, Christian did as he had been ordered and didn't move. Becket was completely in control. What could have been a submissive act was totally dominant.

"Sir... I can't... Oh God!" Christian tried to pull back but Becket grabbed his hips and held him firmly in place. Salty cream filled his mouth and he swallowed it with relish. Becket kept sucking as his sub's dick softened in his mouth. He held Christian's hips too tight, every fingertip digging in. Christian would have bruises. Becket smiled. He liked the thought of his marks on Christian's pristine skin. Belatedly he realized that Christian's thighs were shaking. He lowered him gently, supporting him all the way. "Okay?"

Christian's sated smile was worth the twinges Becket could feel in his lower back.

"Oh yes, Sir."

Becket stroked Christian's abs with the backs of his fingers. "I suppose some conversation would have been polite, rather than me jumping you as soon as I got through the door?"

"I'd greet you like this every day if I could, Sir."

"I'd like that." Becket imagined how wonderful it would be to come home to Christian, naked and ready for him. "You wouldn't be allowed to wear clothes in the house if you lived with me."

"That would cut down on the laundry bills, Sir."

Becket was impressed. Christian didn't seem at all phased by the idea.

"I'm looking forward to spending time with you, Christian. Getting to know you better—and I don't just mean physically. If something good has come from being blown up then it's having a few weeks off to recover."

Christian's face clouded and his clear eyes dimmed. He clambered off the bed. "I should go and clean up. I'll get you a warm flannel first, Sir."

Becket let him go to the bathroom then allowed Christian to clean him up but when he turned to go back to the shower Becket stopped him.

"Are you going to tell me what's wrong or do I have to spank it out of you?"

Christian stopped dead. "What do you mean, Sir?"

"Don't play the innocent with me, sweetheart. Something's bothering you, it's bloody obvious. What are you hiding?"

"I'm not... I mean, it's not something I want to worry you with, Sir."

Becket patted the bed. "Come here." He could see Christian fighting his instinct to obey.

He hesitated for just a few seconds, then his shoulders slumped and he came back to the bed.

"Get under the covers, you're shivering."

Becket shuffled over a little and when Christian slipped beneath the sheets he pulled him close. He stroked his hair slowly. "Now. Talk to me."

Christian kept his face hidden. "I can't stay, Sir. I want to, but I can't."

Becket had to make an effort to keep his voice calm. "Can you tell me why?"

"You shouldn't have to worry about me, Sir. You're here to recover."

"Christian, listen to me. I'm your Dom. Your master. You know how this works, don't you? I want to help you, protect you. If you're in trouble…"

"It's nothing that dramatic, Sir."

Becket started to feel impatient. "Christian, by the end of today I fully intend to have you tied into a contract. A twenty-four seven agreement. You're mine and that makes me responsible for your well-being."

Christian looked up at him from beneath his lashes. "A contract? Really?"

"Really. And whatever you say next is not going to make the slightest difference to that, so tell me why you think you're going to leave me here alone." Becket tightened his hold on Christian as if wrapping him up in a hug could prevent him from escaping.

"If I don't get back to work by tomorrow, I'm going to lose my job. I'm already behind on my rent, so the chances are I'll be homeless too. I don't have any choice, Sir, I have to go home."

"Carey is *not* going to sack you for being here with me, love."

"Oh, I know that, Sir. Carey's been wonderful—he's still paying me even though I'm not there. No, I'm talking about my other job."

"You have another job? How the hell do you manage that with the hours you work at The Underground?"

"I work at a café in the mornings and on my day off, Sir. It's the only way I can make the rent since my flatmate left. I haven't been able to find anyone to share yet."

Becket frowned. It was no wonder that Christian looked tired all the time. "Are you particularly attached to your flat?"

"No, Sir, it's a place to sleep. I like the area because it's within walking distance of The Underground. I can't afford a car."

Becket stroked Christian's shoulder. "You'll move in with me. You'll give up the second job so that you have more time to study."

"But, Sir, I don't want to take advantage."

"It wasn't a suggestion, Christian." Becket gave Christian a cuddle to take the edge off the demand. "I'm possessive. I want you where I can keep an eye on you. I want you happy and healthy."

Christian relaxed and sighed imperceptibly. Becket just felt the little rush of air against his neck. "You've been carrying all this worry around with you for a long time, haven't you, love? And I should have noticed. One more thing to add to my list of shitty behavior."

"None of it's your fault, Sir."

"If I'd been around more… Still, no point in worrying over what's gone. We can make today a new start for both of us."

"I'd like that, Sir." Christian squirmed and cuddled closer. Becket wished he'd taken more clothes off but he didn't want to dislodge the warm, naked body pressed against him.

Chapter Ten

Christian woke feeling cozy and cherished. Becket's arm encircled his waist tightly. He would not be able to get up without disturbing him but he didn't really want to move anyway. He glanced at the clock on the bedside table. Luminous green numbers told him that if he didn't extract himself from Becket's hold he would be late for his gym date with Aiden and Olly. At dinner the previous night it had seemed like a good idea. The Edge had a great gym, and with the latest course group due to leave, Aiden had said it would be empty. Now Christian regretted his enthusiasm. The only physical exertion that he wanted to engage in at that moment involved climbing Becket's solid body.

Becket stirred next to him. Christian gasped as Becket stroked his arse, his fingers brushing the back of Christian's balls.

"Didn't you arrange to meet Aiden and the brat in the gym this morning?" Becket's voice was husky from sleep.

"Yes, Sir. But I can stay here if you'd prefer."

Becket patted Christian's backside gently. "No. You go. I'll sleep in for a bit. If you could just leave my painkillers within reach, that would be great."

"Okay." Christian slipped out of bed reluctantly. He padded to the bathroom for a quick wash and brush up, then pulled on shorts and an old T-shirt. When he got back to the bedroom, Becket was propped up on his pillows, leering.

"You look good in those."

Christian swallowed. The look Becket directed at him was making him hard and there wasn't a lot of room in his borrowed shorts. Becket chuckled. "I think you need to go and work off some excess energy, love."

"That's so unfair, Sir. Look what you've done to me!"

Becket smirked. "Me? I'm just lying here, completely innocent."

Christian choked back a laugh—he doubted Becket had been innocent much past his third birthday. He put a fresh glass of water on the nightstand and shook out a couple of tablets from a bottle.

"Olly left a sheet of instructions." Christian waved a piece of pink paper. "He drew little flowers all over it."

Becket snorted. "He'll no doubt be back to torment me this morning."

"And you'll be nice to him. He knows what he's doing and you wouldn't be here if Olly wasn't around to keep an eye on you." Christian blinked, he wasn't normally so assertive. "Sorry, Sir."

Becket just smiled. "You're my submissive, Christian, not my doormat. I want you to say what you think, and I love how fierce you are when it comes to my well-being." He grinned wickedly. "It's quite a turn-on."

Christian's cock jerked. He groaned. "No! Don't say that..."

"Go. I'll deal with you when you get back." The promise in those words didn't help Christian at all.

With some regret, Christian left Becket in bed and trotted along the corridor from their room to the entrance hall. The Edge's gym was housed in a converted outbuilding just around the corner from Joe and Olly's little house, so he took the back door out of the main building and crossed the courtyard. It was a drizzly morning and Christian had no wish to get soaked, so he picked up his pace and dashed through the gym door bringing a flurry of cold air with him. He caught his breath and looked around. Aiden was already on the treadmill, running at what looked to be a very daunting pace. He still managed a wave. Olly sat on a floor mat. He looked like he was practicing to be a contortionist.

"Wow, Olly, you're flexible!"

Olly beamed. "Have you seen Joe's bondage sling? I need to be bendy, I can tell you!" He unfolded himself and stretched out on the mat. "How's Dave this morning?"

"Good thanks. I left him his pain meds but he was going to go back to sleep for a while."

Olly nodded. "Good. He needs lots of rest and gentle exercise. I'm going to bring him over here for a while later. He can walk on the treadmill if Aiden doesn't blow it up."

Aiden snorted and kept running. "I'd rather be outside but I haven't got time. Have to get to work soon."

Christian looked on in admiration as Aiden turned the machine to a faster speed.

"Ignore him, Christian, he's just showing off." Olly got up and fetched a giant purple exercise ball. "He needs to be able to run fast to get away from Heath."

Christian did a few stretches then input some settings to the Stairmaster. He started slowly, letting his muscles warm. There was music playing in the background with a nice regular beat and he soon got into his stride. "It feels good to move. Since Becket's…accident, I've been wading in treacle. Everything slowed down."

Olly sat on his ball and bounced a little. "Well, from what Joe tells me you've been running yourself ragged for months. Slowing down will do you good, even if it's not under the best of circumstances."

"I feel so useless, Olly. Becket has rescued me from being homeless. Carey is practically supporting me financially, even though I've left him in the lurch, and I've given up my second job now too. I called the café owner last night. Joe and Heath are feeding me and I'm wearing Aiden's clothes. You look after Becket much better than I can. What use am I?" He kept pumping his legs up and down—it was a useful distraction.

Aiden powered down his machine and slowed to a walk. "You really are an idiot, Christian. Who do you think Becket would rather have in his room with him, you or motor mouth?"

"Hey!" Olly protested.

"Well, me I suppose, but…"

"No buts. We're your friends and this is what friends do. Look after each other. Joe and Heath would be mightily pissed off if they thought you'd rather be anywhere else, and Carey… Well, Carey's loaded. He can afford to give you paid time off. And anyway, can you imagine the grief Alistair would give him if he did anything else? Alistair loves you to bits. We all do."

Christian stopped his machine. "I don't want to seem ungrateful. I can't believe how wonderful you've all been. I'm just used to being busy. You both have important jobs and I can't even keep a roof over my head."

Olly started doing press-ups on his ball. "You have an important job too. The Underground would fall apart without you. Next to Carey, you're the glue that holds that place together. I'll bet you have no idea how many friends you have at that place—Doms and subs."

"All I do is let people in. Anyone could do that."

"No they couldn't. Can you imagine Heath trying to do your job? Smiling and welcoming people? The Underground's membership would halve overnight he'd frighten so many people away."

Aiden chuckled. "Olly's right. Heath's far too intimidating. You have a knack of making everyone feel good. You put people at ease." He grabbed a towel from where it rested on a weights bench and slung it around his shoulders. "Don't put yourself down." He rubbed at his face and neck. "If you like, I can talk to Heath and see if there's anything he needs doing around The Edge. Business is growing all the time thanks to the contract we have with the security services and I know he's really busy."

Christian wandered over to the treadmill that Aiden had just vacated. "That would be great, Aiden. Thanks."

"You know he'll discuss it with Becket first?"

"Of course. I'll tell him when I get back to the room anyway. I'm sure he won't mind."

"Okay, well, I'll see you both at lunchtime hopefully. Don't let Olly anywhere near the weights. He's a danger to himself and others if he gets a set of barbells in his hands."

Olly huffed. "It was one time. My hands were slippery and it wasn't my fault that your foot just happened to be in the path of the trajectory."

"Olly, you were swinging that thing backwards and forwards and having a conversation with yourself about the merits of hanging weights from your balls."

Christian nearly fell off the treadmill.

Olly glared at Aiden. "Well, Joe used those dangly little lead ones on me and it felt really, really good and I was just wondering how many more he had hidden away and the barbell just got away from me. How can that be my fault?"

Aiden just raised an eyebrow. "I'm going for a shower. Christian, you have been warned." He got to the door then turned back. "Oh, and don't let him use his big puppy dog eyes on you either." He slipped around the door before Olly could respond.

Christian jogged steadily, smiling. "Look on the bright side, Olly. Aiden thinks you have puppy dog eyes."

Olly batted his lashes. "I do, don't I? They just don't work on Mr Brain-the-size-of-a-planet."

"Do they work on Joe?"

"Nope, and if I try it, he blindfolds me. He's such a spoilsport."

Christian laughed. "He really has your number, doesn't he?"

"He's a psychologist. He has X-ray vision. He can see right into my mind, I swear."

Christian started to feel a little breathless. His calves and thighs burned and he was sweating freely. "I don't think it has anything to do with psychology, it's a Dom thing. Becket always seems to know what I need, sometimes before I know myself."

Olly pushed his ball into a corner. "You love him."

Christian put the treadmill into a cool down mode and slowed his pace. The truth of Olly's words sent a pulse of desire to his cock. "I do."

"There, that wasn't so hard, was it? Have you told him?"

Christian shook his head. "No. I think I've been denying it until now."

Olly giggled. "Look at that... I've given you a revelation moment! Becket gave you a contract last night, didn't he?"

Christian shut down his machine. He stepped off the belt then did a few gentle stretches. "He gave me the paperwork and said I should think about it overnight. We're going to talk about it this morning. I have to admit, I'm a little nervous about it. What if I have a limit that Becket doesn't like, or he has something non-negotiable that I don't want to do?"

Olly looked serious. "You shouldn't worry. Becket wouldn't have offered you a contract if he didn't think you were compatible. You've already played together enough times to give you an idea of what he likes— has Becket ever done anything that wasn't your thing?"

"No... But..."

"But nothing. Becket loves you. Even his poker face can't hide it. He'll want your contract to be something you are both happy with."

Christian chewed on his lip. "I think I'll go back to the room to shower."

"You do that! Get all wet and soapy. Forget to take shampoo or something into the bathroom so you have to wander out to the bedroom, all glistening and naked. Make sure you have to bend over to fetch it... Then give Becket one of those sweet little smiles you're so good at. He'll melt into a big macho puddle of goo. Guaranteed."

Christian rolled his eyes. "Olly, you should be ashamed of yourself."

Olly flicked a curl away from his eyes. "I have no shame. Everyone knows that."

Christian left Olly in the gym and headed back to the main building. He missed Becket, even though they'd been apart less than an hour. When he pushed open their door he was surprised to see the bed empty. "Sir? Where are you?"

To his relief, Becket emerged from the bathroom, shirtless and gorgeous. For a moment, Christian was too tongue-tied to speak. "You're up!"

Becket grinned. "Evidently. As are you, it seems."

Christian immediately covered his burgeoning erection with his hands.

"Hands behind your back, sweetheart. There's nothing you should be hiding from me."

Christian grasped his wrist to stop his hands from shaking as he did as he'd been told. An order from his Dom just made him harder and he really wished his borrowed shorts were made of less flimsy material.

"That's better. Now, did you enjoy your session in the gym?"

Christian shuffled his feet. "Yes, Sir, running felt really good, though I'm not nearly fit enough. Did you know that Olly once dropped a barbell on Aiden?"

Becket chuckled. "I didn't, but nothing Olly gets up to could ever surprise me. Remove your shorts and T-shirt."

Christian was certain that interspersing regular conversation with orders was Becket's way of keeping him off balance. He kicked off his footwear then stripped down to his jockstrap. His dick was tenting the triangle of white cotton. He shivered, but it had nothing to do with the temperature in the room, which was pleasantly warm. He wished Becket would put a shirt on because it was really, really difficult to concentrate on presenting himself properly with that muscled chest on display. "I do love the way a jockstrap displays the arse, don't you? Nicely framed, but accessible." Becket prowled. There was no other way to describe the way he moved, circling Christian as if he were prey.

I'm probably blushing all over – my arse cheeks feel as hot as my face. Christian swallowed back a moan as Becket brushed his fingers across a bare shoulder.

"I really need a shower, Sir."

"All in good time. I think I'd like to warm that pretty backside of yours first. When we are negotiating our contract later, I want you to be very aware that I already own you. Nothing on a piece of paper will change that. If you suddenly decide to convert to vanilla, you'll still be mine."

Christian felt warm inside as well as out. "Even if there are things you like that I don't, Sir?" He cast his eyes down.

Becket lifted his chin and met his eyes.

"Have you been worrying about this since last night?"

"A little, Sir. I don't want to disappoint you."

Becket stroked his lips with the pad of his thumb. Christian opened for his master and was rewarded with a thorough kiss that set his groin to tingling. Becket was very close. Christian wanted to touch, but didn't dare. Becket stepped back and smiled. Before Christian could analyze the look, Becket slipped his hand down the front of Christian's jock and grasped his rigid cock. "Stop worrying. That's an order." He started to play with the tip of Christian's dick, circling the head with his thumb.

Every muscle in Christian's lower body locked into place. He knew that even a millimeter of movement would push him over the edge and Becket hadn't given him permission to come. It was so hard not to thrust into Becket's warm grip. Christian moaned. "Sir, please... I'm going to come if you keep doing that."

"No, you're not. You'll come when I say you can and not before." Becket gave Christian's dick a little tug.

Christian followed him meekly to the end of the bed.

"Spread your legs and bend over. Brace yourself on the bed." Becket didn't let go of him. He kept one hand wrapped loosely around Christian's aching cock and stroked his arse with the other. "It's a double-edged sword, isn't it? You want to come but you know you'll disappoint me if you do. You crave the release but submitting to my will gives you an even bigger rush."

Christian whimpered as Becket circled his hole with a blunt fingertip. "Sir! Please..."

"I know you love this, Christian. You enjoy strict control more than any sub I've ever met and you are beautiful in your submission. You are perfect for me."

Trapped between Becket's hands, Christian felt lightheaded. He was close to subspace. Only the vague anxiety in the back of his mind that Becket shouldn't overdo things stopped him from giving up all control.

"Stop worrying about me and let go, Christian. The only reason you're not over my lap right now is because I'm being careful."

Becket pushed the dry tip of his finger into Christian's hole. The slight burn of the penetration served its purpose. Becket had control of Christian's pleasure and his pain. The last shreds of worry faded and Christian let himself drift into semi-awareness. When Becket's hand connected with his arse for the first time, the warmth that blossomed across his skin also filled his heart. Each blow took him deeper. The intimate sting was delicious and he pushed his arse out to meet Becket's hand, craving the contact. Becket's judgment of how much he could take was perfect.

As pleasure began to edge into pain, Becket landed a final hit that caught the back of Christian's balls. At the same time, Becket grasped Christian's cock and squeezed. "Come for me, love."

It was a command that Christian had no problem obeying. He shot hard, the fire of release just as hot as the skin on his backside.

"There now. Come to your master." Becket guided him round to sit on the edge of the bed and wrapped him up in a warm hug. Christian registered the soreness as his arse made contact with the bed but it didn't matter because Becket's bare chest was pressed hard against him. He was safe. Held tightly by the man he loved. It took Christian a while to come back to the real world. Becket soothed him with whispered words and gentle strokes.

"I'm so proud of you. You gave me everything."

Christian mumbled a thank you and Becket chuckled. "You're not quite back yet, are you? Let's get you in the shower and then I'll rub some salve into your skin. We can rest together."

It was the beat of hot water on his sensitized skin that gently pulled Christian out of subspace. The spray wasn't hard, but it still stung. Becket angled the spray away from the cubicle door and leaned into the shower to soap him down. "If it wasn't for the dressings, I'd be in there with you. Can you manage the shampoo?"

Christian nodded. The soft lather slipped between his fingers like a caress. When Christian was done, Becket held his hand as he stepped from the shower onto the bath mat. A warm towel was ready and waiting and Becket patted him dry carefully. Christian rubbed the drips from his hair until it was just damp.

"Leave the towel, I want you bare."

Christian followed Becket back to the bed and lay down on his front, cushioning his head on his arms. Becket retrieved a tube of salve from the dresser and smoothed it into Christian's skin. "How's that? I think you'll feel me for a while."

"S'good, Sir. Like feeling you." Christian felt sleepy and content. "You want my mouth, Sir? Or my arse?"

"This was for you, sweetheart, I'm good. Stop thinking and sleep."

There was rustling as Becket undressed, then the mattress dipped. Christian turned onto his side and wriggled back until he made contact with Becket's body. He needed as much contact as possible. Becket pulled him close. "There now. Your master's here. Rest."

His mind clear of worry, Christian smiled to himself and drifted off to sleep.

Becket shifted a little, getting as comfortable as possible. Even with the painkillers he'd taken numbing his senses, the bruising that patterned his back was sore. He allowed a small, self-satisfied smile to play over his lips. Christian was incredibly responsive and beautifully submissive. He wasn't over-trained, which Becket liked. He wanted to mold Christian carefully. He wasn't the heavy clay of stoneware, more the fine china clay of delicate porcelain and he needed gentle handling.

Becket let Christian sleep for an hour. Though he closed his eyes, he didn't sleep himself. His body still needed rest but his mind was far too awake to shut off. He was tempted to ring Aiden and ask about the Temple Church investigation but Christian stirred and as he gradually came back to the land of the living he pressed even closer to Becket. Becket grinned. In his semi-awake state, Christian didn't temper his embrace in concern for Becket's injuries, he clung on like a limpet and it felt good.

"Hello, Sir." Christian's stomach growled. "How long have I been asleep?"

"Only an hour or so. If we're lucky we can probably still get some breakfast in the restaurant."

"Mm. Sounds good. Crispy bacon… Hot buttered toast… Oh, and coffee! Lots of strong coffee." He rolled over and fixed Becket with a stare. "You're not going to stop me drinking coffee, are you, Sir?"

"Is that one of your hard limits?" Becket laughed.

"I like my coffee, Sir." Christian mumbled. "Joe doesn't let Olly drink it."

"That's because caffeine turns Olly into even more of a menace than he already is. He shouldn't be allowed to sniff a coffee bean, let alone take a sip."

"True. He does get a little…hyper."

Becket snorted. "You are the master of understatement, but to assuage your fears, no, I won't stop you drinking coffee."

"Thank God!" Christian sagged back against his pillows with a relieved sigh.

Chuckling to himself, Becket swung his legs out of bed and got up carefully. "I have a couple of phone calls I need to make. Heath said I could use his office this morning, so I'll see you downstairs in twenty minutes."

"Okay, Sir. If I'm there first, what would you like me to get you?"

"I don't eat a lot of eggs, but everything else is good. I feel hungrier than I have in a while—must be getting better! Oh…and a nice big mug of coffee."

Becket pulled on a T-shirt over his jeans and dug around for some socks. He sat on the edge of the bed and looked at his bare feet in annoyance. They were too far away. "Christian, could you help me? Socks are still something of a challenge."

He'd barely blinked before a gorgeous, naked Christian was kneeling at his feet.

"My pleasure, Sir. I like your feet."

What could have been a humiliating experience turned into something vaguely erotic as Christian rolled the socks on almost as if he were rolling a condom onto Becket's shaft.

Instead of getting up, Christian crawled across the room and fetched Becket's boots. Becket ripped his gaze away from Christian's still pink arse and looked studiously at the ceiling. He shoved his feet into his boots and Christian did up the buckles. "All done, Sir."

"I don't know how you managed it, but I think you just turned black wool socks into sex toys." Becket stood up and had to reach into his trousers to adjust his swelling cock.

Christian giggled. Becket looked down at him and was satisfied to see that Christian was also hard. "You did that on purpose, didn't you? Well, I will have my revenge. No touching yourself. If you come before you meet me downstairs, you *will* be punished. That's a promise."

Christian cast his eyes down meekly but Becket caught the twitch of a smile. As he left the room, he wondered just how much advice Christian had been taking from Olly.

Chapter Eleven

Becket walked steadily along the corridor to the entrance hall. His measured pace was carefully chosen. Any slower and he would feel like an invalid, quicker and the twinges of complaint from his back and legs made him bad-tempered. He hated the idea that he couldn't protect his beautiful lover. Becket grunted, "Couldn't protect a cabbage at the moment. Christian thinks he should be looking after me. The world's been blown upside down by that fucking bomb."

Heath's office door was ajar but Becket knocked before he pushed it open. "Heath? Are you in here?" Rustling and cursing said that he was.

Heath's dark head appeared from behind the desk. "Hey, Becket, come on in. There's so much paperwork around this place and I just knocked a whole pile of it onto the bloody floor. I'll get out of your hair in a minute — you still want to use the phone?"

"Please. Need to call the boss in London. I can come back…"

"No, no." Heath stood with an armful of folders and papers. "It's fine. If I don't get out of here soon I'll go crazy. I swear I have enough paper cuts that they're turning into a life-threatening condition."

Becket chuckled. "That busy, huh?"

Heath dragged his fingers through his hair. "I need a secretary. Actually… Aiden mentioned this morning that Christian asked if there was anything he could do around the place. I said I would have to talk to you…"

"He's feeling guilty. Thinks he's taking advantage of everyone's generosity."

"Bollocks. I hope you've put him right?" Heath scowled.

"Of course, but helping you out might be the perfect solution. Did you know he's nearly finished his degree with the Open University?"

"Impressive. What subject?"

"History."

"Excellent. If he can get his head around civil war battle strategies he can get his head around my admin. The two topics are remarkably similar."

"There speaks a desperate man." Becket grinned. "I'll send him to see you this afternoon, if that's okay. We have some contract negotiations to sort out first."

"Between four and five would be good, I'll have time then to give him the quick and dirty introduction to management at The Edge. He can decide his working hours with you, but any time he can contribute will be gratefully accepted. Now, I will go and hunt down a decent cup of coffee in Joe's office and put my feet up while you make your call. He's teaching so he'll probably blame Olly when he comes back to an empty coffee pot. Life is good." He sauntered out of the office with a wicked smile and pushed the door closed.

Becket took the seat behind Heath's desk and glared at the telephone as if it were a mortal enemy. He rolled his shoulders then picked up the receiver and dialed Josephine Cornish's direct line. His boss was a formidable woman and even a phone conversation had to be taken seriously. She picked up the phone after two rings.

"What?"

"Morning, ma'am. Sounds like you are your usual cheerful self," Becket said.

"Becket. All your important parts still intact?"

Becket knew that was as close to sympathy as he was likely to get. "Yes, ma'am. Everything's in working order."

"Glad to hear it. When are you coming back to work?"

"The doc says it will be another five weeks before she'll sign me as fit."

"Five weeks! I don't recall any amputations. I need you back, Becket, even if I have to park your arse behind a desk. Your protégée makes slower progress without you breathing down his neck and we still haven't caught those bloody terrorist wannabes."

"Well, that's partly why I was ringing you, ma'am. Perhaps we can come to some kind of compromise?" Becket held his breath then exhaled slowly.

"Spill it, Becket. Wait, am I going to need to get the bottle out of my bottom drawer?"

Becket sighed, "Probably, ma'am." He paused, not for effect but because he needed to summon his courage. "I want to give up fieldwork."

Becket heard the sound of a drawer sliding open, then the clink of glass. He grinned and waited for a verbal response.

"Way to make a girl's day, Becket. What the hell? You were born for fieldwork. You love it and, much as it pains me to say it out loud, you're bloody good at it."

"What can I say? Things change. This latest incident has been something of a wake-up call."

"Don't bullshit me, Becket, this has nothing to do with a sudden aversion to danger, does it?"

Becket felt hot. He didn't really want to discuss his private life with his boss, but she was like a terrier down a rabbit hole. She wasn't going to give up.

"I have someone else to consider now."

"And he's pressuring you to park your arse in a nice cozy office, is he?"

"No, ma'am! He doesn't even know I'm making this call."

"Is anything I say going to make any difference to your decision?"

"No, ma'am, I'm afraid not." Becket pressed the handset to his ear so hard that he risked a headache.

"Fine. I'll move you to a desk job. It'll probably be something really hideous, just to make me feel better. Oh, and if that boyfriend of yours talks some sense into you, let me know. I assume I'll be getting a security clearance form for him?"

"Yes, ma'am. No secrets from this one. He'll be moving in with me—to my real home, not the fake one."

"Can I be happy for you and pissed off at the same time?"

"Yes, ma'am."

"Fine. Get back to recuperating—I want you back in three weeks, not five. Bloody quacks get commission on every week they sign people off for, I swear. Call me next week."

The dial tone told Becket that the conversation had ended.

Frowning, Becket replaced the receiver and slumped back in Heath's chair. He felt no relief and a little knot of disquiet settled in his gut. "It's for the best." Perhaps if he said it often enough, he'd be convinced. Regardless, it was something he had to do for Christian. His gorgeous sub was worth a lifetime of paper-pushing boredom. *Lifetime – that has a nice ring to it.* The tension eased a little. "Breakfast is calling. Better go before Christian eats all the bacon." Becket stood up, accepted the slight twinge his body rewarded him with and strolled out to the hall. He tapped on Joe's office door and pushed it open. "Hey, Heath, I'm done, thanks. You want to come and join Christian and me for a late breakfast?"

Heath looked up from the papers he was reading. "It's tempting, but no. I need to get on and I haven't quite drained Joe's coffee supply yet. Good luck with the contract negotiations."

"Thanks. See you later." Becket pushed the door to then headed for the restaurant.

He spotted Christian straight away, sitting with Olly.

"Hello, Sir. Is everything all right at work?"

Becket nodded. "Fine. Have you eaten yet?"

"No, Sir. I put an order in with the chef but said to keep it warm until you arrived. I hope that's okay?"

"Perfect. Olly, do you have some place to be?"

Olly giggled. "You are the master of subtlety, Becket. I was just keeping Christian company because you left him all alone. I will make my cute self scarce. Don't forget you have physio this afternoon."

"Scram, brat."

Olly poked his tongue out and ran.

Christian pushed his chair back and stood up. "You love him too, don't you, Sir?"

"I'm not admitting to anything that may later be used in evidence against me. He probably has the place bugged. Now, let's get our food, I'm starving."

There was no queue at the serving counter but one of Emile's staff was hovering expectantly.

"Hi, you should have our orders somewhere," Christian said.

"*Oui*. Just give me a minute." The server disappeared through a swing door into the kitchen. He reappeared a few seconds later hefting a tray laden with food. "Emile thinks the both of you need feeding up, so there are a few extras on here. *Bon appetit!*"

Christian took the tray and staggered under its weight. "Oh boy, this should keep us going for a while!"

Becket patted his shoulder. "I'll get some drinks — juice okay?"

Christian swung back toward the table. "Orange, please."

Christian put the tray down and began to unload the various plates with their metal covers. Becket joined him and took a seat, placing two brimming glasses of freshly squeezed juice on the table.

"I think Emile has a soft spot for you." He lifted the lid of a plate of blueberry pancakes. "I can put up with that so long as the side benefits keep landing in my stomach."

"Wow! Eggs Benedict... I just asked for poached, and look at this crispy bacon. Yum."

Becket laughed at Christian's enthusiasm. "We'll both be the size of houses."

Christian started pushing a portion of fried potatoes, grilled tomatoes and mushrooms onto his plate.

"You'll just have to make sure I get plenty of exercise, Sir." He looked up innocently but Becket detected the glint of humor in Christian's eyes.

"I've heard that sex burns loads of calories."

Becket grinned. "Well, in that case, don't hold back."

Fifteen minutes later, Becket wiped the last smear of ketchup from his plate with a corner of toast and sat back with a sigh. "I may not eat again for a week."

Christian laughed. "I definitely need to keep on Emile's good side."

"And mine." Becket sat up straighter. "We have some paperwork to discuss."

Christian instantly became more serious. "Yes, Sir."

"Let's head back to our room so we can talk in comfort." Becket got up and Christian followed, walking precisely at heel.

"One day soon, I'll clamp your nipples and attach a chain to lead you with. Would you like that?"

"If it gives you pleasure, Sir."

Becket chuckled. "A lot of things give me pleasure, Christian, as you're about to find out."

Their room had been cleaned while they'd been gone and the bed freshly made. Becket nodded his approval. The Edge was an efficiently run organization, something that showed in a myriad of tiny details.

"Plump some pillows and make yourself comfortable on the bed. For the duration of this discussion, we are not master and sub, simply two men agreeing some boundaries for our relationship. You must be honest, Christian. Your wishes in this are very important to me."

"Thank you, Sir." Christian sat on the bed and hugged his knees.

Becket fetched the contract document from a dresser drawer and joined him. "You had enough time to read this thoroughly last night?"

Christian nodded. "Several times."

"It's the standard contract that Carey uses at The Underground. It's up to us to customize it as we see fit. There are spaces to list our hard and soft limits and room to change some of the commitments, though from my point of view all the sections on care and responsibility are very thorough."

"I don't think there's anything there that needs changing, though it does seem weighted in my favor." Christian stretched his legs out.

"Exactly how it should be. Your well-being and safety are not things to be taken lightly. Just like your safe words. Non-negotiable."

Christian blushed. "I love that you want to take care of me. Is it okay that I want to look after you as well? I want to take care of your comfort and pleasure. It makes me feel...content."

Becket put his arm around Christian's shoulders and pulled him closer. Christian snuggled against him.

"Of course it is. It's on my list of hard limits... Receipt of TLC and cuddles on demand is obligatory."

Christian giggled. "I think I can cope with that."

"What are your hard limits then, love?" Becket felt Christian tense just a little in his arms. He petted him until he relaxed again.

"No cutting. No breath play. Nothing related to toilet functions."

Becket shifted. "Fine with me. What about sensory deprivation?"

"Oh that's fine, but not asphyxiation."

"We're on the same page then. What about body mods? Piercing? Tattoos?"

"A soft limit. We'd need to discuss what you want first."

"Absolutely. Now, I know you're not heavily into pain, which is good because neither am I. I won't draw blood but I will use whips, paddles, canes and crops. I have a very nice collection at home. Heavy bondage and chastity are favorites. I might want to display you, but I will not share you. I expect obedience and respect at all times."

Christian whimpered.

"Are you okay?"

"You're making me hard, Sir."

Becket chuckled. "Well, as soon as you sign this paper, your cock and your arse belong to me. You don't come unless I say you can."

"Yes, Sir." Christian's voice sounded a little strained.

"We can write in the finer detail later, but there's just one more thing. It's normal to set a time limit on the contract—three months, or six. I don't want to do that. I want this to be permanent. You will be able to request a review at any time but I don't want either of us thinking about this in terms of a defined period. Would you be comfortable with that?"

Becket felt dampness seep through his shirt as Christian snuffled against him. "Oh Lord, I didn't mean to make you cry. Only what you're comfortable with, remember?"

"Oh, I'm not upset, Sir. You make me so happy! Sorry, I'm acting like a soppy girl. It's just that I've wanted this, wanted you, for so long and now all my dreams are coming true. I keep thinking that I might wake up at any moment and find out that it *is* all just a dream."

"Hmm. Now that is soppy. I think I may have to tie you up and fuck you. Just to prove that this is all real, you understand?"

"That might just convince me, Sir."

"So be it. You've got two minutes to strip."

Becket relaxed back against his pillows and took in the view as Christian slipped off the bed and discarded his clothes with impressive speed. As soon as he'd finished, Christian assumed a classic presentation pose, legs apart and hands clasped behind his neck. Becket licked his lips. "Beautiful. From now on I would like you to present yourself on your knees with your hands behind your back. Try it now."

Christian dropped to his knees. He kept his head up but cast his eyes down.

Becket got up and went to stand in front of him. "That's good. Spread your legs a little wider, cross your ankles and rest on your heels."

After a little bit of shuffling, Christian settled into position. It had the pleasing effect of thrusting his groin forwards, displaying his cock and balls nicely.

"Have you ever had dance training?" Becket asked.

"No, Sir, I get asked that a lot. I was a gymnast through school, though."

"That explains it. You move so gracefully."

"Thank you, Sir."

"It shows you can control your body and that's a talent you will find very useful."

Christian nibbled his lower lip. Becket hid a smile. Christian was hard, his cock jerking every now and again, betraying his arousal and his need.

"Unfortunately, when my brother packed my bag he didn't include the set of custom leather cuffs I had made for you."

"That is a shame, Sir."

"It is. However, in my job I often have to improvise."

"Like MacGyver, Sir?"

Becket choked back a laugh. "Jesus, I hope not."

He looked around the room, seeking inspiration. His first source of equipment was easy. The two white, fluffy dressing gowns hanging on the back of the bedroom door had nice long belts. "Perfect," Becket muttered. "Soft but strong. They'll do for your ankles." He pulled the two belts from their loops and threw them on the bed. "Now, something for your wrists. Towels are too thick. Electrical flex bruises too quickly. Were you wearing a belt?"

"No, Sir. I don't like them."

"I don't have one either. Wait, I have just the thing." Becket pulled his holdall from under the bed and detached the carry strap, which was hooked to D-rings on the bag by removable clips.

"Stand at the foot of the bed, back to me and spread your legs wide."

Once Christian had moved into place, Becket tied one end of each of the white belts around the feet of the bed. The other ends he secured around Christian's ankles. "There, beautifully spread for me." He knew there was no way Christian would be able to get free without help, or bring his legs any closer together. He used the bag strap to bind Christian's wrists tightly together behind his back. The stiff fabric was wide enough that it wouldn't dig in, but Christian would be in no doubt of its presence.

Becket was banking on the fact that the bed was unusually high. The mattress came up to his hips and was nicely cushioned by the covers. He pushed Christian gently forwards until his chest rested on the bed. If Becket's rough calculations had been correct, the position should put Christian's sweet little hole at the perfect height for penetration.

"You look stunning and Heath has left something very useful in the bathroom." Becket slipped into the en suite and grabbed a tub of lube and the thick dildo that had mysteriously appeared next to the sink. He sat on the bed where he was sure Christian could see what he was doing, took the toy from its packaging and began to slather it with the thick, shiny lubricant. Christian made the sweetest little whimpering noises that hardened Becket's dick in an instant. Not that it needed much help. The sight of Christian tied down, arse exposed was torment enough.

Becket felt happier than he had in a long time. He shook his head, wondering how long it might be before everything came crashing down around him. *Focus on the now, idiot. You have a sub that needs you.*

He stood and moved to the end of the bed. He trailed his fingers across Christian's creamy skin, enjoying the subtle warmth. "So smooth. So tempting." The dildo was tapered, the rounded tip widening to a thicker girth. He pressed the end of it against Christian's hole. "This will be much easier on you if you relax. Let it in, sweetheart."

He pushed gently but persistently and Christian's body submitted to the toy with only brief resistance. Becket probed gently until the full length of rubber disappeared then he pulled it back and began to fuck Christian slowly.

"How does it feel? Is it stretching you? Making you ready for my cock?"

"Yes, Sir. Need you. Feels good, but I want you inside me, filling me."

Becket grinned as Christian thrust his arse back as much as he was able, taking the toy deep into his body. Becket rotated it and jiggled the end, seeking Christian's sweet spot. He knew he'd found his target when Christian's breath hissed from between tightly compressed lips.

"You are not to come without my permission," Becket snapped. He seated the full length of the toy and stepped away. "Keep it inside you and don't move."

Christian's glutes tensed beautifully as he strained to keep the dildo inside his passage.

Becket stripped his clothes off. Thankfully, taking off his footwear was a hell of a lot easier than putting it on. He took his time and listened to Christian's soft panting. As much as he wanted to hurry and bury himself in Christian's tight passage, he found it much more rewarding to torment his sub for a little longer. He checked Christian's position, looking for any excess strain on his limbs or signs that his circulation was restricted. Everything looked good, but Becket still grabbed a pillow. "Lift up, sweetheart. I don't want you hurting your neck." He positioned the pillow so that Christian could rest his head on it. "Better?"

"Yes, thank you, Sir."

Becket sighed. "I'm not making a very good job of being a big bad Dom at the moment, am I?"

Christian's breath hitched. "Feels pretty good to me, Sir. Please…"

Becket lubed his cock slowly. He didn't dare move too fast or he wouldn't last long enough to get inside Christian at all. He jiggled the end of the dildo before withdrawing it in tiny increments. Christian moaned and wriggled but didn't protest. Becket dropped the toy on the bed and grasped Christian's hips.

"I have a nice leather harness that will keep a plug inside you all day. It's lockable."

"Oh God! Sir... I'm going to come... Please!"

Becket gave Christian's arse a light slap. "No. You're not." He lined up his cock and pushed forwards. Christian's body welcomed him with a snug grip. Becket had doubts that he could hold off for very long. He snapped his hips a little tentatively, expecting it to hurt, but there was no pain. He smiled. *No need to hold back. Thank God.* He focused on making Christian feel as good as possible.

"Sir! Oh..." Christian's body jerked under Becket's thrusts. "Please let me come, Sir, please!"

Becket reached beneath Christian's body and grabbed his cock. As he pounded Christian's arse, he squeezed and released in time. The surge of orgasm rushed through him and at the crest of the wave he snapped, "Come!"

Christian screamed and the heat of cum filled Becket's hand. Christian's inner muscles tightened around Becket's dick and he came with a shout, pushing hard into Christian's body. Beneath him, Christian sobbed. "So good. Thank you, Sir. Thank you."

Becket sucked in some air and waited for his heart to stop pounding before pulling out. He grabbed some tissues and cleaned Christian up before releasing him from his bonds. "Come here, love."

He welcomed Christian into his arms and held him tightly, soaking up the young man's warmth. "Let's snuggle under the covers for a while. We still have to discuss a few of my favorite toys before you put your signature on our contract. There are so many things I want to do to you..." Becket pulled back the covers and got Christian settled. He took his medication then climbed into bed as well. Christian shuffled close and cuddled against him.

"I think I still qualify for daytime naps. A snooze won't hurt either of us." Becket closed his eyes and listened as Christian's breathing slowed. "We have plenty of time."

Chapter Twelve

Christian glanced around Heath's office and felt a deep sense of satisfaction. He had brought order from chaos, and that made him settled and calm. It was the same when Becket issued commands—it took all the uncertainty from his world. Heath had had systems— they just made no sense. Christian had set up processes for dealing with bills, bookings and enquiries that streamlined everything. He'd even borrowed Aiden for a few hours and got him to set up a proper database so that everything could be cross-referenced. He still felt a little anxious, as Heath looked it all over. Heath sat in his leather swivel chair and clicked on file after file on the computer while Christian stood in front of the desk, shifting his weight from foot to foot.

Eventually, after what seemed like an age, but was probably more like five minutes, Heath sat back in his chair and rolled his shoulders.

"I'm going to miss you, Christian. In four weeks you've achieved more than I've managed in years. You have a real talent for organization."

"I just like things to be ordered, Sir." The carpet became fascinating.

"Well, The Edge will become a much more efficient business because of your efforts, so thank you. If you and Becket didn't have to get back to London, I'd offer you a permanent job. Of course, I know I can't compete with the Imperial War Museum."

"It's just a junior archivist position, Sir, and Carey pulled some strings for me."

"Carey may have got your details in front of the right people, Christian, but it's your hard work and talent that got you the job. Don't put yourself down."

"I am looking forward to getting started, and I'll still be covering weekend shifts at The Underground—just Friday and Saturday evenings, though."

"Well, I'm sure Becket prefers you to be available to attend with him as a member rather than as staff."

Christian nodded. "We'll be able to go more often now that he'll be doing a desk job with regular hours." He sighed. "I know he's made the change for me, but I'm not sure it's the right decision for him."

"Have you talked to him about it?"

"I've tried to, Sir. He just says it's for the best and changes the subject."

Heath grunted. "Us Doms can be stubborn arses. Even if Becket thinks he's made a mistake, I doubt he'll admit it. Anyway, he wants to do what's best for you. He doesn't like leaving you alone."

Christian started to reply but the door swung open and hit the wall with a bang. Aiden stood there looking a bit frazzled, his dark hair stuck up all over the place and ink staining his lip.

"You've been chewing your pen again, love, what's up?" Heath said calmly.

"Where's Becket?" Aiden sounded panicky. "I've been looking for him everywhere. I need him."

Heath stood up, came around the desk and put his hands on Aiden's shoulders. "Calm down and tell me what's going on. Christian can find Becket for you."

"It's the Templar bombers. I think they're back. Fuck, I shouldn't be talking about this to you."

"Christian, I think you'll find Becket in the gym with Olly having a final physio session. Go and fetch him please. Tell him to meet us in the basement, in Aiden's room."

Christian didn't wait to ask questions or hear more about the crisis, he ran through the hall and across the courtyard to the gym. He burst through the door and took in Becket's and Olly's startled faces. In an instant Becket moved toward him and pulled him into a hug. "What's wrong, love? You're white as a sheet."

"Sir! Sorry. Aiden needs you downstairs in the basement. There's something going on with the bombers. Heath sent me to fetch you."

Becket kissed him. "Stay here with Olly. I'll be back as soon as I can." He disappeared at a run and Christian sagged against the wall, all his energy gone.

"Trust Aiden to cause another riot, I swear he's more of a drama queen than I am." Olly rolled his eyes theatrically and stuck his hands on his hips. "Now we get to pace and fret while the big boys play spies." He pulled on his black fleece. "Bugger that for a game of soldiers. Come on, let's go and dig Joe out of the library and make him find out what's going on." He grabbed Christian's hand and pulled him toward the door. "I am not going to be left out of all the fun again!"

Christian had little choice but to follow as Olly towed him back to the main house. He felt weird.

Worried. Annoyed. Scared. "Olly, Becket doesn't go back to work for another two days. He shouldn't be getting involved." Even to his own ears he sounded shrill.

Olly skidded to a halt. "Hey, everything's going to be fine. Becket is big enough and ugly enough to look after himself."

"And I'll bet that's what everyone said last time and look what happened then. He nearly died, Olly."

"But he didn't, did he? Apart from a few sexy scars, he's completely back to normal."

"He's going back to a desk job. He's not supposed to be doing fieldwork anymore."

Olly patted his shoulder. "Stop worrying. We don't know what's going on yet, so don't jump to conclusions." He started tugging again. "Come on. The quicker we get to Joe, the quicker I can bully him into eavesdropping for us!" As the two of them reached the library door, they met Joe, already coming in the opposite direction.

"Heath called me. Come on." Joe went past them, his long strides unhurried but determined.

Olly and Christian raced to catch up with him. They piled down the basement stairs and along the long corridor that led to Aiden's workspace. When they got there the door was firmly shut. Joe lifted a hand to knock but Olly snuck under his raised arm and tapped in the security code. He turned and pushed the door open with his arse, giving Joe a guilty look. "Can we discuss this later, Sir?"

"I think that would be a good idea."

Christian couldn't remember Joe ever raising his voice. He didn't need to. His low tones exuded such command that he could whisper and everyone listened anyway. Olly kept backing into the dark room and Christian craned his neck, trying to spot Becket. Joe gave him a comforting smile. "Come on. Olly's already in there, we both need to go in and start damage control."

Christian smiled anxiously back. His stomach knotted. The thought of Becket getting anywhere near the people who had already hurt him once made his gut churn. He slipped just inside the door. Aiden sat at his desk frantically typing at two keyboards in turn. Three large flat screens glowed and flashed in front of him. Christian couldn't see much but the images on the screen looked like gaming sites. Becket stood at Aiden's shoulder, talking urgently into a phone. Neither of them looked around.

Joe stood waiting patiently, holding onto Olly with a tight grip. Olly practically bounced with excitement, only Joe's restraining arm kept him in place. Heath moved from his position at Aiden's side and came to lean on the wall next to Christian. He started talking in a low voice, "Aiden picked up some chat on the same gaming site as before. Indications are that the bombers are planning another hit. Becket's on the phone to their boss in London."

Christian shivered. "Does Aiden know where the bomb is?"

"Better. He's caught up with them much earlier. Since last time, he's been working on code that can track the locations of the people logged into The Crucifix game. You see the screen with the world map on it? That shows all the active users on the site."

Christian squinted, trying to bring the screen of blinking lights into focus. "There are players all over the world."

"There are, and most of them are completely innocent. Well, as innocent as anyone on that site is likely to be. You can't exactly reach it via a Google search. Most of them go to great lengths to hide their identities."

"But Aiden has managed to track them?"

"Apparently. Brains as well as looks. I'm a lucky man."

"I think I'm glad that I'm not that clever." Christian frowned. "Aiden is a bit scary."

Heath chuckled. "Aiden's mind works differently to the rest of us mere mortals, but believe me, if I were in Becket's place, he'd feel just like you do."

"Scared out of his mind then." Christian ducked his head and looked at the floor.

"Absolutely."

Becket put the phone down and turned around. He raised an eyebrow. "What the hell? I thought this room was secure, Aiden?"

Aiden kept tapping at his keyboard. "It is."

"Then why do we have a fucking audience?"

Aiden whirled around on his chair. "Olly! You told me you'd forgotten the code. This is not a spectator sport—it's called the *Secret* Intelligence Service for a reason!"

Olly hid his face against Joe's chest. Joe ruffled his hair. "Sorry, Becket, but we all have a vested interest in this, so unless you want to throw us out we need to know what's going on."

Becket scowled. "You guys are going to get me fired before I'm even officially back at work. Fuck."

Christian caught Becket's eye and moments later he found himself in a tight embrace.

"You shouldn't be here, love."

"I know, Sir, but I couldn't stay away."

"You deliberately disobeyed me. You'll have to be punished for that." Becket kissed him hard, nipping at his bottom lip.

"Yes, Sir."

Becket took a step back. "I have a disobedient sub to punish. So, I imagine, does Joe."

"No change there then," Heath grunted.

Olly turned in Joe's arms and stuck his tongue out at Heath.

"So time is of the essence," Becket continued. "Aiden called me in here because he needed a field agent's perspective on how to move on this situation. I've been in touch with central command and given my take. Our boss is coordinating with local police to pick these jokers up after initial surveillance confirms they are where Aiden thinks they are. That's it."

"Aw, Becket, that's so not fun. I was hoping for a good car chase at the very least." Olly sulked and still managed to look pretty.

Joe gave his sub's arse a firm smack. "Quiet, brat, we should be grateful that ninety-nine percent of Becket's job is more boring than watching you clear out your wardrobe. Now, you and I need to have a serious conversation about your memory for numbers." Joe slipped a finger through one of Olly's belt loops and towed him out of the door.

Heath walked across to Aiden and bent to give his sub a kiss. "Upstairs. As soon as you're done here."

Christian wondered how Heath always managed to sound so menacing. Aiden certainly responded to the tone. He pulled his black fleece lower to cover his groin and chewed on his lower lip before swiveling back to his screen. Christian pressed against the wall as Becket advanced toward him.

"I have to stay here to make sure everything goes down okay. It won't take long. Go back to our room and prepare yourself. I want you clean inside and out, Christian, understand?"

"Yes, Sir." Christian trembled, not from fear but from anticipation.

Becket reverted into his official role. His stance, the set of his shoulders, his voice — everything about him oozed dominance and it was unbelievably sexy. It also made Christian think. Becket slotted naturally into the world of espionage. It suited him. Christian hadn't asked him to give it up but Becket had done it anyway. Riding a desk did not have a place in his master's future and Christian resolved to do something about it. He slipped quietly away and headed back to their room.

After taking care of himself, Christian took a quick shower, checking that his shaved groin was still nice and smooth the way Becket liked it. He toweled dry, cleaned his teeth then spent a couple of minutes giving his hair a quick once-over with the dryer. He debated whether or not to dress, but decided against it. Christian dropped to his knees, facing the bedroom door, and arranged himself in the 'present' position that Becket preferred. Hard and aching, his cock bobbed slightly as he settled down to wait. He took a few deep, cleansing breaths and closed his eyes.

Christian didn't mind waiting. It felt as if Becket were controlling him from a distance as he knelt there. The more he thought about it, the more he realized that control didn't have to be about physical presence. State of mind was just as important. He trusted Becket to be a good Dominant. *I'm still his submissive whether he's right here with me or halfway around the world,* he thought. Contentment radiated throughout his body as he accepted this new understanding.

When the door finally opened, Christian's cock stiffened. He looked up through his lashes to see Becket heaving something into the room. Christian couldn't quite see what it was. Becket's body blocked his view and he didn't dare make his curiosity too obvious. Becket went back out to the corridor and returned with a black canvas bag that clanked when he dropped it onto the bed. He closed the door and locked it, then turned to look at Christian.

"Do you have any idea how stunning you are?"

Christian nibbled his lip and pushed his shoulders back a fraction more. Becket crouched in front of him and Christian couldn't help but gasp as Becket grasped his cock and gave it a couple of strokes.

"Beautiful. Such a shame you've earned a punishment."

Christian thought that Becket looked pleased rather than disappointed, but he bowed his head subserviently just in case. Becket moved away and began to rummage in his bag.

"I know you want to look, Christian, it's fine. I'd like you to see what's coming."

Becket's light blue eyes sparkled and Christian thought he looked particularly handsome. His short blond hair had grown out a little during the weeks of his recuperation and the softer style suited him. Christian shivered. To him, Becket was gorgeous. He could shave his head and grow a handlebar mustache and he'd still be striking.

"You'll love my house, Christian, I've converted the cellar into a dungeon. All state-of-the-art equipment I can't wait to try out on you." Becket pulled a spreader bar from his bag and locked the steel into its widest position. "Stand up and spread your legs."

Christian swallowed hard. "That sounds wonderful, Sir. I'm glad the flat you took me to isn't your real home. It was rather…sterile."

Becket chuckled and started to fasten the spreader bar's steel cuffs around Christian's ankles. "Well, now you've passed the security vetting procedures, we'll never have to go back there again. You are officially registered as my partner."

Being restrained did nothing to ease the ache of Christian's rigid cock. The touch of cold metal against his skin sent tiny bolts of pleasure lightning to his balls. Becket pulled Christian's arms behind his back and locked them into rigid cuffs.

"There, nice and secure."

Christian focused on keeping his balance but almost toppled as he realized what the heavy object that Becket had manhandled into the room was. Becket steadied him. "I won't let you fall. Take a couple of steps for me."

Christian shuffled forwards until he straddled a square metal plate from which rose a vertical steel pole topped with a thick rubber plug. A circular rubber base separated the plug from the stand.

"I borrowed this from one of the playrooms in the basement. It's called an anal impaler," Becket said conversationally. "It's going to keep you exactly where I want you while you take your punishment."

Becket slathered the plug with a thick coating of lube. He wiped his hands on a towel then began to turn a small knob on the vertical pole. Slowly it began to extend, bringing the plug closer and closer to Christian's body. When the end of it touched his hole, Christian gasped. Becket kept turning.

Christian had never wanted to close his legs together so much in his life. His every instinct told him to get away from the invader pushing into his body. Becket put a hand on Christian's backside and stroked him gently. "Take it for me, love. This is my will. Submit."

It took all Christian's willpower to relax. As soon the tension left his arse, the thick plug penetrated the protective ring of muscle and pushed its way into his passage. It truly was an impalement. Christian tried to rise onto his toes but the spreader bar was too rigid. Becket just kept turning the little wheel until the full length of the plug filled Christian's channel. It didn't hurt, the plug wasn't the biggest Christian had taken, but the frustration of being locked in place in such a way was delicious torture.

"I have one of these at home. It vibrates," Becket commented.

Christian whimpered.

Becket patted his arse and circled around to face him. He cupped Christian's neck and ducked his head to kiss him. Their lips met and Christian opened to the insistent pressure of Becket's tongue as it filled his mouth, just as the plug filled his arse. He thought he might come from that kiss, but Becket pulled away. He stripped off his shirt and shoes, leaving on just the black trousers he'd been wearing for his physio session. The soft fabric tented at his groin, displaying his arousal. Christian looked down at his own dick. The impalement had done nothing to deflate his erection. The head of his cock gleamed with pre-cum and his balls felt hot and tight against his body.

"Sir, please..."

"Oh no. No relief for you just yet. Punishment first and if you are very good, there may be pleasure to follow."

Isn't this punishment enough? Christian desperately wanted to come but with his hands cuffed he could do nothing to help himself. He tried to wriggle, but the fat plug filled him so well and his legs were spread so wide that he could hardly move at all. Becket smirked.

He knows exactly what he's doing to me and it's not going to stop until he wants it to.

Christian felt lightheaded and weightless. He had no decisions to make. Everything had been taken away from him — even his ability to move.

At that moment, his master owned him completely. Christian floated as Becket used a narrow leather strap to bind his cock and balls in such a way that they stood proud from his body. The ends of the ties were drawn back over his hips and fastened behind him, lifting his dick higher.

"Perfect." Becket smiled. "Looks like you're heading for subspace, sweetheart, let's see if I can help you fly." He went back to his bag and pulled out a short-handled flogger. He hefted it and did a couple of figures of eight in the air. The leather fronds made a soft swishing sound but Christian knew their impact on his skin would be anything but soft.

As the strands of the flogger brushed his skin, Christian sighed. Becket whirled the implement expertly, raising a warm glow with each touch. The strokes grew gradually harder until each contact left a sharp sting. Becket focused on Christian's shoulders and thighs at first but moved around to face him. "That's it, love, your body is mine to punish. Surrender to me."

Becket landed repeated strokes on each of Christian's nipples. His aim was perfect — just the tips of the fronds striking flesh. The pain was exquisite and Christian knew that if it were not for the bindings on his cock and balls he would be coming in streams.

"Disobedience has consequences. Learn from this. Orders keep you safe, they are not to be ignored."

The flogger moved lower, catching Christian's dick. "Please, Sir! I'm sorry!"

"I'm sure you are. You'll remember this next time you are tempted to disregard my instructions."

"Yes, Sir. Oh…"

Christian's muscles tensed. Endorphins flooded his body. He screamed as the flogger connected with his balls. Pinned in place, utterly at Becket's mercy, Christian rode a wave of pleasure unlike anything he'd ever experienced before. Becket's attention switched to his arse but Christian felt no pain, just euphoria. He didn't know when the flogging ended. He didn't feel a thing as Becket released him from the bondage and carried him to the bed. On the fringes of his consciousness he recognized the sensation of suction on his aching cock and the agony of release as he spilled into Becket's mouth, moaning his gratitude.

Christian had no idea how long he drifted in semi-awareness. The world around him didn't matter. His master kept him safe. He didn't have to worry. Slowly his brain began to function again and he found himself wrapped in Becket's embrace. Becket was naked. Christian sighed happily.

"There you are. Back with me." Becket maneuvered him onto his back and lifted Christian's legs onto his broad shoulders. Without speaking he eased his cock into Christian's receptive passage and sank deep with a series of leisurely thrusts.

Christian looked into Becket's eyes. "I love you, Sir." The words slipped out before he could stop them.

Becket just smiled and kept moving at a steady pace. His strength and power enveloped Christian in a feeling of safety, security and love. With a slight shift of his hips, Becket pegged Christian's prostate. Christian arched his back, trying to draw Becket even deeper into his body. Becket responded by plunging into him aggressively, grunting as he drove home his claim. Christian gasped as Becket flooded his channel with the warmth of his seed. Christian flailed, trying to get hold of his cock, but Becket beat him to it. A couple of short pulls had him tumbling over the edge into another orgasm, muscles straining as the shock ripped through him.

Becket moved them over so that Christian lay on top of his master, Becket's softening cock still inside him. "There now. Rest a moment."

Christian had no problem obeying that instruction. As he relaxed against Becket's warm body he began to feel the ache of the flogging he had taken. He smiled — Becket's punishments were not an incentive to behave. He nuzzled Becket's shoulder. "That impaler was kinky as hell, Sir."

Becket's laugh rumbled through Christian's body. "You enjoyed that, didn't you? You looked spectacular. And I am kinky as hell. We're a good match."

"Perfect, Sir."

Christian made little complaining noises as Becket rolled him off. He plumped the pillows and patted them. "Sit up here. I have something for you."

Christian shimmied into position, wincing as his sore arse rubbed against the sheets. He raised his knees and let Becket clean him up a little.

"Thank you, Sir. I like it when you take care of me."

The covers sat in a pile at the bottom of the bed and Becket made no attempt to pull them up. Christian admired his master's arse as Becket walked across the room to the canvas bag and pulled out a couple of items. He returned to the bed and put two boxes down between them. Becket took the lid off the first box and Christian stared. Nestling inside on a bed of black tissue paper sat a shiny steel chastity tube.

"This is designed for long-term wear," Becket said happily. "The cutaway pattern in the metal means you can wash and dry yourself without removing it and it won't prevent you using the bathroom. I had it modified so that it locks around the base of your cock but also separates your balls."

Becket warmed the metal in his hands then slid it into place. He locked it with two tiny padlocks. Christian looked down at his imprisoned dick and squirmed. The device was comfortable but quite heavy. It wasn't something he would be able to forget he was wearing.

"You will wear this at all times. Only two things will get you out of it — me or your safe word."

Christian had no idea what to say. He was horrified but totally turned on. "Sir, I don't... I mean you can't..."

"I can. Now, are you ready for your second gift?"

Christian wasn't sure he wanted to know what the second box contained, but couldn't look away as Becket opened it. Inside lay a thick band of black leather. A collar.

Tears welled in Christian's eyes as Becket lifted the collar from the box and fastened it around his neck. The clasp clicked shut with finality. Becket ran his finger around the leather, testing the fit. Christian touched it tentatively with trembling fingers. "It's beautiful, Sir." He bit his lip and tried not to cry.

Becket kissed him gently. "A symbol of my love, sweetheart. I have something less obvious for you to wear to work, but otherwise this stays around your neck."

Christian couldn't stop the tears overflowing. "Thank you, Sir. I love it." He flung his arms around Becket and hugged him hard. When he pulled himself together enough to speak he sounded a bit snuffly. "You told me once that life is a double-edged sword. Damned if you do, damned if you don't."

"All decisions have consequences, love."

"They do, and that's why when you go back to work next week I want you to tell your boss that you'll return to fieldwork."

Becket brushed the hair out of Christian's eyes. "Why would I do that? It might take me away from you."

"I know, and I hate it when we're apart, but you were made for that job, Sir. Watching you earlier, taking charge, that's who you are. What happened with the bombers, Sir? Are you allowed to tell me?"

"I sent police and bomb disposal. They caught them red-handed assembling the next device. Ironically, it was wired wrong and they probably would have blown themselves up if they had managed to detonate it. The idiots will be taking a very long break at Her Majesty's pleasure."

"That's fantastic! But listen to how satisfied that makes you. Fieldwork may be dangerous, but a desk job will kill you and I've come to realize that the control I crave is not dependent on your presence." He touched his collar and the metal encasing his cock.

"Don't you see? You own me. I'm yours. Where you are doesn't change that."

Becket gave him a hard look. "It seems that Heath is not the only Dom whose sub has a brilliant mind. Are you sure about this?"

"I'm sure. The last few weeks have shown me that life's too short for compromise. We are so lucky. We have each other. We have amazing friends. Self-imposed unhappiness should not be part of the equation."

Christian gasped as Becket took his mouth for a punishing kiss. The gasp turned into an unmanly squeal as Becket pressed two fingers into his still slick hole.

"I love you. I'm going to fuck you, then I'm going to plug you. It's likely that I won't let you come for days."

Christian squirmed, impaling himself farther. "You've been sharpening that sword, haven't you, Sir?"

Becket gave his arse a slap. "Double-edging. A technique every Dom should master. On your knees. Now."

Christian giggled and did as he'd been told.

About the Author

Lucinda lives in a small village in the English countryside, surrounded by rolling hills, cows and sheep. She started writing to fill time between jobs and is now firmly and unashamedly addicted.

She loves the English weather, especially the rain, and adores a thunderstorm. She loves good food, warm company and a crackling fire. She's fascinated by the psychology of relationships, especially between men, and her stories contain some subtle (and not so subtle) leanings towards BDSM.

L.M. Somerton loves to hear from readers. You can find her contact information, website details and author profile page at http://www.totallybound.com.

Totally Bound Publishing

Home of Erotic Romance